SURVIVING MIDAS

find more from RW Hague

www.rwhague.com

SURVIVING MIDAS

RW Hague

Young Adult

Suspense

ISBN: 979-8-9892705-0-7

To Josiah—

May your years be blessed.

ACKNOWLEDGEMENTS

This book has had a long and eventful journey filled with hope and heartbreak, but thanks to a bevy of support from friends and family, it has made it to the finish line!

To all those who had a direct hand in making this dream a reality, I offer my love and sincere thanks. To my beta readers and critique partners: Cheri1000, Kale Sartor of the Chattanooga Writers Guild, Sarah Hughes, and Sagar Megharaj. A special thanks to Andrew Rucker Jones, who has been there from the beginning and continues to be one of my greatest supporters – all of the technical aspects of the Midas franchise hang on your expertise.

With all my heart, I thank my family, especially my husband for listening patiently to twenty different versions of the same chapter without spontaneously combusting or walking away from my nonsense. Thanks to my mom for putting up with my never ending questions about children's responses to trauma, and to my sister for cheering me on, even when things got rough.

During birthdays at Katie's house, Dad always had one rule: don't check the mailbox.

The rule stood for the week before and the week after one's birthday just in case out-of-town family decided to send a surprise gift through the mail. But when Katie got off the bus the day after her fifteenth birthday, she was thinking more about her final exams tomorrow than the mailbox rule. By habit, she stopped by the box and pulled out a wad of letters and coupons on her way to the door.

As she walked down the sidewalk and climbed the porch steps, Katie flipped through the stack of letters. Most of them were junk mail or bills, but one letter was addressed to her with her name written in swirly calligraphy. No return address was listed on the otherwise blank, white envelope and the postmark was missing as if it had been hand-delivered. Since her closest relative lived fifty miles away, she doubted it was from them. The envelope was square and firm, not the typical rectangle bills came in. She guessed it to be a birthday card from a school friend or an invitation to a party. Graduation was coming up for some of her friends on the softball team after all.

Katie glanced back at the mailbox, wondering if she should put the mail back, but it seemed silly to pretend that she had not seen it. The surprise gift rule itself was silly, especially since she was no longer a little kid. So, Katie tore open the back of the envelope.

A mass of gold glitter shot from the envelope, showering her in golden flakes.

"Crap!" shouted Katie as the glitter bomb struck. As she shook her hair and wiped her face, flakes of gold floated in a cloud around her. The stuff was everywhere! She'd have to risk tracking glitter through the house like a blood trail in order to shower to get rid of it. Thankfully, she was still standing on the porch when she opened the envelope and the majority of the mess could be swept up before Dad arrived.

Who the heck sent this anyway? Her suspicions were drawn to Alec, her older brother. This was the type of prank he would pull, especially since the mailbox rule would guarantee his presence at the dinner table when she opened it. Her best defense, in that case, would be to clean up everything and never mention it.

Katie shimmied the card out of the envelope. The outside of the card had more swirly font but this time written in gold on a black background. "Happy Fifteenth Birthday!" it read. "It's been such a joy watching you grow up, Katie Belle! Here's to many more."

Katie Belle was the nickname Dad used for her, but she doubted he would send glitter bombs to his own house. Or to any house for that matter. But when Katie opened the card, mere annoyance turned to cold fear.

"To the girl who's always on my mind . . .

Midas"

Katie swirled around looking for anyone who might be watching her as the card tumbled out of her hand. With her heart thumping, she backed away to the front door, grasping behind her for the knob. With fumbling fingers, she worked her phone from her pocket and dialed for Dad.

*   *   *

Dad showed up minutes after the squad cars and ambulance. With a wave of his FBI badge, the emergency responders let him through to where Katie sat on the wicker chair beside the front door. A blood pressure cuff hung from her arm as a paramedic pressed his stethoscope to her chest.

Squatting beside her, Dad took Katie's hand. "Are you alright, sweetheart? How are you feeling?"

Katie shrugged in reply. After the initial terror, a sort of numbness had fallen over her. The police, who were the first to arrive on the scene, asked questions about the envelope, and she answered as best as she could. It was clear the officers didn't understand the significance of the letter, but why would they, considering it was a decade-old, yet still ongoing, federal investigation?

"Dad," said Katie, "why would Midas send me a birthday card?"

"I don't know, honey," said Dad with a sigh. "It's going to be okay though."

"We got the preliminary report on the suspicious substance," said a portly man in a white button-down shirt. The shield on his shirt and the badge on his shoulder marked him as a captain of the Nashville Fire Department. "It doesn't appear to be anthrax or anything poisonous, just glitter. But we'll send it off for further testing."

"Thank you," said Dad, shaking the man's hand. "I appreciate all of you responding so quickly. The team from my office will take over the investigation, but I can't thank you enough for coming."

"Of course," said the fire captain, patting Dad's shoulder. "We're all in this together."

The paramedics finished up their assessment and were soon on their way apart from a patrol car that remained in their driveway until the FBI showed up. Katie knew most of the members of the Nashville FBI office, and they each came by to check on her. Soon,

Alec arrived as well, having canceled the date with his girlfriend after receiving Dad's text.

Under Dad's instruction, Alec took Katie inside while the investigation team collected samples of the glitter and bagged the envelope and card. Katie expected to feel better in the house, surrounded by the familiar walls and furniture. Mom's old piano, which Katie now played, stood in the corner with its same dents and chipped varnish. The missing knob on the stair railing was still missing. The scrapes and flaws of the faux leather couch on which they sat had been there for years, and the water stains on the coffee table marked many a meal in front of the TV. This was the house in which Mom had lived before she died two years ago from cancer, and Katie still felt her presence like a warm embrace.

But Midas had somehow corrupted this protective barrier, destroying it with his letter. He knew not only that she existed, but also her name, her birthday, and her address. What did it all mean? Was she next?

"What does Midas want with me?" asked Katie.

"This has nothing to do with you, Katie," said Alec, draping a protective arm around her shoulders. "This is about Dad."

"The letter was addressed to me!"

"But you're not investigating Midas. Dad is. And this isn't the first time Midas has sent us mail before."

"It-it's not?"

"Midas sends us birthday cards every year, Katie. The FBI screens all of Dad's letters, but this isn't the first to have slipped through the cracks."

Katie shrugged off Alec's arm and turned to face him. "Why didn't anyone tell me?"

"I don't know. You were so little when the first one came. Mom and Dad didn't want you to worry about it at the time. After that, I guess no one got around to it. But it's why you're not supposed to check the mail around your birthday."

"So let me get this straight. Some psycho has been sending our family creepy birthday cards since forever, and the FBI hasn't done anything about it?"

"We have been doing something about it," said Dad as he closed the door behind him and joined Alec and Katie on the couch. "We've been trying to catch him."

"Yeah, for over ten years, Dad!" cried Katie, standing. "Am I the only one worried about this crap?"

"I'm not *un*worried, sweetheart," said Dad, pulling Katie back down and into a hug. "But we've had the FBI behavioral analysis unit review the letters, and they're pretty sure these aren't threats, just taunts. Midas is trying to scare us by making a connection between our family and one of the kidnapping cases I'm working on. The Kelley victims would be close to the same age as you and Alec. Not only that but the case was linked to Midas personally."

"Linked to him?" asked Katie. "I thought Midas took only contract kidnappings like for mobsters and stuff."

"Usually, yes," said Dad. "But this time it was different. We caught a money launderer who had direct contact with Midas. In order to get his guy out of jail, Midas kidnapped the children of the assistant district attorney overseeing the money launderer's case. In order to protect his children, the attorney blew the case and the money launderer was acquitted. The children were never found, and this is how Midas taunts us about it. But Katie, this was all ten years ago. The pattern of the letters has been the same ever since. We have no reason to think he's targeting or threatening you or Alec."

Katie did feel a little better knowing how old this case was, but it was still creepy.

"In the future, however," Dad continued, "If you come across a letter with no return address, give it to me, please."

"You won't have to worry about me finding any more of Midas's letters," said Katie. "I'm not going anywhere near that mailbox again."

With a laugh, Dad squeezed her knee and stood. "That's fine, Katie Belle. Before the FBI goes, however, I need you to go upstairs and change your clothes. Put your shirt and pants into this bag." He handed her a giant zip lock. "Then we can put this whole thing behind us."

Katie changed into sweatpants and an old t-shirt, her favorite lounging clothes, before returning to the buzz of activity downstairs. "Agent Watts, can I give this to you?" Katie asked Dad's partner who stood by the front door.

"Certainly," said Agent Watts. Like the other agents, he wore a white button-down shirt with a black tie and coat. He was in his mid-thirties, clean-shaven with curly, brown hair. His strong Detroit accent stood out from the usual southern accents Katie was used to. As he extended his hand to take the bag, a golden watch peeked out from beneath his shirt cuff.

"Nice watch," said Katie. It looked expensive—unlike anything Dad could afford.

"Why thank you, Katie," said Watts. "It's an old family trinket."

For an old family trinket, it sure did sparkle, but Katie assumed he just made a point to keep it nice.

"Do you know where my dad went?" asked Katie.

"He's out back speaking to Rogers," said Watts.

Rogers was Dad's supervisor and old mentor. If Dad was out back speaking to him, he didn't want to be interrupted, but that didn't mean Katie didn't want to listen. While she warmed up a couple of Hot Pockets in the microwave, she listened through the cracked backdoor.

"Just because one letter slipped through—" said Rogers.

"It didn't slip through," said Dad. "Did you see the envelope? There was no postmark. Midas either hand-delivered this letter himself, or he paid someone else to do it. He's escalating."

So Dad was worried, just downplaying it for her sake. How old did she have to be to get the truth from him?

"We have no indication that this is the case," said Rogers. "It's probably a fluke."

"For ten years he has held pattern: same font, nearly identical contents, always postmarked Connecticut. This is a break in pattern. And I don't care what the BAU says, these are more than just taunts. They're threats, like if I get close again, he's going to take my children."

"I think you're reading too much into it, Thompson," said Rogers. "It's been ten years, and we have no leads. Why would Midas threaten you now?"

"I don't know," said Dad. "But what other reason would he have to break pattern other than to send us a message? Is he back in Tennessee, about to work a new job? Is that why he just— dropped it off?"

"In all likelihood, it wasn't even Midas who delivered it," said Rogers. "We don't know what this means, but if you'd like, I can place your family into protective custody for a week or two."

Dad sighed. "I don't know. Alec and Katie are finishing up school in the next couple of weeks . . ."

"How about I put a uniformed patrol on your house for the night," said Rogers. "Then we'll see what tomorrow brings."

The backdoor started to open, and Katie turned back to her Hot Pockets. Agent Rogers, an older man with salt and pepper hair, gave her a small smile before joining Watts by the door. Dad wrang his hands as he entered the house. Upon seeing Katie nearby, he cleared his face of worry and draped his arm over her shoulders.

"How are you holding up, sweetheart?" Dad asked.

"You sounded worried talking to Rogers," said Katie. "Tell me the truth, Dad. Should I be worried?"

"You were eavesdropping?"

Katie put a hand on her hip and cocked her head to the side. "Wouldn't you?"

Dad let out a long sigh. "Ever since you were little, I taught you not to talk to strangers or to get into strange cars. Use your head and do all the things I taught you, and you will be okay. Then tomorrow, when you get off school, I'll be there to pick you up. Sound like a plan?"

Katie nodded, still unsure, but feeling a little better. At least she knew Dad was taking this seriously. His job might be important, but he wouldn't let it put her in harm's way.

Would he?

Dad wrapped his arms around Katie in a tight hug. "That's my girl. Don't worry. I promise I won't let anything happen to you."

*　　*　　*

All through the next day's biology exam, Katie kept thinking about glitter exploding in her face. How could she think about cephalopods and crustaceans when she kept finding gold flakes in her hair and on her backpack? The patrol car had stayed all night and even followed her to school the next day, although when she checked last, it was no longer in the parking lot. All of her teachers had been told about the incident, which meant all of the students now knew as well.

"That's soooo creepy," said Laney, Katie's best friend, when she told her about it at lunch. "I'm glad my dad's just a sous chef. I couldn't deal with that sort of stuff."

"I think it's totally cool!" said Calvin, who sat across from Katie that meal. Calvin had deep chocolate brown eyes and coiffed black hair. Even as a freshman, he was already third-string wide receiver for the varsity football team, second-string first baseman, and lead guitarist for his garage band, *The Haflings*. The kid was going places, and Katie hoped to go there with him. Last week she had danced with him at the spring formal and he promised her a spot in his band on the keyboard after his sister went to college in the fall.

"You know what I would do?" said Calvin. "I'd take an ad out on Facebook inviting Midas to come at me. Then I'd shoot him in the face."

"Do you really think a super-criminal like Midas is on Facebook?" asked Laney.

"You could put it on Instagram too!" said Calvin.

Katie laughed. "You're such a dork, Cal."

Calvin was right about one thing: having a super-criminal stalker did make for a cool story that drew a level of popularity to Katie thus unprecedented. In that one day alone, she got twenty followers on social media, many from upperclassmen. But now as she chewed on the back of her pen trying to concentrate on the lifecycles of Lepidoptera, her thoughts kept coming back to that card.

"I've enjoyed watching you grow up," Midas had said. Was he really watching her little family? What else did he know about them? Was it a taunt like Dad had said, or something more?

Katie placed her exam on the teacher's desk just as the bell rang—the last of the class to do so. She hoped the results wouldn't wreck her straight-A record. If it did, she wondered if would they let her try again, considering the circumstances?

Thankfully, biology was the last class of the day, and, after stopping by her locker to get her backpack, Katie headed to the front of the school in search of Dad's car. Instead of his blue SUV, however, Alec's ten-year-old Camry sat in line outside.

Although Alec was a high school senior, he attended a 'middle college' that applied dual credits for high school and college. He also got to get out of school earlier than Katie.

The rain, which had misted for most of the day, turned into a steady drizzle, and Katie pulled her jacket close as she darted through the parking lot to the car. "Where's Dad?" she asked as she closed the passenger-side door.

Alec looked at Katie apologetically, and she rolled her eyes.

"If it makes you feel any better," said Alec, "I'm supposed to go straight to FBI headquarters. Dad says we'll be safe there until he gets back from Memphis."

"What's in Memphis?"

"Some new lead," Alec sighed. "Something about an ambassador kid getting kidnapped. Dad thinks it might be Midas."

"What if this case is the reason for the threat? What if Midas is warning Dad to stay away because of this kidnapping?"

"Dad doesn't think that's the case," said Alec. "He says the timeline doesn't add up for that or something. Look, Katie, I know all this is freaky, but you don't think Dad would put us in danger, do you?"

Katie sighed and pulled her seatbelt across her chest. "I suppose not. I guess we're going to be sitting in swivel chairs and munching on vending machine food until Dad gets back though, huh?"

"Rogers has offered to go get us some take-out, so it won't be just potato chips tonight."

"Great," muttered Katie. "Because MSG-filled Chinese food is so much better."

"Katie, I know you're upset, but Dad's—"

"Dad's job is important," she grumbled. "I know." Katie turned to watch the rain drip down the window. Sometimes she wished her dad were a sous chef too.

When Katie turned back around, Alec gave her a look of sympathy and she felt guilty for her bad attitude. None of this was Alec's fault. Before Mom died, Dad's work-life had not been as intrusive nor his absences as obvious, but now . . .

"Alec, I'm sorry. I know—" but Katie paused as headlights grew beyond the driver's side window. A car was heading straight for them, fast. "Alec!" Katie screamed.

Alec jerked the wheel, but it was too late. The vehicle smashed into them, metal crunched, and tires squealed against the wet pavement. Katie's head struck the window and glass shards showered her. As the car skidded to a stop, darkness crept across her vision. Her eyelids drooped and threatened to close, but she shook her head, clearing the cobwebs. Her vision pulsed with the throbbing in her head, but she knew she had to stay awake.

Katie fumbled for her phone, but it had fallen to the floorboard. Beside her, Alec slumped across the wheel, blood oozing from a wound on his forehead. Feebly, she gripped his sleeve. "Alec . . ."

A gloved hand reached inside her busted window and unlocked the door. Through bleary eyes, Katie watched the woman in black open her door and slash through her seatbelt. Paramedics already?

"Fifteen seconds!" someone cried out. But fifteen seconds until what?

A man in black opened Alec's door and placed the blade of a knife under his nose. The reflective surface fogged lightly as Alec breathed. "Alive, but unconscious."

The woman seized Katie's shoulders and pulled her toward the door.

"Ow! Wait! What?" Katie cried. Her head pounded, and her face stung like fire.

"Twenty seconds!"

The woman tugged harder, pulling her from the car and into a maroon panel van that had pulled up beside them. Katie lay flat on her back and stared up at the metal ceiling. The pain continued, and so did the swimming in her head. As she rolled to her side, she came face-to-face with a girl. Blank, lifeless eyes stared up from her pale face.

Shocked, Katie scooted away from her. Something was wrong. Very wrong. But she couldn't think clearly enough to do anything about it. *Run*, came a fleeting thought, but her legs felt like lead and her head continued to swim.

The man rounded the car and scooped up the dead girl. She flopped like a ragdoll over his shoulder.

"Thirty seconds!" someone cried.

"Where's the boy?" the woman asked.

"Leg's too damaged," the man said as he positioned the body into her seat. "I left him on the sidewalk."

"Alec?" Katie tried to sit up.

The man frowned. "Why haven't you sedated her yet?"

"I was getting there." The woman pulled a syringe from her pocket, grabbed Katie's ankle, and pulled her close.

"No!" Katie cried as the needle sank into her thigh. But her vision clouded further and she fell back.

"Forty-five seconds!"

The world crumbled and spun around her. Just before her vision faded, a man in a suit appeared near the van door. His eyes pulsed, or was that the drugs? "Light it," he said.

Flames erupted from Alec's car as a smile spread across the man's thin lips. Then everything went black.

Her aching cheek was the first sensation to cut through the fog that swirled about Katie's head, but for a few moments, it was all she could register. It did not take long, however, for that ache to grow. Darts of pain, beating in time with the pounding of her heart, shot through her face and echoed down her neck and into the rest of her body. She tried to lift her heavy eyelids but could only do so for blinks at a time.

Finally, she forced them open, but the blackness only continued. Something covered her face – a cloth of some sort? It smelled of sweat, metal, and foulness.

A strange rumbling sound filled the space that served only to worsen the ache. Something else was hurting now too though. Her legs?

More specifically, it was her knees that ached as she sat upon them. She tried to shift off of them and onto her hips, but her hands remained suspended above her head, holding her in place. She could not feel her fingers.

As she shifted to sit up, pins and needles shot through her fingers. Her wrists were stuck to something—a rod of some sort?

Katie tucked her fingers down to her wrist, feeling the handcuffs secured around them.

She yanked against them only to jar her arms, and she felt a flicker of pain somewhere about her wrist. Grabbing the chain, she teetered to a stand on her cramped, bound legs. "Help!" she screamed.

An echo replied.

"Somebody! Please?"

The floor pitched beneath her, and Katie toppled over. The restraints cut into her wrists and her arms twisted unnaturally. A brash squeak penetrated the darkness, and the room came to a stop. The noise diminished, giving way to the rattle of a diesel engine.

She stood again. When the ground shifted this time, she braced against the metal rod holding her hands in place. The noise resumed.

Road noise?

Slowly, feeling returned to her fingers once more, and she tried to pull the bag off her head. Pain erupted from her cheek, stabbing and burning. Gentle pressure sent fire deep into the bone. The bag was too moist to be just from her breath and was also sticky. Blood?

Her chest heaved. Was this real? This couldn't be happening. *Where am I? What happened to Alec?*

An answer came, solid and resounding, and with it, an increased level of dread.

Midas.

Katie's chest tightened, and her throat threatened to close. Midas had come for her after all. Despite all of Dad's reassurances, all his promises, she had been kidnapped by one of the most elusive criminals known to the FBI. A man whose victims never went home.

Her head grew woozy, and Katie clung to the chains to keep upright. But she couldn't panic now! What would Dad do?

The first thing Dad would do would be to remove the bag from his head, but as she tugged on the base of it, even the slightest touch caused too much pain for her to continue. In a fit of terror and rage, she yanked and pulled against the chain, but it held firm. Sobbing, she fell to her knees. Her thoughts continued to swirl, but her mind was so foggy that she could not latch on to one. Instead, she sat crying in the dark, praying to wake up.

When the sound of the engine ceased, Katie straightened, ears piqued for any other sounds. The pins and needles returned to her hands. A horrible screech erupted from some place in front of her, and light filtered through the bag on her head. Footsteps echoed off the walls.

Katie tried to back away, but the chain around her wrists held firm. Warm hands gripped her arms and undid the handcuffs, allowing them to drop from the bar. Her feet were unbound next.

"Alright, come on," a man's voice spoke with a Southern drawl. He pressed a hand against her back, forcing her toward the door. Katie tried to scoot away from him, but he grabbed under her arm and dragged her down a ramp into the sun.

"What's her name?" another male voice asked, also twangy but less pronounced.

"Hell if I know," said the first as he yanked the bag off.

Katie howled as the cloth ripped from her face. Clutching her cheek, she collapsed into the gravel, screaming.

"Geez!" the second man cried. "What'd you do Clark?"

Clark, a tubby man in a white undershirt, gaped at her. "She had the bag on her face before I got her! How should I have known?"

Katie sucked in air. Blood soaked her hand, rolling down her arm. The second man pressed the bag to her face. She glanced up at him, then had to look again. The man was a kid—a teenager no more than a couple of years older than herself, maybe the same age as Alec. He was short and slender with blonde, matted hair piled on top of his head.

"Michelle!" he called over his shoulder. "Get me a wet cloth. And someone find Addison!"

"What-what's going on?" Katie managed. "Where am I? What happened to my brother?"

"We're going to deal with your face first," he told her. "You can ask questions later."

A moment later, a girl near the same age returned with a wet washcloth. "Oh dear," Michelle said. "Is she a Greenie?"

Katie frowned at the word, not understanding.

"I think so," said the boy, then looked at Clark. "We'll take it from here."

"I expect payment!" declared Clark.

The boy's lip twitched as if suppressing a sneer. "I have no business in that." He took her arm and helped her stand. The white rag was quickly turning red.

"Make sure your bosses know!" Clark insisted.

This time, the sneer turned into a scowl. "I'll get right on that," he muttered. As they stepped away, however, he muttered, "Moron."

"Shh!" Michelle whispered. "Goldie, I swear, sometimes—"

"Your bosses . . ." Katie said. "Who are your bosses?"

"Questions after, remember?" The boy—Goldie? prodded her toward a door. But the shock had worn off a little and she lingered to take in the surrounding area. She needed to know where she was. Dad would learn where he was.

The door led to a brick mansion commanding a hillside. A few roughly built structures sat at the base of the hill, and fields lay beyond this. Several U-shaped greenhouses ran along the sides of the compound, and a chain-linked fence enclosed the area with a shield of trees beyond that. Her nose crinkled. The place smelled like a skunk. She had smelled it before, in the stairwell at school during a football game. Was it—?

Goldie tugged on her arm, not allowing her to linger any longer. As they entered the house and into a kitchen, Goldie called, "Clear a path!" and kids of various ages parted before them. Katie's mouth popped open at the sight of them all. A boy standing on a stool drying dishes could not have been more than five. The children were thin and wore clothes so tattered and filthy, they belonged in the trash.

Goldie and Michelle led her down several passageways until they stopped in a white-washed infirmary. Four beds lined one wall and a medicine cabinet stood across from them. An executive desk stood next to the cabinet. The wall behind the beds was lined with tall windows overlooking a courtyard.

"Have her sit on the bed," said Goldie. "Did you send someone for Addison?"

"I did." Michelle aided her to sit on the crisp sheets as she continued to hold the rag to her face. The wound still throbbed, but Katie was too busy sorting through these strange surroundings to focus on it. Where was the dark dungeon? The duct tape and ropes? Where were the freakin' adults? Surely this kidnapping gig wasn't run by a bunch of teenagers.

"Will someone please tell me what's going on?" Katie demanded.

"Explain it," Goldie said as he moved behind the desk and tugged on locked drawers.

"Me explain it?" Michelle said, turning to him. "Why do— Goldie! What are you doing? If Addison comes in here, she'll catch you!"

He harrumphed and continued to tug on the drawers before moving to the medicine cabinet, inspecting the lock.

"Goldie!" she cried.

The door to the infirmary opened, and Goldie straightened and stepped away from the cabinet to join Michelle and Katie beside the bed. A woman in her early twenties with purple and white hair fixed in an androgenous style entered. On her hip sat a holstered weapon. The yellow tip marked it as a taser. "What happened?" she asked.

"She came like this, Addison," Goldie said.

"I was in a freaking car accident, idiots!" Katie cried. "Your car rammed into our car?"

"That wasn't us," Addison muttered, almost to herself.

Katie guffawed. "What are you talking about? You kidnapped me!"

Addison ignored her statement, speaking instead to Goldie. "I don't have the key, Dad's in town running errands, and Barb's at her grandkid's birthday party until Tuesday. Can you manage with what you have lying around?"

"Like what? The sheets?" he answered.

"Maybe we can find some Bandaids . . ."

Goldie rolled his eyes, shoved his hand in his pocket, and pulled out a paper clip. "May I?"

Addison balked. "Right in front of me?"

"Do you have a better plan?"

Katie's gaze darted between them. Who the hell was in charge here? Judging from the woman's well-fed body and the unhealthy, scrawny state of the teens, she would have guessed that Addison was in charge. But the boy spoke boldly, borderline snarkily with the woman. Meanwhile, Michelle stood silent, not even raising her gaze.

Addison narrowed her eyes but glanced at Katie once more. "Fine. Do it."

Goldie unwound the paperclip and brought the two ends together in parallel lines. In less than ten seconds, the cabinet was open.

"That was a bit scary," Addison said. "Have you gotten in there before?"

"Nope," said Goldie as he set the supplies next to Katie and wheeled over a metal tray. He was about to open the packages when Michelle stopped him.

"Wash your hands," she said.

Katie grimaced at the dirt caked beneath his fingernails and between his knuckles. The boy spent some time at the sink before he returned with clean—albeit red hands. She relaxed further when he donned a pair of gloves.

"This is going to hurt," he warned, and Katie sucked in air as he removed the washcloth and poured water over the wound. Michelle reached for her hand, and Katie flinched. But then she allowed her to take it. Of all of those present, she feared her the least.

"That's pretty gross," said Addison as she leaned over Goldie's shoulder. "I might get sick."

"Trash can's behind you." Goldie took a wetted gauze and pressed it against Katie's cheek. "She's going to need stitches."

"Stitches?" Katie repeated. But who was going to do that? Were they going to take her to a hospital? Call in a doctor?

Addison dragged the trashcan closer. "Dress it as best you can, and Barb will get to it when she gets back."

"On Tuesday?" said Goldie. "Judging from the needle marks on her arm, she's already been out for over twenty-four hours. The longer this thing waits, the more it will scar."

Katie jerked her hand from Michelle to see the oval red mark in the crook of her arm. How long had she been sedated? She could be anywhere! Panic clutched her chest again and her breathing quickened. The others continued to talk, discussing what to do, but it felt as if they were far away now.

The boy opened a packet and dumped out a needle and thread onto the metal tray. He picked it up and advanced toward her, but Katie retreated, nearly falling backward off the bed.

"Hey, it's okay," Goldie said, setting the needle back down. "I'll numb the area first."

"No freakin' way," she said. "You're not touching me."

"Hey, honey," Michelle said. "I know this is tough, but Jared and I are just trying to help. You don't want to walk around with a gaping wound, do you?"

Katie glanced at the boy. Jared now? Not Goldie? Her head swam.

"It won't take but a second," said Goldie. "No more than five minutes, I swear."

"I said no, asshole!" Katie shouted.

Goldie looked to Addison. "Have any sedatives?"

"No! We're not sedating her!" said Michelle. "Look, honey, I know this is really scary. And I know that there's nothing I can say that will make it better. But I'm going to have you look into this tray here and see your face, and then I think you'll agree with what needs to happen here."

"I don't know you!" she cried. "I don't want you anywhere near me!"

"You're right," Michelle said. "You have no idea who we are. And you're also right in saying that Goldie here is an asshole."

Goldie frowned at this part.

"But he's also super smart and knows what he's talking about," Michelle continued. "Let him fix your face. Then we'll do everything we can to explain all this to you, okay? Now come on, honey. Just look in the tray and you'll see."

Hesitantly, Katie moved to the edge of the bed and peered into the reflection. The cut ran from her eye to her chin in a semi-circle, and as she leaned forward, a flap of skin pulled away from her face. "Oh my gosh!" she cried, leaning back. Blood dripped from the wound, and Michelle pressed the cloth back to her face. "Oh my gosh, do it. Freakin' just do it."

"Alrighty then." Goldie pulled a set of glasses from his pocket, dragged over a stool, and leaned in, inches from her face. He peeled back the rag and rummaged through the supplies on his tray. Up close, he looked even younger, except for his eyes. A piercing green, his eyes looked old and tired.

After filling a needle with some liquid from a vial, he said, "Try to sit still. The medicine is going to sting." As he drew near with the needle, however, it jumped and jolted in his hand as if his hands were shaking.

"Are you nervous or something?" Katie asked, clutching the sheets.

"Nope." Before Katie could protest further, the needle pierced her skin, and he pressed his thumb upon the plunger. The medicine did sting, and she resisted the urge to recoil, but eventually, the skin grew numb. He injected the medicine a few more times down the edges of the wound. The suture needle trembled in his hand as well, but as soon as it went into the skin, he controlled it with precision. His tongue protruded out the side of his mouth as he created little knots.

There were only a handful of people with whom she had sat so close before, all of them family. Being this close to him, a stranger, felt more than awkward. She could feel the heat from his body and smell his odor too. That and the cigarette stench clinging to his clothes.

His shirt, a previously red tee, was frayed around the seams and was scattered with little holes. His jeans fared better, although several places had been patched. She could see actual dirt within his hairline, among the twists and matts. More than once, Katie forced herself not to crinkle her nose and risk insulting him.

The girl, Michelle, looked a little better. Her hair was not matted and her face was clean. The clothes were old, but she did not smell like he did. Both had sharp jawlines and were thin to the point of gaunt.

Judging by the starch sheets and well-stocked infirmary, this was not a poverty problem, and Katie grew more confident in her determination of who the enemy was, and it wasn't the teenagers.

Five minutes was a lie. Thirty minutes passed before the boy put in the final stitch and knotted it off. "That went better than I thought it would," he said, pressing a swath of tape over the edges of the gauze bandage.

"Why is that?" Katie asked. Her words were slurred due to her numb cheek.

He shrugged in reply.

"This was your first time putting in stitches, wasn't it?" Addison asked.

"Yup."

"What?" Katie cried. "You said you knew what you were doing!"

"And I did a good job too." He scraped the wrappers off into the trash.

"Goldie!" Michelle smacked him on the back of the head, but he grinned.

"Relax," he said. "I've seen the nurse do it a thousand times. Addison," —he turned to the adult— "the stitches usually come out in ten to fourteen days. I'm putting her in Dakota's hut. What else do you want me to do with her?"

"Give her the tour." Addison pulled a green plastic band from her pocket. Taking Katie's wrist, she secured the band around it. "But ten to fourteen days? I was hoping you could do it in seven. That's when we make first-contact."

"I don't make the rules." He pushed the metal cart back to its original place. "I suppose you'll have to talk to God on that one. I'm not sure you still have his number though."

"Funny. I've got to go deal with the moron out back, so—do your thing." Addison moved to the door. "Oh, and Goldie, lose the paperclip."

"Sure thing, boss," he said, and she left. Goldie stuffed the paperclip back into his pocket.

The pounding in Katie's head returned, and she pressed her hand to her good cheek. "Can someone please give me some answers?"

"Michelle can," Goldie said, turning for the door.

"Oh, we're back to that now, huh?" Michelle protested. "You know I'm busy too!"

"Then complain to your boss." The door clicked behind him.

"Goldie, you jackass!" she shouted after him before turning back to Katie. "Alright then—oh geez, I realize I don't even know your name." Her voice changed to an unnatural calm after shouting at Goldie, and Katie staggered from the shift.

"I—uh—Katie," she muttered.

"Katie, right. Look, the thing is, I know you have a lot of questions, but I don't have time to answer them either."

Katie's mouth popped open. "But that was the deal!"

"Yeah, I know. And I'm really sorry, but lunch is about to start and I have to be in the kitchen. I'm going to take you to Dakota and he'll have to give you the rundown."

"But—I—"

"Come on." Michelle moved to the door and opened it for her. "If you talk fast, I'll answer as many questions as I can."

"I . . ." The pounding in her head intensified. Where to even start? Katie wanted to lay down and pretend like none of this ever happened, but Michelle continued to wait for her by the door. Hesitantly, she rose and followed her out into the hallway, wrapping her arms around herself.

"No questions?" Michelle asked as she turned a corner.

"No," Katie said. "I mean, yes—I . . ." She buried her face in her hands. "I don't know. This can't be happening—this can't be..." Katie placed her hand against the wall and slid to the floor.

Michelle's eyes darted down the hall, but then a look of sympathy filled her face. "Katie . . ." She knelt next to her. "Come on, Katie. You can't sit here and cry. You have to get up."

Katie cried louder.

"Dammit, Goldie," Michelle muttered under her breath. "Katie, are you hungry?"

Katie paused at the question, noticing the rumbling in her stomach for the first time. She nodded.

"I thought so," said Michelle. "Let's get a hot meal in you, and we'll go from there."

What the heck was this stuff? Katie stared at the unrecognizable gray mush Michelle had called food. Raising the spoon, she let the lumpy substance fall back into the bowl. Perhaps it was better than it looked? With an upturned lip, she brought the food to her mouth and tasted it.

"Blah!" Katie threw the spoon back into the bowl. It was acrid. Was Michelle serious? She looked over her shoulder to the girl, but she was busy talking to some long-haired boy.

Michelle had taken Katie down the hill from the mansion to the largest of the outbuildings. Inside were twelve long wooden tables set in two columns. Here other children gathered to eat their porridge-like substance. The children were filthy like Goldie, and baths seemed to be a distant memory. If the food was not disgusting enough, the scent of sweating bodies would churn the strongest stomach.

At least fifty other kids were packed in the mess hall, a number that amazed Katie. Had all of them been taken like her? Was this Midas's collection?

The fact that they were still alive was comforting, but the sheer number of kids present startled her. Fifty kids meant fifty kidnappings. How did someone get away with that? For ten years, Dad had been chasing this guy. What were the odds of him finding her now?

"You must be the new girl." Katie startled as a girl with golden hair braided to her waist took the seat next to her. Although the girl smiled at her, Katie offered a trembling lip in return.

"I'm Leida," the girl said. "What's your name?"

"K-Katie," she whispered.

"Are you going to be in our hut?"

"I-I don't know." Katie brought her shoulders to her ears. The girl, freckle-faced and young, seemed nice enough, but Katie was wary nonetheless.

Leida placed her dirt-covered hand over Katie's. "It's going to be okay."

"Is it?" Katie asked, pulling her hand away. "This can't be real." She pressed her hands to her eyes, wishing to wipe away the vision, but it was still there when she brought her hands back down.

"I know this is tough," said Leida.

"So how does this kidnapping thing work?" asked Katie. "Does Midas send proof of life through a picture with a newspaper or something? Or am I going to get to talk on the phone to my dad?"

"When Midas is ready, he'll set up a video call," said Leida.

"Then what? I'm assuming Midas wants something from my dad, but my dad would never betray his country. His job is too important. What if—what if?" Katie wrapped her arms around herself, unable to say what she truly feared. What if Dad chose the FBI instead of her?

"I've been here for a while," said Leida, "and I've never seen a parent choose their job over their kid."

Tears edged across her vision as she shook her head. "You don't know my dad. Will Midas kill me?"

"He'll threaten to, but Midas doesn't kill his captives," said Leida. "You'll just lose your armband is all."

Katie clamped her hand around the green plastic band the purple-haired woman had placed on her. As she looked down the table of kids, she spotted only a couple of others who had an armband. That wasn't a good sign, but more reassuring than the prospect of imminent death.

"My brother was in the car with me when it crashed. What happened to him?" Katie asked, swiping tears from her eyes.

"I'm sorry, Katie," said Leida. "I don't know anything about your brother. We aren't told much about what happens outside of here."

"This can't be happening," Katie breathed again, but the ground beneath her feet was so solid, the table before her so firm. This was real. And she didn't know what to do about it.

"Tell me about yourself," said Leida. "What line of work is your dad in?"

"My dad's an FBI agent," said Katie, then she let out a weak laugh. "He's the one supposed to be investigating Midas's kidnappings."

Leida's mouth dropped. "Come again?"

"Dad's the lead agent in the Midas investiga—"

"Jared!" cried Leida and stood. Waving fervently, she beckoned Goldie over from a nearby table. "Her dad's a Fed, did you know about this?"

With Leida's loud announcement, the heads of all the nearby kids turned to Katie, and she felt a warmth rise into her cheeks.

"Addison mentioned it, yes," said Goldie, hands in his pockets.

"Midas wouldn't risk taking a Fed's daughter unless the Fed was close to finding something!" said Leida. "That's great news!"

"And since his daughter is now stuck with us, we know that lead is dead," he said.

"My dad would never intentionally ruin an investigation," said Katie. "He's a good agent."

Goldie shoved his shoe into the dirt floor and nodded. "Of course." And with that, he strolled back to his seat.

"But he won't," said Katie to Leida.

Leida, however, just smiled, patted her on the shoulder, and retook her seat.

*   *   *

When the meal was over, Katie followed the others from her table outside. Per Leida's prediction, Katie had been assigned to her 'hut' or sleeping quarters. Each hut stayed together throughout the day, as well as when they performed their work assignments. The other kids, seemingly adapted to their current state, joked and prodded with each other, like kids do, as they made their way to the fields and greenhouses. A pair of boys even sword-fought with sticks, oblivious to the chain-link fence and three adults following them with tasers.

Katie gulped upon seeing the weapons. Tasers were better than lethal weapons, but not by much. Dad once taught a class for the FBI where the new recruits practiced firing tasers at each other. It was supposed to create a level of empathy in the agents for those at whom they fired their tasers.

They had videoed the whole affair, and Dad, although he wasn't supposed to, had shown the video to Katie and Alec. The 'victims' were held up on either side by their fellow agents while a fourth agent fired the taser into the victim's back. Invariably, the victims would spasm and crumble, and their fellow agents would lower them to the mat below. One guy peed his pants.

It was not something Katie ever wanted to experience.

Leida directed Katie to the field ahead, which dominated the majority of the property. The field was gridded into perfect rectangles filled with rich, dark soil and mulch bordering the rectangles. Inside the beds, shoots of green protruded from the ground.

"What is all this?" Katie asked.

"This is cannabis," Leida said. "That's the other side of the business. Instead of having us sit around all day, our captors decided to have us grow pot. Go ahead and grab a shovel."

Katie took the shovel from a pile of tools lying in the grass, but her thoughts were far from gardening. "I thought Midas kidnapped kids for ransom and stuff. He's a pot grower too?"

"Midas does a little bit of everything," said Leida. "If you can make money from it, he's involved in it. Listen, no one is expecting you to do much today, but you do need to look busy. If that means moving dirt from one pile to the other, knock yourself out, but do something."

"Why?"

"Because of the Watchers." Leida gestured to a man standing a few yards away. The man was in his mid-thirties with close-cut hair. He stood with his muscular arms crossed, and Katie was able to make out a tattoo of a globe with an anchor through it and an eagle on top. A marine? Her dad was a former marine. Surely not this guy too. When he saw Katie looking at him, he glared back. Katie dipped her head.

"Stay away from the Watchers," Leida said. "Especially Matt. He's a bit—grumpy."

"He's one of the kidnappers?"

"Kind of?" Leida said. "The people who run this place aren't actually kidnappers. Not really. People get kidnapped for all sorts of reasons. Political, financial—but the kidnappers all need some place to stash their victims. That's where Midas comes in. They hire him to keep us at these camps during the operation. The risk of kidnappers getting caught or prosecuted goes down when they can't find the victims. But we're getting off track here. The Watchers are the guards."

"Wow," said Katie, then laughed feebly. "This is so much more organized than I imagined."

"It's a business," said Leida. "And we're the Commodities."

Leida instructed Katie to dig little holes along the row. Following behind, Leida planted the cannabis seedlings. It was good the work was monotonous and uncomplicated, because Katie's mind would not allow for much else. Every so often, she would look back at Leida, and the girl would smile at her.

As her body continued to move down the row, Katie felt as if she were floating above it, looking down on the world as if from afar. Surely this was a dream. This place was too strange to be real. And yet, an overwhelming sadness filling her heart weighed like a stone, pulling her back to earth.

*   *   *

"How's she doing?" The boy behind Katie in the meal line asked. Work for the day had ended, and Leida had led her to the mess hall once more. The speaker was the long-haired boy Michelle had been talking to earlier, but now his hair was tied up with a bit of twine. He wrapped his arms around Leida and smiled affectionately at her.

"As well as expected," Leida answered and wiggled out of his hug. "No thanks to Michelle or Jared. Or you for that matter."

"You seemed to have it under control." He tried to kiss her, but she gave him her cheek. The boy rolled his eyes and looked at Katie. "I'm Dakota, your hut leader. How's your face doing?" He gestured to her bandage.

"It hurts." Katie sniffed, running her fingers against the gauze. "But not as bad now that it's not gaping."

Dakota spoke with what Katie initially thought was an Australian accent. But that wasn't quite it. Typically, this would have intrigued her, but she wasn't in the mood. Nor was she intrigued by his firm jaw and easy smile. Nor the muscles rippling beneath his shirt. Okay, so maybe that did intrigue her a bit, but still, not in the mood.

The line pushed them forward to a table at the front of the mess hall. Katie sneered as another bowl of unrecognizable mush was handed to her. Next was a boy pouring the beverage of the day. Water. Katie took one of the cups and followed her hut to a table near the door.

"Would you like to sit next to me?" Leida asked, and Katie shrugged and joined her.

Leida and the others dug into their meal with vigor while Katie let the mush drop from her spoon. "What is this?"

"Gruel," Leida said. "It's corn and soybeans mixed with vitamins."

"It's disgusting."

"Since we're Greenies, we get a double portion." A boy a couple of seats away shoveled in food with a wry smile.

"Greenie?"

"Your armband," said Leida.

Katie inclined her head in understanding. "Why were you kidnapped, Leida?"

"Midas wanted one of his buddies out of jail," said Leida. "And my dad made it happen."

"And after that, Midas just cut off your armband?"

"Mhm," said Leida. "But that was a long time ago."

Katie ran her fingers over the smooth surface of the band wondering how long she would be able to keep it. Addison had said first-contact was due in a week. Why so long from now? Couldn't they contact Dad now?

Spoons were soon laid next to bowls as the others finished eating in a matter of minutes. Katie, however, continued to contemplate her meal. Her previously hungry stomach was silent.

"I don't think I can eat this." Katie slid it away, and the other Greenie reached for the bowl.

"No, Eric." Leida slid the bowl to the center of the table. "Everyone put your bowls in."

The boy glared at Leida as his and ten other bowls moved to the center. The others waited silently as Leida divided the portions.

Once the job was completed, Leida slurped down the extra bite. "How old are you, Katie?"

"Fifteen."

"Only a year older than me," Leida said. "And a year younger than Dakota."

Who cared how old she was? But then she considered the others. Dakota was the technical leader of their 'hut,' but as far as Katie had seen, Leida called the shots. He was the oldest and a boy. Katie estimated those were his only qualifications for his current position.

Where were the guards? Finally, she spotted a Watcher leaning against the doorpost checking his phone. Another stood against the opposite wall looking equally bored. Whenever a kid would make a loud noise their attention shifted, but they remained otherwise unengaged. The one closest to her was a man in his late twenties, and he looked like a normal guy. A normal guy with an evil job.

"I want to talk to my dad," Katie said abruptly.

"And I wanted steak and potatoes for dinner," Eric said.

"When they set up the call," Leida said, "they'll come get you."

"I'm not waiting on that," she said. "I'm a hostage. They need me. I'm going to demand they contact my dad." Katie moved to stand.

"That's not a good idea." Leida grabbed her hand. "You don't want to go talk to the Watchers. You don't even want to look at them."

Her brows knit. "Dakota, you'll go with me to talk to them, right?"

Dakota laughed, but then his smile faded. "You're serious? Katie, you don't want to do that. Trust me."

She studied the nearby Watcher once more. Perhaps she didn't see what they did. "Well, then, I'll talk to you, and then you'll talk to them, right? You are the leader after all—"

"Uh, no," Dakota said. "That's not how it works. As a hut leader, I get an assignment from Goldie and break it up from there like—who gets to hoe or who gets to weed or water. Talking to the Watchers is not my job."

"That's Goldie's job? Then I'll go talk to him." This time she yanked her arm away before Leida could stop her.

"No!" Dakota protested, but the Watcher's attention swerved to him. He ducked his head.

Goldie sat alone at the table across the aisle with papers scattered before him. Although he wore his glasses, he continued to squint at his work. He did not acknowledge her as she approached, but shuffled a few papers instead.

Katie cleared her throat.

He turned a page.

She repeated the action.

"Pollen count was seven hundred and twenty-three today," he said. "I hope that's what that is, and you're not coming down with something."

"Huh?"

"Your throat. I'm assuming it's giving you trouble since you keep making that noise."

"I want to talk to you."

"No." He turned to another page. "I don't think you do."

Dakota arrived and took her arm. "Come on, Goldie's busy."

"Hmm." He scribbled something illegible.

"I get that you've got this sort of tough guy, 'I don't care' attitude going on," said Katie. "But I also saw your face when the truck driver ripped that stupid bag off my face. You're one of us, aren't you? Please, help me."

While he continued to stare at the papers before him, a wry smile appeared on his face. He set the pencil down, folded his hands, and looked up. "So you've got it all figured out, do you?"

"How do I go about seeing my dad?"

He glanced up to Dakota. "Explaining stuff like this is your job, remember?"

"I tried," said Dakota. "But she's not a good listener."

Goldie sighed. "Katie, I know this place is weird, but this isn't some summer camp where you play in the dirt with your friends and make good memories. You might not be tied to a chair right now, but believe me, you're in no position to be making demands."

"I know how this works," she said, taking the seat across from him. "These people need me alive and healthy, so I'm not going to eat, I'm not going to work, and I'm not going to cooperate unless I see my dad."

"*Healthy is a relative term.*" He tilted his empty bowl up for her to see. The bowl was so clean, it could have been put on a shelf without anyone knowing it had ever been used. "Do you think they care about your caloric intake? If you don't eat, they'll ignore you. And if you don't work, they'll flog you. And then they'll still contact your dad on their timetable. You'll just be a little sorer and hungrier than if you had done as you were told. But by all means—it's no skin off my back. Dakota . . ." He slid his glasses back on and returned to the papers in front of him.

Katie sat startled for a moment. By the way he had talked to the purple-haired Watcher, she had assumed he had a bit more clout, but the kid was eating the same rations as everyone else. Maybe she was wrong.

"Come on." Dakota jerked his head back to their table.

With no other play to make, Katie obeyed. Upon returning to her table, she found her bowl as clean as the others and wondered if she should have tried harder to eat.

After dinner, Leida ushered Katie inside a long rectangular building, a "hut" as Leida called it, across the way from the mess hall. There were four huts, two on either side of the mess hall. Katie was not quite sure why they were called huts, as there was nothing hut-like about them. The roof was made of shingles instead of grass, and the walls were made of plywood, not canes. The floor was made of hard-packed dirt. There were no glass panes in the windows, but instead, a shutter filled the hole. Two rows of bunk beds lined the walls with blankets wadded on top of bare, gray mattresses.

Leida handed Katie a thin blanket before leading her to a wooden bunk bed at the end of the row. "If you need anything, let us know."

That was a strange thing to say. The boys lay in the middle of the floor tossing rocks into a circle as part of some game, while most of the girls played with each other's hair. Judging from the complete lack of 'things' in their hut, Katie could not imagine how they intended to fill even a single need. Maybe it was just something people said.

Leida moved to the single twin bed at the front of the hut where Dakota sat, and Katie sat down on her hard bunk and watched her hut-mates for a time. Occasionally, she would receive a glance from the others but was otherwise left alone.

The exhaustion from the day, the sedatives, and the shock caught up to Katie now that she was sitting still, and she began to nod off as she leaned against her bedpost. With nothing else to do, she climbed beneath her blanket and pulled it over her head. But as she wrapped the covers close, the tears started again. Less than two days ago she was home with her family, but now?

What about Dad? What about Alec? Was he even alive? A vision of flames erupting from their vehicle crossed her vision. As she wiped a tear from her eye, her fingers brushed against the bandage. Pain roared from the site, and Katie let out a moan.

"Katie?" Leida's voice came from above her, and she pulled the blanket down. "Do you need anything?"

What a stupid question! Katie shook her head.

Leida was about to leave but paused at the foot of the bed. "I have some Tylenol buried underneath my bed. Would you like some?"

Buried? That thought had never occurred to Katie. A commodity like that had unquestionably been stolen. And with dirt floors, what better place would there be to hide it? "Yes, that would be great."

Leida smiled and went back to her bed. After a few minutes, she returned with a couple of white capsules, and Katie downed them dry.

"You don't happen to have a satellite phone buried somewhere, do you?" Katie asked, and Leida giggled.

"I wish," she said. "But if you find one, let me know, won't you?"

The lights in the hut went out, and Katie jumped.

"That's just the cue for bedtime," said Leida with a pat on Katie's knee. "I know it's been a hard day, but try to get some rest."

One-by-one, the kids moved to their bunks, and blankets were pulled over heads. Soon soft snoring spread throughout the hut as kids drifted off to sleep. Katie laid quietly on her bunk, but she was sure sleep would never come. The sedatives from the journey here must have had some lingering effects, however, because soon she was fast asleep.

*   *   *

When morning came, an air raid siren blasted from the Big House, and Katie woke to a pounding headache. Her foggy brain took time to recall the events of yesterday. The headache intensified once the memories returned.

"Good morning." Leida sat on the edge of her bed. "How are you doing?"

Katie pressed her hands to her eyes, from where the headache seemed to radiate the most. Part of her wished to cry, but that would make the headache worse.

"It will get better," Leida said. "I promise, but we need to get moving. You're going to get thirty seconds at the water spigot, then we have breakfast."

Since 'getting ready' entailed putting on shoes and nothing more, Katie trudged out of the hut behind the others in short order. A Watcher outside counted them as they exited, then all the huts meshed together on the journey to the water spigot outside the mess hall.

"Time's up," the Watcher at the spigot said after she had only wet half of her face, and Katie glared at her.

"Hey, don't sass me, little miss," the Watcher said.

Leida dragged her away as she kept her own head lowered.

At breakfast, Katie stabbed her gruel as she ate. She managed to get the whole bowl down, but her stomach groaned louder. How did these kids live off this stuff?

They continued planting seedlings in the field that morning. The boy Eric went behind her with the tiny plants as she dug the holes. Already, the heat was rising, and the air grew muggy. As she worked, her frustration grew. Katie had finished half a row when she slammed the shovel into the ground. "That's it! I'm done. I'm not digging one more darn hole until somebody calls my dad. And I'm going to walk up to one of those Watchers and demand it unless one of you can give me a good reason not to!"

Dakota and Leida exchanged glances before ambling over from a few rows away. Eric knocked dirt off his hands. "Here we go again."

"Show her," Leida said when she arrived.

"Are you sure?" Dakota said. "She's so new."

"She's not a young one. Show her."

Dakota bit his lip, but then removed his shirt turning his back to Katie. White lines crossed at odd angles where the flesh had been torn.

"What-what happened?" Katie said.

"That's what happens when you cross the Watchers," Leida said. "They're flogging scars from the whip they keep at the Big House."

"But . . . but I'm a hostage. I'm . . ."

Healthy is a relative term, Goldie had said. Katie gulped.

"Look," said Leida, "I'd love to set fire to this entire field, but we can't. The Watchers leave us alone for the most part, but only if we do our jobs. We have quotas to meet, we all pitch in, otherwise, this happens."

Dakota slid his shirt back on.

"You don't have to work fast," Leida said. "But you do have to work."

She handed Katie back the shovel, and Katie stared at the tool as the vision of Dakota's back played in her mind. Katie slammed the blade into the dirt and tore a hole in the earth.

* * *

That night, Katie picked at the cloth Leida had wrapped around her now blistered hand. Hours had passed since the Watchers cut the power to the huts, but still, she could not sleep. As she tossed and turned on the thin mattress, she cursed the shovel and the marijuana and the Watchers. Even Clark, the truck driver, received his own special curse.

Around one in the morning, Katie settled into a comfortable position. As she was drifting off, however, she suddenly had to pee.

She tried to ignore the call of nature, but it persisted. At home, a trip to the bathroom was a quick dart across the hall, but the outhouse was almost to the fields. She was so tired. Surely, she could wait until morning. Katie wrapped the thin blanket closer and nestled her head onto the flat pillow, but her bladder protested even stronger.

Katie flung back the covers and slid her feet to the dirt floor. The sound of gentle snoring reached her ears, and envy grew in her. Sighing, she shoved her feet into her sneakers and resigned herself to her fate. After wrapping the blanket around her, she slipped past the rows of sleeping kids, slipped through the front door, and closed it behind her.

As she stepped onto the moonlit path, however, the door opened once more. "Where are you going?" Leida, also wrapped in a blanket, followed her. With a pang of jealousy, Katie realized the blanket was a fraction thicker than her own.

"I have to pee," Katie said.

Leida studied the shadows cast by the outbuildings. "I'm coming with you. Make it quick, and next time go before lights out."

"Sure. Sorry." Katie frowned. What was her deal?

As the two girls walked the well-worn path in silence, Leida continuously peered over her shoulder, and Katie grew nervous. Both girls jumped when Katie's stomach growled.

Katie laughed. "Sorry."

"Come on. Hurry up and pee and let's get back."

"Okay." Katie held her breath and ducked inside the dark outhouse at the edge of the buildings. She took her breaths in gasps as she tried not to breathe in the smell. As soon as possible, she got out of there. When she rejoined Leida, the younger girl drew her blanket close and stared down the dark lane.

"What is it?" Katie asked.

"Nothing," Leida said. "I thought I saw something."

"One of the Watchers? If we weren't allowed outside, wouldn't they lock the door?"

"We're allowed outside." Leida started back up the path.

"Then why would it matter if we were caught?" Katie joined her.

Something moved across the path, and both girls stopped.

"Who's there?" Leida called out.

A dark figure stepped from behind one of the buildings and stood in the middle of the path. The hairs on the back of Katie's neck raised. As she turned around, another shape rounded the edge of the hut on their left.

Leida grabbed her wrist. "Run."

Leida's fingers tightened around Katie's wrist, and they darted alongside the mess hall instead of down the path to their hut.

"Where are we going?" Katie cried. Was Leida trying to make it to the huts on the other side of the mess hall?

When they reached the corner of the building, Leida continued. Katie gasped as one of the figures reached the opposite corner at the same time as them. Only the short side of the mess hall was between them.

Katie slipped on the damp grass, and Leida yanked her off the ground. Precious seconds were lost. He was gaining on them. They weren't going to make it in time.

"Jared!" Leida cried as she neared a cluster of sheds. Something brushed against Katie's hair. A hand grabbed her arm, and Katie stole another look over her shoulder. Then a force hit her from the front, and she collapsed into a heap.

As Katie lay on her back staring up at the stars, a man with crooked teeth moved to stand over her. The other Watcher joined him, bellowing with laughter. She scooted away from them until her back jutted against two poles.

Katie looked up—they were not poles. They were legs. A shirtless man looked down at her.

She gasped and tried to launch herself away, but he grabbed her arms and shoved her into the shed. The door slammed behind her.

Disoriented, Katie lay upon the cold, hard dirt as the world spun around her. A hand touched her, and she pulled away.

"It's me," Leida said.

Katie clutched her head and rolled to a sit. Her eyes strained to adjust to the darkness. The place reeked of cigarettes.

A light flashed to her left where an oil lantern ignited. Leida set the lamp on a table next to a cot, extinguished a match with a shake of her hand, and tossed a blanket from the floor onto the bed. Between the cot, the table, and a row of crates along the wall, the shed was tightly packed. Voices leaked through the thin walls, but Katie couldn't make out what was being said. One of the Watchers cackled with laughter once more.

"Are you okay?" Leida said. "You sort of smashed your face into the door."

Katie shook her head to clear the pounding.

"Sit here." Leida helped her to the cot and wrapped the blanket around her shoulders. Yet another blanket that was thicker than her own.

"Where are we? Who helped us?" Katie said.

"Jared." Leida sat next to her. "This is his hut. Let me see your head."

Katie winced as Leida pressed her fingers to Katie's temple.

"Jared?" Katie asked.

Leida frowned. "Goldie."

"Goldie?" Katie said. "This is Goldie's hut?"

The door opened, and a shirtless Goldie stepped inside. Katie could make out each of his ribs in the lamplight. With a sneer, he surveyed Katie as he leaned against the door and folded his arms. "How's her head?"

"I'm fine," Katie said.

Leida stood. "What the hell did Tweedle Dee and Tweedle Dum want?"

"I think they're a bit too high to answer that," Goldie said.

"Assholes," Leida said.

"What the hell were you thinking?" He strode toward Leida. "You were out walking in the open? What'd you do, look outside and think, 'Gee! What a nice night for a walk!' Have you lost your mind?"

"Katie needed to pee," Leida said.

"Are you freaking kidding me? That's your excuse? Have her piss in a corner and get a shovel in the morning," he said, and Katie curled her lip.

"They aren't supposed to be working today." Leida balled her fists.

"Newsflash! They are! You're getting soft."

"You're one to talk!"

"Stop yelling at her!" Katie shouted back and winced from the effort. "It's not her fault. It's my fault."

"But you—" he pointed at her, "—you don't know any better. Leida, you know better."

"And what about you, Jared?" Leida asked. "You don't know better? You're out here roaming the camp every night. What's your excuse?"

"Stop it!" Katie rubbed the knot already forming on her head. "Stop it. You two fight worse than a brother and sister."

Leida and Jared looked at her oddly. Their identical blonde hair and green eyes caught in the lamplight.

She paused her rubbing. "You two—you two are brother and sister, aren't you?"

"Deductive reasoning," Jared said. "That's a trait you've yet to manifest. Glad to know it's among your capabilities."

Katie should have been insulted, but the revelation of the two's relationship roused another memory. Dad had talked about a pair of siblings taken ten years ago, but what was their name again?

"You are such a jerk," Leida continued arguing with her brother, but Jared waved her off.

"In all this, where is Dakota?" he asked and Leida's mouth formed a line. "He never woke up. Damn him."

"You chose him."

"Kelley," said Katie, and both of them paused to look at her. "Leida, you said your dad helped Midas get his buddy out of jail. Was your dad a district attorney? Is your last name Kelley?"

"Holy crap," breathed Leida.

"You know us?" asked Jared.

"Are you kidding?" asked Katie. "Your kidnapping was my dad's first case with the Bureau! He told me about you the other day. Midas threatened your dad to get his money launderer acquitted. My brother and I are close to the same age as you two, so it made a big impact on my dad—and Midas apparently."

Jared pressed his hands against his face and leaned against the wall. "Tell me everything you know."

"I—uh—I just did," said Katie. "My dad only told me this much because of the birthday cards."

"Birthday cards?" Leida asked.

"After my dad took the case, Midas started sending birthday cards to my brother and me to taunt my dad. This last one though, I think it was a threat against me."

"That's super creepy," said Leida.

"That's what I said!"

"Did your dad say anything else about our family?" asked Jared. "Are they okay?"

"I'm sorry, I don't know anything else. The conversation was more about Midas than you."

Jared nodded, seeming to accept this. In any case, he returned to the situation at hand. "It's time to get you back to your hut. You did pee, didn't you?"

Katie nodded.

"Wait," said Leida. "If you don't have more questions, I certainly do. How close was your dad to catching Midas?"

Katie shook her head. "As of the other day, Dad said they had no leads. But he was called away to Memphis to follow up on a missing ambassador's kid the day I was kidnapped."

"Not that it matters," said Jared. "Like I said before, whatever leads were there, they are dead now."

"Why do you have to be like that?" asked Leida.

Jared said nothing but dug his toe into the dirt floor instead.

"I'm sorry," said Katie. "Really—"

"It's not your fault," muttered Jared.

"But I feel responsible . . ."

"Our dad blew the biggest lead the FBI ever had in catching Midas. We weren't responsible for that, and neither are you for this." Jared snatched his dirt-stained shirt off his chair. As he drew near the light, Katie saw flogging marks on his back, and her stomach churned.

"Now come on," he said, turning for the door.

What a hellish place to spend a decade.

Goldie escorted the girls back to their hut in silence. If there were any other Watchers around, they left them alone. Before they entered their hut, however, Leida stopped him at the door. "Jared, leave it, please."

He pushed the door open. "Go inside."

Leida's shoulders sagged as she entered, and Katie followed her toward their bunks. Goldie gave a sweeping glance across the room of sleeping children before stepping to the single bed at the front of the room. Taking the edge of the mattress, he flipped it and the sleeping occupant to the floor.

"Whaa?" Dakota cried as collided with the cold ground.

Goldie grabbed him by his shirt, pinning him to the side of the bed.

"Goldie?"

"Perhaps," Goldie said in a lowered voice, "you can explain to me why my sister was out there tonight doing your frickin' job, you lazy sack of shit."

"Whoa, man! I don't know anything about that."

"You are the hut leader, Dakota. Not her. Do your job, or I swear, you will wish your mother had smothered you the minute she laid eyes on you. Do you understand?"

"Yeah." Dakota rubbed the back of his head. "Sure, yeah. Sorry."

Goldie shoved him back to the ground and left, slamming the door behind him.

Dakota nursed his shoulder as he looked to where Katie and Leida stood a couple of bunks down. "Can someone explain to me what the hell just happened?"

*   *   *

"Do the Watchers often enjoy terrorizing people on their way to the bathroom?" Katie asked as she swiped sweat from her brow. An hour had passed since they were sent to the fields, and Katie was ready to be done. It had rained last night after their escapade, and now the mud was trying to eat her sneakers. Her frustration grew as she watched Leida move her rake over the woodchip mulch with ease. Katie didn't know someone could have magic rake powers, but Leida used that tool as if it were an extension of her own arm. The girl was a machine, leaving behind an even cover and healthy stock while Katie struggled not to hit the plants. She should have helped Mom more in the garden.

"Most people don't leave their huts until morning," Leida said. "You shouldn't be going anywhere without a buddy, even in the middle of the day."

Katie nodded and silence fell between them once more. In the quiet, her thoughts grew louder, but the questions were the same ones that repeated over and over. What about Dad? What about Alec? What do they want with me? Questions no one had been willing or able to answer.

She longed for her iPod. At least music would have pushed these thoughts into the background. How did Jared and Leida survive so long with so many unanswered questions?

"I'm sorry about last night," said Katie. "Midas has been sending me birthday cards for the past decade, but this was the first birthday I ever knew about them. If I had known about the threats, I would have demanded Dad tell me everything he knew. Now . . ."

"Well, it's not like you knew you were going to be kidnapped," said Leida.

"To be honest, I can't imagine living in a place like this as long as you or Goldie have."

"I don't call him that," Leida said. "The Watchers gave him that nickname. His name is Jared."

"He seems—interesting . . ." The vision of Goldie's scars in the glow of the oil lamp flashed through her mind and she shuddered.

Leida groaned. "Can we please not talk about my brother? I hate talking about him. He is his own person, and I am in no way responsible for the questionable stuff he does."

Questionable stuff? Perhaps she was referring to dumping Dakota out of bed last night. "No, I get that," said Katie. "I would feel the same way about my brother."

The vision of the scars reappeared—only this time it was Alec's back. Katie gripped the rake tighter as she shoved the thought from her mind. It was replaced by Alec's face as he lay slumped over the wheel of their vehicle. Katie shoved her pile of woodchips forward with the back of the rake and rolled her shoulder across the moisture in her eyes.

"Oh no, Katie," Leida stopped mid-shove. "You've just covered up three plants. They'll suffocate like that." Leida looked back down Katie's row to find a few other plants with leaves barely visible from their mulch cover. She grimaced.

"I'm not very good at this, am I?"

Leida bit her lip. "Ivy?" she called over a five-year-old girl who was busy watering behind them as they went. "Swap with Katie, will you?"

Who the heck was bad at raking? Distracted or otherwise. But Katie relinquished her rake to the five-year-old, and Ivy continued on ahead of her, controlling the rake with precision. Having not even the distraction of the rake to aid her, Katie followed behind dangling the water hose over the plants as the knot in her throat grew. Would she ever see her family again?

*   *   *

Wincing, Katie leaned against Leida's bedpost. They had just had dinner. Why was she still so hungry? She recalled Mom's homemade ravioli, and her mouth started watering. Had it really been over two years since Mom had died? She wished Mom were here now.

No.

Katie wouldn't want anyone to be here with her. Not Alec. Not Dad. She wanted desperately to be with them, but not the other way around. Never the other way around.

"It gets better," Leida said.

"So you keep saying," Katie mumbled.

Leida shrugged. "At least, you won't think about it as much."

Katie pressed her forehead into the bedpost. Somehow, she doubted this.

"Would you like me to teach you the rock game?" Leida pointed to the boys lying on their bellies in the dirt. They had drawn a circle in the dust and took turns tossing rocks at a central rock. "Eric thinks he's reigning champion, but that's because he's never played against me. I'll take back my title, and you'll learn how to play."

"I'm good," Katie said. "No offense, but that sounds terribly boring." She would prefer watching Alec create mods on his videogame—which was saying something.

Leida laughed. "I agree completely. Maybe I'll read tonight instead." She pulled a hardback book out from beneath her pillow.

"They give us books?" Katie straightened.

"Jared worked out a deal with one of the Watchers," Leida said. "She smuggles in a book from the library, and he passes it on to me."

Some of the girls took notice of Leida's new book and joined her on her bed. Katie soon found herself in the back of the crowd as she continued to lean against the bedpost.

"Can I sit in your lap?" Ivy, the five-year-old, asked Leida.

"Sure," Leida said. "But there aren't any pictures."

Ivy snuggled up nonetheless.

"Chapter one." Leida looked over the pages with an enticing smile. "My mother drove me to the airport with the windows rolled down . . ."

Katie laid down on the bunk and closed her eyes listening to Leida's melodic voice. Soon her depressing surroundings faded away as she became immersed in the tale. She had read this book before, but any distraction from this horrible place was most welcome. They were getting to the good part when Leida stopped.

Katie sat up and looked around. Everyone's attention was on the newcomer leaning against the door.

"What brings you to our humble hut?" Dakota greeted Goldie.

"Katie," Goldie said, "you wanted to see your dad? Now would be that time."

A smile erupted across her face, and Katie leapt to her feet and joined him at the door. Goldie held it open for her, and they stepped into the evening light. "I get to see my dad?"

"You get to video call your dad," he said. "But don't get too excited. You're going to be reading from a script. Follow it to the letter."

Katie didn't care. Other than the gnawing in her stomach, her father and brother had been her only thoughts.

Goldie led her through the kitchen and into the large dining room. After a few turns, the hallway emerged from beneath a staircase at the main entrance. Although the door was unguarded, the Watchers had placed metal rods across the exit, making it part of the wall.

Two separate staircases with polished banisters ran along the walls, and an oriental rug covered the hardwood floors. An enormous chandelier caught the light from the stained-glass windows mounted over the door.

Goldie followed her gaze. "Don't get any ideas," he said. "There's a pane of reinforced glass fixed over the stained glass."

Katie, who was admiring the glass, not hatching an escape plan, inclined her head. That sounded like first-hand knowledge, and the scars on his back made a little more sense. "They don't miss a thing, do they?"

"They've had years of kids banging on things and picking locks. They've adapted." He rolled his shoulder, and Katie wondered more about those scars. "Now, come on. You're not going to want to keep these people waiting."

They continued up the elegant staircase and down yet another hall. When they passed a Watcher on the way, Goldie bowed his head. The Watcher didn't acknowledge their existence. Once they stopped at a door with a keypad and fingerprint scanner, Goldie knocked.

A balding Watcher ushered them inside. At the far end of the room, a long black sheet hung on the wall, and two chairs stood in front of the backdrop. A video camera was mounted on a tripod next to a table full of electronics. The purple-haired Watcher, Addison, smiled at Katie, a gesture that confused her more than comforted her. In the corner sat a black-bearded man in a gray silk suit, his arms fixed over his chest as he studied them in silence. Katie's eyes widened as she recognized him as the man from her kidnapping.

"Did you brief her?" the balding Watcher at the door asked.

"I told her there was a script, and she was to stick to it," Goldie said.

"You have a list of approved questions. Any questions not on the list do not get answered."

"But what do I say to those questions?" Katie asked.

"You say 'I can't answer that question. Okay, princess?" he asked, and she nodded. "Then take a seat. And don't think about trying anything. Don't try to tap Morse Code with your eyelids or anything like that. We've seen those tricks before."

Adapted . . .

Hesitantly, Katie walked past the table of electronics to the chair. The man surprised her with a pair of zip ties. "Hands on the armrests."

Katie looked to Goldie, who nodded. The balding man, however, glared at Goldie.

"Don't look at him," sneered Baldy. "Look at me. You do as I say, is that clear?"

Trembling, Katie obeyed, and the Watcher secured her hands. The sneer held as he turned back to Goldie, and the teen studied the floor with intensity.

"Richard, she's all yours," Baldy told the man in the corner.

"We've talked about this," the bearded man said. "You call me Midas in front of them."

The balding man paused, his hand on the electronics table. "Sorry, but don't you think that's weird? Everyone already knows you're my brother."

Uh, not everybody, thought Katie as her eyes widened. So not only was this the elusive Midas, but he had family! In just one sentence, she had gained more information than the FBI had acquired in ten years.

Midas scowled, and Baldy held up his hands. "Fine, whatever. Are you going on or not?"

"I'm not going on," Midas said.

"But I thought—? You called the father . . ."

"Yes, but I can't go on film, Ian I've already taken enough risks by being at the kidnapping. If it weren't for the Chinese case . . ."

"Fine, I'll do it," Ian sighed and grabbed a Guy Fawkes mask from the table. As he sat, he pulled the mask over his face.

"What's your name again, girl?" Addison asked.

"Katie," she said.

"Katie, I'm going to turn on some bright lights. I want you to tell me if you can still see the screen here, okay?" Addison tapped on a television screen where a list of questions and correct responses were displayed. Two bright lights then blinded Katie.

"Can you still see the script?" Addison asked.

Katie blinked several times, and her vision cleared some. "Yes."

"What do you think, guys?" Addison said. "Bandage or no bandage?"

"Bandage," the others said in unison. Goldie taped some gauze to her face and stepped back behind the lights.

"Remember, Katie, stick to the script," Addison said. "Anything off-script will be dealt with severely. Everyone ready?"

Another screen lit up with an image of a phone ringing. After a few seconds, the image turned into the face of her father.

"Katie?" her dad burst out.

"Dad?" she cried as her heart leapt into her throat. "Dad!"

"Katie! Where are you, honey?"

"I'm—" she started, but Addison tapped loudly on the screen. She pointed to the top line. "I can't answer that," Katie read.

"Are you—are you okay, honey?" Dad said. "Are they treating you well? Are they feeding you?"

She snickered. "The food sucks." The ever-present ache in her belly continued. "I mean—yes. They are taking care of me very well."

The sound of shuffling was heard from behind the lights. She shouldn't have said that.

"Katie, what's on your face?" Dad squinted at the screen. "Is that a bandage?"

Her eyes scanned the panel. "It's nothing. Just a scratch."

"I love you so much, Katie Belle. And Alec loves you too. We're going to do everything we can to get you home, do you hear me?"

"Yes, Dad. I hear you. I love you too."

The camera swiveled to the masked Ian. Midas stepped into the light and placed a strip of duct tape over her mouth, but tears of relief streamed down Katie's face. Alec—Alec was alive.

"You son of a bitch!" Dad shouted at Ian. "What have you done to her? What's wrong with her face?"

"Relax, Agent Thompson," Ian said. "I assure you, it's nothing but a scratch. And as you can see, she received the appropriate medical attention."

"Proper medical attention? You bastard!"

"Your daughter is fine, Agent. We've proven that to you. Now, you need to keep your end of the deal. And remember, keep your daughter's survival to yourself. If anyone finds out she's still alive, you'll be no use to us. You'll be hearing from us soon."

They cut the feeds, and Katie sat numbly under the bright lights. He was gone so quick. There was so much she had wanted to say, so much she wanted to hear . . .

The tower lights turned off, and Midas strode toward her. His steps were deliberate, his expression taut. Katie squirmed and pulled against the restraints. Midas ripped the duct tape from her mouth and Katie whimpered.

Softly he said, "Was it not clear that you were to follow the script and only the script?"

"I'm sorry! I got—" Katie said, Midas slapped her. She recoiled as tears sprang to her eyes. "I'm s-sorry. I-I got carried away."

"You say only what we tell you to say, do you understand?" He leaned in closer, his nose inches from hers.

"I'm sorry!" She tried to slide her wrists free.

"Who the hell do you think you are?" Midas shouted and slapped her again. "Do you think you are above the rules?"

"No," she said through tears.

The next blow came so hard, the chair wobbled backward. Midas grabbed hold of her throat and squeezed.

Katie gasped as her eyes bulged. She pulled against her restraints, and the ties cut into her wrists. Her feet scrambled against the tile floor as the world started collapsing. Vaguely, she heard voices behind him, protests perhaps. Yet still, he squeezed. Only when she neared unconsciousness did he release the hold.

Katie gasped and choked, her lungs bursting for air. Midas shoved her in the chest, and the chair teetered backward. It struck the wall, but the momentum slid the legs out from the chair, catching the curtain and tearing it during the descent. Katie struck her head on the floor.

"Well done, Rich," Ian said somewhere above her. "You tore the curtain."

Dazed and choking, Katie lay upon her back while shadows moved above her. Someone cut her wrists free and rolled her to her side. She was yanked up by her arm. Katie tried to protest, but Goldie ignored her, slinging her arm over his shoulder and hurrying her to the door. Although her chest was racked with coughs, he did not stop until they were down the stairs and in the kitchen. A couple of kids still lingered there cleaning, and he ushered her to a swivel stool in front of the workbench.

"Take some breaths," Goldie said as Katie continued to cough. He raised her chin gently, but Katie pulled away.

"I'm just looking." He pressed his shaking fingers against her throat.

"Here's some water." A cold glass was placed into Katie's hands. It took her a moment to recognize Michelle, the girl she had met on the first day. "Sip it slowly," Michelle said.

The coughing started again, but the water felt good gliding down the back of her throat. Her teeth chattered, and she hugged herself and rocked.

"Ian?" Michelle asked Goldie.

"Midas."

"What happened?"

"A misstep. Ian didn't flinch, but Midas . . ."

"He just looks for an excuse."

Tears slid down Katie's face. She felt like a little girl again with her parents talking over her. Ian entered the room, and the hairs on the back of her neck stood up as she stifled a cough. Michelle and Goldie fell silent and lowered their heads.

"How bad is it?" Ian lifted Katie's chin. She pulled away, but he advanced further. "Damn. It's going to bruise. Get some ice on it, Goldie."

"It's locked," Goldie said.

Huffing, Ian rounded the corner with Goldie and returned a few moments later with a bag of ice. Katie jumped as the cold hit her neck.

"Get her back to her hut," Ian said. "We'll put some make up over it if it's still there next week."

"Yes, sir." Goldie took Katie's cup and washed it in a nearby sink.

While Goldie finished tidying up, Ian slid his hands over Michelle's petite frame. Even in her dizzy state, Katie sat up straighter as the grown man nestled his chin onto the teen girl's shoulder.

"Are you about finished here?" Ian said.

Michelle stiffened at his touch but smiled falsely. "Yes."

"Then I'll see you in a bit." He pecked her on the cheek.

Goldie stared after him as the water poured over the full glass and onto his hand. Michelle looked at him, and he turned away, set the clean glass in the drying rack, and dried his hands. "How's your voice?"

For a moment, Katie did not realize the question was directed at her. She ripped her eyes from Michelle and answered, "It hurts to talk."

"Then try not to for a couple days," he said. "We need to get you back."

Katie stood from the stool but had to grip the counter to stay upright.

Goldie took her arm again, guiding her through the kitchen. "You can rest in your hut. It's safer there than in the house."

As they reached the door, Katie passed a final look over her shoulder to Michelle. The girl looked away.

Clutching her throat, Katie followed Goldie halfway down the path before stopping suddenly. Goldie tried to prod her along, but Katie needed to know something and was determined not to let him push the question off onto someone else.

"Why are you the oldest kid here?" Katie asked.

Jared cocked his head to the side. "I'm not. Trevor's a couple months older."

"But there are no kidnapped adults," said Katie. "Midas has been at this for ten years. Surely, there were others older than you. Did Midas kill them when they grew up?"

"Midas doesn't kill his victims," said Goldie. "You don't have anything to worry about."

Katie stamped her foot. "Don't do that to me!"

"I—uh—what?"

"Minimize!" she said. "My dad does that to me all the time. Tell me the truth, Jared! What happens to us once we lose the armband?"

Jared bit his lip and scuffed his shoe repeatedly against the grass, ripping up the blades. Then, after a long deep breath, he said, "Midas doesn't kill his victims, but he doesn't save them either.

Between the lack of food, sickness, and exposure, our people die one by one. The reason adult victims don't exist is not because Midas kills them; it's because no one has survived long enough to grow up."

"So, the fifty kids here now?"

"Are just the tip of the iceberg," said Jared. "There are more buried in the woods than living in the camp."

Katie's chest began to ache as tears re-emerged. "But why wouldn't they just kill us?"

"Because there's no money in that," said Jared. "They keep us here on their farm and use up what little profit is left from us through slave labor. But the armband is the key. As long as you have the armband, they'll do whatever they can to keep you alive."

Katie tried to be strong, to keep her head up in the face of such news, but the dizziness returned. "Jared, I think I'm going to be sick."

"Alright," he said, taking her arm once more. "Hang in there. I'll get you to your hut."

The next morning, Katie woke to another pounding headache. As she sat up rubbing her head, her surroundings further disoriented her. Why was she so close to the front?

"Good morning." Leida sat up on the bunk next to her and slid her feet into old, mud-caked shoes.

"Did I sleep in your bed?" Katie asked.

Leida shrugged. "You were kind of out of it when Jared brought you back last night. How's your neck?"

She brushed her fingers over the injury and winced. "It hurts, but I think I'll be alright. My throat's a little scratchy though." Katie sat up and stared down at her own shoes, waiting to receive her feet. But what was the point of getting up? Getting out the door? It didn't matter if she played nice with these Watchers, the end was still the same.

"It gets better," said Leida.

"No, it doesn't," Katie said. "You just get used to it."

Leida bit her lip, glanced down the row of kids, and lowered her voice, "No, it doesn't. But I've got a whole hut of young ones here that are depending on us to keep it together. I know you're hurting, but you need to keep what Jared told you last night to yourself, okay?"

Beyond her, kids continued to rub sleep from their eyes as they stumbled out of their beds and into their worn shoes. More than one watched Katie and Leida's exchange through sleep-weary eyes.

"Okay?" prodded Leida.

Katie hugged herself and nodded.

"But," Leida said in her normal, sunny voice, "if you want, you can take the bed beside me."

"What?" cried Eric as he approached from behind. "She can't take my bed!"

"I couldn't take his bed," said Katie.

"Sure, you can! Right, Dakota?"

"Eric," Dakota said lazily, "you're swapping with Katie."

"Oh, come on!" cried Eric before trudging toward the door, muttering unkind words beneath his breath.

*   *   *

At breakfast, Katie wolfed down her morning gruel and stared at the bottom of the bowl, wishing it would refill itself with pancakes drizzled with blueberry syrup. Katie shoved the bowl away and rubbed her weary eyes. Or eggs mixed with cheese covered in sausage gravy . . .

Stop it! She ran her fingers through her greasy hair and stared at the table. The knowledge of the missing food hung heavy on her shoulders knowing the greater truth behind it: her captors wanted her dead, and they were going to bring about that death as slowly as possible.

"How many know?" Katie asked Leida, who sat beside her.

A few of the other kids raised their heads, and Leida cast Katie a side-glance. "About the number of crops we planted last year?" Leida diverted the question. "I'd say only Jared knows the actual number, but numbers are kind of his thing. Things have improved since he took over two years ago."

"I don't think you understood my question," said Katie.

"I understood your question perfectly," said Leida evenly, and Katie inclined her head in understanding. Only Jared knew how many dead lay buried in the woods.

"Hey, Michelle!" Dakota greeted.

Katie jumped to find the girl from the kitchen standing directly behind her. The image of the bald Watcher's fingers on her shoulders flashed to mind.

"Good morning," Michelle said. "Katie, you've been sent for at the Big House. After breakfast, meet me at the kitchen and I'll take you from there."

A knot formed in Katie's stomach. "Why?"

"I'm supposed to take you to Addison. Other than that, I don't know." Without waiting for a reply, Michelle walked away.

Dakota shrugged. "It might be about your dad."

Katie leaned in to the table and whispered, "What's up with Michelle and the bald Watcher?"

"Ian?" Leida asked.

"Yeah, sure." Katie shrugged. "He got all weird and handsy with her yesterday. He kissed her on the cheek and put his hands on her shoulders?"

"Uhm," Leida said. "Yeah, she and Ian are sort of sleeping together."

"Voluntarily?"

Leida scratched her head. "I don't know the details, but it's part of some deal. Ian is the camp head, and there are certain—perks— to being with him."

"That's disgusting," Katie said. Yeah, their situation was bleak, unbearable even, but to sink so low that you would sleep with a Watcher for 'perks?' "Is that why she's the only girl hut leader?"

"I don't know about that," Dakota said. "Michelle does a pretty good job. I don't know if that's the only reason."

"I ain't sayin' she a gold digga," Eric muttered, and a couple other kids laughed.

*   *   *

After breakfast, Katie trudged up the hill to the Big House. The hairs on her neck rose once more as she surveyed the massive structure. Suddenly, Midas had his hand around her throat again, and the light started to fade.

"Katie?" The vision stopped. "Are you alright?" Michelle watched her from the kitchen door. Katie didn't know how to answer, and Michelle frowned. "If it makes you feel any better, Midas left this morning."

Katie gulped. "He's gone?"

"Midas doesn't stick around long. Thank God." Michelle held the door open for her. After giving a couple of instructions to a young teen stirring a giant pot, Michelle led Katie out of the kitchen.

Katie studied the petite girl as she followed her through the maze of halls. Michelle was a beautiful girl with straight, dark hair and flawless, pale skin. Katie guessed she was southeast Asian but could not place her ethnicity beyond that. So far, Michelle had been kind to Katie. Of all the people in the camp, Katie would never guess her to be a gold digger.

Not that Katie knew how a gold digger would act, but still. And was that even the case considering her actions were taken in the face of sheer survival? But Katie was saving her first kiss for someone special. No matter what this place was like, she would not be trading that for 'stuff.'

Michelle led Katie to an office on the first floor. Inside, Addison sat behind a desk, her purple hair now pink. She was surrounded by stacks of files and folders. Dishes tottered in unstable towers across her desk, and no less than three coffee cups sat before her—one in use and two others hidden among the mess. The couch next to the door was nearly invisible, and a printer lay in the walkway.

Two upholstered armchairs sat across from the desk. One was filled with a box of papers and a cheerleading trophy, in the other sat Goldie. He turned in his seat as Katie arrived.

"You've got to be kidding me," he said. "Her? You want me to work with her?"

Katie stopped short in the doorway. What had she done to deserve that level of animus? Even without knowing the underlying context, the disgust in his voice was clear.

Addison thumbed through a few pages on her desk. "She's the oldest kid with the most recent arrival, which means she's had the most schooling to date."

"Her though? Seriously?"

"Well, let's ask her. Girl, what grade are you in?" Addison asked.

"What are you talking about?" Katie asked.

"Grades," Goldie said. "Years of school. Are you eighth grade? Ninth grade?"

"I was about to finish ninth grade, but what does that have to do with anything?"

"See?" Addison said. "Ninth grade. That's pretty good."

"She's a moron," Goldie said.

What had earned her that reputation? Sure, she might be having a little trouble adjusting, but . . .

"That's not very nice." Addison smirked.

"She is," Goldie continued. "Second day here, Tweedle Dee and Tweedle Dum chased her into my hut because she decided to go for a nighttime walk. Then yesterday, well, you were there. It's a bad fit. Won't work."

"How the heck should I have known he was going to strangle me?" Katie cried. "And like you said, how could I have known the outhouses were no-go zones at night? Nobody told me that stuff!"

"Stop talking," Addison ordered, before turning back to Jared with clenched teeth. "I don't care about your drama, Jared. You need to make this work because if I get one more phone call about your illegible writing, you're out of a job. Do you understand me?"

Goldie stared at his hand as Addison's gaze bore into him.

"What's her name?" Addison asked Goldie.

"My name is Katie," she said.

"She asked me, not you," snarled Goldie. "You don't get to talk unless you're invited to."

Again, Katie was taken aback by the sharp response.

"She's green," said Addison. "That's obvious enough without pointing it out. So, train her."

"This is nuts," he muttered, pressing his hands to his face.

"Girl," said Addison, turning to Katie, "you're being reassigned to work as Goldie's scribe."

"What?" Katie asked. "I don't understand."

"Goldie can't write anymore because his hands shake."

"Hey!" he protested.

"She needs to know. And she'll find out sooner or later if she's got the job."

"Your hands shake?" Katie asked.

Goldie stared at Addison's desk, and she didn't think he was going to answer. Then he raised one hand. It vibrated uncontrollably. "It's getting worse, and some people say they can't read what I write."

"It's not some people," Addison said. "It's everyone."

"Why do your hands shake?" Katie asked.

Goldie was silent for a time. "I don't want her," he said eventually.

"I don't care," said Addison. "You're taking her."

*   *   *

"It's not much to look at," Goldie said. "But it's my hut. Don't mess with anything unless I give you explicit permission."

Katie had only observed his room in the semi-darkness and didn't notice how clean the space was. Compared to Addison's cluttered office, his seemed impeccably tidy. There was a work table next to the cot, and on the wall opposite the bed was a waist-high bookshelf made from crates. The books and notebooks in the shelves were sorted by size. The selection, however, mystified her. *The Complete Works of Tacitus* was sandwiched between *Principles of Basic Botany* and *Interpreting Soil Samples*. Open on his desk was a textbook entitled *Organic Chemistry*.

"You can sit there, I suppose." He pointed to the chair at his table, and he sat on his cot beneath a window.

Chewing on her nail, Katie took a couple of wandering steps. She was doing her best not to be insulted by being called a moron. The conversation between him and Addison seemed to have very little to do with her, but the name was still uncalled for.

"To be honest," he said. "I don't know what to do with you."

"I'm supposed to write for you, aren't I?" Katie asked. "Sounds straightforward."

"Yeah, but it's not like I'm writing every second of the day. Am I supposed to have you follow me around until I need you or something? This is so stupid."

"What if I copied over whatever you were trying to write?" she suggested.

"Hmm, that's an idea." Goldie took a notebook from the table and flipped through it. "I'm going through the soil samples in Camp 7 trying to figure out why their growth rates are down from the previous two years. It's something to do with the pH . . ."

"There are other camps? How many camps are there?"

"Ten." He found the page and handed the notebook to her.

"Ten?" she repeated, taking the notebook numbly. Ten other camps like this one? Tip of the iceberg indeed. How had such places gone undetected by the FBI?

He pointed to various boxes on the page. "This section is pH. This is nitrogen. N is the chemical abbreviation." Using the lines of the spiral-bound he had created a grid, but the verticals lines bounced in all directions. A string of what appeared to be numbers filled the little boxes, but the writing was nearly illegible. She squinted as she tried to decipher the text.

"What is this—M?" Katie turned the notebook sideways. "Mg?"

"Magnesium. This is the amount of magnesium in the soil samples from the past eight quarters. Here's calcium." He pointed to the next row.

"It says 'Cat', only spelled wrong."

"No, it's 'Ca++.' It's the chemical abbreviation for calcium."

"I thought it was just 'Ca.'"

"If it were stable," Goldie said. "But this is calcium ion—after it's given away two outer valence electrons."

"What?"

"I thought you were in high school. Have you had chemistry yet?"

Katie bit her lip. "No, I was supposed to take that this fall."

He huffed. "Of course you were."

"Is this what you do? Evaluate soil samples from other camps?"

He took the notebook back. "It's part of what I do."

"How do you even know how to do all this? You've been here for ten years, but you've kept up on your school work?"

"It's a long story." He rubbed his eyes. "This isn't going to work. You think I'm talking about cats rather than calcium."

"Look, I'm not a moron," Katie said. "So, I don't know anything about calcium ions, but I'm a straight-A student, and I can figure it out."

"We'll see." He picked up another notebook. "Come on. Let's go."

"Where are we going?"

"It's Wednesday. Measurement day."

Goldie led Katie to the greenhouses. As she had only seen them from the outside before, she was surprised to see mushrooms being grown instead of marijuana. Several waist-high grow beds were lined in rows. Irrigation pipes ran along the ceiling. A handful of kids were in the room chatting to amongst themselves as they worked. They fell silent as she and Goldie entered.

Katie followed him to a grow bed separate from the others where a grid created with string marked off 10x10 sections. On the wood of the bed, he had carved "A-J" down one side to mark the columns and "1-10" to mark the rows.

"I'm going to call out the measurements," he said, "and you copy them down. Sound simple enough?"

She glared at him in an attempt to scorn his patronization. Last night she felt as if they had bonded in a way. Clearly, she was wrong.

Goldie ignored her glare, opened a box at the end of the row, and removed a ruler. "Box A-1. Plant color normal. Root depth 0.75. Plant height 1.5."

Katie jumped into action, but she was already behind. She scribbled as quickly as she could but missed a few entries. "I'm sorry, I didn't catch that," she said, and he repeated himself quickly. "Please, slower."

Goldie sighed and said it again, this time with exaggerated slowness. Biting her tongue, Katie wrote down the numbers.

"What are you doing?" He peered over Katie's shoulder. "Soil temperature here and plant height there."

"Sorry." She erased the numbers.

"Box B-1."

Katie didn't anticipate him going by letter instead of number and couldn't find the row.

He didn't slow down. "Soil temperature: 65. Plant height: 3.6. Root depth: 1.25. Grid C-1. Plant height—"

"Hold on, hold on. Did you say 1.75?"

"Are you even listening? I said 1.25. Not there. There."

Sweat broke on her brow. Katie felt the workers' gaze on them as he corrected her clumsy work. Even the Watcher in the back of the greenhouse shifted from one foot to the other.

"I'm sorry," she muttered for the twelfth time.

"This is taking twice as long as it should," Goldie said. "You need to keep up."

Katie stopped, pencil on paper, and glared at him. "I'm sorry, but I thought you were supposed to make this work. Slow down."

He turned back to her, nostrils flared. "And you said you weren't a moron, but I could get a first grader to write faster than you. So, keep the hell up."

Katie lip quivered, but Goldie turned back to the rows, listing off numbers as she struggled to keep up. Finally, they reached the end of the box, but they weren't done. There were two more gridded boxes and three more greenhouses awaiting them.

*　　*　　*

When the lunch siren sounded, he said they were done for the day and that she was to return to her hut.

"You're under strict order," he told her before leaving, "not to mention my hands shaking. If anyone asks, you are my new assistant. Nothing more."

"Sure," she sighed. "Whatever."

She shouldn't care so much about what Goldie said to her, but spending time with him emphasized the loneliness that had been slowly swallowing her soul. Besides this, the work felt so insignificant considering the weight of their situation. Shouldn't they be trying to escape or something instead of tracking plant growth?

Katie joined her hut-mates for lunch and laid her head on the table. She was exhausted from maintaining constant focus and felt as stupid as he said she was. How hard could it be to fill in little boxes?

"How did it go?" Dakota asked.

She groaned in reply. "Leida, no offense, but your brother's a jerk."

Leida laughed without humor. "I know. He made you feel dumb, didn't he?"

"How does he know how to do all this stuff?"

"Jared's a genius, so . . ."

Katie laughed. "I'm sure he thinks he is."

"No, I mean like—he's an actual genius."

"What?" Katie sat up.

Leida shrugged. "He can read something and quote it back a month later. He runs numbers in his head like a calculator. He can list the atomic number of every element on the periodic table. He's a genius."

"You're kidding."

"I know. Makes him twice as annoying, doesn't it?"

Katie groaned and put her head back on the table. "He doesn't have to be such a butt."

This time, Leida did laugh. "No, he does not. But, it's also the reason why we're both still alive."

Katie cocked her head to the side. Even if the others didn't fully know how dismal their state truly was, Leida and Jared were commonly revered for their longtime survival. She had a point. "This work we're doing, what is it for?"

"He's set up experiments all around camp where he adds a certain fertilizer or uses a certain amount of water to see what works best. Then all the Watchers do that in their own fields, and they have a great harvest."

"He works for them?"

"In a way," Leida said. "Not for free, though. He gets stuff like the heaters in the huts and the upgraded food. It used to be only corn. People were getting sick."

"He's evening the odds," Katie said beneath her breath. So, part of him did care. Maybe that's why he was so annoyed by her. Did he think she would screw with his survival plan?

"He also gets drugs," Eric smirked. "Only guy here with permission to light up."

"They let him smoke the weed?"

"He gets a monthly allotment," Eric said. "Of weed and—other things."

"Look," Leida said, "I'm not my brother's keeper. Jared does what he wants. Sometimes he does good things, sometimes not so much. But you're right. He does have a tendency to be a jerk."

*   *   *

After breakfast the next morning, Katie went to Goldie's hut on her own. She wanted to quit, but the flogging scars on her friends' backs showed that it was not an option. Beads of sweat slid down her brow as she knocked.

"Hey."

Katie's heart leapt into her throat as Goldie's voice came from behind her.

He nodded to the house. "We've been summoned."

For the third day in a row, she was hauled into the belly of the beast. She didn't know which was preferable: being berated with the abusive mocking of a tyrant or being in close proximity to her captors.

"Yesterday," he said as they climbed the stairs within the Big House, "I told you to keep your head down and to wait until you're addressed before speaking. Do you remember that?"

It was not something she would forget. "Yes."

"Yeah, I was being a dick. But today, I mean it. Addison is less uptight, but we're going to see Ian. It'd be best if you didn't say anything at all."

"At least you acknowledge it," she sneered.

"What's that?"

"That you're a dick."

"Hmpf."

When they reached the door to the office, Goldie knocked. After a few moments, Michelle exited the office, and Katie's mouth popped open. The girl looked down at her feet.

"Michelle," Goldie said flatly. "Good morning."

"Morning," she whispered and kept walking. His gaze lingered after her as she quickened past them.

"Come in," a voice from inside ordered, and Goldie ripped his gaze from Michelle's back before gesturing Katie inside.

The office overlooked a courtyard in the front of the mansion framed by the mansion's two wings. Here, the cobblestone driveway circled around a fountain before disappearing into a line of trees. In the center of the fountain was a statue of Goddess Diana. There was no view of the camp from here.

Ian, the balding man from Katie's video call, glanced up from behind his desk to see them enter before returning to his newspaper. He pointed to a corner, although two chairs sat at the desk. Goldie moved to the indicated spot in front of a bookshelf and lowered his head, and Katie copied him.

The only sound in the room was the man turning pages. After they had been there a while, Goldie nudged Katie and sat. She followed suit. While they waited, Katie picked at loose fibers on the carpet, but Goldie stared at the floor. Katie thought Goldie had fallen asleep, but when the door opened, he leapt to his feet. She rose too, with a little less haste.

Addison and the guard from the greenhouse yesterday, a middle-aged man with a crooked nose, entered. Ian rounded the desk to perch on the edge. As he studied Katie, she looked to the floor.

"Bartram tells me things aren't going well with the current arrangement," Ian said.

"I'm not sure it's going to work out," Goldie said.

And whose fault was that? Jerk.

"Pity," Ian said. "Do you have another in mind you would rather work with?"

"No, sir. I prefer to work alone."

Katie smirked. Let him work alone and get his butt fired for all she cared. His not being able to write was not her problem. Unless . . . unless they took the heaters out of the huts and reverted the food back to corn. The smirk died.

"That's not an option." Ian picked up a paper from his desk. "Because this—chicken scratch—is unacceptable. And it's getting worse."

"I will try harder," Goldie said.

"No, you will make it work."

"I don't know if that is possible. The girl's a moron."

Katie glared at him. She opened her mouth to retort, but Addison met her eye. She shook her head slowly, and Katie stifled it. Once again, she was more confused than comforted by Addison's intervention.

"Hmm." Ian narrowed his eyes. "That's one way of looking at it. Or perhaps you don't want this to work at all. Bartram says you acted rather harshly toward the girl and exhibited behaviors that seemed—how did you put it Bartram?"

"A bit over the top," the man said. "He was calling her names. Intentionally throwing a lot of numbers at her so she couldn't keep up, yelling at her."

Katie frowned as Goldie's ears grew red. Had all of that been for show? It didn't feel like it.

"Goldie does numbers fast," Addison said. "He always has."

"But he doesn't talk to the other workers like that," Bartram said.

"Perhaps this one is especially dull?" she asked, and heat rose to Katie's cheeks. Had Addison silenced her to be further insulting?

"I doubt it," Bartram continued. "We've all heard him yell at people before, but this—like I said. It was over the top."

Goldie glared at Bartram, but he only shrugged. Clearing his throat, Goldie asked, "May I?"

Ian waved a hand in his direction.

"I could try typing out the—"

"No," Ian said. "You're not going anywhere near a computer."

"Perhaps one that's not able to connect to the wi-fi?"

"I said no." Ian's voice grew agitated.

"Or hell, a typewriter?"

Ian backhanded Goldie across the face, and he stumbled back. Blood appeared at the corner of his mouth, and Katie retreated deep into the corner, touching the bruises on her throat.

"I said no!" Ian shouted. "You're lucky I don't fire your ass, do you hear me? Out of my good graces, I have let you keep this position. Hell, I even allowed you to have a damn assistant. And this is how you repay me? By trying to manipulate me this way?" He smacked him again. This time, Goldie's back hit the wall, and he shrunk from him. Ian struck him yet again, and Goldie pulled his shoulders to his ears.

"Dad!" Addison said, and Ian stopped, hand raised. "You made your point."

Blood ran down Goldie's lip and cheek. He trembled violently, and Katie gripped blindly onto the shelf behind her.

"She stays," Ian said coolly. "Now, get out."

Goldie's shaking hand took Katie's arm and ushered her to the exit. Without a word, he headed back the way they had come.

Katie chased after him. "Are you okay?"

"I'm fine," he snapped, but he touched the corner of his lip, leaving blood on his fingertips. He smeared it with the back of his arm and continued down the stairs. Unsure what else to do, Katie followed him.

"I guess that's that," Goldie said when they were outside. "You're stuck with me."

Katie silently followed him back down the path. Her cheek stung as if she had received the blows instead of him. They reached his hut, and once again, he held the door open for her.

"Go ahead and have a seat." He knocked his shoes off and sat cross-legged on his bed, but Katie stayed near the door, still stunned by the encounter and not feeling at all trusting.

"Sit." He pointed to the chair. She didn't move, and he rolled his eyes. "I don't have the plague, and I'm not going to hurt you. Sit."

Reluctantly, Katie moved to the chair as Goldie rubbed his hands together. "It's a bit stuffy in here." He pushed open the window above his head.

"Was the Watcher right? Were you trying to get me fired?"

He pinched the bridge of his nose and nodded.

"But—why?"

"I like my privacy."

Katie bristled. "Your privacy? This is about your privacy? We're freaking hostages in a camp run by a bunch of psychos, and you're worried about your privacy?"

Goldie ran his fingers through his hair.

"So, to protect your privacy, you tried to get me in trouble."

"You wouldn't have gotten in trouble," he muttered.

"You're an ass, do you know that?" she said. "You've been mean to me ever since I got here. You've called me stupid and a moron and foolish. You freaking stuck a needle into my face and told me you knew what you were doing the first day I was here!"

Goldie leaned against the wall and scraped the blood off his fingertips. "Are you finished?" he asked.

Katie scowled at him. Her scowl diminished in short order, however. It was hard to scowl at someone with blood smeared across his face.

Goldie sighed. "I'm sorry. I know I'm an ass, which is why I didn't think you'd like to work for me. I thought getting you fired would have been a favor to both of us. I didn't mean to hurt your feelings. But if we're stuck together, we should try to get along. I won't overwhelm you next time."

Katie raised her brows. Was that a sincere apology? She didn't know what she had expected, but an apology was not it. "I-I'm sorry I couldn't keep up." She wasn't really sorry, but she felt like she had to contribute to the moment.

He smiled wryly.

"Are you going to wipe the blood off your face?" she asked.

Goldie touched his lip. "I didn't know there was any there." Taking a rag from his desk, he tried to wipe the blood away, but without a mirror, he couldn't see what he was wiping.

"Let me help." Katie took the cloth and dabbed his already swelling lip. His privacy must have been important to him since he took such a beating for it. As Katie removed the last of the blood, Goldie winced.

"Thank you," he said. "Would you like me to take out your stitches? It's about time."

"Uh, no," Katie said. "I'd rather see the nurse."

"Really?" he said. "She was sued three times and lost her medical license after overdosing some poor schmuck."

"Are her hands cleaner than yours?"

He looked down at his dirt-stained hands. "Most days."

"Then I'd like to see her."

"Hey, Katie." Dakota approached as she put her dish on the long table at the front of the mess hall the next day. "Are you heading to Goldie's hut this morning?"

"Unfortunately," she said.

"Might as well hang around here then. We have a hut leader's meeting on Friday mornings, so he's going to be coming soon."

After the other kids exited, the hut leaders sat at a table in the back, and Katie took a spot next to Dakota.

"Morning, Katie." Michelle smiled, and Katie smiled vaguely in return, still unsure what to make of the girl.

"She's a hut leader now?" A broad-shouldered boy named Trevor sat down next to Michelle.

"Goldie's new assistant," Dakota said.

"Assistant?" Trevor sneered. "That's what they're calling it these days."

"Shut up, meathead," Michelle said. "The Watchers selected her, not him. From what I hear, he wasn't fond of the arrangement."

"He tried to get me fired," Katie said.

"Was this before or after he banged you?" Trevor said.

"Excuse me?" Katie's voice squeaked. "We are not sleeping together."

"Who's not sleeping with who?" Another boy with dark, curly hair, slid in next to Trevor.

"Goldie's new assistant says she's not." Trevor grinned.

"Nah, man. She's telling the truth. He can't stand her. You should have seen him the other day in the greenhouse. It was painful to watch. I'm Bryan, by the way," he said, reaching across the table to shake her hand.

Thank you, kind sir, Katie thought. She didn't even know the guy and he was coming to her defense. Bryan's name she had heard before in passing, usually lumped in with people who had been here a long time. She guessed his age to be between hers and Goldie's.

"A little advice," Bryan said, "don't take anything Goldie says personally. This whole hand tremor business has got him a bit rattled, ya know?"

"You know about that?" she asked.

"Everyone knows about that," Bryan said. "He's had it for years now, but it's gotten worse recently."

"Of course it's got him rattled," Michelle said. "It'd freak me out. Especially since he has no idea what's causing it."

"It's guilt that's causing it." Trevor leaned back in his seat. "That or the drugs."

"It's the drugs. Totally." The final hut leader joined them at the table. He wore a pair of eyeglasses with tape around the middle. "I'm Sam."

"I don't know," Michelle said. "If weed caused you to shake, I'd think Bryan here would be rocking and rolling by now."

Bryan shrugged but didn't deny this.

"Then it's guilt," Trevor said. "From whacking that guy, Landon."

Michelle and Bryan rolled their eyes.

"He didn't whack Landon," Bryan groaned.

"Then what happened to him?" Trevor asked. "They cut through the fence, Goldie gets hauled back, but no one ever sees

Landon again. I'm telling you—something happened, and he gave up his buddy to save himself."

"We know what happened to Landon," Bryan said. "They shot him. He's buried in the cemetery."

"But you didn't see it." Trevor smiled. "Could have been Goldie who shot him for all you know. I mean, think about it. Everyone who gets caught outside the fence gets a bullet to the back of the skull. And yet, he didn't. He's still walking and talking. Not only that, but they make him the head of the camp? He totally sold him out."

A chill ran down Katie's spine. The guy had chosen to work for the Watchers to survive. Just how far had he gone that day?

"He did not sell him out," Michelle said.

"Then what happened?" Trevor asked.

"I don't know, okay?"

"What do you think happened, Bryan?" Trevor asked. "You've been here the longest."

"Jared didn't shoot him," Bryan said.

"Come on, how do you know that?"

Bryan leaned back in his seat and shook his head. The corner of his lip turned up as if the whole conversation were beneath him.

"See," Trevor said. "You don't know."

"You want to talk about somebody who wasn't there?" Bryan asked. "You weren't there when he came back covered in blood."

"Look, I know he's your friend," Trevor said. "Don't you think that's clouding your judgment?"

"Shut the hell up!" Bryan rose out of his seat. "Two of my friends walked into the woods that day, and neither of them came back. I don't want to hear another word of your conspiracy bullshit."

The table fell silent, and Katie turned to see Goldie standing in the doorway. Bryan paled. For a moment, Katie wondered if he was imagining the blood on Goldie's clothes now. A person could get blood on their clothes without killing the victim, right? Or did his hands shake because he murdered his friend?

"Sorry, I'm late," Goldie said as he took his seat. As he set a spiral-bound notebook on the table; his hands wavered until they disappeared into his lap. "I was called into the office before breakfast. We've got new arrival coming around one."

A groan came up from the hut leaders, and the weight of the previous conversation dispersed. Dramatic hands flew to faces, and Trevor flung himself back in his chair. Katie couldn't help but smile as she considered the trouble she caused since being there.

Goldie continued, "He's some ambassador's kid, so Addison said to pretend he's got three armbands on. The kidnappers have had him for a while, but they screwed up and got one of their trucks caught on a surveillance camera. The Feds were watching their properties, but they got their new recruit in the FBI to kill the lead, so he's arriving today."

"Do you mean my dad?" Katie blurted.

"Addison didn't know, but probably."

Michelle nudged Katie. "At least you get to keep the armband."

"But he—" Katie gulped, looking around at the bare arms of those around the table. "I'm sorry. I know what this means for all of you, for all of us."

"Katie," Bryan said, "your dad has guaranteed your survival for who knows how long."

Tears sprung to her eyes. "But he compromised his investigation. Without his investigation . . ." Without his investigation, more graves were going to be filled.

"Listen to me," said Bryan, gripping her hand from across the table. "Your dad chose to keep you alive for as long as possible. Is it great for all of us? Not really, but each of us would want our dads to make the same decision. So, if anyone gives you grief about that, tell them to get bent. Do you hear me, Katie?"

Katie bit her lip and nodded, but she still felt like dirt. What if Dad had killed the lead that would bring them all home? If any more of them died, how could she not be responsible?

Goldie cleared his throat. "Anyways, there are a couple of complications with this kid. He's been sitting with a bag over his head for weeks now. And he doesn't speak English."

The hut leaders groaned once more in unison, but this time, Katie could not manage a smile.

"And who, might I ask," Bryan asked, "is getting this shit storm?"

"That would be you," Goldie said.

"What? Why am I—?"

"Because Dakota got the last one. You're up."

"Aw man," Bryan said. "But what does he speak? Spanish or something?"

"Chinese."

"Chinese?" His brows raised. "Man, this is getting better and better."

"Woo!" Dakota raised his hand to high-five Katie. "I'll take you any time, girl!"

She obliged with less enthusiasm. The poor kid was bound to be traumatized, but all they cared about was their jobs.

"Freakin' Chinese?" Bryan muttered to himself. "What's his name, anyway?"

Goldie looked down at his notebook and laughed. "Zuh-hang Jeng," he butchered.

"Fantastic," he muttered. "Triple green armband that can't speak English. This is great."

"Now that's settled—" Goldie said.

"Settled my ass . . ."

"Sam, your hut's on kitchen duty next week. Everyone has met Katie?" The hut leaders nodded, and she smiled tersely. "That's all I have on my end. Anything else?"

"Eric's running low on his seizure medication," Dakota said.

"Okay, I'll send that one to Barb." Goldie slid a notebook and pen to Katie. After a puzzled moment, Katie realized she was supposed to write that down.

Bryan rubbed his eye. "My ladies are telling me they need more—feminine supplies. Apparently, they're all 'on it' at the same time. Because screw me, right?"

Despite herself, a grin crept across Katie's face, and she wrote this down too.

Trevor laughed. "Geez, Bryan, you are having a bad week."

"Shut up, man," Bryan said.

"You got that, Katie?" Goldie asked.

"I've got that." She set the pen down.

"I hate my life," Bryan muttered.

"This is from Leida." Dakota slid over the novel she had been reading.

"That was quick," Goldie said.

"It was a good book."

"Goldie," Trevor said, "how come we can't get some books to read?"

"Because you're not my sister," Goldie said. "And Addison only lets me check one out at a time."

"So, you admit there's a bit of favoritism going on then?"

"Are you asking if I prefer my sister over you?" Goldie said. "Yes, Trevor, I most certainly do."

"Trevor has a point," Michelle said. "I know my girls would like a book to listen to."

Goldie frowned. "Okay, I'll have her send the books to the other huts after she's finished. Good enough compromise?" Everyone nodded. "Alright then, we're done. You know where to find me."

Goldie stood, and the hut leaders started to disperse. He indicated Katie should come with him, and his hand was on the knob when Sam approached. "Something going on?"

Sam rubbed his glasses on his shirt. "I got a bit of a problem."

Goldie sighed. "Of course you do. What is it?"

Sam eyed Katie suspiciously.

"Katie has taken a vow of silence. Isn't that right?"

"Uhm, sure," she said.

"She's going to be around a lot. Get used to her."

"Okay," Sam said. "It's my girlfriend. You know her—Paulina?"

He narrowed his eyes. "Yes."

"We broke up," he said, and Goldie rolled his eyes. "Now she won't stop going through my stuff, and I've already lost half my hut's respect from the crap she's been spreading about me, and—"

"And you want her transferred," Goldie interjected, shaking his head. "Every time. Every single time. I always tell you guys, don't date someone from your hut, but what do you do?"

"Is that a no?" Sam asked.

"No," he sighed. "I'll transfer her to . . ." He looked around the room. "Dakota. Come here for a sec."

Katie's brows raised as her hut leader trotted over.

"Yeah, boss?" Dakota said.

"I'm moving Paulina to your hut."

"Okay." He furrowed his brow. "Can I ask why?"

"No. Don't date her and you should be fine."

Dakota scratched the back of his head. "I'm dating Leida right now."

"Then that's two reasons why you shouldn't date her. First being that if you cheat on my sister, I'll kill you." Dakota laughed, but Goldie didn't. Surely, he was kidding, but his eyes bore into Dakota as if issuing a challenge.

"Okay, sure," Dakota said. "I guess I'll go see if we've got a bed ready."

*   *   *

Zhang Jing Xi arrived at one o'clock as predicted. Katie was busy plucking heads off of clover flowers when the transport truck rumbled up the drive. She moved to stand, but Goldie put a hand on her arm. A Watcher exited the kitchen with an AR-15 slung over his shoulder.

Katie started at the sight of the weapon, but Goldie remained cool. The gate rolled open, and the gunman glared at the two as if daring them to rush him.

"Afternoon, Matt," Goldie greeted, but the man didn't reply. "Dickhead," he muttered.

"Is there a reason he's staring at us like that?" Katie asked.

"I tried sneaking out the gate a few years back when he wasn't watching. Well, I may have tried several times to sneak out. He doesn't like me much."

The transport truck backed into the yard, and the mechanical motor brought the gate closed. Only then did Goldie stand and wipe the grass from his pants, and Katie did the same. AR-15 guy continued to glower at them.

Goldie greeted the truck driver as he stepped from his cab, "Howdy, Clark."

The man spat tobacco into the grass. "Goldie. Who's your fri— wait! Aren't you the girl from last time? Damn, that little thing on your face ain't nothing but a scratch. And here they docked me by half. I ought to sue somebody."

"Took thirty-eight stitches to fix it," Goldie said.

"Hell, that ain't nothing. I fell off a boulder when I was out hunting a few years back, and gashed my leg up something good. Took fifty-two stitches to fix that." He raised his pant leg to show a nasty scar that appeared to be twenty years old. With Clark's current weight, Katie would have been surprised to see him anywhere near a hunting blind. She forced herself not to roll her eyes. Unexpected hatred flowed from her toward this man she barely knew, a man who participated in this horrible venture with such a casual attitude.

"As I've said before, your payment has nothing to do with me," Goldie said. "I'm only here for the kid."

"He's in the back." The tubby man waddled to the back of the truck and lifted the lock. The hatch went up with a terrible screech, and the boy in the middle of the trailer trembled and pulled away from them. Goldie and Clark pried him out of the truck as he kicked and screamed.

"Just drop him," Clark said when they got to the end of the trailer.

Goldie scowled at him and forced the boy down the ramp. Katie's own face puckered as she followed Goldie's instructions to say nothing. Clark and Goldie set the boy on his knees.

"Take his hood off. That will help," Goldie said.

"No—wait!" Katie said, but Clark was already lifting the hood. He didn't yank it this time, though. The boy screamed as the hood came off.

"What now?" Clark said. "He ain't got any marks on him."

As the screaming continued, the boy kept his eyes sealed shut.

"He can see your face," Katie took Zhang's hands into her own, but he pulled away. Sliding her fingers beneath his balled fists, Katie whispered, "Hey."

The screaming diminished some.

"Zhaing," Katie said, using a long 'a' instead of an '-ong' sound. "Look at me."

The boy whimpered.

"Zhaing," she said.

"Zhang." He finished the sentence with what Katie assumed were some choice words.

"Zhang," she repeated. "Katie."

He frowned at the word, then his eyes flitted open. His brows rose soon after.

"Zhang." She placed a hand on his shoulder. "Katie." She placed it on her chest.

A stream of questions in Chinese poured out, and Katie shook her head. "English."

"No English!" he said. "No English!"

"Okay. It's going to be okay." She raised his hands to Clark, and he unlocked the cuffs. Zhang tried to run, but Goldie grabbed him across the chest and pulled him back.

"No." Goldie pointed to the fence. "Zz-zz," he imitated electricity.

"Zz-zz, Zhang." Katie mimed touching the fence then getting shocked and dying. Zhang nodded, and Goldie let go of his chest. Zhang's eyes darted around.

"Whelp," Clark said. "You've got it from here. I'm going to go get paid." He stepped past them.

"I hate him," Katie said as Clark disappeared into the mansion.

Goldie swiveled his head about, then spoke in a lowered voice, "So do I, but I don't say it out loud."

"Does he even know what he's doing? Bringing kidnapped kids to their deaths?"

"Even if he does, I doubt it matters to him, Katie."

"I'm sorry, I just—I disliked him before, but now that I know…" She shook her head. "How do you work with the Watchers knowing what you do?"

"Yeah, I'm going to table this discussion until later," said Goldie, nodding to the door as Addison stepped outside and joined them on the hill.

Katie bit her lip, but her hatred still gathered in her belly like simmering coals.

"So, this is Zhaing," Addison said.

"Zhang," Katie corrected.

The scared boy looked between the teenagers and the grown woman. As Addison approached, he pulled away. "It's an armband." She showed him the bit of plastic, but when she tried again, he pulled further back.

"Give it to Katie," Goldie said.

Addison did so, and Katie showed Zhang she had one too. As she took his hand, however, she saw his entire wrist was an open wound. "Goldie?"

"He's been tied up all this time, remember?" he said.

Katie winced and secured the band above the wound.

"Her." Zhang pointed to Addison. "Asshole. Us—no asshole."

Katie and Goldie burst into laughter while Addison tried, and failed, to hide a smile.

"Quick learner," Goldie said, and Katie slapped a hand over her mouth. Addison whacked Goldie playfully on the back of the head before walking away.

Zhang looked around once more, his eyes settling on the gunman. "Asshole."

"Yes," Katie said as Matt frowned. "Watcher."

"Wa-ter?"

"Wat-ch-er."

"Wah-ter."

"Sure." Katie patted him on the shoulder.

"Wahter asshole?"

"Yes," she said.

Goldie smiled. "This is going to be fun."

"So, he's allowed to say it, but I'm not?" she asked.

"Eh, for now. But they won't tolerate it if it lasts forever."

"No asshole." Zhang pointed at Michelle as she exited the house. She frowned in confusion.

"No," Katie said. "No asshole—worker."

"Wer-core."

"Sure." She patted him on the shoulder again. "Zhang—Michelle." The girl smiled at him, and he ran off a string of questions in Chinese again.

"You don't speak Mandarin, do you?" Goldie asked.

"My mother is Korean, not Chinese." Michelle shook her head at Zhang. Zhang ran his hands through his hair as his eyes darted about. He turned around and saw the camp stretched out behind him for the first time. Putting his hands to his head, he made a strange noise.

"I think he's overwhelmed," Katie said.

Zhang rattled off more words, but then he formed a ball with his hands. "China." He pointed to one side of the ball. "China."

Goldie mimed the same ball. "China." He pointed, and Zhang nodded enthusiastically. "America."

"America," he repeated. "America? Oooohh!" He rubbed his head. "America assholes—America—" Zhang picked up a nearby twig and drew a stick person in the dirt. Using stick figures and hand gestures, they communicated that Zhang was being ransomed. Then Zhang pointed to his eyes and then the Watchers. He mimed being dead.

"He's asking about him seeing the Watchers again," Katie said. "He thinks they'll kill him now."

Goldie shook his head. "I don't know how to explain that one."

"That's pretty heavy," Michelle said. "Perhaps we should wait?"

"He needs to know," Katie said.

"Let him learn English first," Goldie said. "We'll tell him later."

Zhang mimed himself being dead again, and Goldie shook his head emphatically. Relief shone on the poor boy's face.

*　　　*　　　*

After treating his wounds, Katie and Goldie took Zhang to meet with Bryan in the greenhouses. The hut leader's eyes grew wide as Zhang gestured wildly and repeatedly called out, 'asshole,' again and again. Goldie slapped his bewildered friend on the back. "You've got it from here."

Katie smiled sadly at Zhang and placed a hand on his shoulder. "Stay with Bryan." She pointed to the hut leader. "He'll look after you."

The Chinese boy shook his head. She rubbed his shoulder and smiled with encouragement before turning back with Goldie. As he and Katie stepped away, however, Zhang followed them.

"No." Goldie pointed at Bryan. "Stay."

Zhang complained, but Goldie turned to go again. Zhang followed once more and made pleading gestures to Katie.

"He wants Katie to stay," Bryan said.

"What?" Goldie said. "Why?"

"Because she's nicer than us," he said, and Katie laughed.

"You wanted to be reassigned?" Goldie said. "Here you go. Stick with Zhang for the day. I'll catch up with you this evening."

"Sure thing." She smiled. The boy deserved to have at least one friendly face around.

Throughout the day, Katie picked up a few Mandarin words, and they established basic mimes. This allowed her to communicate that Zhang was to stay with his hut, but not much else. He stopped calling the Watchers 'assholes,' which was an improvement. All this time, Katie had been feeling sorry for herself. Now, she felt horrible for Zhang.

When the siren sounded for dinner, Katie trudged back up the hill from the greenhouses. Her brain was exhausted from trying to communicate all day. As she entered the mess hall, however, Goldie motioned her over to his table.

"They're going to video call Zhang's parents tonight," he said. "But we've got a problem. The script is in English, and they're going to gag him," he said.

"Poor Zhang."

*　　　*　　　*

"Zhang?" Goldie and Katie arrived at his table after the meal, and Goldie gestured for him to follow. He did so willingly until they reached the communication room. When Goldie led Zhang to the chair, he tried to bolt.

"Nope." Goldie caught him around the middle. "Relax. Katie!"

She took Zhang's hands in her own, inhaled, then motioned for Zhang to do the same. The boy did, but a cry escaped his lips.

Goldie led him to the chair, and Ian zip-tied his wrist above the bandages. A single tear fell from his eye as he was tied down once more. Katie stood behind the lights and indicated she wouldn't leave. Zhang bounced his leg up and down.

Things had been bad for Katie, but at least she spoke the language. At least she had a clue as to what Midas was and what he did.

"Has he been like that all day?" Addison whispered to Goldie.

Goldie nodded. "Stuck to Katie like a leech."

Ian tried to slide the gag into his mouth, but Zhang moved his head around.

"Zhang," Katie tried, but Ian socked him in the belly. While Zhang was reeling, Ian secured the gag, and Katie held a hand to her mouth as the boy choked.

Ian picked up his mask and took his seat. "Ready."

"Give him a minute," Addison said as Zhang caught his breath. "Can't have him looking like that." Tears streamed down his face.

"Like what? Tears are fine. Might even be beneficial. Roll it."

Reacting to his indifference, anger boiled inside Katie, but Addison shook her head and turned on the lights. At least the woman felt something. Behind the lights, Katie had a clear view of the open laptop. The picture of Zhang sat in the bottom right corner while a gray avatar filled the majority of the screen. The customary ringtone was soon heard, and then the screen filled with a face from the other end of the call.

Dad stared back at them.

"Da—" Katie's voice was silenced as Goldie clamped a hand over her mouth. She tried to argue through his hand, but he pressed firmly.

"This is Agent Thompson with the FBI. I'm contacting you on behalf of the Xi family. I see young Zhang Jing on the line, but who else is there?"

Katie bit Goldie's hand and struggled to move away. He grunted but held on to her. The motion caused one of the lights to teeter and fall. Ian drew a line over his throat repeatedly, but Addison was too busy fixing the light to see.

Goldie grabbed Katie's hair. His hand remained like a steel trap over her mouth as he dragged her into the hallway. The door shut, and he released her. Katie grabbed the doorknob, but it was locked.

Goldie made the guttural sound again as he examined his hand. Her teeth had broken the skin along the web of his hand, and blood dripped from the wound.

The door opened, and Addison exited.

"I want to see my dad," Katie demanded.

"Out of the question," she said. "What happened to your hand?"

"She bit me!" Goldie exclaimed.

"Explain it to her."

"You explain it to her! She doesn't listen to a freaking thing I say."

Addison rubbed her eye. "What do you think you're going to accomplish, Katie? You're going to bust out on screen and show yourself to your dad? The only thing that will do is earn you is a bullet to the brain, and your dad will never see you again. Do you understand? They will kill you."

"You say they as if you're not one of them!" Katie shouted. "But you are."

"Get her to her hut," she told Goldie. "Now."

"I'm not going!"

Ian opened the door, and Katie retreated to Goldie's side.

"Get rid of her," he told Goldie. "Then get back here immediately."

Goldie slid his arm around Katie's and led her away. This time, she did not resist.

*   *   *

When they entered the kitchen, Trevor and Michelle were the only two finalizing the cleanup. Goldie pushed Katie further into the room. "Watch her and make sure she's here when I get back."

"What's going on?" Michelle said. "What happened to your hand?"

"Let her tell you."

Michelle smiled sadly at Katie as she wiped away a tear. "Have a seat," she said.

Katie sat on the swivel stool, and the boy went back to scouring a metal tray. While she recounted the events upstairs, sobs interrupted her tale intermittently. "He was so close. I . . . I couldn't help myself."

Trevor placed the last dish into the rack and shook his hands out over the floor. "If you've got this?" he asked Michelle as if Katie's troubles were far beneath him.

"We're good." Without missing a beat, Michelle dismissed him with a wave, and he stepped out into the yard. "It's a good thing Goldie was there. Even if you did bite him."

"I can't believe I did that." For the first time, she felt guilty. He was only trying to protect her.

"Yeah, and I'm sure he's thrilled about the situation too . . ." she muttered.

There was noise in the dining room followed by Goldie dragging Zhang into the room by his shirt. As soon as Zhang saw Katie, he erupted in a smile. "Katie!" he started talking rapidly.

Goldie scowled as he stepped past them toward the sink in the back. The area around his eye was red where a new shiner was forming. Michelle fetched a fresh rag and followed him.

Katie didn't hear their conversation as Zhang continued to mime and talk at her. Seeing his parents had helped him. Seeing her own father had not. A stone settled in her stomach as she realized her father was handling the negotiations for the Xi family. Is that what they had wanted all along?

Katie wondered if she should try to explain what happened: explain who the FBI agent was and what this meant for him. But it was too much. Their primitive mode of communication would never be enough.

"You two!" Goldie called, and they joined him by the back door. Katie winced as she saw perfect little teeth marks lining the web of his hand. "Let's go."

After dropping Zhang off at Bryan's hut, Katie expected to be thoroughly chastised, but he never said a word.

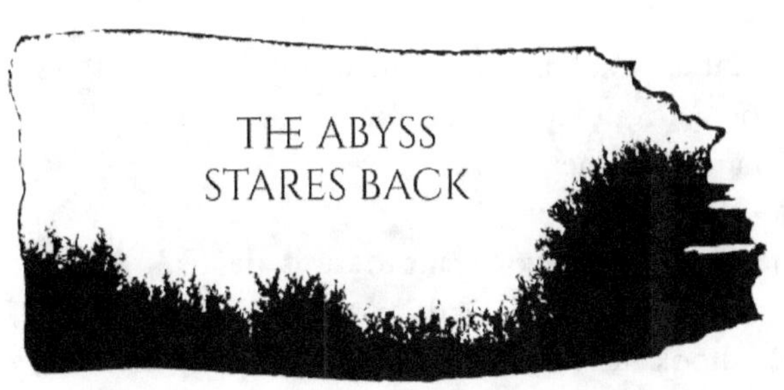

Goldie dropped Katie off at her hut as the sun sank behind the trees. On her way to her bunk, she stepped over the rock game taking place on the dirt floor and a couple of her hut-mates greeted her. Upon reaching her bed, she collapsed onto her mattress, and a girl dropped down from the top bunk.

"Hi, you must be Katie." The girl smiled at her. She had brown hair frizzing about her face despite it being contained by a loop of twine. "I'm Paulina. Your new bunkmate. You're Goldie's new assistant, right? How's he treating you?"

"I don't know," she sighed. "He hasn't yelled at me lately."

"Don't let him get to you. If he tries to act all big and bad, it's because he's trying to compensate for something." She giggled and Katie frowned at the odd insinuation.

Leida joined them, and Paulina quieted. "Paulina, are you settling in okay?"

"Fine," she snapped. Katie cocked her head at the curt response.

"Oh-kay." Leida frowned.

"So, Katie," Paulina said, "Since you're Goldie's assistant and all, can you get your hands on some paper? I managed to snag some weed." She tapped her pocket.

"Like, as to smoke it?"

"Uhm, yes? Unless you want to eat it, that is."

"Don't do that," Leida said. "You'll get caught."

Katie shook her head. "I don't do drugs, Paulina. Besides, he's super particular about his stuff. He'd notice."

Paulina shrugged but said nothing else on the matter. "When are you getting your next book, Leida?"

"Who knows? A couple of weeks before Addison has a paper due, she'll head to the library."

"Is she in college or something?" Katie asked.

"The more correct way of looking at it is that Jared is in college." Leida bounced on Katie's bunk and leaned against the post. "He does the work, and she gets the credit. But that's been going on since Addison was in sixth grade. Katie, what happened to his hand?"

Warmth flooded her cheeks. "I—might have bit him." She relayed the story and Paulina laughed. Leida did not look as entertained.

"Leida," said Katie hoping to change the subject, "the hut leaders mentioned Goldie had once gotten beyond the fence, but I was told anyone who did that would get shot. What happened?"

Leida studied the grains on the wooden bunk bed. "He refused to tell me. I know they shot Landon, but Jared wouldn't say why they let him live. All I know is he stopped stealing and stopped trying to escape. Then he started talking more and more to the Watchers about how to grow their product better. And then there were the drugs."

"It's only weed, right?" Paulina said.

"I've seen pills," Leida said. "He tried to hide them from me, but I saw them. We got into a fight and he moved out. Who knows what he's on now though? I don't even know him anymore."

Katie placed a hand on her shoulder.

"I still can't believe you bit him." Paulina laughed.

*　　　*　　　*

The next morning dragged on as Katie copied measurements into a notebook and Goldie spooned soil into plastic cups. Data from the other camps were sent to Goldie for recommendations on how to increase crop yields. For each page that came in, he had Katie make a copy into a notebook. The work was easy but monotonous, and Katie grew bored.

"Don't you ever feel guilty helping these people make money?" Katie asked.

"Yes," he said as held the soil up to the light of the window.

The pile of papers stared up at her from the old folding table he had brought down from the Big House. She sighed loudly, but he ignored her. "And why can't we stick these in a binder?"

"Because I like this method better."

Katie rolled her eyes. Starting a conversation with him was frustrating and pointless, but only three pages remained on her desk. As she sifted through them, however, she frowned. Her fingers ran against strange bumps on the underside of the pages—the bumps were holes the size of a pinprick.

Goldie continued to pour water into each of the cups, not observing her actions. She didn't know what he was doing, nor did she care. Tilting the paper, she allowed light from the window to pass through the bumps. Several numbers were illuminated at odd intervals. Goldie continued to stir his dirt water. Did he know about this?

She opened her mouth to tell him, then stopped. It was possible that he did, but what if he did not? He was a survivor. What if surviving meant selling someone else out? What if he had sold out that Landon guy after all?

Goldie dipped a tan strip of paper into the soil water, then squinted at the strip. "What the hell? That can't be right." Holding up the strip, he turned to her, and Katie dropped the papers.

"What color would you call this?" he asked.

"Orange?"

"Damn it. I need it to be yellow or yellowish green. At this color, the pH is like a 4, which is way too acidic." He rubbed the area where Katie had bitten him. Goldie still hadn't said anything about it, and now she was afraid to bring it up.

Goldie raised the other cup. "Then this one is reading too alkaline. The two samples come from supposedly the same geographical area, but . . ." He resealed the baggie full of dirt and stood. "I'm going to have to send these off for further evaluation—again. Come on."

They made the hike to Addison's office, but she wasn't there, so Katie wrote a note and fixed the sample to her door with a thumbtack. By the time they returned to the yard, a crowd had gathered on the hill.

A Watcher Katie recognized as Tweedle Dee held onto the shirt collar of a twelve-year- old boy near the center of the mob. Tweedle Dum stood nearby, like always. Their real names were Derek and Dumar. Dumar was speaking with Bryan, who waved Goldie over.

"What's all this about?" Goldie asked. "What did Randy do?"

Randy refused to meet his eye.

"Found him smoking one of these." Dumar held up a half-burnt joint. "Do you recognize it?"

Goldie slid on his glasses and examined the joint end with a sniff. When he saw the writing on the outer wrapping, his brows shot up. It was his own. "Where in hell did you get this?"

Katie's stomach clenched as the boy shuffled his feet. Surely he wasn't stupid enough to steal from Goldie, was he?

"Did you steal from me, Randy?" Goldie asked.

"N-no!" He rubbed his arm. "I f-found it."

"Bullshit," Goldie said, and Katie winced.

Dang it, kid!

"We were going to flog him, unless you had something better in mind?" Derek said.

"Sir—Goldie—please—I didn't steal from you," Randy said.

Goldie glared at him. "It seems to me two crimes were committed. Theft and unauthorized possession."

Derek grinned. "You know, you're right. I guess that means a double flogging."

Katie gawked at Goldie.

"No! Please!" Randy pulled against Derek. "Please! I'm begging you. Bryan—Bryan please."

Bryan glared at Goldie, but Goldie stared at the ground and dug his toe in the dirt.

"I'm sorry, Randy. I can't help you," Bryan said.

"No!" cried Randy as Derek dragged him to the post. Although he struggled, he was no contest for the grown man.

"Goldie!" Katie touched his arm. He turned to her with brows raised. Had he forgotten she was there? "He's only a kid."

The Watchers secured Randy to the post, and he tugged against his restraints. Derek uncoiled the whip.

"You have to do something."

"People don't steal from me," he said.

Katie shoved him in the chest, forcing him back a step. "You son of a bitch!"

"Goldie," Dumar said, "get your puta under control."

Goldie's gaze darted to Dumar. "Be quiet."

"Be quiet? What the heck is your problem? You can't just stand here while they—"

"Stop arguing and shut up," he hissed.

Katie sneered. "If you won't do something, I will!" She pushed forward from the group, but Goldie grabbed her around the middle. He dragged her back from the post as the crowd parted before them. Flailing, she shouted, "Put me down!"

Someone held the door to the kitchen open for him, and he brought her inside. "Don't you dare bite me again."

"No! I have to help him."

"Michelle!" Goldie shouted into the nearly empty kitchen, then swore as Katie continued to kick and beat at him. She pulled at his hair.

"Ow!" Goldie dropped her, and Katie scrambled for the door. He held the knob closed with one hand. With the other, he turned on the water tap of the adjacent sink. "Calm down."

"This is your fault, you son of a bitch!"

"This is getting ridiculous," Goldie grabbed her around the waist and shoved her head underneath the flowing water.

Katie clawed against him as she sputtered beneath the cold liquid. "Get off me!"

"Not until you calm down," Goldie said, hand clasped around the back of her neck, fixing her in place.

Katie pressed with all her strength against the sides of the sink, but his grip did not budge. She floundered behind her, trying to grab his wrists, scratching at him. Water poured across her face, and she inhaled some through her nose. "You're drowning me!" she cried, coughing.

"Bullshit!" he said. "Calm the hell down."

Calm down? Was he insane?

The door beside the sink opened, and Katie saw Michelle through her strands of wet hair. "Help me!"

"What the hell is going on? Let her go!"

"She needs to calm down," he said with frightening calmness.

"And she will if you stop drowning her!" Michelle pulled against his hands, and finally, he relented.

As Katie came up gasping, she smacked her head on the water spigot. Sinking to the ground, she continued to cough and sputter. "What is wrong with you?" she screamed.

"What's wrong with me?" he returned. "What the hell is wrong with you? First, you take a chunk out of my hand trying to jump in front of a camera, and now this? You're going to get yourself killed!"

"Well, if you hadn't doubled some kid's flogging!" said Katie.

"You what?" cried Michelle.

"I just—it," he floundered. "Go to my hut."

"What?" said Katie. "No, I'm not—"

He opened the door. "Go now, Katie. I'll be down there soon."

Katie looked to Michelle, expecting her to back her up, but her lips were tucked beneath her teeth. Sealed.

Clutching the edge of the sink, Katie stood, but her legs felt like jelly. With a huff, she shoved past Goldie out of the kitchen. On the hill, the crowd still gathered, and a sharp *crack!* sounded. But she didn't linger around to watch; she couldn't bear it.

Katie paced Goldie's hut, waiting on him to return. How could he do such a thing? That poor kid . . .

She prepared a speech for him while she waited on his return, all the while allowing her hair to drip on his blankets just for spite. If he was particular about his stuff to the point of insanity, then he deserved to have a wet blanket. In fact, she considered tearing apart his room, just to make him angry.

But then she recalled how easily he had picked her up and held her beneath the sink faucet. For a little guy, he sure was strong. Years of hard labor would do that, she figured. No, she would stick to the passive-aggressive drips and a possible tongue lashing.

Finally, footsteps were heard through the thin wall. The doorknob twisted, then froze half-turned. "Look, man, I know what you're going to say," said Goldie, still outside.

Katie climbed onto Goldie's bed and peeked out the window to see Bryan approach the door, fists balled, seething.

"You arrogant, son of a bitch," said Bryan. "Who gave you the right to do something like that?"

"I'm sorry," said Goldie. "I just—I freaked."

"You freaked, huh? That's your excuse?"

Goldie removed the half-burnt nub from his pocket and tossed it to Bryan.

Bryan dropped it in the grass. "I already know, jackass, but Randy didn't steal it." He waved a notebook he had tucked under his arm at Goldie's face. "Someone else stole it and gave him the blunt. They're kids, dammit! Poking the bear is what they do. But you are the one responsible for this. If you don't want people stealing your shit, then hide it better." He shoved the notebook against his chest.

"I know, but . . ."

"But what? You're distracted? High?"

"No."

"Look man, you're my best friend and the closest thing I've got to a brother, but if you pull something else like this, we're not going to be stopping at words, do you understand me?"

"I-I just . . ."

"Do you understand me?"

Goldie bit his lip and nodded, and Bryan stormed off, making his way back up the hill. After watching him go, Goldie picked up the nub and placed it back into his pocket. As he entered the hut, Katie spun around, plopping down on the cot. His brow furrowed to see her sitting suspiciously beneath the window, and his ears turned red.

For a moment, he said nothing as his gaze lingered on the floor and he dug his duct-taped shoe into the dirt, creating a sizeable crater. "It has been made abundantly clear by Michelle and now Bryan that errors were made in the handling of today's situation."

"Errors?" Katie balked. "You call doubling a flogging and—"

"I screwed up, alright?" His eyes flashed. "I never wanted this job! I'm in this position because—" But his words died on his tongue and he pressed a hand to his face.

"Whether you wanted the job or not doesn't matter," said Katie. "What you did just now was straight-up evil. You were as bad as them. No, actually, you were worse."

"Don't talk about worse," he snarled. "You haven't seen worse."

"Growing up around a lot of psychos doesn't give you an excuse to become one."

"I screwed up," he said. "But don't talk to me like you know you would have done better. You haven't been here long enough to—"

"But Bryan has," she said.

"Bryan watches over twelve kids." He slammed his fist onto the papers on her desk. "I watch over one hundred seventy-two. And I'd like to see you decide whose life is more important." Grabbing a pack of cigarettes from his table, Goldie made for the door, the notebook still tucked under his arm.

The pin pricks!

"What's in the notebook?" Katie asked.

"Bake sale recipes," he said, then slammed the door behind him.

Katie's stomach growled as the smell of bacon swirled around her. The greasy morsel sizzled in the frying pan, tempting her with every pop. This week was her hut's turn in the kitchen, and Goldie told her to join them.

Five of the bacon strips finished; their texture just the right side of crispy, and she fished them out onto a plate.

"Excuse me, Katie," said Eric, reaching across the stove. "I need this pot."

When Eric returned to the commercial dishwasher in the corner, only two bacon slices remained. She glanced over her shoulder, and Eric tapped his finger to his lips. The supervising Watcher's head was lowered as she sat in a swivel stool at the prep table playing a game on her phone, so Katie slipped one of the bacon slices into her pocket as well.

The kitchen was spacious but crowded with twelve kids running the show. Katie didn't think it would take all twelve of them to cook for the Watchers, but she wasn't about to complain as it brought the food within arm's reach. Each of the four huts took a weekly rotation in the kitchen, and Katie suspected Goldie to be behind this. It was a brilliant way to make sure every kid had an opportunity to steal real food—an opportunity she took full advantage of.

Later that morning, Katie entered the adjacent storeroom to restock ketchup dispensers. Three walls were lined with canned goods, dried beans, rice, and cereal with a refrigerator and freezer filling the final wall. She was pouring the red goop into a funnel when Eric joined her at the work table to stock cereal into smaller tubs. After placing a large quantity of cereal in his mouth, he stuffed another sizeable portion into his pockets, and Katie helped herself to a handful.

The kitchen door opened with a pop, and Eric grimaced as he swallowed the remaining bits of dry cereal. Katie peeked around the corner. "Goldie," she whispered, feeling less worried.

"Don't let him catch you," Eric said. "You never know what he'll do."

Katie bit her lip. Perhaps she was wrong about the origin of the kitchen rule. Eric sure didn't trust him. And after Randy, maybe she shouldn't either.

"Dakota!" Goldie called across the kitchen.

"Yup." Dakota trotted over. "It's in here." Dakota led Goldie toward the store room, and Katie returned to her work. Eric passed Goldie at the door and crunched with every step.

"When did it stop working?" Goldie moved to the refrigerator in the corner.

"It was off when we came in this morning," Dakota said.

"There should be a manual around here somewhere . . ." After not finding it on the shelves, they returned to the kitchen. Katie plunged her hand into the cereal. As she shoved the handful into her mouth, they came back.

Dakota winced while Goldie's mouth hung open. Katie put her hand down, but her cheeks still bulged. The food tasted like ash in her mouth as she recalled the marks on Randy's back from yesterday.

Goldie, however, rolled his eyes and looked to Dakota. "Will someone, please, teach her how to steal?" He shoved past Dakota to the refrigerator.

"I'm sorry," Katie mouthed to Dakota with crumbs spilling out of her mouth, but she was also pleased that her original suspicions concerning her boss were accurate.

Dakota waved her off. "I guess I can give you some pointers?"

"Teach her the clothespin game." Goldie unscrewed the back panel of the refrigerator.

"The clothespin game?" Dakota asked. Goldie looked to Dakota with disbelief, but the hut leader shrugged. "Didn't have it where I came from."

Goldie removed a clothespin from a shelf and set it next to Katie. "Try to steal the clothespin without me noticing it."

"But you're staring at it."

"Then wait for the right moment." He returned to the refrigerator and pulled a flashlight from his pocket. Katie reached for the pin.

"Saw it," Goldie said without turning around. "Go back to refilling your ketchup. The more movement going on, the less your theft will stand out."

"I'm gonna . . ." Dakota jerked his thumb to the kitchen and exited.

Katie picked up the funnel with one hand and reached for the pin again.

"Saw it," Goldie said, pressing on the wires.

"How? You're not even—"

He looked over his shoulder as if to say *Really?* On the panel, he pressed a something to another thing, and the refrigerator started humming.

"That'll do it," he said, smacking the dust off his hands. He was about to stand when the panel sparked and cracked. Flames leapt up from the wires. "Whoa now!" He yanked the cord out of the wall and kicked the flames out.

"What happened?" Katie asked.

Goldie shook his head and studied the blackened wires. Then he laughed. "I think I killed it. That's just great."

"But I thought you knew what you were doing."

"I don't know how to do half the things I'm told to do. You should know that by now. I guess I'll go find Addison."

On his way out, he stopped at her table to find the clothespin missing. Katie smiled in triumph.

"Good job," he said. "If you can do that without Leida seeing, you'll be well on your way."

*   *   *

"You did pretty good," Leida said when Katie showed her the pocketful of cereal, three granola bars, and two single-serving packs of peanut butter. "Especially for your first day. We'll keep up the clothespin game for the rest of the week. You'll have a blast when we get to pickpocketing."

"Pickpocketing?" Katie said.

Leida smiled and tossed her braid over her shoulder. "Here, I'll show you how to stash your stuff."

Katie watched with amazement as Leida popped a board off the base of Katie's bunk to reveal the cubby. Hidden inside was a bunch of junk: bottle caps, paper clips, safety pins, bobby pins, pens, staples, ends of tape rolls.

"I have a box under my bed," she said, "but you have this. Jared called it his klepto- stash."

"This was Goldie's bed?"

"Yep." Leida dusted the dirt from her knees. "If you need any help, let me know."

After stashing away her treasures, Katie examined her bunk closer to find what other oddities might be present. She crawled underneath and found carvings of random strings of numbers and letters. The first two letters at the beginning were familiar, however: TN, GA, CO, MA—state abbreviations. They were license plate numbers. Also written on the wooden slats were the names of all the Watchers. Some she recognized, others she didn't. Bartram was listed with the name Theodore Bartholomew Dyer in parenthesis.

On the wall beneath the bed was written "Jared Adam Kelley and Leida Marie Kelley. Children of Wayne and Marie Kelley were here." Dates of birth, an address, and phone number followed. This part had been gone over and over again, as if in a sense of desperation.

They were still here.

"Hey there, Katie Belle." Dad's voice sounded so sad as it came across the speakers. Katie forced her voice to sound normal as she greeted him in return, but her heart nearly shattered. How much older Dad looked. The hair around his ears had begun to turn gray, and dark circles collected under his eyes.

And what must he think of her? Katie could see from the picture in the corner she was thinner than before. The pink crescent moon scar was ever-present. Every time she saw the scar, it surprised her. During the day, no one mentioned it, but as she looked into the screen, it stared at her.

It was ugly. It made her feel ugly.

"Are they still treating you well?" Dad asked.

Katie didn't have to look at the prompts anymore to answer, "Yes, they're treating me very well."

"That's good." Dad nodded. "Are they giving you any sunscreen? You look a bit red, honey."

Katie looked to Ian. The man shook his head behind the mask. "I can't say anything about that."

"Of course," Dad said. "Don't do anything to get yourself in trouble. Alec and I love you."

Her eyes blurred with tears. "I love you both so much."

Addison turned the camera to Ian, and the tears slid down Katie's cheeks. Dad cursed at Ian like usual, but she didn't listen to what else was said. The call ended, and the lights went down. Addison cut her restraints, and Katie followed Goldie into the hallway.

Katie sniffled as she walked beside him. She wouldn't trade these calls for anything, but the sadness that followed was overwhelming. They made their way to her hut in silence, and Goldie opened the door for her. When Katie reached her bed, she pulled her blanket to her chin. Homesickness swept through her.

The end of her bed bounced as Eric plopped down. "I wish I had popcorn."

Katie peered over the covers. "Why?"

"So I could watch what's about to go down with a snack. Just wait."

Dakota and Leida spoke near his bed. She couldn't hear what was said, but the conversation was animated. Suddenly, Leida slapped Dakota and stormed away.

"Oooohh," Eric said.

"Come on now," Dakota said. "We can still be friends."

But Leida stormed to her bed and pulled her blanket over her head. The rest of the hut was silent as they looked between her and Dakota. Then Paulina dropped from her bunk and joined Dakota, wrapping her arm around his waist and whispering something in his ear. They slipped out into the evening.

"Apparently," Eric said, "Dakota wants to date a girl closer to his own age. Told you it would be good." He returned to his own bed.

Jackass. Dakota didn't have to dump her in front of everybody like that. Across the way, tears slid down five-year-old Ivy's face, and Katie's heart broke. It wasn't just a breakup. Not for the little ones. It was like watching their parents split.

Katie scooted over to Leida's bed.

"I don't want to talk about it," Leida said from beneath her blanket.

"You don't have to," Katie said. "But come out for a second, and I'll give you a hug."

Leida pulled back the covers and Katie embraced her.

"She's such a whore," Leida cried.

As they were leaving breakfast the next day, Goldie approached Leida while she was still with her hut. Dakota dropped Paulina's hand, but Goldie stepped past him and slipped something into Leida's pocket. Later, she showed Katie three Hershey's Kisses.

"He's under the impression," Leida said, "that chocolate fixes everything."

"Doesn't it?"

Leida laughed, but over the week, Katie saw her nibbling on the tiny morsels with a look of divine pleasure. Chocolate didn't fix everything, but it did help.

Katie stopped before the little shed and looked up to see legs dangling off the rooftop of Goldie's hut. "What are you doing?" she asked.

Goldie leaned out over the edge of the roof and let out a large puff of white smoke. "I'm smoking."

"Are you high?"

He chuckled. "Nope. It's a cigarette."

"Then why are you on the roof?"

"Because it's a beautiful morning. Come up if you'd like."

It was that. Blue skies with no clouds, but still, what a strange place to be! Katie found a pile of wood around back stacked into a makeshift staircase. Carefully, she mounted the woodpile and clambered to the top. Goldie offered her the cigarette.

"I'm good," Katie said. "Besides, don't you know those things will give you cancer?"

"You still think we've got that long of a life expectancy?"

Katie opened and closed her mouth a couple of times. She frowned, watching the end of Goldie's cigarette grow red. He handed her the cigarette, and she took a small puff, but coughs racked her chest.

"Why do you like that?" she gasped.

"It's calming, but, unfortunately, a nicotine habit is not a great thing to have around here."

"Better than a pot habit," she said, and he took another drag. "Are we going to get yelled at for being up here?"

"Nah, as long as I get my stuff done, everybody's cool. If anyone asks, I can say I'm overseeing processes to ensure the camp is functioning at maximum capacity."

"Is that what you're doing?"

"Nope. I'm taking a smoke break."

"It is nice up here," said Katie. The morning was still crisp and cool, although the muggy heat was coming soon. Temperatures were starting to push into the 90s. She knew this because, like everything else, Goldie kept track.

It was odd to find Goldie loafing. Katie still wasn't sure if he was high, but his eyes were not red, and the only smell on him was cigarettes. An airplane flew overhead, its propellers barely audible from the distance. "Do you ever wonder where in the world we are?"

"Nope," he said. "I know where we are."

"Really? Where?"

"Hell."

"Ha-ha, funny."

"Seriously, though," he said. "We're in the Cherokee National Forest about forty-five minutes from a tiny town called Reliance, Tennessee."

Her mouth parted. "How do you know that?"

"The Watchers talk." He shrugged. "And they bring in coffee cups and receipts from town. It's a poorly kept secret. And then there's this."

Goldie opened the library book he had brought with him and showed her the back page. Stamped on the inside were the words: "Reliance Public Library" with the address to follow.

Katie laughed. "Nice. I've never heard of Reliance before. I'm from Nashville. How far away is that?"

"Exactly? I don't know. But Reliance is in the southeast corner of the state. I'm from Chattanooga, and Reliance is about sixty miles from there."

"You know, I'm not that far away from my dad. I'm still in Tennessee." That was a strange thought indeed. There was nothing but woods and mountains between them. No oceans.

He dragged on his cigarette in reply. If this news had shocked him before, it was clear the shock had worn off.

A soft sound mingled with the wind, and Katie craned her neck to listen better. It was somehow familiar.

"It's a train," Goldie said. "It comes through every Tuesday, Thursday, and Saturday at the same time. But you can only hear it if the wind is right."

"How far away do you think it is?" All she could see was a mass of trees beyond the fence.

"About five, maybe seven miles."

"You can tell from listening?"

"No," he said. "I've been to the tracks before. A buddy and I got out of the fence a few years back. First place we ran to was the tracks. They follow a river until they come to a campground and a store with a bunch of rafts. We got caught there." He sighed. "The store was closed for the winter. We broke out at the wrong time of the year."

"Who did you break out with?" Katie knew the answer from the hut leaders meeting, but she wanted to see what he would say. This was the most she had heard him speak about himself, and she wanted to keep it going.

Goldie smashed his cigarette into the shingles. "A guy named Landon."

"I don't think I've met him."

Goldie narrowed his eyes. He was on to her. The kids talked, and the story was too big for her not to have heard it by now. She expected him to shut down, but he continued.

"Landon didn't make it. They shot him," he said. Katie didn't feign surprise, and he studied her from the corner of his eye. "And the next question is why didn't they shoot you too, Jared?"

"I'm sorry," she said. "I know this is not something you want to talk about. I was just curious."

"Sometimes the Watchers make decisions on a whim. Look, I don't need you right now. After lunch, I'll have a job, but you're good to go with your hut for this morning." Goldie slid off the edge of the roof, and Katie frowned at his abrupt exit. She didn't know what she had expected.

*   *   *

Katie shoveled compost onto the rows and wished for lunchtime. The day grew steamy, and crickets screamed as if to complain about the heat. She had been spoiled by her time writing for Goldie. While the others were adept at their monotonous chores, she always lagged behind.

She had been with her hut for over an hour when Paulina called out, "What's going on over there?"

Katie plunged the shovel into the ground and raised a hand to her eyes. A girl her age came running from the huts, looking over her shoulder repeatedly.

"Courtney?" Paulina stepped over the knee-high rows. "Courtney, what happened?"

When Courtney reached Paulina, she fell into her arms sobbing. Katie laid down her shovel and joined them.

"I have to—I have to find Trevor," sobbed Courtney.

"What's going on?" Dakota asked upon reaching them. "Was she attacked?"

Courtney's shirt was ripped, and she kept rubbing her arm. Dakota took her hand revealing a bruise around her wrist. Katie looked back up the hill, but she couldn't see anyone.

"I need Trevor," Courtney said.

"Eric!" Dakota said. "Go get Trevor. Now."

The boy ran toward the greenhouses. Courtney sank to the ground as she continued to cry, and Paulina wrapped her arms around her.

"Who hurt you?" Katie squatted next to her. "Was it one of the Watchers?" Sobs caught in Courtney's throat, and Katie patted her shoulder. "Take your time."

Trevor ran from the greenhouse with Eric on his heels. He was one of the hut leaders, and also Courtney's boyfriend. He bent at the waist to catch his breath. "Courtney, were you attacked?"

Courtney's gaze flashed to Leida. "Goldie! He attacked me."

Leida paled, and Katie's mouth parted. She looked up to the huts once more, but there was no sign of him.

"I-I was coming back from the house after dropping off the drying cloths and he—" she covered her mouth, "he told me to come inside. I thought he had something for me to take back to the greenhouse, but he attacked me. I tried to get away but he . . . he raped me!"

Katie flinched. "He what?" she muttered. For over a month, Katie had worked with the guy and she had never witnessed him act suggestively to anyone.

Trevor, however, rose to full height, his teeth barred as he turned toward the hill. "I'm going to kill him."

"No, you're not." The crooked-nosed Watcher, Bartram, had approached while the others were distracted and now stood with one hand on his taser. Although Bartram was not small, Trevor stood a few inches taller than him and was wider in the shoulders.

"This has nothing to do with you, Bartram!" Trevor shouted.

"Goldie is protected."

"He raped her!"

"It doesn't matter. He's worth a hell of a lot more than you."

Trevor started up the hill anyway, and Bartram raised the taser. "Last warning before I put a thousand volts through you and rip the flesh from your back," said the Watcher.

Trevor's fist clenched, but he stood still. Abruptly, he turned back to Courtney who continued to sob on the ground, holding her torn shirt close to her neck. Katie rubbed her back, but her brow crinkled. Her story wasn't impossible. The guy was stronger than he looked, but still . . .

"He can't get away with this." Trevor looked over the group, but everyone's heads were lowered. Then his gaze rested on Leida. "What about her? Is she protected?"

The Watcher's brows pinched, but he shook his head. Trevor's hands clenched into fists once more.

"Wait, what?" Katie stood. "Leida hasn't done anything."

"I don't care!" Trevor shouted.

"Trevor," Dakota said. "You're mad. I get that, but Leida is innocent."

"He hurt Courtney," Trevor said. "I can't touch him, so I'm going to hurt him the only way I can."

Leida scooted back into the group.

"Trevor!" Katie said. "Trevor, you can't!" She reached for his arm, but he shrugged her away.

"Leida," Dakota said, "go find Goldie. Now."

Leida's wide eyes looked from the hill to Trevor. There was no way she would be able to outrun this boy.

"Leida, Go!" Dakota said.

"No, I'm not going to him." Leida took a step forward. "He's not my brother, Trevor. Not anymore. Not after what he's done. I hate him as much as you do."

Trevor clenched and unclenched his fist. With a terrible moan, he ran his fingers through his hair and cast another look toward Goldie's hut.

"Trevor," Courtney said. "Let's go. Please? Leave Leida alone. It's not her fault."

Trevor cast a longing gaze toward Goldie's hut but nodded. He picked up Courtney and carried her back to the greenhouse. Katie turned to Leida, but she pushed through the rows away from them.

*   *   *

The mess hall buzzed at lunch. Word had already spread among the huts, but no one had seen Goldie that morning. After eating, the hut leaders convened a meeting in the corner of the room. Trevor, however, stayed next to Courtney with an arm around her.

"Do you think he did it?" Katie asked Paulina at her table. Leida raised her head up at the question before continuing to stab her gruel with her spoon.

"You don't?" Paulina asked. "Why would Courtney lie?"

"I don't know," Katie said. "It just seems—weird."

"Look, I don't know if your creep sensitivity is turned to zero or what," Paulina said, "but that guy's got issues. He's a sellout to the Watchers for starters. Mix that with drugs and a short-guy inferiority complex, and stuff like this is bound to happen. His biggest mistake was picking on Trevor's girlfriend, though. He's bound to kill him!"

"But he's never acted that way toward me."

"You mean other than the time he about drowned you in the sink?" Paulina asked.

"I mean, you know—like that."

"Maybe you're just not his type."

Bryan left the hut leaders and beckoned for Katie to join him away from the others. "Were you with Jared this morning?" he asked her.

"He was on top of his hut smoking a cigarette after breakfast," Katie said. "We talked briefly, then he sent me away."

"Did he seem high?" Bryan asked. "Drunk? Anything weird like that?"

"No," Katie said. "In fact, he was in a good mood, but I left an hour before any of this took place."

"Katie, I'm going to ask you a question, and regardless of any promises he's made you keep, you need to answer honestly."

Where the heck is this going?

"Have you seen him take any pills?" asked Bryan. "Or smoke anything more than a cigarette?"

"I mean, Leida said she saw some pills when he moved out, and…"

"I don't care about the rumor mill. Did you see him take anything?"

She shook her head. "I haven't seen any pills."

"Okay," Bryan breathed. "Okay, at least that's something."

"You don't think he did it?"

"For the most part, I'm convinced that Jared is a good kid. But he does forget it sometimes. I don't know what happened, Katie, but I also think he should be given a chance to say something before we draw conclusions."

The door opened, and all eyes turned to watch Goldie enter. He, however, was too busy reading his mail to notice. After a moment of silence, he peered over his glasses with furrowed brow. Michelle rose from her seat, crossed the hall, and cupped her hand around his ear.

"She should have let him squirm," Paulina said loud enough for the other tables to hear.

Goldie's eyes grew wide as Michelle spoke. He pulled away before she finished and approached Courtney, but the girl stared at her hands. When Goldie was a table away, Trevor barred his path.

"I need to speak with Courtney," Goldie said.

"Not going to happen." Trevor's voice shook as he crossed his arms over his chest. He stood a foot taller than Goldie.

Bartram, the Watcher, moved from the wall to stand behind Goldie and rested his hand on the taser.

"I don't give a crap about your bodyguard," Trevor said. "If you come near her again, I'll kill you."

"I only need to talk to her," Goldie said.

Trevor leaned forward. "No."

"Stand down," Bryan breathed beside Katie. "Just stand down."

"This is how you want to play it, Courtney?" Goldie said. "You want to sit there and hide behind your boyfriend?"

Courtney stole a quick glance over her shoulder, and Trevor advanced a step. "Don't speak to her. Don't even look at her. You've hurt her enough for one day."

"I didn't touch her."

"I've seen the bruise on her arm!" he said.

Goldie stammered for a moment. "Okay, so I threw her out of my hut, but I didn't hurt her like—like that."

Bryan winced. "Shut up, man. Just shut up."

"I'm tired of your shit. And your lies!" Trevor shoved Goldie in the chest.

The Watcher raised his taser, and Goldie took two steps back. "Nope! We're good." He stared at Bartram. "We're good."

"Then get your food and go," Bartram said.

Goldie rubbed his eyes. "I'm not hungry."

"Then get out."

With a sigh, Goldie nodded and left.

"Coward!" Trevor yelled as the door shut, and the Watcher slid his taser back into its holster and stood against the wall once more.

"I'll catch up with you later," Bryan muttered as he followed Goldie out the door. When Katie returned to her seat, Leida had thrust her bowl into the middle for the table to swallow up.

Katie didn't go back to Goldie's hut after lunch that day, nor the next morning. Every time someone passed by their table at lunch, she would jump, thinking it was him about to yell at her for her absence. She just wasn't sure about what had happened to Courtney, but each time she thought of facing Goldie, that squeezing sensation around her throat, like Midas's fingers crushing her neck, returned.

"I don't blame you for not going back," Paulina said with a mouthful of gruel. "I wouldn't go anywhere near that creep."

"I'm surprised he hasn't said anything."

"I totally thought you were sleeping with him before I moved into your hut," Paulina said. "Afterall, it's a cushy job, and people don't get favors from him for nothing."

"I haven't seen anyone come by for that sort of thing." She hadn't seen him do any pills, either, but that didn't mean he wasn't taking any.

"People don't go to him for the little things," said Paulina. "They go for, like, transfers and stuff. Or job changes. Things he's in charge of. I thought that's how you got the job. No judgment or anything. A girl's gotta do what a girl's gotta do, you know?"

"That's not how you got your transfer though," Leida said as she picked at her food.

"Gosh no. I didn't have to. After Sam and I broke up, I simply made it awkward for me to stick around. Goldie will do anything for his bros."

Leida stabbed her spoon into the gruel, and Katie rested her head in her hand. What was true? Everyone thought they were sleeping together, but they were not. Could he have done it? Sure. Strength wasn't an issue; she knew that first-hand. But had he?

She didn't know, but not even his own sister was defending him.

Michelle slid into the seat next to Katie. "I'm here on behalf of Goldie. He says you're to go to his hut after lunch."

"And why doesn't he come himself?" Paulina asked.

"He's trying to avoid a scene."

"Doing his dirty work, Michelle?" Paulina said. "Katie doesn't want to go back. If you don't have a problem with him, then maybe you should work for him."

"Paulina," Michelle said through tight lips. "You are the last person anyone at this table should listen to. Shut your mouth, or I'll shut it for you."

As Paulina's mouth parted, Katie's brow furrowed. What was that supposed to mean?

"Katie," Michelle continued, "this is not an option. You need to head to his hut after lunch."

Katie played with a splinter on the table and nodded. After the way Ian reacted to Goldie trying to get her fired, she doubted the camp boss would think warmly of her trying to shirk her chores.

Dakota leaned in across the table. "Katie, if he causes you any trouble, come find me, alright? Or any of the hut leaders. We've got your back."

*　　*　　*

After the meal, Katie entered Goldie's hut once more. As she stepped through the door, he glanced up from his desk and said, "The newest numbers from four and six are in. I put them on your desk."

She glanced at the door, thankful that this new table was near it. Six sheets packed with numbers looked up at her, and she estimated at least a couple of hours to transcribe them into the notebook.

Goldie opened a textbook on his desk but didn't look at it. Instead, he studied something in his hand. Katie strained her neck to see what it was and was surprised to see a silver cross sitting in his palm. She continued her writing, and he continued in silence. Then, abruptly, he tossed the cross into the small box on his desk and stood. "I'm going for a smoke."

Once he was gone from the room, Katie felt as if she could breathe again. A few minutes later, a thump sounded on the roof. She tried to concentrate on her work, but the cross kept intruding her thoughts. Unable to withstand the temptation any longer, Katie crept to his desk and opened the little box, finding a Celtic cross with a blue sapphire in the center sitting at the bottom. The piece was tarnished but still beautiful. Beneath the cross was a broken, beaded chain. A rosary?

Was he religious? Katie ran her fingers over the chain, and a brown substance flaked off the beads. She dropped the rosary back into the box. It was blood.

Goldie shifted above, and Katie jumped. She listened for any other sounds, but there was only silence, so she resumed studying the box. It was made from wood scraps, but the inside seemed too shallow compared to the outside. Besides the rosary, there were four cigarettes, a bunch of screws and nails, five paper clips, and two buttons. All this she poured out onto the desktop to find a small hole at the bottom of the box. After bending one of the paperclips, she slid the narrow wire into the hole, and the floor pried up easily.

Inside were three Hershey's kisses, two sticks of gum, and two caramel candies. Underneath the Hershey's kisses were two straightened foil wrappers and a stick of gum. He also had money tucked inside: fifty-seven dollars and thirty-two cents.

Once a klepto . . .

Other than the box on the desk, there was a green bean can full of pens and pencils, a couple of library books, the open textbook, and a stack of spiral-bound notebooks in the corner. Katie hoped to find the ever-elusive blue notebook from Randy's flogging, but these were just old crop record books. The one on bottom was different and older; the cover was bent, the edges frayed.

Katie flipped open the cover, and a cardinal sitting on a fence post looked up at her. Beneath the bird, written in elegant cursive was *"Cardinalis cardinalis."*

The drawing beneath this was a strand of flowers Goldie had captured well. *"Solidago virgaurea"* it said. Goldenrod, a common flower around the camp.

Katie found page after page of stunning images and elegant cursive, but the drawings soon became poor. The tremor had entered his art until finally, the drawings were hard to identify. Entire pages were scribbled out. Others were torn where he had erased too heavily. She closed the notebook and slid it beneath the others. What had destroyed him?

Recalling the secret compartment on her bunk, Katie slid her fingers around the edges of the table and found a hidden latch. She disengaged it, and a false bottom detached. Inside were bags and bags of dried green leaves.

Goldie shifted on the roof. With haste, Katie closed the compartment and returned to her desk. The door opened, and the smell of cigarettes filled the room. As he approached the desk, Goldie looked back at Katie.

Had she left something out of place? Was she paranoid, or did he know she had been prying?

He said nothing but returned to the textbook still lying open before him. After fifteen minutes, he had yet to turn the page. "I've decided to call a hut leader meeting after dinner."

"Are you sure that's a good idea?" Katie asked.

He rubbed the bridge of his nose. "Trevor needs to hear what I have to say."

Katie shrugged. It wasn't her problem.

*　　　*　　　*

After returning her bowl to the front after dinner, Katie joined the other hut leaders. No one spoke above a whisper as they waited on Goldie, and Trevor leaned back in his seat, his brow creased. Finally, the door to the mess hall creaked on its rusted hinges.

Trevor leapt to his feet as Goldie stepped inside. The bigger boy's fists clenched, and he stepped into Goldie's path. Through gritted teeth, he said, "You've got some nerve, I'll give you that. But I have no interest in hearing a damn thing you have to say."

"Sit down," Bartram said as he slipped in behind Goldie. "And shut up."

"Ha!" Trevor cried. "Brought your bodyguard, did you?"

"I didn't ask Bartram to come," Goldie said.

"Bullshit."

"Sit down!" Bartram barked. "I'm here to make sure you two don't kill each other."

"Each other?" Trevor said. "You mean to make sure I don't kill him, because the only reason his insides are not on his outside is because of you."

Bartram crossed his arms, his brows raised as he looked to the short and slender Goldie. "Don't underestimate him."

"We should all sit down." Goldie gestured to the table. "We need to talk."

Trevor glared at him. Finally, he yanked back the chair and dropped into the seat. Bartram stood behind Trevor.

"First off, I need to make something abundantly clear," said Goldie as he sat. "Trevor, I know you hate me, but this stays between us. You will not threaten Leida again."

"I won't?" Trevor said. "And what if I do?"

"I will kill you."

Bartram cleared his throat. "No, you don't mean that. You're exaggerating."

"And how do you expect to kill me, you little shrimp?" Trevor asked.

Goldie leaned forward. "Stay away from her, and you won't have to find out."

"Goldie, you're not going to kill him," Bartram said. "You were exaggerating. I need to hear you say that."

He narrowed his eyes. "I'm exaggerating."

Awkward silence followed. Nobody at that table believed that to be an idle threat. Katie also wondered how, but she never considered he wouldn't try.

Finally, Bryan adjusted in his seat and said, "Trevor, whether or not Goldie gets his ass kicked the second Bartram goes home is still to be determined. But he's right in this: Leida's off limits."

Goldie gawked at his friend. "So, it's like that, huh?"

"You know I don't say it lightly," said Bryan.

The awkward silence returned as Goldie slumped further in his chair as he pressed his hands against his face. Bryan had warned Goldie after Randy's flogging that he wouldn't stop at words if he tried to pull something else. Perhaps that time had come.

"I have no interest in harming Leida," Trevor said. "I wouldn't stoop to your level by hurting an innocent girl."

Katie laughed aloud at this bull crap. When Trevor turned to her, however, she stifled it. There were too many threats going around for a new one to be aimed at her.

"Trevor, I didn't rape Courtney," said Goldie. "I swear to God, I didn't. And if all the evidence you have to show I did is a little bruise on her arm, then I'd say that's not worth a whole lot."

Trevor leapt to his feet. "She told me what you did, you lying sack of shit! How you threatened her!"

Bartram kicked him in the back of the knee, and Trevor collapsed into his seat. The Watcher pressed the taser against his skin. "Get yourself under control."

"Bartram, please." Goldie raised his hand. "Trevor, listen for two minutes. Can you give me two minutes?"

Trevor glared at Goldie but was silent.

Goldie looked to Michelle, and she smiled encouragingly. "Courtney was in my hut yesterday. I didn't ask her to come by, she just showed up. And—" He gazed at to Michelle again. "Dammit, this is going to sound nuts, but she came on to me!"

Trevor's face grew red, and Katie's mouth parted.

"She was rather assertive," he continued. "And I told her to leave. When she didn't, I grabbed her arm and removed her from my hut."

Michelle continued to nod with encouragement, but Bryan winced at the explanation. Trevor leaned across the table with a snarl. "You son of a bitch. She came on to you? You . . . you pathetic piece of shit!"

"The other day," Michelle said, "Courtney asked me for a transfer to the house, but we're full right now. Perhaps she thought Goldie would give her a transfer if she . . . you know . . ."

"So, she's a whore? You didn't just hurt her. Now, you're making her out to be a whore!" Trevor stood again. Bartram raised his taser, but Goldie motioned for him to wait.

"If you value your life, you will stay away from me. And her." Trevor stormed out of the mess hall. He slammed the door, and it bounced off the frame.

Sam shook his head. "Dude, you are one messed up son of a bitch." He shoved his chair back and followed Trevor. Dakota excused himself next. Katie considered leaving, but she wanted to know more. She was stuck working with the guy after all.

Paulina did say girls came by for stuff like that. Maybe things didn't go according to plan for Courtney. Could there have been a misunderstanding of some sort that led to Courtney feeling violated? Or had Goldie turned her down as he said?

If this were the case, both would be motivated to lie given the threat Trevor's jealousy created. At this point, though, Katie didn't know who to side with, so she kept her mouth shut.

"That went well," said Bryan. "Truly. I didn't think he could hate you more than he does."

"Yeah," Bartram said, still staring at the door. "He's going to be a problem."

Goldie straightened. "He's not going to be a problem."

"Right," Bartram said. "At this point, I'm surprised he hasn't bludgeoned you in your sleep. He's out of control."

"I will handle him," Goldie said.

"Like you did now? No, we need to consider transferring him to another camp."

"I don't want him transferred," Goldie said. "He hasn't done anything wrong."

"He's threatened to kill you."

"Well, I'd want to kill me too," Goldie said, and everyone cast him a strange eye. "If I had done it. But I didn't."

Bartram shook his head. "Look, I've been off the clock for about an hour now, so I'm gonna go, but you need to figure this out. Or we will, understand?"

Goldie studied the table, and Bryan rose. "I'm going to go find Trevor and talk with him. Maybe I can convince him not to murder you tonight."

*　　　*　　　*

Katie moaned as the morning siren erupted over the camp. Gray light crept through the shuttered window beside her bed. Surely, the sun had sped its arrival to deprive her of much needed rest. As she stretched her weary muscles, nagging hunger clawed her belly. She nibbled on the dry cereal hidden in her pillowcase.

Over on her own bunk, Leida ran her fingers through her long hair. Within moments, she created a masterful fishtail braid running the length of her back. Every morning she managed a fantastic creation out of meager means. Unable to compete with Leida's expert fingers, Katie settled for a ponytail.

Katie was third away from the spigot when Goldie passed by, and he inclined his head in vague greeting. At first, Katie thought he was greeting her, but then she remembered Leida was next in line. Although Leida saw him, she did not return the gesture, and

Katie frowned. Leida always had a smile for Goldie, albeit often a small one.

Goldie continued on. Either he did not notice the change, or he ignored it. Katie reasoned after the hostility Leida had received from Trevor, remaining distant would be in her best interest.

Two Watchers approached from the house. Katie recognized Bartram as one, but she had never seen the other. He wore a tan cowboy hat, dark brown cowboy boots, and a silver revolver hung on his side.

Leida inhaled sharply. "What is he doing here?"

Bartram pointed to Trevor exiting his hut. Trevor saw the gesture and tried to bolt, but he was intercepted by another Watcher who shoved him back. The teen's head swiveled until he spotted Goldie only feet away. "You son of a bitch!" He lunged for Goldie, swinging at him.

The smaller boy ducked under the wild haymaker and danced back several steps. Enraged, Trevor moved to charge him again but froze with one foot out. Volts of electricity flooded his body as the cowboy held down the trigger on his taser. Trevor fell to the ground twitching.

"And enough of that." The cowboy pulled the trigger again. "You two—Tweedle Dee and Tweedle Dum. Get him up and packaged. He's riding in my trunk." He sniffed and spat tobacco onto the ground.

Derek and Dumar glowered at the names, but they tied Trevor's hands and feet. As they passed by him, the cowboy dangled his keys in Dumar's face. The Watcher snatched them and shoved them into his pocket. Grumbling, he continued on.

"You owe me, Goldilocks." The cowboy tilted his hat to Goldie.

Goldie kept his head down, but his hands were balled into fists. The cowboy sauntered up the hill after Derek and Dumar. As soon as he was out of earshot, Goldie approached Bartram, seething. "You said you'd let me handle it!"

The Watcher's eyes grew wide as he looked around at his peers.

"I told you not transfer—" Goldie continued.

A backhanded slap landed across Goldie's face, and he stumbled back, his head lowered.

"I don't take orders from you!" Bartram lifted his hand to strike Goldie again, but a flash of sympathy crossed his face. He shook his head and walked to the house.

Goldie stood rooted as his shoulders heaved. When he raised his head, he spotted Courtney hiding behind her hut-mates and marched to her.

"Is this what you wanted?"

She retreated until her back was against the wall, and a pitiful cry escaped her lips.

"Because this," he pointed toward the house, "this is on you." Goldie left her cowering against the building.

DISBANDED

With her eyes sealed, Katie imagined the literary scene as Leida's voice filled the otherwise silent hut. Three weeks had passed since Trevor had been transferred, and work had been stressful. No one blamed Katie for Trevor's transfer, but her position as Goldie's assistant had put her at the center of the conflict.

Goldie had tried to fill in as a hut leader, but the animus from the hut was too great. Bryan slept in Trevor's hut while his number two, Olivia, handled the nighttime duties of their own hut. The hut limped along without a leader during the day. Katie had seen their latest projected work output. If something didn't change soon, they were going to fall short of their quota.

"'Will tried it that way,'" Leida read. "'He turned his back on Tug, seized the rope firmly and began walking.'"

A knock pounded on the hut door, and Katie sighed as the fantasy ended. As was expected at this time of night, Goldie stepped inside. But this time, Ian joined him.

Katie had never seen Ian out of the house, and her unease intensified when her hut-mates turned to look at her. Leida slid her hand into Katie's.

Goldie bit his lip as he surveyed the hut. "Eric."

"Noooo!" Eric moaned from the next bunk. "No, no, no. Please, Goldie!"

Goldie pinched the bridge of his nose. "I'm sorry. Come here, please."

Eric searched the faces of his friends, but there was no help to be found. Tears poured down his face.

"We don't have all day." Ian stamped to the bunk.

Eric covered his wrist. "Please—please, there must have been a mistake. Whatever it is, it can be fixed, please!"

Ian yanked his hand free and sliced through Eric's green band with his knife. Eric cried out as if Ian had cut through his very arm. Ian shoved the broken plastic into his pocket, and Eric fell over on the bed weeping.

"You—girl—come with me." Ian grabbed Katie's wrist and pulled her off the bed.

Katie's heart pounded as she looked back at Eric. What happened? Would they ever tell him? Ian shoved her forward, and she stumbled to Goldie. He held the door open for them, and they walked up the hill together.

The drill was sealed into Katie's mind. Sit in the chair. Put your hands on the armrests. Ignore the zip ties. Wait for Dad.

It didn't matter. Every time she sat in that chair, butterflies swarmed her stomach. After witnessing Eric's band being removed, the butterflies felt like hornets.

Goldie stared at the floor in the back, arms folded across his stomach, and looking paler than normal. As Addison logged into the program at the table between them, a chime sounded on Ian's phone. He nodded to Addison and tucked the phone back into his pocket.

The familiar ringtone brought Katie's attention back. The lights came on, and it was her and Ian at the front of the room. But after the fourth ring, Katie frowned. Dad never let the call ring so long. Then a face appeared on the screen. It wasn't Dad.

Katie squinted at the man on the screen. He had wide shoulders and wore a white button-down shirt with a thin tie. And he had spent many meals across the table from Katie. "Agent Watts?"

Ian leapt up and turned the camera to himself. "What the hell are you doing?"

"We've got a problem," Agent Watts said.

Katie's eyes bulged as she looked between the two. Ian knew him?

"No shit! Where is our guy?" Ian asked.

"He's tied up in the bathroom," Watts said. "He and the son were acting strange. I tried getting him to talk to me, but he wasn't biting. I was unable to maintain my cover when things escalated, but I was right to be suspicious. Apparently, his son is some whiz kid and set up a program on the computer to—" He looked to something off-screen. "To be honest. I have no idea what he did. But something just churned out your approximated location."

The room started spinning as Katie continued to gape at Agent Watts. He was betraying them? Or had he been an imposter all along? She strained to see Goldie beyond the lights but could only make out shadow.

"That's not possible," Ian said. "We have a VPN."

Watts laughed. "I don't know, Ian. I'll get my tech guy to look at it and see what he's done."

Ian ran his hand over his balding head. "This guy isn't connected to one case. He's part of the Chinese case too."

"Believe it or not," Watts said, "I know what's on his desk. I'll take care of it."

"No, we're shutting this down. We never should have taken this job. Kill him and the kid."

"No!" Katie shouted.

Ian pointed a meaty finger at her. "Shut it!"

"I said I would take care of it, and I will," Watts said. "I'm not one of your damn amateurs."

"I'm not taking any chances," Ian said.

"It's not your damn call, Ian. It's Midas's. Don't do anything until you talk to him."

The screen went black, and Ian swiped the computer and electronic devices off the table. A stream of expletives poured out his mouth, and he threw his mask across the room then kicked over a chair.

Addison slipped a pair of scissors to Goldie, and he cut Katie's bonds. Taking her arm, he escorted her out of the room before the raging bull could turn his sights on her.

"Are they—are they going to kill my dad?" Katie said once they reached the hallway. "And Alec?"

"It's going to be okay." Goldie looked over his shoulder, eyes wide as they climbed down the stairs. He clutched her arm so tight it hurt. "Nobody has decided anything. We don't know what's going to happen."

"But Ian—" Katie pulled her arm away as they reached the bottom of the stairs.

"The guy on the screen was right. Ian's not in charge. Midas is, and he decides when this op ends."

"I'm so scared." Katie hugged herself. "They're going to cut off my armband too, I know it!"

"You don't know that." He placed his hands on her shoulders. "You're not the first to have issues like this, and the Watchers will handle it."

"That doesn't sound good either!"

"I'm just saying—never mind. It sounded better in my head. But did I hear correctly? Did your brother run a successful hack on them?"

Katie shrugged. "Alec was always good at computers."

"No one has ever been able to do that. What if your dad told someone from the FBI what they were going to do?" he said. "What if they are able to . . ."

"You don't get it, Goldie!" she said. "Watts is FBI. He's my dad's partner!"

Goldie's mouth fell open. "Oh, shit."

*   *   *

"Kill him and the kid." Ian's words rattled in Katie's head during breakfast even a week later. The Watchers had told her nothing. She glanced down the table at Eric, and her throat nearly closed. Was she next?

Across the table, Ivy coughed and laid her head on her arms. The five-year-old's face was flushed, and she had only picked at her food.

"Are you feeling alright, sweetie?" Leida nudged her.

"My throat hurts," Ivy said.

Leida felt her forehead and frowned. "Let me see your mouth."

Ivy opened her mouth, and the table behind took notice. The workers nearest Ivy went to sit on the other side.

Goldie approached their table with furrowed brow. "Is she sick?" He placed a hand on her forehead.

"She has white spots on her throat," Leida said.

"Quarantine her. I'll send over fresh sheets."

"Sweetie." Leida's voice cracked. "We're going to go back to the hut now." She took Ivy's hand, and the girl's shoulders slumped as she followed her.

"It's probably just strep throat, right?" Katie asked.

Eric tugged at his collar. "It's not just strep when you don't have antibiotics. Goldie, we could have an outbreak quick. She's been in here almost the whole meal."

"They won't save us," Katie breathed, recalling what he had told her before. Goldie bit his lip, and she stifled everything else.

"They'll save you," Eric said bitterly. "You're a Greenie."

"He's right," Goldie said. "Katie, it will be safer for everyone if you watch over Ivy instead of Leida. Swap with her."

"But . . ." Katie paled. "I don't know what to do."

"Unfortunately," he said. "There's not much you can do."

*　　*　　*

When Katie returned to the hut, Leida had stripped the sheets and piled them on the floor. Ivy sat naked on her bed as Leida gave her a quick, cold bath with a tiny bar of soap. She redressed the girl in different clothes before leading her to the furthest bunk. A sheet was hung between Ivy and the rest of the hut.

"Where did you get the clothes?" Katie asked.

"One of Michelle's girls snuck me a change for such an occasion," Leida said. "There's a giant box of used clothes at the Big House they will trade for tattered ones. In my opinion, this is worse than tattered." She tossed the clothes into a pile at the foot of the bed. "In the box buried under Dakota's bed, there's a bottle of rubbing alcohol. Take the cloth next to it and wipe down the bed frame and anything else you think she might have touched."

"I'm here to swap with you," Katie said.

Leida spread her arms wide in exasperation. "Why does Jared think I can't do this?"

"It's not about that. I'm a Greenie."

She bit her lip then sighed. "Okay, you can stay with her, but if you need help or don't know what to do, come find me." Leida ducked behind the curtain. "Ivy, Katie is going to stay with you, alright?"

The girl coughed in reply, and Leida returned to watch Katie wipe down the little girl's belongings.

"If she gets hot and shaky," Leida said, "give her some of the Tylenol under my bed. One pill at a time."

Katie agreed, and Leida left. Once alone, Katie put her hands on her hips and surveyed the empty hut. It was odd knowing she was the only one safe enough to look after Ivy. During her own bout with strep throat, she was completely well after a couple of days of antibiotics. How long would this take?

Ivy called from behind the curtain, and Katie sat on the edge of the bed.

"Can you tell me a story?" Ivy asked.

Katie smiled at the simple request. "Sure. Have you ever heard the story of Beauty and the Beast?"

*   *   *

Nine others fell sick over the course of two days, and Dakota's hut became the official quarantine. Only Katie and Noel, another Greenie from Bryan's hut, entered. They had tried to get new sheets and a blanket to separate the bunks, but Ian had cut them off at three. He didn't want to waste detergent.

The worst off were the young ones—those under twelve. To the touch, the fever didn't seem too high, but still, they shivered. None of the others wanted to lend out blankets for fear of contamination, so the sick suffered quietly beneath their thin, gray blankets.

Ivy was the sickest of their patients. After the first day, a white, strawberry film had coated her tongue, and a bumpy rash broke out over her body.

Goldie entered and leaned against a bunk, chewing on his nail for a half hour. He didn't bother himself to help but just watched. His inactivity annoyed Katie, but she kept her mouth shut about it. Eventually, he slipped out while Katie was helping a kid with a cup of water.

"Finally," Noel said once he was gone. "He's such a creeper."

Noel was a thin thing, all knees and elbows. Her brown, straw-like hair was cut raggedly and was held up by twine. The green band hung loose around her wrist. Katie speculated she was not a good thief.

"He's something else," said Katie. More than one person had commented about Goldie's level of creepy, and this had become her permanent answer. He continued to deny anything happened with Courtney, and Courtney continued to insist that it did.

Katie chose to remain undecided in her opinion about what really happened that day. So far, Goldie had managed to keep his hands to himself as it concerned her, but she remained wary of the possibility.

Noel smiled at Katie's statement. "I didn't think you'd mind me saying so. Pros and cons, I take it?"

"I'm sorry?"

"If he wasn't a creeper, you wouldn't have the job," Noel said. "No judgment or anything. A girl's gotta do what a girl's gotta do, am I right?"

Katie glared at her and was about to retort when she saw Zhang walking to the door. "Hey now, where are you going?"

Zhang jumped like he had been caught doing something bad. When he turned around, he raised the plastic cup in his hand. "Water."

"I'll go get it." Katie took the cup and pointed to his bed. "Go lie down."

Zhang frowned. "I okay." He flexed his muscles then mimed getting a shot in the arm. As a Greenie, he had received a trip to the infirmary for a nice dose of antibiotics that morning.

"Then are you ready to get back to the fields?" Katie pointed in that direction and mimed a shovel.

Zhang shook his head.

"Then get back to bed before the Watchers send you there."

Zhang sighed but trudged back to his bunk. Stinking noobs. Had to spell everything out for them. She was heading out to the spigot when the door burst open.

"Clear that bed!" Goldie shouted as he and Dakota entered. Eric hung between the two teens. His body thrashed, and his eyes rolled back. Katie snatched up the pile of blankets from Dakota's bed.

"What's wrong with him?" she asked.

"He's having a seizure." Dakota worked in tandem to get the boy on the bed. "And it's not stopping."

"Put him on his side," Goldie said and touched his brow. "He's burning up. Katie, get some cold washcloths. Noel, take two of the Tylenol and crush them as small as you can. Dakota, do you have any weed on you?"

Dakota produced a joint from a hidden pocket in his sleeve. Goldie ripped the roll open and chewed the contents. When he had a nice paste, he slathered it against the inside of Eric's cheek.

"Will that work?" Dakota asked. "I know marijuana is supposed to help with seizures, but—"

"Well, I can't have him smoke it, can I?" Goldie interrupted. "When did he have his seizure medicine last?"

"Yesterday, I think," Dakota said. "After he lost his armband, we tapered the dose, but this is his third seizure, and it's been ten minutes!"

"I have the crushed Tylenol," Noel said. "How are you going to give him that?"

Goldie scratched his head. "There is another entrance."

Dakota turned to Goldie with a quirked brow.

"What do you mean?" Katie asked. "Are you going to put it up his nose or something?"

"You want him to keister it?" Dakota said.

Goldie spread his arms wide. "I'm open to suggestions."

"Guys, he's stopped," Noel said.

Eric lay still upon the bed.

"Okay," Goldie sighed and wiped his brow. "Okay, he's stopped. That's a good sign—I guess. Eric?" He shook him, and Eric's eyes opened then shut. "Noel, when he comes round, put the Tylenol in some water and have him drink it. Dakota, the weed seemed to work. I'm going to have you start giving him a small dose." Goldie and Dakota wandered off to a corner of the room to discuss a regimen.

Eric's chest rose and fell weakly. His eyes were dark and sunken, and his skin a shade paler. Katie felt for the mattress on the adjacent bunk as her legs grew weak.

Wake up, Eric. Please. Please, God, let him wake up. He's my friend. Katie blinked back tears. Across the room, Ivy was propped on her elbow, watching them, her face flushed.

Katie watched Eric's chest go up and down. Up, then down. Up. Down. Then it stopped.

Katie held her own breath as she waited for the chest to rise again. Her eyes burned as she willed for it to go up. *Please, go up.*

"Goldie!" she screamed.

Dakota and Goldie raced to the bed, and Goldie felt for a pulse. "Shit!" He tilted back Eric's head and breathed into his mouth. Goldie's face turned red as the boy's cheeks puffed and chest rose. His hands shook so badly, he could barely hold onto Eric's nose.

Folding her fingers together, Katie prayed. Tears slid down her cheeks. *Come on. Come on.*

Goldie lowered his face next to the boy's lips to offer his next breath but paused. Closing his eyes, he shook his head.

"What are you doing?" Katie said. "Don't stop."

Goldie rubbed his brow. "There's no point in continuing. Even if I got him back, what the hell are we going to do with him?"

Dakota shoved Goldie out of the way, bent over Eric, and continued the breathing. Finding a place midway on his chest, he pressed up and down several times before attempting more breaths. With a sigh, Goldie held up a hand to Dakota and performed the breaths himself, allowing Dakota to continue the compressions immediately thereafter.

For ten minutes, they continued like this, pressing on Eric's chest, breathing for him. Goldie coached Dakota on hand placement, and twice they switched roles. Still, nothing happened.

Dakota's compressions became frantic as tears poured down his face.

"Dakota," Goldie said as he brushed back Eric's hair from his face. "Dakota—come on, man. You know as well as I do."

"Shut up."

"Dakota."

With a strangled cry, Dakota relented, shoved his hands into his pockets, and turned away.

"What?" Katie cried. "B-b-but . . . he can't be gone. You have to try harder. He wasn't even that sick. You brought him in from the field. He had to have been fine this morning. He can't—he can't be gone!"

Goldie rubbed his shaking hands. Then he took a blanket from Dakota's bed and unfolded it.

"No, no, no," Katie whimpered as the blanket was laid over Eric's still body. "This can't be, this can't be!" Hot tears streamed down her face, and she moved toward the body.

"Katie." Goldie took her arms.

"No!" Katie shoved him away. She ran to the door but stopped with her hand on the knob. Where could she go? All that waited for her beyond the door were the Watchers and more death. She slid to the dirt, pulled her knees to her chest, and wept.

She barely noticed when Bryan entered the hut and set shovels against the wall beside her. He joined Goldie standing over the body and spoke in whispered tones while Dakota sat on his bunk with his head between his knees, shoulders heaving. Bryan placed a hand on Dakota's arm and squeezed, and Dakota gripped the hand.

Goldie rubbed his toe in the dirt. "Are we ready?"

Bryan sighed. "Just a moment." He held his hand out over Eric and said, "May Adonai bless you and keep you. May He make His face to shine upon you and be gracious to you. May He lift up his countenance upon you and give you peace."

Dakota scooped up the body shrouded in the blanket and carried him out as the other boys followed behind with shovels.

*　　*　　*

The next day, a scratching sensation crept up Katie's throat. Visions of Eric lying on the bed the day before flashed through her mind. Upon her request, Noel peered down Katie's throat.

"Yep," Noel said. "You've got it. Do you want to tell Goldie? Or should I?"

Tears sprang to Katie's eyes.

"It's going to be alright," Noel said. "We're Greenies, remember? We can get antibiotics."

So was Eric a couple of weeks ago.

When he arrived, Goldie felt Katie's forehead. "Come with me," he ordered and turned on heel for the door. As she moved to the door to follow him, Katie passed by sleeping Ivy. The rash was ever present on her little face, but now whenever she coughed, it seemed deeper than her throat.

She couldn't lose another friend. Not like this.

Goldie tapped his fingers on the door as he held it open for her. The trip to the Big House was silent. When they arrived, the nurse was sitting behind her desk, reading a fashion magazine. The beds around her lay untouched, their starched sheets unwrinkled.

"Another Greenie with the plague, I see." The woman was near her seventies with spiked, bleach-blonde hair, and she waddled out from behind her desk. After rummaging through multiple cabinets, the nurse produced a tongue depressor and a pen light.

Katie rolled her eyes. The woman was not familiar with her own infirmary. But when the nurse asked her to open her mouth, Katie complied.

"Yup, you were right, Goldie. Looks like Strep," announced the nurse. "Same symptoms as the rest?"

"Seems to be," he said.

"Let's go ahead and nip this thing in the bud, shall we? They give me a bigger budget than I know what to do with, so we'll bring out the big guns."

Katie curled her lip in disgust. They had the budget and the supplies to treat everyone in that hut. Only they wouldn't. Eric was dead because of them.

From her locked medicine cabinet, the nurse removed a vial with powder and another with liquid. Her hands being full, she did not lock the case. After setting her equipment on her desk, she reconstituted the medicine and pulled it up in a syringe. "Turn around girl and pull your pants down."

Katie looked to Goldie, but he stared blankly at her. "Oh," he said finally and turned to face the medicine cabinet.

She pulled down her pants, and the nurse wiped down the area before inserting the needle. She jerked; the medicine felt like glass.

"Is there a reason you went on the side and high like that?" Goldie said. "It seems there would be more padding toward the center."

"You watched?" Katie gawked over her shoulder. Goldie's mouth parted, and he turned red.

The nurse erupted in laughter. "Honey, don't pretend like he hasn't seen your rump before."

Katie's mouth fell open as heat rose to her cheeks and she pulled her pants up in haste.

"But to answer your question—" The nurse wiped away a tear as her belly jiggled. "There's a nerve going right through that area." To Katie, she said, "If your symptoms don't go away in 24 hours, come see me again."

Once outside, Katie sped up her pace. "I can't believe you. You watched? What is wrong with you?"

Goldie shrugged, hands in pockets as he strolled behind her.

"Do you know everyone thinks I'm sleeping with you?"

"That doesn't surprise me."

She halted and turned, and Goldie lurched back to keep from colliding with her. "I don't like people thinking that," she said.

"I don't know what you want me to do about it. I can't control what people think."

"You can deny it," she said.

Goldie rolled his eyes. "If you hadn't noticed, people have a tendency not to believe me."

Katie opened her mouth to retort but couldn't think of a good comeback.

"Why does it matter so much what people think, anyways?" he asked.

"That's easy for you to say. Your reputation is trash. I don't think it could sink any lower, so why would you care?"

Goldie sighed. "You know, Katie? I'm tired of this conversation. I'm sorry I looked at your ass." He shoved past her.

*　　　*　　　*

Ivy's deep cough began producing thick mucus. Her fever climbed even with the Tylenol, and they were running low on the precious pills. The other patients had gotten better after three or four days, and Noel had been sent back to her hut. It was now day eight, and the girl showed no signs of improvement. She was the first and now the last of the sick.

Katie dabbed a wet rag across the shivering girl's face. She cooed at Ivy, telling her to relax. "Everything's going to be fine," Katie lied. The girl was dying and the helplessness was unbearable.

"Katie," Ivy managed a whisper past her chapped lips. "Can you tell me a story?"

Katie pressed her forehead to Ivy's sweat-covered brow. "Yes, I can. Do you have a certain story you'd like me to tell?"

"Can you tell me about Belle and the Beast again?"

"I most certainly can." She smiled. "Once upon a time . . ."

Ivy fell asleep before Belle reached the castle, and Katie pulled the covers up to her chin. She kissed her on her head and leaned back in the chair.

"How is she?"

Katie jumped as Goldie's voice drove her from her own thoughts. She didn't know when he had snuck into the room and didn't like that he had. "Terrible."

Goldie sat on the next bed and stared at his hands. "I need you to keep a secret."

Katie narrowed her eyes. She blamed him for Ivy being sick but wasn't sure why. Perhaps because he was here and wasn't helping. Perhaps because it felt good to blame somebody. "What kind of secret?"

He surveyed the room, then reached deep into his pockets and pulled out two vials. One with liquid, one with powder.

"Is that?" Katie started. "Did you steal it?"

"Of course," he said. "Now, your back was turned, so I need you to watch as I mix the medicine and give the shot. You're going to have to do this tomorrow."

After reconstituting the medicine, he drew a syringe full of yellow liquid. Goldie slid down Ivy's pants enough to expose the needed area. She barely flinched as the needle went into the muscle.

With a jolt of guilt, Katie realized how Goldie knew where to give this medication. That was why he had watched.

"Can you do this tomorrow around the same time?" Goldie asked, and Katie nodded. "Hide this inside your mattress. And here." He produced a bottle of pills. "After tomorrow, start these. She needs to take one in the morning and one at night until they are all gone."

Swallowing hard, Katie accepted the pills. "You're helping her."

Goldie glanced over his shoulder. "Yeah. Now, keep your mouth shut."

After he left, Katie sat dumbly holding the medicine. Finally, she returned to reality and hid the supplies.

*　　　*　　　*

"Where did you get the pills?" Ivy whispered loudly into the empty hut.

"Shh!" Katie looked about. "Just take it."

"But where did you get them?" Ivy's voice hissed at the same volume only at a higher pitch.

"It doesn't matter."

Ivy's petite mouth turned down. "You stole them, didn't you?"

"Yes, now take it."

After tossing her head back dramatically, Ivy swallowed it. "It tastes bad."

"You're not supposed to taste it, silly." Katie kissed her head and felt her cheek. Yesterday, the rash had abated. This morning, her fever had broken, and now the cough was resolving. Katie shook her head at the nearly miraculous transformation. "You go ahead and get some rest today, Ivy. If you need me, I'll be a few doors down."

Ivy slid further beneath her covers. As Katie moved toward the door, she paused at Eric's bunk. A few magic pills would have been enough to save him too. With clenched teeth, she continued on.

*　　*　　*

"How's Ivy?" Goldie removed a rusted bolt off of a set of pruning shears at his desk. The pile of papers on Katie's desk had turned into a small tower stacked neatly in the corner. Goldie's hut was generally tidy, but today it appeared to have been straightened by a drill sergeant. He had even managed to fix his flimsy blanket tight against the mattress.

"Better." Katie closed the door to his hut behind her. "A lot better."

He nodded approvingly.

Katie took a seat on his bed. "Jared, why do people call you Goldie? What does it mean?"

He leaned back in his chair. "It's short for 'Golden Boy.' Midas makes a lot of money from me, so Tweedle Dum thought it would be funny to start calling me that."

"Do you like to be called that?"

Jared narrowed his eyes. "It's not really a compliment, is it?"

"People say horrible things about you, Jared, and you let them. But a little girl is alive because of you. Why don't you let people know you are still on their side?"

His eyes widened. "What did you tell them?"

"What will happen if the Watchers find out you stole the antibiotics?"

"What did you tell them?" His voice shook.

Katie frowned. "Nothing. I told them nothing. But Ivy thinks I stole the drugs. It's only a matter of time before everyone else does too."

Jared ran a hand through his shaggy blonde hair. "Good. It's better that way."

"Why?"

"Because." He slammed the pruning shears on the table and rubbed his shaking hands together. "Because if the Watchers find out I stole the drugs, they won't flog me, Katie. They'll kill me."

"But you're valuable to them. Why would they?"

"Because I'm smarter than them," he said. "Because . . . because Ian thinks it was a mistake to keep me alive in the first place, while all Midas sees is dollar signs. But if I get caught stealing again, I'm a dead man." He ran his hands over his face. "I'm a dead man."

"Are you sure?"

"Yes, dammit!" He leapt from his chair. "I'm sure."

Katie studied her shoes. "I won't tell anyone."

"See that you don't," Jared said. "Oh, and Katie—don't tell Leida I said all that either. She'll only worry."

"She's doing plenty of that already," she said, and Jared opened his mouth to protest, but she held up her hand. "But I won't tell her."

"I know this has been delayed longer than it should have been," Jared said at the next Friday meeting. "But I've come to a decision regarding the new hut leader. It's going to be Olivia."

"Finally," Bryan said, resting his head on the table. As senior hut leader, he had spent more time in Trevor's old hut than his own. Bryan was a capable leader, but even he had his limitations. But there was a catch to this assignment, one Katie knew Jared had been worrying about all week.

"Since she'll be new to the job, though, I want her to take over her own hut," Jared continued. "Bryan, I'm moving you to Hut 3."

"Sure. Fine. Whatever. As long as I'm not dancing between the two."

Katie bit her lip and shared a look with Jared. Bryan didn't get it.

"I take it you haven't looked at my projected outputs yet," Jared said.

Bryan sighed. "There's been a lot going on."

"You're under by a quarter."

Bryan's mouth dropped. "A quarter? But we harvest in two weeks! Jared," he paused, brow furrowed, "are you setting me up as the fall guy?"

Jared's lips drew taut. "I'm sorry."

Bryan opened his mouth to speak but shook his head. With curled lips, he scraped his chair back against the dirt floor and walked out. The shaking of Jared's hands worsened, and he hid them in his lap.

Katie knew why Jared had done this: it would be unfair to put Olivia in charge of a failing hut. The question was, would Bryan understand? Even Katie would hate to see Jared lose that friendship.

After the others left, Katie gathered her papers and stood to join Jared at the door. As she did, she racked her mind with something comforting to say but could think of nothing. When Jared sent her to her hut, she was not surprised. He didn't like to have her around when he was feeling poorly.

The next day, Katie rejoined Jared to help write one of Addison's papers. When she arrived, he promised he would be ready to dictate everything after a few more minutes, but thirty minutes passed as he scribbled illegible notes. As she leaned back in her chair, she watched dust flakes dance in the light of the window. The window did nothing to dispel the heat, but at least it caused the smell of cigarettes to disperse.

Katie had caught Jared on the roof more and more often lately—ever since Trevor had been transferred. His tremor had worsened too. More than once, she had seen him shake gruel out of his bowl during their meals and Katie doubted even he could decipher the notes he took today.

Katie let the silence drag on for some time, not wishing to interrupt his concentration and cause the process to take even longer, but she grew tired of the quiet and finally broke it. "Leida is pretty upset she didn't get the hut leader position."

Jared didn't pause in writing his illegible notes. "I know."

"You know she would have done a great job. She practically runs our hut as is."

"I know."

Katie cocked her head to the side. "You know? Then why didn't you pick her?"

Jared set his pen down and turned to her fully. "Leida's already a hut leader. What she wants is the status, not the job. Adding the title will just put a target on her back."

"A little bit of recognition goes a long way. You really hurt her feelings."

"Her feelings?" said Jared. "My job is to keep her alive, not worry about her feelings."

"Fine, but you could—" Katie was going to continue, but the door to Jared's hut opened, and Bartram entered, taser drawn.

"Up!" Bartram nodded to Jared. "Hands on the wall."

With slow, deliberate moves, Jared obeyed while Katie sat on the bed, mouth ajar, wondering if she should stay or run.

Bartram patted him down. "Where is it, Goldie?"

"Where is what?" Jared spoke calmly, but beads of sweat broke on his brow.

"Don't screw with me. I will find it with or without your help." After searching his person, Bartram rummaged through the contents of his desk. Jared turned to watch, and Bartram turned the taser towards him again. "Hands back on the wall."

"Okay, okay." Jared obeyed.

Then Bartram nodded to Katie. "Your turn."

Hesitantly, she stood and placed her hands on the wall, allowing him to search her.

"Now you may go."

Katie glanced to Jared. She felt like she should help in some way, but what could she do? Jared nodded his head toward the door, indicating for her leave.

So, she obeyed.

Katie headed down the path toward the field but was stopped by a "psst." Bryan beckoned her into a shadow. "What do they want?"

"I don't know," she said. "They were looking for something."

"Shit," he said. "I thought we would have more time. One of Michelle's girls nicked a cellphone while cleaning Ian's office, but Goldie had a meeting with him this morning, and Ian probably thinks he took it."

"Ian's phone? They couldn't pick anyone else to mess with?"

"Ian's phone is the only one that will send or receive calls. Everyone else's phones are basically toys while they are at the camp."

"Bryan, if they think Jared stole the phone, they're not just going to flog him!"

"I know," he said. "Who do you think has been watching his back all these years? But if Bartram searches Jared's hut—and I mean really searches it—he's not going to find a cellphone. But he will find a shitload of other stuff. We need to work fast."

The door to the hut opened, and Bartram led Jared up the hill in handcuffs. Bryan picked up the five-gallon bucket full of dirt he had brought with him.

"What's with that?" Katie asked.

"It makes it look like I'm doing something rather than roaming around the camp. We need to talk to Sam."

When they reached Sam's field, Bryan set the bucket down and turned to Katie. "How's your pickpocketing?"

*   *   *

"It doesn't matter." Sam continued to weed between the rows, refusing to meet Bryan's gaze.

"What the hell do you mean it doesn't matter? Ian will kill him." Bryan said through clenched teeth. He pinched off another discolored leaf from the plants.

Katie searched the area for something to do to look busy but was at a loss. She feigned checking the stakes for instability—if that were a thing.

"This is bigger than Goldie," Sam said. "This isn't about just one guy—it's about all of us. Besides, even if we fail, you'd be next in line, and I don't see how that's a downside."

Katie cocked her head in question. Jared was unpopular, but she did not know how deep the animus went. Sam caught her gaze and looked away.

"We're not killing anyone over this," Bryan hissed. "And if you think I want that job, you're out of your mind."

Sam barked a laugh.

"Sam," Bryan urged. "When an op goes bad, it gets scrapped. You know this. Are you even close to cracking the phone?"

Sam stared at the ground as he continued weeding, and Bryan rolled his eyes.

"Where is it? Down here?" Bryan slipped between a couple of massive cannabis plants to a denser part of the crop.

"Don't—Bryan!" Sam chased after him, and Katie followed. Several rows over, shrouded in plants, sat a girl. When she saw them coming, she hid the phone behind her back.

"It's fine," Sam grumbled. "They know.

"How far have you gotten?" Bryan asked, squatting before her.

"I got past the fingerprint scanner no problem from the prints you gave Sam, but I can't get through the passcode. It's not his birthday, Addison's birthday, or any of the other combinations. It could be random alphanumerics for all I know."

"Can I see it?" Katie sat next to her, and the girl handed it over. That was easy.

"Alphanumerics meaning?" Bryan asked.

"Random strings of numbers and letters," the girl said.

Bryan sighed and looked to Sam. "So, it's hopeless."

"It's not hopeless," Sam said. "We just need more time."

Standing, Katie rubbed her brow with one hand and slipped the phone into her back pocket with the other. "I'll go talk to Michelle. Maybe she'll know what's up with Jared, then we can go from there." She moved back through the rows.

"We've talked about this, Sam," said Bryan behind her.

"I can't live like this!" Sam cried. "Hell, this isn't even living. It's because of your damn rules that we're all still here, anyways. The only way we're getting out is by taking chances!"

Katie didn't hear the end of his rant as she moved through the plants quickly, but not so quick as to draw attention from the Watchers. She was three rows away when she heard Sam shout behind her.

Katie shoved the branches away. Bryan said he wouldn't follow her past the cannabis forest for fear of the Watchers. One more row...

"Hey! There you are!" Dumar called as she stepped out of the plants.

"I—uh," Katie stammered.

The brute grabbed her arm like a vise and dragged her away from the field. "You're wanted in the Big House," he said as Katie stumbled along beside him.

Did they know? How could they possibly know? As they passed through the kitchen, Katie caught sight of Michelle washing dishes. Katie widened her eyes, pleading with Michelle.

Michelle splashed the water from her hands onto the kitchen floor. "Dumar!" She stepped in front of them as they reached the doorway to the dining hall. "Will you tell me what was lost? I might be able to help find it."

"Stay out of this, Michelle." Dumar pushed her aside.

"I know you think someone took it," Michelle continued. "But what if it was just lost?"

Sighing, Dumar stopped in the doorway. Katie slipped the phone from her pocket and waved it slightly. The girl's gaze darted to the hand, then back to Dumar.

"If you must know," he said, "it was a cellphone. And if you're going to find it, you'd better do it quick. Otherwise, your current boyfriend is going to kill your ex-boyfriend."

He turned back around, and Michelle took the phone from Katie's hand, slipping it into her pocket. Katie hoped she worked fast. Time was not on their side.

Katie went with Dumar up the stairs to Ian's office. After a quick knock on Ian's door, Dumar shoved Katie into the office.

Jared sat on the floor, his hands chained to the front of Ian's desk. He had a bloody gash on his cheek but seemed otherwise alright. Ian rounded his desk, and Katie's mouth went dry. When she looked back to Jared, he offered a small smile of encouragement, and she was able to swallow again. If he wasn't terrified out of his skull, then she shouldn't be either.

"Goldie insists he knows nothing about the bit of personal property taken from me this morning," Ian said. "Which is bullshit, of course!"

A knock sounded on the door, and they all turned to it. Bartram entered with Michelle, who folded and unfolded her hands.

"They found this in the laundry, sir." Bartram handed over the phone. "Among your personal clothing."

Ian took the phone, studied it briefly, then tossed it onto the desk. "My personal clothes, you say?"

"It was in the jeans you wore last night," Michelle said.

He narrowed his eyes at his mistress. When his gaze turned back to Katie, she dipped her head once more.

"Indeed." Ian spun the phone in a circle. "Goldie, I suppose you're free to go." He tossed the keys to Bartram.

Jared's head dipped in a nearly unperceivable nod as Bartram uncuffed his hands. Michelle returned the gesture with a ghost of a smile.

Ian's face darkened. As the three kids turned to leave, he said, "Michelle, do stay for a moment."

Fear filled her face, but she obeyed, and the door closed behind them. As they descended the stairs Katie asked Jared, "Will she be okay?"

Jared rubbed his wrists. "Ian has to either buy her story, or he has to burn her. He won't do the latter."

"How can you be so sure?"

Jared sighed. "Because he loves her."

Katie's mouth parted, but he just shook his head. As they continued on their way down the stairs, Katie noticed Jared trembling. "Are you okay?"

"This?" Jared touched his cheek. "I've cut myself shaving worse than this." He rubbed his hairless chin, and Katie's brow furrowed.

He cleared his throat. "I saw you with Bryan. Did you two—?"

Katie nodded.

"Thank you," he said.

"Of course. We couldn't just do nothing."

He bit his lip. "Yes, you could have."

"Come to join us today, have you?" Dakota interlaced his fingers over his head and leaned back in a stretch, his muscles flexing beneath his thin shirt. They had finished harvesting the last of the marijuana crop over the past week and were busy hanging the plants upside down in the greenhouses. The mushrooms had been harvested just in time for the hut leader swap.

Katie narrowed her eyes at him and all his muscles. She had the feeling he was doing that on purpose. "Jared has a meeting. Where do you want me?"

Dakota shrugged. "Go find Leida. She actually knows what's going on. But here, take these." He handed her a pair of rubber gloves.

"They're protecting us?"

Dakota laughed. "No, the THC comes off when you touch the plants. It ruins the high."

Katie rolled her eyes. "Figures."

Before she could turn to go find Leida, the air siren echoed through the camp. It quit and started again in three subsequent blasts. "What does that mean?" she asked Dakota.

"It means we need to gather on the hill. I wonder if this has something to do with Goldie's meeting."

Dakota led the way up the hill to where Jared and two Watchers stood waiting at the top. When everyone was present, Jared stepped up onto an old stump and the workers fell silent.

"The quota was low," he said. "Namely in Bryan's hut and Sam's hut. Half-rations are going to be in effect for those huts for the next week."

Grumbling came from those huts, but Sam spoke above the others. "We had sickness! You can't blame us for getting sick."

"I'm just the messenger," Jared said.

"Screw you!" Sam said. "This is your fault, Goldie. You're the one who got rid of Trevor."

"Hey!" Bryan said. "Shut it, Sam. Shut it and take it like a man."

Sam glared at him.

Jared's shoulders slumped, and he rubbed the bridge of his nose. Katie gulped. That wasn't the end of the announcement.

"The leaders of those huts are also to be flogged," Jared said, and Bryan's lip curled.

A grave silence fell over the others as all eyes turned to the two hut leaders. With the near-perfect system of stealing in place, floggings were rare, which increased the dread of those who faced them.

Sam turned pale and looked over his shoulder, his eyes flashing wildly. Katie wondered for a moment if he were going to try and run, but Tweedle Dee moved in behind Sam and seized him by the shirt, dragging him forward. He shoved Sam into the dirt next to the post.

Bryan, however, walked to the post on his own.

"Who wants to go first?" asked Tweedle Dee.

Bryan looked to Sam trembling on the ground, then, without a word, he removed his shirt revealing cruel crossing scars lining his back. The damage far outweighed what Katie had seen on Dakota's back. He wrapped his arms around the post, and Derek fastened them there with rope.

The crowd grew silent as Bryan buried his ears between his shoulders. His back heaved with deliberate breaths as Derek uncoiled the whip. Katie placed her hand over her mouth and pressed her fingers into her cheek.

The whip came down with a sickening smack. Bryan's body jerked at the impact, and a bloody line appeared on the bare skin. Another blow came down, and Bryan retightened his grip on the post. Katie took hold of Leida's arm and held it tight.

Meanwhile, Jared sat on his stump and hung his head between his legs as blow after blow struck Bryan. With each crack, he jumped.

Finally, Derek curled his whip, and Dakota came forward and undid Bryan's hands. As Dakota helped his friend to the hut, Bryan leaned upon him.

Dumar dragged Sam to the post next, and the poor boy whimpered as the Watcher secured his hands. A few silver lines crossed Sam's back. He had tasted the whip only enough to be more fearful of it. As the whip cut into flesh, he released a pitiful cry. Halfway through, he began to beg. Derek ignored his cries, and Sam wept. Katie turned away.

After Dakota hauled away Sam, the crowd began to disperse. Jared, however, approached the flogging post and cast his shirt aside, revealing the mass of contorted flesh that was his back. Jared wrapped his arms around the post and waited, and Derek uncoiled the whip once more. Either they forgot or did not feel the need to tie his hands.

Leida slid her arm into the crook of Katie's. "It doesn't matter how many times. I can't watch this." She buried her head in Katie's shoulder.

The first blow came, and Jared's body tensed, but he made no sound. Leida did, and Katie pulled her in closer. The whip came down again. And again. Still silence.

Katie lost track of how many times. Was Katie imagining things, or was Derek bringing down more blows on Jared than the others? They kept coming and coming.

Two fields. Two punishments. When it ended, Jared leaned against the post as Derek coiled his whip, and Katie and Leida stepped forward to help him.

Jared's chest heaved, and a trickle of blood ran down his lip where he had bitten his tongue. Blood dripped down his back in streaked lines, and he winced as Leida pulled his arm over her shoulders. Katie took the other arm, and he leaned on her heavily.

Once they reached his hut, Jared groaned as the ladies lowered him onto his bunk facedown, but he spoke quickly. "Leida, I want you to take over your hut for now. Send Dakota to Sam's, and tell Michelle to watch over Bryan's while they're in the kitchen."

"Can you shut up?" Leida said. "They'll be fine for five minutes. Katie, grab the med kit from under his bed."

Katie found the kit buried under a thin layer of dirt and set to retrieving it. Jared moaned as he shifted his position, pulling something from beneath his stomach. "New book came in."

Leida rolled her eyes and tossed the book onto the table.

Katie brushed dirt off the box and set it on the bed next to him. "What do I do?"

Leida removed the wooden lid and pulled out clean strips of linen. She doused these with clear liquid from a glass bottle tucked inside. "Go wet these other clothes in the water spigot," Leida ordered.

Katie nodded, took the cloths, and left the hut.

"Are you ready?" Leida asked.

Jared tightened his grip on the pillow and closed his eyes. After his nod, Leida dabbed the red lines.

"Augh!" He squeezed the pillow tighter, and the smell of alcohol filled the hut.

"Shut up, you big baby." A tear pooled in her eye.

"Ha-ha. Big baby, huh?" He gritted his teeth. "You're one to talk. Remember that rotten tooth of yours?" He buried his face in the pillow.

"That was nothing next to when you dislocated your shoulder. I'd never seen such a wimp."

"I had, when you broke your finger. Mmhhhnnn. You'd have thought someone had amputated it."

"About done," Leida said.

Jared nodded as sweat dripped down his face. Katie returned with the dampened cloths, and Leida draped them over his wounds. To his sister, Jared ordered, "Go find Dakota."

Leida took his hand and squeezed it. "I'll be by later," she said and left.

Katie dragged her chair closer. "How are you doing?"

Jared squeezed his eyes shut. "Fine as frog's hair."

"Sorry. That was a dumb question."

Jared's back rose and fell with labored breaths. Intense pain was scrawled across his face. As he tried to adjust his position, he let out a soft whimper. Katie looked anxiously around the room, unsure of how to help, but desperately wishing to. Abruptly, she moved to his desk.

Jared watched her. "What are you doing?"

"I'm getting you some weed." She detached the false bottom.

He closed his eyes again. "I don't do drugs."

"You're kidding, right?"

Jared remained silent, his face pinched in pain, his back trembling as it rose and fell.

"Why ask for them if you weren't going to use it?"

"I didn't ask for it. It's a control."

"A what?"

He sighed. "A control. The drugs slow down how quickly I think, so they got me hooked on the stuff. I quit taking them so I can think clearer."

"Well, you're hurt so you can make an exception, or what are these?" She pulled out a large bag of pills.

"Put them away," he said. "I don't—I don't even want to look at them right now. I'm done with them."

The stash was massive. Bryan was right for being afraid, but still, she wished he would take them now. When she returned to her seat, Katie bounced her leg up and down as she tried to think of something to do. "Jared, how many times have you been flogged?"

"I don't remember," he grumbled.

"Of course, you do."

Sighing, he answered, "Twenty-seven."

"Twenty-seven? How does that even happen?"

"Because I'm a slow learner. Look, believe it or not, Katie, I'm not in the mood to chat. Why don't you go check on Bryan or Sam? Maybe there's something you can do for them."

"Are you sure? Because—"

"Please, Katie—go."

Katie hesitated. She recalled the Tylenols Leida had given her on her first day, but Ivy had used up the rest. She doubted they would even put a dent in his pain, but still, they were something.

Jared closed his eyes tight as he clutched his pillow, his forehead wrinkled. Perhaps, the best way she could help him was to leave, but she felt guilty doing so. Frowning, Katie returned the medical supplies back to the box and covered it with a layer of dirt, then she left.

After the door clicked closed, Jared turned his face to the wall and cried.

"Things are a bit tense, aren't they?" Katie said to no one in particular. The boys were bickering in the corner while the little girls sat together and watched. No one had picked up the rock game since Eric died. Leida had taken over Dakota's bed for the night while he stayed in Sam's hut, and she and Katie sat together at the front of the hut.

"What do you want me to do about it?" Leida asked, running her fingers through her hair.

"Should you read?" Katie said.

Leida sighed. "I'm too tired to read. If you want to, go ahead, but I'm going to lie down." She rolled over and pulled the blanket over her head.

Katie surveyed the others. Paulina sat on her bunk scraping the dirt from her fingernails and toes. Katie cringed at this, but then set it aside. It was the equivalent of painting one's nails in such a situation.

"Are you kidding? Hulk would tear Iron Man's head off!" one boy exclaimed, and Katie rolled her eyes.

Would a story even help? She didn't know, but if anyone needed a distraction, it was this lot. She picked up the book but then paused. "Does anyone want to hear a story?"

The boys stopped bickering and shrugged in response.

"It's called Jonah and the Whale. My mom used to tell it to me."

Ivy climbed into her lap. "I know that story."

"Then, would you like to tell it?"

"No, you tell it, Katie. I like it when you tell stories."

Katie smiled at the glowing endorsement. "Okay, once upon a time . . ."

As Katie told the old story, she could feel the tension release in the room. One-by-one, the kids moved to their bunks. Even Paulina stopped fidgeting and leaned her head against the wall.

"For three days and three nights, Jonah sat in the belly of the whale praying and begging God for forgiveness. Then, on the third day . . ."

The door to the hut opened, and Jared stepped inside.

Leida pulled back the blanket. "Jared!" She leapt out of bed. "You should be lying down."

He held up a hand. "Katie, you're wanted at the Big House."

Katie swallowed hard. The news was either very good or very bad.

"Then I'll take her," Leida said. "You're in no condition to go."

She was right. Jared was pale as he hunched in the doorway. A gentle nudge seemed enough to knock him over. "I'm fine," he said.

"Jared, are you sure?" Katie asked and received a glare for her trouble.

He pushed open the door. "Let's go."

Once the door was shut, Katie offered, "Why don't you stop over and find Dakota?"

Jared shook his head. "Midas is here. He doesn't like surprises."

Katie brought a hand to her throat. "Midas?"

"That's the one."

By the time they reached the stairs in the Big House, Jared's face dripped with sweat. With a stifled moan, he mounted them.

Halfway up on the landing, Katie said, "Stop here. Take a breath."

Jared put his foot on the next step, but then gazed up the stairs with a pained expression. He leaned on the banister. "Michelle will kill me for putting fingerprints on this thing."

"Michelle will forgive you," Katie said.

"I practically built this thing." He shook his head. "Bryan and Leida too. This house was a mess when we came here. We had a hand in rebuilding every bit of it. Installed the damn bullet-proof windows too, but only after we busted out the old ones." He sighed. "Damn, we could have pulled that escape off had we known a bit more. I guess that's what happens when a bunch of nine-year-olds put their heads together for an escape plan."

Katie followed a couple of steps behind as she tried to imagine a nine-year-old Jared climbing these very stairs in disrepair. What a life.

Jared knocked on Ian's door and it opened immediately. "I'm telling you, Rich," Ian said. "This girl—whoever she is—is close to breaking this thing wide open. She knows man. She knows."

"She doesn't know shit," said the bearded man from Katie's nightmares as Jared led them to their customary corner across from the desk beside the bookshelf. "And even if she does, she can't prove anything. She's just another raving conspiracy theorist on the internet."

"But Rich, look at how many followers she has." Ian spun his laptop around. A redhead with familiar green eyes filled the screen. "Three hundred ninety-four followers. Five hundred fifteen people have seen this one video."

"That's nothing, Ian."

"Five hundred fifteen people, Rich. That's not nobody. Listen to her." He clicked play.

"Richard Dunn is the head of the biggest human trafficking cartel in the northern hemisphere. He is the infamous 'Midas' the police have been looking for. This criminal mastermind is responsible for the abductions of my cousins, and I will not rest until he is brought to justice!" The girl slammed her fist onto the table. "And now the bastard is running for Congress? I don't think so!"

Midas clicked pause, and the screen froze with the girl's mouth open. The color drained from Jared's face as he sagged toward the floor. Katie grabbed under his arm, and he looked at her in bewilderment.

"Who is she anyways?" Midas said.

"Sedonya Ryder."

"No, who is she to us?"

"You heard her," Ian said. "We nabbed a couple of her cousins, but who the hell knows who these cousins are? They're probably dead anyways."

"I'll have my guys check into this chick, but I promise you, she has nothing. If she did, do you think I would still be here?"

"Five hundred fifteen!"

"Let's look at the comments, shall we?" Midas said. "Top comment: 'Cute girl. Nuts. But cute.' See Ian, nobody is taking any of this seriously. Let it go, okay?"

Whoever this girl was, Katie wanted to hug her. If only she knew how right she was.

"As if the people wanting to legalize pot weren't bad enough . . ." Ian said.

"Pot legalization won't be a problem after I'm elected," Midas said.

"If you're elected."

Midas glared at his brother. "When I'm elected." Ian played with a pen on his desk, and Midas checked his watch. "Let's get back to the business at hand. I need to be in D.C. by morning."

"Fine." Ian grabbed a newspaper from his desk. "Girl—put your back to the wall."

On the wall beside the door hung a black sheet, and Katie stepped in front of it.

"For the record, Richard, I'm still not on board with this idea either."

"You worry too much." Midas gave the newspaper to Katie. "Goldie, stand over there."

Jared stared at the floor.

"Hey!" Midas shouted, and he jumped. "Move."

Jared slid further away from Katie toward the bookshelf, and Midas picked up a camera.

"Can't be trusted with technology? Then we'll do this old school." Midas snapped the picture. It printed out, and he shook the paper to life. "Okay, we're done. Get lost."

As they left the room, Ian continued to complain, "I still think we should scrap this whole job."

"We're not going to scrap the job," was the last thing Katie heard as Jared shut the door, and she sighed with relief. She headed toward the stairs, but as she reached them, she saw Jared was not with her. He still stood by the door, leaning his shoulder against the wall.

She rejoined him. "What is it?"

"I have to be hallucinating," he said. "What was the girl on the computer's name?"

"Sedonya Ryder. Do you know her?"

"She's my cousin."

"What?" Katie said. "Wow, Jared! That's great!"

He shook his head. "She doesn't even know how right she is."

"But she'll figure it out. It's going to take some time."

Jared buried his head in his hands. "She has no idea what she's up against. If she knows too much, Katie—they'll kill her." Jared paced the hall, his breath coming in heaves.

"Jared, calm down. It's okay!"

He turned and took the stairs at an alarming speed. Katie jogged to catch him as he moved through the kitchen and into the yard.

"Jared!" She placed a hand on his back. He withdrew, and her hand came away wet and sticky. "Stop. Just stop." Katie grabbed his arm, and he tried to pull away. She put a hand on his cheek. "Stop."

"They'll kill her, Katie." His eyes glistened with moisture.

"No, they won't, Jared." She rubbed her thumb over his cheek. "Midas is right. If she had anything, she would have taken it to the police by now."

"I can't let them kill her." Jared hugged himself.

"And they won't. You have to believe that. She's going to be alright," she said.

Jared closed his eyes and placed his trembling hand on hers. His shaking reduced as he stood holding her hand to his cheek.

"It's going to rain," Jared said. "You can smell it."

Katie sniffed the air. He was right.

"You know, there's something else." Jared turned and continued down the path. "Leida and I have been missing for ten years. And we still have someone looking for us."

Katie smiled. "Yes, they haven't forgotten you."

"I need to tell Leida." He quickened.

"Not until I take a look at your back."

"But . . ."

"If she sees what you've done to it—she's going to kick your ass."

Jared winced. "You're probably right."

*   *   *

"Most of these have scabbed over, but this one here is being stubborn," Katie said as she dabbed the wounds on Jared's back. He lay on his stomach with his pillow waded in a ball, staring at the wall. A week had passed since the flogging, and Katie had taken over tending to his back. He had reopened his wounds taking the stairs that fast, and both agreed Leida didn't need to know about it. After all, no amount of lecturing would prevent another panic attack or make the wounds heal faster.

"It's where three, maybe four hits intersected," Katie observed about the wound.

"I can tell," said Jared, wincing.

"You can sit up now."

With her help, Jared shifted to sit on the edge of his bed. Sweat dripped from his brow, and his face was pinched, but he seemed to be getting better. At least, she thought so. Jared didn't talk about the pain, and all Katie had to go by were his facial expressions.

Addison had smuggled in a pack of clean cotton undershirts for bandages. Two went to each of the injured hut leaders: one for morning, one for night. Katie dampened Jared's undershirt with a cup of water and draped it over his back. With a torn bedsheet, she secured it in place before helping him put his shirt back on.

They stopped by Sam's and Bryan's hut after breakfast to collect the soiled bandages hidden beneath their mattress and took them to Michelle to be cleaned. The trek up the hill caused Jared's pain lines to deepen, but he refused to let her go to the Big House alone. Simple errands she had taken over, including collecting measurements on Wednesday, but not even Michelle's girls, who worked the house every day, walked around the Big House without a partner. Thankfully, smuggling in three t-shirts was easy compared to the back-breaking work of the fields.

Leaving the air-conditioned house was the hard part.

"100 percent humidity?" Katie muttered as they stepped back into the sultry heat. "100 percent? For five days straight now! And 100 degrees? Why would anyone ever live in Tennessee?"

"I thought you were from Tennessee," said Jared.

"I am," she said. "But I'm an air-conditioning-loving, city girl."

"Then what are you complaining about?" he asked. "You get to hang out every day in the cool crispness of a shed."

"You mean your little outdoor sauna? I swear, I'm not sure if I'm losing weight now due to the food, or because I'm sweating it off."

Jared tried to grab the doorknob of his hut and hold the door open for her, but Katie beat him to the punch. She stopped short, however, when she saw Courtney sitting on Jared's bed. Her face was red and tear-stained.

Jared's lip curled to see her. "Get out."

"Goldie . . ." Courtney stood. "I am so sorry. I don't—I don't even know what to say. I never meant for any—"

"Get out!" he snarled.

"Please, I'm desperate. I'll do anything." Courtney reached for him, but he swatted her away.

"If you touch me again, I'll do more than bruise your damn wrists," he said. "Get out of my hut."

"Please!" Courtney said.

Jared raised his hand, and Katie grabbed his arm. "Jared!"

"You want to talk to her? Fine. But I'm not having any part of this." He turned on heel and slammed the door behind him.

Courtney collapsed back onto his bed. "Why does he hate me?"

Katie stood with mouth ajar for a moment, then she cleared her throat and said as calmly as possible. "Well, Courtney, judging by what you just said, it sounds like you told quite the whopper about him. Do you even know what you've done?"

"I never meant for any of this to happen!" she cried. "It was just a small favor! I don't know what I did to make him react like that."

"Like how?"

"Just—badly. You saw the bruise on my wrist. He literally dragged me out of his hut."

"After you did what, exactly?"

She shrugged. "Oh, you know—flirted."

Katie cocked her head to the side, and Courtney added, "Aggressively."

"So, to be clear, you came in here—" Katie paused as a scraping sound came from the roof. Was Jared really climbing up there to smoke with his back the way it was? Katie cleared her throat and continued, "You made a pass at him, he turned you down, and then you ran with the 'he raped me story?'"

"He threatened to tell Trevor!" she cried. "He would have killed me!"

Katie pressed her hands against her face. "Jared's right," said Katie. "You've got a lot of nerve showing up here."

"Look, I don't know why you're giving me the third degree," said Courtney. "We all know how you got the job. What I don't get is why he went for you and not me. I'm obviously prettier than you since you've got that scar and all."

Katie took a long, deep breath. "Courtney, why are you here?"

"I have to get a transfer to the house. I can't be in the greenhouses anymore." She pulled an inhaler from her pocket. "I have asthma and I'm down to my last refill. I'm not a Greenie you know."

Katie pressed her hand to her forehead. "All this is about your asthma? Courtney!"

"Everyone knows what he's like. He doesn't give out transfers for nothing. After Paulina told me what she did—"

"I'm sorry, what Paulina did?"

"Sure." Courtney shrugged. "She shagged him to get rid of Heath, her old hut leader. She was dating Sam and wanted him to have the job. After she bedded Goldie, he transferred Heath and..."

And suddenly all of Paulina's insinuations and comments became clear. But Katie was not satisfied to only receive the abridged version from Courtney, so she turned on heel for the door. After climbing the wood pile around back she sat down next to Jared.

"What did the wh—" Jared started.

Katie snatched his cigarette and took a long drag. She stifled the cough and let out a long puff of smoke as Jared watched her curiously. "Paulina." She handed him back the cigarette.

Jared held the burning roll until the ashes bent and crumbled onto the shingles. Then he swore.

"What happened?" she asked.

Jared took another drag then stamped out the rest. "Paulina told me her hut leader was bullying her and the young ones. I asked the Watchers to transfer him to another camp."

Katie cocked a brow. So, he was intent on giving the abridged version as well. "Was this before or after you slept with her?"

"I didn't know—I thought . . ." He pinched the bridge of his nose.

Katie waited for him to continue. This had festered long enough.

"We didn't make a deal or anything," said Jared. "It just sort of happened. I didn't know she was dating someone else. Dammit, Sam still doesn't know about any of this. I should have spoken to the other members of Heath's hut, confirmed her story. Heath had a temper, but—I don't know."

"You got the Watchers to transfer him," Katie said. "One of your own people, your friend, because Paulina—?"

"I was high. And I should have known better, but . . ." He stared into the tree line. "I didn't want to know. I had moved out of my hut, I was lonely, and I was high."

"What happened to Heath, Jared?"

He pulled out another cigarette, and it shook in his hand.

Katie snatched it. "What happened to Heath?"

Jared slumped. "Last fall, the camp he was sent to was having some issues with blight. The Watchers sent me to check it out. No one had ever heard of him." He shook his head. "I don't know what happened to him, Katie. Heath could be in a shallow grave somewhere. I just don't know."

"And you stopped the weed?"

"The shaking in my hands gets better when I'm on weed, but I can't do this job if I can't think clearly."

"Are you thinking clearly now?" she sneered.

"As clear as I'm going to be . . ."

"Courtney has asthma," Katie said. "The mushroom spores are triggering it. She wants to work at the house to get away from it."

Jared played with loose asphalt on the shingles.

"I'm going to tell Michelle at dinner," she said. "And from now on, if any of the girls need a transfer or an inhaler or whatever the hell else, they come talk to me."

"If you're looking for a way to fix your reputation—"

"Screw my reputation. This has to stop." Katie slid over the edge of the hut.

"Uhm, hey, Katie," Jared called after her.

Katie spun around, hand on her hip. "What?"

"I know, you're wanting to storm off and all, but I'm kinda stuck up here. Any chance you can, you know?"

Katie dropped her head to her chest. Idiot. "Fine, give me just a minute."

*   *   *

"I'm not giving up my bunk." Leida snatched her pillow away from Paulina. "I have had this bunk for years. You're not taking it."

Paulina tried to grab the pillow again, but Leida was too quick. "It's mine now," Paulina said. "You're moving down to the end. Tell her Dakota."

Dakota sauntered over with red-rimmed eyes. "It's her bunk, Leida."

"I'm not moving," Leida said.

"Yes." Paulina snatched the pillow. "You are." She threw it over Leida's head.

"Leave her alone, Paulina." Katie approached from the door. She had stayed late after dinner speaking with Michelle about Courtney only to find this crap on her return. With everything going on, were they really playing 'keep-away' like toddlers?

"Stay out of this," Paulina said.

"This is Leida's bunk," Katie said. "Everyone knows it. You're not moving her."

"Oh yeah? And you're going to stop me, are you?"

Katie bristled. "I am Jared's assistant."

"His little whore, you mean."

She smirked. "He listens to me. He trusts me. What do you think he'll do if he finds out you're bullying his little sister? You haven't forgotten what he does to bullies, have you?"

Paulina hesitated. She looked from Katie to Leida to Dakota. "Fine, you little slut. Keep your bunk. Your mattress smells funky anyways."

Leida frowned as Paulina climbed back onto her own bunk, but Katie rolled her eyes. A few weeks ago, she would have been bothered by the name-calling, but now it was pathetically insignificant.

"Do you know something I don't?" Leida asked Katie.

Katie bit her lip, wondering what she should tell and what she shouldn't. "Screw it," she said. "Paulina tricked your brother into transferring some guy named Heath out of the camp."

"What?" Paulina gawked. "That's a lie!"

"She came in all 'Help me, Jared! Save me, Jared, from my big bad hut leader!'" mocked Katie. "The skank even seduced him, thinking if he cared about her, he'd do anything she wanted him to!"

"You are a liar!" shouted Paulina, dropping to the floor.

"And then, she convinced Courtney to try the same damn thing!" said Katie, pointing an accusatory finger at Paulina. "When Jared turned Courtney down, who did she come running to? You! Shouting rape! Now Trevor's gone, dead for all we know, and whose fault is it? Yours!"

Leida's mouth hung open as she stood gaping at Paulina. Paulina's bottom lip, however, started trembling. She burst into tears and ran from the hut, sobbing.

"The little bitch!" said Leida.

"Oh, shut up, Leida," said Dakota. "Well done, Katie. You handled that well."

"I told the truth!" said Katie. "If you can't see what she is . . ."

"She was desperate, is what she was!" said Dakota. "You didn't know Heath, but I did. He was horrible to the kids in his hut, and he forced himself onto Paulina more than once."

"I see she's convinced you too," said Katie, folding her arms.

Dakota jammed a thumb against his chest. "I saw what he was first hand. And if Goldie didn't see it, it's because his eyes were closed. Paulina did what she had to do, and the rest of us are better off for it."

Katie opened her mouth to argue, to insist that Paulina should have spoken to him instead of resorting to such means. But she also knew her boss. For all she knew, Paulina could have tried that first and met the wall that could be Jared, especially if he was as high as he admitted.

Dakota rolled his red-rimmed eyes at the pair before turning to the door to go after Paulina. So much for a neat, all-encompassing answer. Could this world get any more screwed up?

GOLD DIGGER

Sweat rolled down Katie's neck and she cringed as it glided all the way down her back. For the fifth time in the past ten minutes, she wiped her forehead. Unable to concentrate, she picked up the notebook and used it as a fan.

Jared noted the movement and smiled at her. "Want to take a break?"

"Yes!" She hopped to her feet. "This heat is incredible. How are you not dying over there?"

Jared was, in fact, covered in sweat, but he shrugged in reply. "Let's go see if Addison has any mail for us."

Going up the hill got easier for Jared with every passing day, which eased Katie's nerves. As they entered the kitchen that afternoon, the air conditioning hit them sending goosebumps across Katie's arms. She closed her eyes to take in the moment.

"Ya ready there?" he asked, his mouth raised in the corner.

"Just a second," Katie sighed.

Jared tapped his foot impatiently, but his smile betrayed him. He had been smiling more and more the last few days.

They were on their way back from Addison's office with the mail when voices came from down the hall. Both paused for a moment, heads lowered, expecting to let Watchers pass by. It was best to 'think wall' whenever any of the guards were near, and this was no exception, as it was Midas who turned the corner.

Beside him walked Michelle, carrying a basket of cleaning supplies and leaning away from him as best she could. Not seeing them, Midas stepped in front of her, placed his hand against the wall, and blocked her path. Looking past Midas, Michelle spotted Katie and Jared down the hall, and her gaze pleaded to them as he brushed a hair from her face. He then slid his arm around her waist and put his scratchy, black beard against her cheek.

"Do something," Katie hissed.

Jared's gaze ripped from Michelle to Katie. He swallowed hard and studied his shoes.

"Hey!" A voice boomed from behind, and Ian sped past them. "Get your hands off her!"

Midas jumped back and raised his hands as if from fright. "Sorry there, little brother." He turned away from Michelle, laughing halfheartedly.

"You don't get to touch her!" Ian said.

Michelle pushed past him, sped down the hall, and turned the corner.

"Sorry," Midas said. "Didn't mean to get your panties in a twist. I didn't realize you were so territorial."

As Ian stepped past Midas into one of the offices, he glared at his brother. Midas, however, turned to Katie and Jared, his brows raised, noticing them for the first time.

"Hey there, Goldie," he said. "Enjoying the show, are you?"

Jared kept his gaze fixed downward.

"I want you to have that Chinese kid—Zang, Wang, whatever his name is, here at 7:30 sharp." He studied Katie up and down. "It seems our proof of life photo did the trick. Daddy's back on the straight and narrow. Well done, beautiful."

He brought a finger to Katie's chin. She withdrew, but his smile grew. "7:30, champ." Midas slapped Jared on the back, and Jared gasped.

Midas turned toward the stairs but glanced back, his eyes filled with mirth. "See you then. Ciao!"

Jared pressed his hand against the wall and inhaled deeply.

"I hate that guy," muttered Katie.

"I'm going to kill him one day," said Jared. "I have no idea how I'm going to do that, but someday . . ."

*   *   *

The siren sounded as they were going down the hill from the Big House, and Katie and Jared diverted their path to the mess hall. Katie joined her hut to eat, and Jared moved to sit at his usual spot alone.

Halfway through the meal, Katie noticed Michelle kept touching her eyes. Six other girls were in Michelle's hut, but none of them sat with her. Instead, they scattered themselves around the dining area. The girls who worked the house shared sleeping quarters with Bryan's hut, and even though Michelle sat at his table, she was by herself at the end.

Gathering her bowl, Katie stood and migrated to sit beside Michelle. All the while, she felt the eyes of the other workers on her as she slid into the vacant seat, but she ignored them, finding once more her concerns about reputation slipping away.

As Katie sat, Michelle cleared her throat and wiped her eyes as if to hide the fact she had been crying. "What's up?"

"How's Courtney fitting in?" Katie asked casually.

Michelle glanced over to the girl sitting at the end with Bryan's hut. She pressed her hand to head, as if doing so would clear her thoughts. "Surprisingly well. She's still on my 'watch closely' list though."

"And how about you, Michelle? I mean, after earlier . . ."

Michelle moved her spoon around the empty bowl. "I'm fine."

"Midas is an ass."

"You've got that right," she sighed. "Thank God he's leaving tonight. This political campaign has him traveling a lot."

"He and Ian don't get along much," Katie said.

"I suppose not. Can't control who you're related to."

"You know, if I had to picture someone who would willingly get involved in this, I could see Midas. But Ian is a bit—nervous—you know?"

"Ian is an accountant," Michelle said. "He never wanted to get involved in this, but Midas got him wrapped up in some money laundering thing, and Ian was arrested. Midas being—well, Midas—he kidnapped a district attorney's kids and blackmailed him to get Ian off. Eventually, everything came out. Ian was being followed by the FBI, and it was only a matter of time before they would be able to pin something on him, so he went underground. He's been hiding in these mountains ever since."

"The district attorney—you're talking about Jared and Leida's dad, aren't you?" asked Katie.

Michelle cocked her head to the side. "You already heard this story, huh? But what I just told is Ian's version."

"Why did Ian bring his daughter along too?"

"That was Midas. They're only half-brothers, but Ian doesn't have any other family. Midas got custody of Addison while Ian was in jail. He brought her here. Now, Addison is wrapped up in this too, and she's being used to keep Ian in line."

"He's using his own niece?"

"Midas doesn't care about anyone but himself. Ian is a pawn to him."

Katie tried to wrap her mind around such a creature. How could you not care about your brother? "And how did you end up with Ian?"

Michelle rested her head in her hand. "Why are you asking me all this?"

Katie considered this for a moment. It was a fair enough question, and one Katie didn't quite know the answer to herself. "I'm trying to understand," she said finally.

"Understand what? How a nice girl like me ends up shagging an incel like Ian?" Michelle said. "I'm a power-hungry slut, didn't you hear?"

"I don't believe that."

Michelle slid the spoon around the empty bowl once more then shoved it away. "A Watcher named Clayton used to work here. He started stalking this girl. Real obvious stuff: leering and blocking her way out of doors. Then one night, she didn't make it back from the kitchen. We found her dead the next morning. Of course, the Watchers never figured out what happened, but everyone knew. Beth was—Beth was the sweetest person I've ever met. For him to have . . ." She cleared her throat. "A couple of weeks later, he started stalking me. I've never been so scared. To have someone hunting you like that . . .When Ian found out, he approached me with a deal. Now here we are. Clayton got a promotion, and Ian got me."

"I'm sorry."

"I guess it could be worse. At least he doesn't snore." Michelle forced a laugh. "And of course, there are other perks. I shower regularly and have access to the occasional scraps. I know I don't have a right to complain."

"Michelle, you have every right to complain," Katie said. "And anyone who tells you otherwise is a moron."

She smiled sadly. "Thank you, Katie. You know, Jared is lucky to have you."

"Michelle—we're not—"

"Oh, that's not what I meant. I meant as a friend."

"Friend?" she said. "I'm not sure he considers me that."

"I disagree."

"Thank you," Katie said. "I think you're full of crap, but thank you."

Michelle laughed.

*　　　*　　　*

Jared held the door open as Katie ducked into the sauna-like shed. "I thought they were spiders," Katie said. Lunch had just ended, and unfortunately, not too much work remained. Soon, she'd be sent to join her hut in the field during the hottest part of the day. With the harvest drying, her hut had moved on to next season field prep, back-breaking labor she had thus far avoided.

"Not technically," he said. "Ticks aren't insects or spiders. They're mites."

"You don't see any more, do you?" She lifted her hair for him to look.

"Nope." He studied her neck. "Only the lice."

"Lice? I have lice?"

"Everyone has lice."

Katie scratched her head all over. "Lice? Really?"

Jared laughed and took his seat. "What? You don't like having a million close friends?"

She laid her head on her desk and moaned. Her copy work looked up at her, and she slid it away.

Jared gazed out the window. "I have to meet with Addison to take a test around three."

Katie perked up. "Do you need help studying?"

"No, I read the chapter last night. I'm good."

She sighed. "Of course, you don't study. Fine, I'll finish my work."

Jared nodded and opened the envelope from the Big House. "By the way Katie, thanks for checking up on Michelle."

She studied him curiously, but he continued to look at the mail.

"Labs came back," Jared said. "Looks like I was right. The pH is doing some funky things in Camp 7."

"You knew that Beth girl, didn't you? I mean the camp's not that big, you had to have."

"Yes," he said, continuing to thumb through the letters. "I knew her. She was my hut leader."

"Did Michelle leave you for Ian?" Katie blurted.

The thumbing stopped. "You're a bit nosy, you know that?"

"I'm sorry. I'm just trying to understand. Tweedle Dum called you Michelle's ex the other day, and now I get an I-can't-be-seen-talking-to-her-because-her-boyfriend-will-kill-me kind of vibe from you, and—"

"Yes, I was dating Michelle before the Ian deal," he interrupted. "That's not a secret."

"Wow. That had to hurt."

Jared set the envelopes down. "Are you coming to a point there, Katie? Or are you just trying to make me feel like shit? Yeah, I was dating Michelle, and yeah, I tried to protect her. When Clayton was stalking her, either Bryan or I would stay by her side 24/7, but what the hell were we supposed to do?"

"I'm not blaming you, Jared. I'm just saying 'wow, that sucked.' I'm empathizing."

"Well, do it quietly or something. This is my life we're talking about after all. I don't enjoy remembering this shit." Jared resumed sorting the mail, but slower.

No wonder he was angry all the time. Katie hugged herself as she imagined what that did to Michelle, too. What that continued to do to her. *A girl's gotta do what a girl's gotta do.* The mantra rolled through Katie's head. Noel had said that. So had Paulina. A great homesickness swept through Katie—deeper than she had felt before.

"You're still over there doing it, aren't you?" asked Jared.

"What?"

"Empathizing. Seriously consider doing that on your own time, please."

Jared folded the letter and slid it into the envelope before tearing into the next one. Katie tried, and failed, to think about something else, until the paper started rattling that is. The letter Jared was reading quivered in his hands. Light filtering through the paper illuminated four circles on the page.

Jared noticed her gaze and folded the paper. He shoved it into the envelope and cleared his throat. "On second thought, we'll stop for now and pick up some time this evening. It will be cooler."

"You have the meeting with Zhang."

"Oh." He stacked the papers, but they slid off each other. As he was trying to right them, he knocked over the green bean can, and Jared swore under his breath.

"What's the matter?" Kate placed a hand on his shoulder. His whole body shook.

"Nothing, just clumsy."

"Does it have anything to do with the coded messages in the data sheets?"

Jared straightened. "I don't kn-know what you're talking about."

"Oh my gosh," Katie said. "Is this—is this you lying? Because you suck at it."

Jared balked.

"I'm not an idiot, Jared. That's why you've been having me transfer the originals into the notebooks, so the little holes aren't there anymore. You've been communicating with someone."

"Do you ever mind your own business?" he demanded. "You come in here asking prying questions. You've been through my stuff, and now this?"

"I wasn't searching for it. I stumbled upon it. And it's not like I've told anybody."

"Get out. Get out!"

"You want me to leave now?"

"Yes!"

"What good is that going to do? I already know. Let me help you."

Jared stopped, his face red and contorted, his eyes wide, his jaw set. "Fine," he sneered. "I doubt the Watchers would believe you weren't involved now anyways. At least if they execute you, you'll know why."

Suddenly, Katie wasn't sure she wanted to know after all.

"And this is why I didn't want a damned assistant. They can't help but stick their noses into shit. Or at least 'empathize' their way into it."

He ripped the paper she had been copying off her desk and held it to the window light. Little stars dotted the page. "See each number indicated? It correlates to a gridded code. This is camp 3 so their code is . . ." He drew a grid of five rows and five columns. He tried to add letters but was too flustered to make it legible.

Jared threw down the pencil. "They prick two numbers, and the first number correlates to the 1-5 on top, while the second number correlates to the 1-5 on the side. When paired, the numbers correspond to a letter in the grid. Understand?"

"Simple enough, yes."

"Well then, now you have it." He fell into his seat, grimacing as his back struck the chair.

"But who are you talking to? What messages do these contain?"

He sighed and shook his head. "I'm talking to the workers at the other camps. I'm not going to tell you their names, but they send me information."

"What kind of information?"

Jared stared out the window for a time, then he sighed once more and turned back to Katie. "Any information that might lead to their location. License plate numbers, addresses and phone numbers from receipts left in the trash. Anything at all that might help them be found someday. Then I take it and send it to the other camps. There are nine other camps out there. Eventually, someone is going to escape."

"How do you give them the code?" she asked.

"Whenever there's a problem at one of the camps that I can't fix by looking at the datasheets, Midas sends me to that camp. So far, I've been to six other camps and they all have the code now."

"What did they send you this time that has you worried?"

Jared held the new letter up to the light. "The message says help."

Katie scratched her head. "That's vague. We could all use a bit of help."

"That's not the freaky part. They shouldn't be saying anything. I've never been to this camp."

"But—but then how . . .?" Katie took the sheet from him and held it up, illuminating the four dots.

"This isn't the first message they've sent either. A few weeks back the message said 'Hello,' and I sent back 'Hey,' with my initials. I figured it would look like gibberish."

"Do you think it's a trap?"

"I don't know. I guess I'll go convince Addison to take me on a field trip. Good thing their lab results came back so abnormal."

Jared collected the notebook for Camp 7 on top of a botany textbook as he glanced about his shed, making sure he had gathered all his meager possessions. "If there's any mail, put it on my desk until I get back."

"You haven't memorized that yet?" Katie asked.

"Not quite," he said distractedly. "Bryan's going to be in charge, so if anything goes down, find him. He also knows about the—you know—so if I don't make it back, he can help with that."

"Is there a chance you're not coming back?"

"I never know what's going to happen on these trips, but I should be back in a week."

"Have fun."

"Unlikely." Jared closed the door, and Katie found herself alone in his hut.

She glanced around the room wondering if she should tackle the pile of datasheets that had arrived that morning, but the boss would be gone for a whole week. If she needed a break, she would come back. Instead, Katie left the muggy hut and strolled down the well-worn path with familiarity.

The world was already heating, but a nice breeze flowed over her, and she closed her eyes to take in the moment. As she passed the final building, a hand grabbed her, and she screamed.

"What are you doing down here?" Bartram asked.

Katie yanked her arm away. "I'm heading to the field."

"No, you're leaving with Goldie," Bartram said. "Go to the house. They're loading by the fence."

"Oh—kay." Katie turned back around but looked over her shoulder as she went.

Jared frowned when she arrived at the top of the hill but kept loading bags into the backseat while Addison leaned against the car, smoking.

"There she is," Addison said when she saw Katie.

"She's coming?" Jared closed the car door.

"Of course, she's coming."

"I am?"

The kitchen door popped on its hinges as the man with the cowboy hat stepped out the kitchen door. Jared tensed, and Katie's mouth parted as she realized this was the man who had tased Trevor. Was he coming with them too?

"Hey there, Goldilocks." The cowboy smacked Jared hard on the back of the head as he passed, and the boy glared after him. "Are we ready to go?"

"Yep." Addison tossed the keys to him. "Clayton, you take the first shift."

A knot formed in Katie's stomach. This was Clayton. Michelle's Clayton.

"Come on Goldie, Katie, let's get you two loaded up." Addison beckoned them to the rear of the car.

"Clayton's coming?" Jared whispered once behind the vehicle.

"This is a cartel camp we're visiting," Addison said. "He's our lead negotiator."

"I don't want to come," Katie said. "I don't think you'll need me."

"Tough," she said. "I didn't plan this trip, but Ian thinks you'll be needed. Now, will someone, please, give me your hands."

With a look of dread, Jared put his hands forward, and Addison slipped a set of zip ties over his wrists. She pulled them down snug. Katie swallowed hard but followed Jared's lead.

Clayton popped the trunk. All the bags had been placed up front leaving a wide, empty space in the back. "You've got to be kidding me," Katie said.

"Sit," Addison said.

Jared perched on the bumper, and she secured his feet and eased him into the trunk.

"Oh, come on," Katie muttered as the trunk shrank before her. Jared scooted against the wall. There was space for her, but it would be cramped.

"We don't have all day!" Clayton shouted from the driver's seat.

Hesitantly, Katie sat on the bumper. After securing her feet, Addison helped her inside, and the lid closed above them, plunging them into darkness.

"I'm sorry," Jared said. "I never meant to drag you into this."

"This is going to suck," she grumbled. Rolling on her side, Katie felt along the soft wall of the trunk. She found the crease to the lid, but it was too narrow to slide her pinky through. "Shouldn't there be tail lights or wiring or something?"

"They sealed it off with this box," Jared said. "It's soundproof in here too, so if you're considering screaming, I would appreciate it if you refrained."

"Jared," she whispered. "How long are we supposed to be in here?"

"I don't know. I didn't get an itinerary."

"I can't do this," she said.

"Do what?" He shuffled beside her, and his warm, cigarette-smelling breath struck her.

"Ride like this. We're going to suffocate in here. It's already getting so much hotter." She tugged at her throat. "I'm—I'm losing air."

"No, you're not. You're panicking," Jared said, but Katie pushed up on the roof as hard as she could. When nothing budged, she collapsed down panting.

"Katie, air gets pumped in here when the car is turned on. It will cool down. You need to take some deep breaths."

"We're going to run out of air before they turn the car on." She licked her parched lips. "What is taking them so long?"

"Katie, roll over and face me."

"What? What are you going to do?"

"I'm going to help you, roll over." Jared took her hands in his own and placed them on his chest. "Feel me breathe? Match my breathing. As long as you breathe like I do, you will be fine. Come on. In." He inhaled. "Out." The tobacco smell nearly burnt her nostrils.

"This is stupid."

"Do it," he insisted. "In—and out. In—and out."

Katie forced her ragged breaths to follow his. After a few cycles, the air grew cooler.

"How are we doing? Better?"

She nodded and remembered he couldn't see her. "Yes."

"Good." He dropped her hand. "Do that over there and stop freaking out."

Although he couldn't see it, she narrowed her eyes before rolling on her back to continue the deep breaths.

The car shuddered. "What's that?" Katie cried, clutching his arm, and a blast of frigid air struck her.

"That would be the car starting," he said. A few moments later, the car lurched forward, and Katie shrieked.

Jared sighed, "This is going to be a long trip."

*　　　*　　　*

Sighing, Katie twiddled her thumbs as Jared shifted in his sleep. Once again, she tried to close her eyes and drift off, but it was no use. Not in the trunk as cold as the tundra, and not in such cramped quarters.

When she rolled onto her shoulder, his nasty rotting teeth and cigarette breath struck her face again, and she scooted as far away as the trunk would allow. With her own warm breath, she breathed into her palm and regretted it. Her breath was not as bad as Jared's, but close.

Jared jerked in his sleep and let out a small moan. He sat up, struck his head on the roof, and clawed at the low ceiling.

"Jared?" Katie said, and the clawing stopped.

"Ow." His arm brushed past Katie's as he rubbed his head. Every scratch, every adjustment had become a joint experience. "How long was I out?"

"I don't know. A couple of hours?"

"Hey, Addison?" he said.

Was he still asleep?

"Yes?" Addison's voice erupted from a speaker, and Katie jumped.

"Can we turn the air down a bit, please?" Jared asked, and the air slowed.

"They can hear us?" Katie said.

"They can see you too."

"That's good to know," Katie said. "Glad I wasn't picking my nose or something."

"This vehicle is designed to transport people like us," Jared said. "Hence the spacious, soundproof trunk. At least it's usually spacious." He shuffled about to lay on his side facing her. His chest rested gently against her own, and Katie scooted back an inch.

"I wish we knew how long we were going to be in here," she muttered.

"Camp 7 is somewhere in growing zone 6. The reports show cold winters and frequent snows. They also get tornadoes. My best guess is the Great Plains area. Oklahoma maybe, Arkansas." Jared lowered his voice. His warm breath caused her to cringe as he whispered near her ear. "Kansas."

For the next three hours, the two lay practically on top of each other. At first, Katie tried to stay scrunched on her side of the trunk, not wishing to touch Jared. Girls didn't touch boys who weren't their boyfriends, at least that's what had been communicated through Katie's upbringing. But at a certain point, something had to give.

At first, Jared also seemed to show consideration for personal body space as well. If ever he adjusted himself and his hand came too close to her hips or chest, he would apologize. But this seemed to happen so often, the apology became redundant. He didn't seem to be trying to touch her, there just was no escaping each other.

"You know Jared," Katie said, "I thought before that we spent a lot of time together, but this is flat out ridiculous."

The car slowed to a stop, and then the sound of the engine ceased.

"Are we there?" Katie asked, ready to hop out, stretch her legs again, and resume some semblance of personal boundaries.

"Feels about lunchtime," Jared said. "They'll let us get out to pee and stretch our legs for a little bit before going on."

The door of the trunk ripped open and Clayton slung a paper bag inside before slamming the lid shut again. The smell of greasy food filled the trunk.

"What were you saying about stretching our legs?" Katie asked.

"I guess those plans were canceled," grumbled Jared.

The trunk opened again, and this time, Addison appeared. She dragged Katie out first while Jared exited with a little more grace. Addison chained their legs to the hitch, and they sat on the bumper. Gravel was beneath their feet, the road stopping mere yards away. All around were trees. The sound of a highway nearby penetrated the woods, but nothing else was heard.

Addison distributed water bottles before sitting in a camping chair a few feet away. As she set her taser in the cup holder, she looked pointedly at Jared. Jared opened the food bag, and the smell caused Katie's mouth to water.

Katie nearly hopped with excitement. "That looks so good." Licking her lips, she took the shiny package from the bag.

"Wait," Jared said. "When was the last time you had something this greasy?"

"I don't know. Months?"

"Your stomach won't do well if you eat it quickly. Take it slow."

She frowned. Her hopes of cramming the delicious morsel down her throat were dashed. With less enthusiasm, she unwrapped the burger, and her nose hairs raised to capture the smell of the greasy delicacy. "You are such a buzzkill."

Addison smiled as she played on her phone, pretending not to listen.

"I'm only saying . . ." Jared nibbled his sandwich.

Katie took a larger bite but did eat slowly. When she finished, her stomach growled louder than usual.

Jared ate half and wrapped the rest.

"Are you going to finish that?" she asked.

"I'm saving it for later." He set it in the trunk.

As Jared took a sip from his water bottle, Katie remembered her own bottle, and her mouth went dry. She downed it. Meanwhile, Jared stared at her, mouth ajar, and Addison gawked.

"You shouldn't have done that," Jared said. "Clayton doesn't stop for anybody."

"What don't I do?" Clayton closed his flip phone as he came to the rear of the vehicle.

"Nothing," Addison said. "It's not important."

As Clayton rounded the car, Katie could not help but stare at the silver revolver hanging on Clayton's hip. The gun was massive, almost too massive to be real.

He followed her gaze. "Like what you see there, sweetheart?" he said and removed the gun. ".44 Magnum. Like Clint Eastwood."

Katie stiffened as he pointed the gun at her. Smiling, he turned the gun on Jared and mimicked the sound of a gunshot.

"Are you done goofing off?" Addison asked.

"I don't know, are you done being a hard-ass?" He flopped into the other camping chair. "Besides, it's good to remind them of the score. See, little darling, if you cross me, you will regret it. Ain't that right, Goldie?"

Jared stared at the gravel road.

"See? He knows." Clayton kicked Jared's leg with his boot, but Jared kept his head down. The man stood and leaned over him. "How's the shoulder?"

The burger in Katie's stomach turned to lead. She didn't know what he had done to Jared's shoulder. Broken it? Dislocated it? But

Jared's foil wrapper trembled in his hand as he continued to stare at the ground.

Clayton sniffed and wiped his nose with the back of his hand. "Goldie, aren't you going to introduce me to your friend there?"

Jared's brows pinched together, and Katie looked away.

"You know , she'd be kind of cute if not for that hideous scar." Clayton touched her hair, and she withdrew.

"Her name is Katie," Addison said. "And she's a Greenie, so don't get any ideas."

"Relax. I'm just having a bit of fun, isn't that right, Goldie?"

Jared's ears turned red.

Clayton lit a cigarette and took a couple of puffs. "We need to hit the road if we're going to make it there tonight. Let's wrap it up."

As Clayton moved to the front of the vehicle, Jared let out a ragged breath and rolled his shoulder. Katie attempted to give him a reassuring smile, but he looked away.

"You heard him," Addison said. "Time to pack it up."

"I'm sure it's not much further," Jared said. "They rarely go over four hours at a time."

"And you've been counting?" Katie gritted her teeth as she wiggled like a little kid. "Oh gosh. I don't know if I can hold it any longer." Why had she drunk all that water?

"Ha! You'd better hold it. That's all I'm going to say about that."

"Rrrrrrrr."

The car came to a stop, and both paused to listen. It lurched forward again, and Katie let out a stream of curses. She knocked her head on the floor of the trunk to regain focus.

"Hold on," Jared said. "I think we've turned off the highway, so we're almost there."

To Katie's relief, as Jared predicted, the engine cut off a couple of turns later. She rolled onto her side, poised to hop out of the trunk, but Jared placed his bound hands on her shoulder. "Don't rush it. If you climb out too fast, he'll shoot you."

The key turned in the lock, and the trunk opened. Clayton grinned down at her wickedly. Clearly, he had been listening.

"Are you two ready to get inside?" he asked. "Get some rest?"

Beads of sweat formed on her brow. Was he seriously going to keep her from the bathroom? But, in short ado, he grabbed her arm and pulled her out of the vehicle.

They had parked in a residential garage. Katie wondered how close the nearest neighbors were, but Clayton's fingers rested on the revolver as he watched her closely. He'd shoot her dead before she could inhale enough to scream.

Turning to the door, Katie started walking in that direction, but Clayton grabbed her arm. "What's the rush?"

"I can take her in," Addison said as she mounted the three steps to the house and unlocked the door.

"She can wait."

Jared maneuvered out of the vehicle while carrying his hamburger.

"Midnight snack?" asked Clayton.

Addison put a hand on her hip. "He always does that. He won't eat it until the next meal."

"Afraid we'll forget to feed you, Goldie?"

"Of course not," Jared muttered.

Katie bit her lip and looked pleadingly to the door. Clayton narrowed his eyes but nodded toward Addison. "Go on."

As Jared tried to move past him, Clayton blocked his way. "That hamburger is all cold by now. Let me throw it away for you."

Jared extended the hamburger to him, but Clayton slapped his hand, spilling it. Jared's lip twitched and his ears turned red once more. Frowning, he bent, collected the scattered pieces, and moved to follow Katie to the door. Clayton shoved him in the back, and Jared barely dodged the side mirror, his cheeks growing continually red.

On the left side of the drab house was a living room with an old couch and an up-to-date gaming system. On the right, a small kitchen. As soon as he entered, Clayton threw himself onto the couch and flipped on the TV while Addison led them down a narrow hallway past two bedrooms. Katie eyed the bathroom, but they kept going to the back of the house. Hidden behind a normal door was a steel door with three locks. Addison unlocked these using keys from a giant keyring. Katie breathed a sigh of relief when she saw the toilet mounted to the floor.

"Y'all got a mattress in here," Jared said. "Nice."

The mattress was a shabby thing with a divot in the center. Besides the toilet, it was the only thing in the room. Cinder block walls sealed them in on all sides with one frosted window. The last few rays of light filtered in the depressing cell. In the corner was a video camera.

"You know the drill." Addison nodded to Jared. "But I'll lay it out for Katie. The walls are soundproof, but we can hear you through the door. If either of you try to escape, you will be punished, and Goldie will be shot. Do you understand?"

"Even if he doesn't help?" Katie said.

"Yes," Addison said. "You are responsible for her, Goldie. Don't let her do anything stupid."

Jared rubbed the bridge of his nose and nodded.

"I'm going out for food in a bit," Addison continued. "Any requests?"

Katie eyed the toilet.

"Are you talking about food?" Clayton hollered from the couch. "Have Goldie cook!"

"Seriously?" Jared whispered. "He hates my cooking. It's a trap."

Addison held up a hand. "I'll make a show of looking through the kitchen. When I don't find anything, I'll suggest we eat out. What do you want?"

"How should I know?" he said. "It's not like I'm up to date on my options out there."

"I'll bring back some burgers, okay?"

"Sure," Katie said. "I have to pee."

Addison undid her hands. "I'll see you in a bit."

Katie looked sheepishly at Jared, but his expression was blank. "Oh!" he said finally and sat on the mattress with his back to her and the toilet.

"I guess that's as good as it's going to get."

*　　*　　*

Jared slid his half-burger and water from lunch between the mattress and the wall. "Just in case they forget about us, or Addison gets killed in a car wreck," he explained. "Clayton won't care whether or not we eat."

Katie wished she hadn't eaten all of hers too, but there was nothing to be done about it. Instead, she stretched her weary muscles and walked around the room, examining the walls. "Jared, what are all these names?"

He lay on the mattress and stared at the ceiling. "They're the names of the other kids that came through here."

Katie studied them closer. "There's so many of them." Each had been carved into the cinderblock, some more than once.

"I'm on there somewhere," he said and pointed to a corner. "This safe house is on the way to Camp 9 as well."

"Jared Adam Kelley," Katie read. "You put your address and phone number on here too."

"I didn't want to get confused with some other Jared Kelley," he muttered. "There's usually something in here to carve your name with if you want to leave your mark too. Rock, piece of metal, old nail." He felt along the edges of the mattress.

"Old screw?" Katie found it on the window ledge. They found a blank spot, and Katie carved her information into the stone. As she stood back to admire her work, the door clanged open, and Addison entered with another paper bag.

"I thought about getting some chicken nuggets," she said, "but hamburgers seemed more filling."

"Cheeseburger too expensive?" Katie asked.

"Goldie's lactose intolerant." She tossed him the bag. "I'm going out for a drink. Clayton will be here, so don't get any ideas. I'll see you in the morning."

Jared sat on the mattress and dug through the bag. "Be careful."

"Worried about me, Goldie?" She winked at him.

"Should I not be?"

"Hush, you." She closed the door. He shook his head and brought out another hamburger.

"So, because you're lactose intolerant, I can't get any cheese," Katie complained as she unwrapped her burger. "How does Addison even know you're lactose intolerant?"

"Because I told her," he said.

"And she remembered? It took her three weeks to remember my name."

Jared shrugged.

"You're kind of friendly with each other, aren't you? I mean for a captor and captive relationship."

"A few trips back, she got me a cheeseburger, and I scraped the cheese off. Clayton beat the crap out of me for being 'ungrateful.' After that, he hog-tied me and left me in the trunk overnight."

"Oh. I'm sorry."

"It's fine." He picked at his food. "Addison feels bad, so she's left off the cheese ever since. She tries to be a good person, but the business she's in sort of makes it a one-step-forward—two-steps-back-situation."

"But she looks out for you, doesn't she?"

"She's not very good at it, but yes. She tries. And in another life, we might have been friends. But as for now, she's holding the keys, and that makes her my enemy."

"I've never had enemies before," Katie said, wiping her greasy fingers on the mattress. "I mean—there have been people I didn't like, but not real enemies. Not like this."

"That's because you're a nice person. I've always had enemies."

"What'd you do, get into with your kindergarten teacher?"

He smiled mischievously. "Mrs. Blanchette, my Sunday School teacher. I put purple ink in her coffee, and it stained her dentures."

"You what?" Katie laughed. "Why would you do that?"

"I don't know. I was seven. It seemed like the thing to do."

Katie laughed so hard she snorted, and Jared started laughing too. But then he grew quiet.

"Sometimes it feels like my life out there was just part of some good dream, you know?" Jared said. "I remember my parents, but sometimes it's like they're characters in a book or something. Still, I miss them, all the time."

"Leida told me it would get better, but I don't know believe her," Katie said.

"It's like missing a limb, I reckon. You don't forget it's missing, but you get used to the hole in your gut. Even if we were freed tomorrow, I don't know if that hole would ever really go away. Too much has happened. I'm not some seven-year-old kid anymore."

"A seven-year-old kid wouldn't think to send coded messages like you have." She nudged him in the side. "I think you're onto something with this one, Jared."

"Only three more camps to go, thank God," he said. "I hate these trips."

"Then all the camps will know where we are?" she asked.

He nodded. "And then maybe I'll never have to see that son of a bitch Clayton ever again. He can go off and do whatever the hell it is Midas's cronies do when they're not torturing us."

"He really is a tool, isn't he?"

Jared laughed. "Clayton's beaten me more times than I can recall—literally. Like there are times where all I remember is ending up on the ground after he walked past. Didn't do anything either. He just felt like hitting someone." He took another bite of his burger. "No, he makes me regret what I said about Addison. She can hold the keys all day. She's the only Watcher who hasn't hit me."

"Even Ruby has hit you?" Katie asked.

"Oh Ruby? She's the worst, don't you know? Got a mean right hook."

Katie laughed, and his grin grew. Ruby, the kitchen Watcher, barely noticed the world beyond her phone. If a fly landed in front of her, she wouldn't swat it due to laziness.

Jared said, "If you think I shake normally, you should see me around Ruby. People wonder if there's an earthquake going on."

Katie jabbed him playfully in the arm, and he laughed. Then his face grew distant once more. "Addison saved my life."

"How?"

"I have been begging Addison for years to go to the cops, but she's too scared. And sometimes I hate her for it. But if anyone knows her uncle and what he would do if she betrayed him, it's her.

She says there is nowhere on earth she could hide from him, and he would cut her apart slowly once he caught her."

Katie shook her head. "Children around her are dying."

"Yeah," he said. "Which is why she still works for Midas. She could have left years ago, gotten a job on the other side of the country and never looked back, but she has stayed for a reason."

Katie cocked her head in question, and he continued, "How many supplies go missing from the kitchen because of us? Enough to be noticeable, but Addison orders the supplies. Hell, she's been sneaking in food for us since she was in middle school. Addison replaces Tylenol, blankets, and antibiotics—anything else that goes missing without question. I say that she has saved my life once, but she's done that a hundred times by now." He shook his head. "When Landon and I got past the fence—they should have shot me—they would have shot me if it hadn't been for her."

"Jared, what happened?"

Jared crumpled up the thin sheet from the mattress. "Landon's plan was one in a million. He rigged an upstairs toilet to leak onto the breaker box below. It was a dumb plan and never should have worked, but it did. The whole camp went dark, and we cut through the wire. We were so close!"

"That's when they caught you at the rafting shop?"

He nodded. "When they brought Landon and me back, Midas took us to the cemetery. The whole time, Landon kept telling me not to worry. To be brave. He told me he would see me on the other side."

A tear slid down his cheek. "Midas made us dig a grave big enough for both of us, then he had us kneel. I can still taste the gunpowder in the air." He ran his hands through his hair. "Midas shot Landon in the back of the head, and he fell into the grave. He was my best friend, Katie, and Midas shot him like he was a dog. Like some pest that had cut through his precious fence."

Moisture filled Katie's eyes, and she leaned her head on his shoulder.

"And then he put the gun to my head, and he pulled the trigger," Jared said. "When nothing happened, he told me I had one more chance. I had the time until he loaded the next bullet to convince him not to kill me."

"What did you tell him?"

"I told him I would double the camp's output by the next harvest."

"And that worked?"

Jared sneered. "He asked me why I couldn't triple it. I told him I didn't want to promise what I couldn't deliver. He laughed and put the gun away." Jared leaned his head against hers. "I was taking Addison's college classes in exchange for food at the time. She told Midas about our little deal. When he found out that a fourteen-year-old was taking collegiate courses, he saw dollar signs. After the harvest, Midas came back and told me I had earned one more year, but I had to convince him again to give me another. I told him I could improve the other camps as well, and he started sending me the data sheets. Of course, if I try to escape or start stealing again, the deal is off."

"But he also gives you favors and stuff, doesn't he?"

"During the second year, I told him there was no point in helping him if I was going to die of cold during the winter. In exchange for each special job, I get a request. The proceeds from this job will buy windows for the huts just in time for winter."

"Midas must find you very valuable if he's willing to trade favors."

He shook his head. "What I do isn't rocket science, Katie. It's basic botany. Eventually, I will become expendable again." He laughed. "Not to mention I'm falling apart."

"You're still making profits!"

"Katie, I can't write anymore. I can't sleep. I have trouble eating. You saw how close I came to getting fired when you started."

"But you have me now. I can help you."

"What happens if something else slips or I start making mistakes?"

"Teach me how to analyze the data sheets, how to collect the information."

He laughed, and she turned his face to hers.

"Don't act like that toward me, Jared Kelley. I am not as smart as you, but I am no idiot either. If you teach me, I will learn, and we will do this together. You don't have to do this on your own."

His mouth parted, then he smiled. Jared slid his hand behind her head, brought her face near his, and kissed her.

Katie's eyes grew wide as she pulled back from the kiss, and Jared's popped open.

"I—I uh." Jared muttered and rubbed the back of his head. "Sorry."

Warmth flooded Katie's cheeks, and she looked away. He liked her? How had she not seen that coming? She bit her lip and cleared her throat. "Jared," When she turned back to him, his face was red. "I'm sorry, I just . . ."

He frowned and shook his head. "Clearly, I misread that. It's my fault."

"Can we just pretend it didn't happen?"

Jared winced but nodded. "Yeah. Yeah, sure."

"Aw, come on!" Clayton's voice called from the hallway. "That's it? Goldie, you're such a pussy!"

Katie looked to Jared in shock, but his head fell into his hand as he pointed to the camera mounted in the corner of the room. "I am so sorry."

Katie glared at him, slid beneath the covers, and rolled onto her side away from him. So that's how her first kiss went. An unwanted disaster in front of a psychopath. The mattress shifted as Jared slid beneath the blanket, his back to hers. Her heart panged with guilt, but it was his fault. What was he doing, kissing her like that? A tear slid down her cheek, and she swatted it away.

When the sound of the key in the lock woke Katie the next morning, Jared was awake, looking out the frosted window. Clayton's head popped inside the door, and he lobbed a paper sack at Jared's head. Jared caught the bag, and Clayton slammed the door. Was the psycho incapable of doing anything without being as obnoxious as possible?

Jared brought over the bag and handed Katie a chicken biscuit before joining her to sit on the bed. Katie ate as normal, but just as she reached the halfway point through her biscuit, Jared was already crinkling up his trash.

"You ate the whole thing?" Katie asked.

Jared stared down at the tinfoil ball in his hand. "Damn, I wasn't thinking." He threw the trash in the corner and stood to study the names on the walls.

Addison entered the room some minutes after. Her hair was wet from a recent shower, but the dark circles beneath her eyes betrayed her. She winced at the bare bulb in the center of the room.

"Rough night?" Jared asked.

She put a hand to her head. "Don't talk. You know the drill."

Jared put his hands out in front of him. Katie followed suit, and Addison removed zip ties from her back pocket.

"How long this time?" Katie asked.

"Three more hours," Addison said. As she led them out, the bonds on Katie's wrists burned against her raw wrists.

Once in the trunk, Katie dozed for the first few hours and woke to find her hip completely asleep. She turned on her other side discovering that hip to be sore from yesterday. Katie flipped to her back, jostling Jared as she did.

Jared shoved her. "Can you find a comfortable spot already?"

"Geez, sorry."

"If you keep flip-flopping like that, I'm going to jab you in the gut," he said, but then the car engine shut off.

Katie held her breath as she waited for another sound to follow. "What's going on?" her voice cracked.

"We're here," Jared said.

They waited for five minutes, then ten, then twenty. The trunk temperature rose to alarming levels. The longer they waited, the harder it was to breathe, but Katie continued to take the deep breaths Jared had shown her yesterday.

Then the trunk started vibrating. Only after a few moments did Katie realize it was Jared shaking.

"Are you okay?" She brushed her hands against his to find his fingertips ground into the carpet.

Jared sucked in air. "I—uhm." He swore.

"They're going to be here soon, right Jared? They haven't left us, have they?"

"They'll be back," he said in a whisper then tugged on his collar. "Damn this to hell!" He kicked on the roof of the trunk with both feet.

"Jared, you're scaring me."

"I just want out too, Katie," came his breath-laden reply. "We won't—we won't suffocate. It's not an air-tight space after all. It's just a little hot."

Katie got the feeling he was talking to himself more than her. Finally, the sound of the key in the latch penetrated their cell, and light cut into their world once more. While they were still blinking, a Watcher yanked them out by the arms.

They stood before a whitewashed wall with a concrete floor beneath. The lighting was low, and the room had a musty smell. Katie craned her neck to look around and saw a few other vehicles nearby.

A hand smacked her face, causing her to yelp. "Eyes down and forward!" the Watcher barked in her ear. Hastily, she complied with the order but cut a side glance to Jared. He offered her the slightest nod of encouragement, but his body continued to shake, and his face was plastered in worry. Then a black bag was pulled down over his head. Before she could react, a matching one was placed over her own. A hand grabbed her arm, and she was led into the unknown.

After a series of turns, they paused for a moment. With a lurch, the floor rose, and Jared inhaled sharply. It was an elevator. How long had it been since he rode in such a contraption? A 'ding' sounded, and they were pushed forward again. The space was cooler than before, the floor softer. Carpet, Katie suspected. After several more turns, the Watchers greeted someone, and a woman replied, "Hello."

The Watcher released her arm. "Stay there."

The longer the wait, the more Katie's previously cramped legs began to ache. Other than a strange intermittent clicking, there was nothing to hear. A terrifying thought entered her mind in the silence. Where was Jared? Surely, she would have heard him again by now. A gasp, a cough, heck the floor vibrating around him? Up to this point, Katie had not realized how much she had come to depend on him. The unknown filled her like an ocean entering her lungs.

"Jared?" She could hear the panic in her own voice.

"Quiet!" the Watcher next to her screamed.

"I'm here." Jared's steady voice came from a few feet away.

The Watcher yelled obscenities at him. *Whump!*

Jared inhaled sharply and coughed. Katie gasped and for the next several moments, she listened as he continued to breathe heavy. That blow was for her. Tears filled her eyes, and she dared not say anything else.

After several minutes, the woman spoke again, "You can go in now." The Watcher pushed them forward.

"What the—?" Addison's voice sounded, and the hood came off.

Katie and Jared found themselves in a large office. A man in his mid-sixties sat behind a beautifully stained executive desk with the emblem of a marijuana leaf carved into the front. The spacious office was lined in bookshelves, not with literature, but with interesting bits of art. Exquisitely glass-blown bongs of intricate color detail were scattered among the mix. A massive hookah sat on a table behind the desk. The entire back wall was made of windows, but long gray shades covered them.

The man behind the desk had a pockmarked face and sported a long scraggly goatee. His button-down shirt opened and bits of gray hair curled out. A thick blunt was clenched between his teeth; the smoke curled and collected on the ceiling.

Addison sat in an upholstered chair in front of the desk. "I'm assuming the hoods have a purpose."

"Oh!" the man said. "Yes, your workers are accustomed to a laissez-faire approach. Here we are stricter. The less the workers know, the less trouble they cause."

"Sounds like a hassle to me, Linus," Addison said, and he narrowed his eyes. "Do you want him to look at the plants now or tomorrow?"

"Tomorrow." The man rubbed his beard as he studied the two. Katie's skin crawled as his eyes lingered on her. She struggled to keep her gaze on the floor as he moved around the desk. At the last second, Linus diverted in his path toward her and moved to stand uncomfortably close to Jared. "He doesn't look like much, does he? Your boy genius."

Addison crossed her arms. "We don't use him for his appearance."

Linus grabbed Jared's upper arm. "Not lacking in muscle though. Like a rock." Jared grew a shade pink. "Open your mouth." Linus grabbed Jared's lower jaw.

Katie forgot all pretenses of staring at the floor and gawked at this man. Jared's eyes flew to Addison.

"Open your damn mouth," he demanded. Hesitantly, Addison gave a nod, and Jared obeyed. "How long has he been with you?" He inspected the inside of his mouth.

"How the hell should I know?" Addison said. "We don't keep those kinds of records."

"Close." He jerked Jared's head to the side and inspected his ears. "He seems well enough trained. Keeps his eyes where he should. The girl's still rather new, I take it." He looked at her pointedly, and Katie diverted her eyes to the floor. "Jumpy. Pretty though. Shame about that scar. Put your arms up."

Begrudgingly, Jared raised his still bound arms. Linus lifted his shirt and inspected the mass of tangled scars covering his back. Some of the fresh ones were still scabbed over, but most of them were pink. Linus let out a low whistle. "He's given you some trouble though, hasn't he? Took a while to break this stallion."

Addison scratched her nose. "Do you want to look at his dick too?"

"Why? Is there something wrong with it?"

Addison's brows shot up.

"How much?" Linus asked, turning back to Addison.

Jared shook his head emphatically behind Linus's back and put his hands together in a pleading form, a gesture he dropped as Linus looked back at him.

"He's not for sale," Addison said.

"Everything is for sale."

"Look, even if I was in a position to make that—"

"Oh, you're not who I need to talk to, are you? You're just a foot soldier. I may have your boss's number here." He turned to his desk.

"I'll let my boss know you're interested," Addison said through clenched teeth. "If he's interested in selling, he'll call you."

Linus scowled. "Fine. There's nothing more I need from you today. I'll have Blakeney and Layne put these two in the cells, and we'll talk again tomorrow."

After one final look of contempt, Addison ushered them into the antechamber where they had waited. The woman behind a desk glanced up as she continued typing away at her computer, and the two Watchers from earlier stood as they entered.

Before relinquishing Jared to them, however, Addison whispered into his ear, "There's no way in hell you're getting sold to that freak."

*   *   *

"Can they even do that?" Katie said. "Just sell you like that?"

Jared cleaned the wounds on Katie's wrists with a bit of cloth they had found in the cells. Gray, moist cinder blocks and cement floors surrounded them making the room seem colder than it was. There were no windows, and the light came from a series of bare bulbs running along the ceiling.

The space was twice the size of one of their huts. Bunk beds fashioned with iron brackets were stacked three high along the wall. Thin, ragged mattresses lay across creaking springs. Each had a rough blanket and a pillow, but they were unable to tell which beds were occupied. They had picked a bed at random to sit on while they waited for the others.

"It's up to them," Jared said. "I have no say in it, but Addison said she'd take care of it."

"And you think she will?"

"I have to, don't I?" He managed to wrap the cloth around her wrist as his hands shuddered. "Damn, I could go for a cigarette."

"How do you pretend to be so calm? Your hands are shaking badly, but your voice is steady. Someone just tried to buy you, Jared, but if I didn't know you, I would think you were totally unfazed by that."

He tied off the wrappings. "When you first come to the camp, no one expects much from you for the first month or so, but I had a terrified four-year-old with me. She needed me, and she needed me not to be afraid. So, I pretended I wasn't. Until I couldn't any longer." He held up his quaking hand.

"How does a seven-year-old take care of a four-year-old?" Katie asked.

He met her gaze with a furrowed brow. "Any way he can."

The door creaked open, and a line of kids entered. For a moment, the kids stared at each other, sizing one another up. Then a boy about the size of Trevor stepped forward from the group. "That's my bunk," he said.

Katie began to rise, but Jared stayed put. "Is it now?"

"Who the hell are you? You aren't new."

"We're here for a couple of days," Jared said.

A murmur spread through the group, and the boy laughed. "Are you on vacation or something? Get off my bunk."

"This bunk belongs to somebody," Jared said. "But it's not you."

"Oh, it's not, is it?"

"Probability, my friend."

"I'm not your friend."

"So be it." Jared stood. He studied the boy for a moment then looked to the crowd beyond. "I need to talk to you." He pointed to a girl near sixteen with braided hair resting on her shoulder. Her brows rose.

"No," the boy said. "You're talking to me. Now, apologize for sitting on my bunk."

"I will not."

"Jared," Katie cautioned.

"Then I will beat out an apology." The boy made a fist.

Jared gestured for Katie to move away and rested his hand in the small of his back. "Try me, but don't expect to be breathing when the dust settles." A glint of metal caught off the light where Jared's hand rested. A knife?

"Stop!" Katie said. "Look, we don't mean to step on any toes here. Okay? We're all prisoners. Why do you two have to fight?"

"You will show me respect!" The boy wagged a finger at Jared.

"I have shown you no disrespect," Jared said. "But I will not bow to some perceived slight. If you feel that requires retribution, I await your move. But do not assume it will go well for you."

The boy squinted. "Do what? What fancy mumbo jumbo was that?"

Jared rolled his eyes. "Come at me bro. See what happens!"

The boy raised his fist.

"Enough!" The girl with the braid stepped forward. "Steve! Stop. He's got a shank in his hand, and he'll gut you if you come too close."

"You serious Claudia?" Steve gawked.

A small smile crept over Jared's face. "There she is. The real power in the room." He lowered his arm to show the thin blade in his hand.

"You son of a bitch," Steve said.

"Relax," Jared said. "I would have just nicked you for starters." With a quick motion, he slid the blade back into its hidden pocket.

"For Pete's sake." Claudia rolled her eyes and stepped to Katie. "While these two figure out who's got the biggest dick, I'll introduce myself. I'm Claudia Vernor."

Katie accepted the hand.

"You'll have to forgive Steve there. He's a bit territorial. And that is, in fact, his bunk."

"Oh, shit," Jared said. "Are you serious?"

Steve folded his arms once more.

"Then, I am sorry." Jared extended a hand. "I thought you were just busting my balls."

Steve eyed the hand suspiciously before shaking it. "You know, I could have still taken you, knife or not."

"That might be something best left for speculation."

"Those words, man."

"I know it's annoying," Katie said. "But he's not messing with you. Jared just talks that way."

Jared frowned at her. "You're annoying."

"What do you mean you're just staying for a couple of days?" Claudia asked.

Jared scratched the back of his head. "It's complicated. We're supposed to be looking at the plants. You guys have a soil acidity issue we had luck solving a few years back. My Watchers are working with your Watchers to fix it, and they dragged us along with them."

"And by 'Watchers' you mean?"

"The guards," Katie said.

"Ah, gotcha," Claudia said. "I like that term, Watchers. We call them the assholes or sons of bitches when they aren't listening, but Watchers is all ominous and shit. But what the hell do you mean 'dragged you along?' Are you two some kind of—I don't know—personal staff of your Watchers?"

"We have an understanding," Jared said.

"With the assholes? What kind of understanding?"

"Windows," Jared said, "for our camp. Right now, our windows are holes in the wall, and it gets cold in the winter. If I can identify and fix the issue, we'll get glass."

"You made a deal with them? What the hell, man?"

"We had two kids die from cold last winter," he said.

"And we had four die of sickness last month."

"And what if they had given you antibiotics to save them in exchange for a job? Would you not have done it?"

"You're dancing with the devil, you know that?" she said.

"When in hell?"

"I don't know about that shit." She held up her hands. "But you do you. Just keep us out of it."

"Shouldn't be a problem," said Jared.

"And what do you do?" Claudia asked Katie.

"I—uh—write better than him, so they brought me too," she said.

Claudia sneered. "Whatever. Bed at the end is open—take your pick of top, bottom, or middle." She walked away, but as they went to their bunk, she cast one more suspicious glance their way.

"How's your—headache?" Jared asked as Addison entered the cell the next morning. He and Katie sat together on Steve's bunk near the door, waiting to be fetched after the others had been sent to work.

"Fine," Addison said. "Gosh, it reeks in here."

"You might not want to come any further," Jared said. "Katie had a discovery last night."

"Bed bugs," Katie said, then let out a stream of curses that rivaled Jared's best. She had been itching all morning after finding little bites on her arms and legs.

Addison's mouth parted. "I am sorry."

"Whatever," Katie grumbled.

"I'm here to fetch you." Addison handed Jared his notebook. "The crops are on this floor, so you won't need any hoods."

Jared and Katie followed her into a hallway. "Where's Clayton?"

"After introductions, he said he was going to take this opportunity to enjoy life," Addison said.

"He's on a bender?"

"He's on a bender."

"The crops are on this floor?"

They came to a large steel door that opened into an enormous warehouse. Rows and rows of marijuana plants in various stages grew underneath artificial grow lights. Some of the plants were almost the height of Christmas trees.

"Holy—" Katie marveled.

"Well, this is just great," he said as he flipped through the notebook. "No one told me the freaking plants were grown inside. Not a word. Not a mention. I have records of temperatures fluctuating as if they were outside, and a weekly rainfall count too. Who the hell has been filling this thing out?"

Addison laughed. "I guess we can't all be geniuses."

"Geniuses? An IQ above seventy would have sufficed."

Addison looked at her watch. "Well, if you need anything, I'll be over there with those two hotties."

Jared and Katie frowned as Addison trotted off to speak with Layne and Blakeney. They were armed with semi-automatic rifles resting on their backs.

"They don't play around," Katie said.

"Yeah, and I wonder how many eight-year-olds they've shot for doing eight-year-old shit."

Katie and Jared spent the entire day as if it were measurement Wednesday. Since the warehouse was so large, Jared assigned each section to a grid. Then he divided the grid into quadrants. Each quadrant had a quarter where at least four plants were evaluated. This included measuring the soil depth, the plant height, leaf color, root depth, as well as about any other thing that could be measured. The missing data was obtained from a couple of Watchers who looked like they had smoked an entire Christmas tree plant.

Katie had never seen Jared so much in his element. He listed off numbers like a song as she struggled to keep up. When he noticed the lower branches were a yellowish color, Jared gave Katie a huge explanation on why that was—which she promptly forgot. Theories regarding the soil irregularities flowed out of his mouth in between numbers. She stopped trying to participate in the discussion about the plants after thirty minutes and just let him talk. Katie began to doubt her earlier promise that she could help him with more than being just his scribe.

Katie also began to wonder if he had forgotten their true mission. Jared appeared oblivious to the odd and sometimes hostile looks they received from the others. Katie attempted friendly smiles but received contemptuous stares. The Watchers let them be, but they too cast their share of curious gazes.

About midway through the day, Jared whispered. "Are you feeling the vibes I'm feeling?"

"The I-want-to-remove-your-liver-with-a-spoon type vibes?"

"You are the empath. Try to hold the notebook facing out so the other workers can see what is written on it. I want it to get back to whoever sent that message what we're carrying."

Katie held the notebook to her side and looked away from whoever might be trying to sneak a peek. The hostile glances did not abate. By dinner time, Katie was relieved the work was over. Jared, however, studied the notebook closely, flipping it back to months past. "Ohh," he said and winked at Katie.

"What?" she said.

"Nothing." Jared closed the notebook. "Nothing at all." The worker closest to them eyed him and wandered off.

*   *   *

"They keep looking at us," Katie said.

"That's because they're talking about us." Jared leaned back against the post of her bunk as they surveyed the other workers chatting in the far corner. He stretched his arms and propped his feet up on the edge of her bed.

Katie glanced at his smelly feet on her already nasty mattress. Jared blushed and put them back on the floor.

"What are they saying?" Katie asked. "Can you read lips?"

"Read lips?"

"Yeah, you're clever. I thought you would know how to do that."

"Even if I were wearing my glasses right now—which are Addison's old pair and not even my prescription—I would only be able to see blurry blobs. You're pretty blurry, and you're close."

"Addison's pair? That explains the butterflies on the rims."

"The what?" He held them to his eyes.

"I'm kidding."

"Ha-ha. Funny."

"I just can't believe I let your blind, shaky-handed self stitch up my face," Katie said.

"And I did a pretty good job, too."

"How would you know? You can't even see it."

He smiled. "Touché."

Katie looked back down the way to see yet another kid look over their shoulder at them before turning away. "Should we go over there?"

"If we go over there, they will consider us interlopers. Hopefully that Claudia girl will approach us soon. Then, if one of them is a snitch, they'll try to lure us into giving something away. And if the message was genuine, hopefully they'll try to get more information."

"So, either way they're going to be asking us questions that could compromise us?"

"Uh . . ."

"How do you tell which is which?"

Jared scratched his head. "It's going to be more or less a feeling?"

"Great. We're trusting your gut now."

*　　*　　*

It took Katie longer to fall asleep knowing her mattress was infested with bed bugs. To add insult to injury, the lice activity was so profound she could feel them skittering over her scalp. After a long time of tossing and itching, she managed to fall asleep beneath her inadequate blanket.

Katie woke to a hand clamping down over her mouth. Hands seized her, and she was dragged out of bed. She tried to call for

Jared, but the hand muted the noise to a moan. As Katie was forced down onto her belly, her hands were secured behind her with a blanket rolled tightly into rope. Someone managed to get a gag in her mouth.

From the continued scuffling, Katie could tell Jared was lasting longer than her, but then someone cried out, "I've got his knife!" The distinctive sound of fist hitting flesh sounded, and her eyes burned as she strained to see. When she tried to wiggle free, the kid on top of her pulled her hair.

*   *   *

While Jared was dazed from the blow to the face, the workers pinned him against the bunk bed ladder, and someone on the other side gripped him around his chest. Another fist flew into his face followed by a body shot.

"You think you can make a fool of me, you son of a bitch traitor?" Steve took another shot, and Jared's stomach heaved. His eyes moistened as he sucked in air through the gag. Think. Think. How the hell to get out of this one?

"Enough," Claudia said.

Steve shuffled back, and Jared relied on the kid behind him to hold him up. A finger, slender and cold, brushed beneath his chin.

"I'm going to take out your gag," said Claudia, "but if you raise your voice above a whisper, I'll slit your throat. Do you understand?"

Jared managed a nod, and she slid the gag down.

"Alrighty then, darling," he said in his best Southern drawl. "Just how can I help you?"

"Do not play games with me," she said. "I will kill you."

"Then do it," he breathed.

Claudia hesitated, and he knew where they stood.

"Where's Katie?" he asked.

"We killed her."

"Bullshit. But I want to hear her voice. She has nothing to do with this. She shouldn't be harmed."

"Do you not think I will kill you?" Sharp metal pressed against his throat nicking his skin.

"You would have already had you wanted to, sweetheart," said Jared. "But you want me to answer your questions first. You need me to answer your questions. You need to know how much I've already told the Watchers."

"Told the Watchers about what?" She pressed the knife firmer, and he winced. His trembling worsened, but he forced himself to focus.

"About what you've done," he said.

Claudia was silent.

"Katie. Now."

When the gag was removed, Katie spoke quickly. "Please, don't hurt him, Claudia. I know he's an ass, but—" The words cut off.

Jared bit his lip then winced as his teeth found a cut. Not the greatest defense from his side-kick, but he'd take it.

"Now, what have you told them?" Claudia demanded.

Jared lunged at her. He had long since worked his way through the thick knot of the blanket leaving only the grasp of the kid behind him. He torqued Claudia's arm backward, wrenching the knife away. Wrapping his arm around her neck, he pulled her to the floor and pressed the blade against the soft flesh of her neck.

The sound of shuffling feet echoed off the concrete walls.

"Stay back!" Jared whispered. "Stay back, or I slit her throat."

The others stopped advancing, and he scooted himself and Claudia along the floor until his back came against the wall.

Claudia tried to elbow him in the gut, and he tightened his grip around her neck. "Stop!" He shook her roughly. "I won't hesitate like you did."

"You scum! You won't do it. Your hands are shaking."

"My hands always shake. That won't stop me from dragging this blade across your throat."

"If you kill me, they will kill you and Katie. You can't take on all of them."

"No, I can't," he said. "But I will take at least three more with me. Don't let it come to that."

That shut her up.

"Now listen to me, Claudia," he said. "I am not a snitch, and I am not your enemy."

"Says the guy with a knife at my throat."

"You had one to mine first, sweetheart."

"You work for the Watchers," she said. "You're a traitor!"

"That's a common misconception," he said. "I work for my people, not the Watchers. If I worked for them, don't you think I would have hollered for them by now? But I'm not here for them. I'm here for you."

"What the hell is that supposed to mean?" Claudia said.

Jared adjusted his grip on the blade. "About a month ago, you sent out a tiny message on one of the data sheets. One word. Hello. That was you, wasn't it? And you got a reply from someone named JAK."

"I don't know what you're talking about."

"Then you sent another word. 'Help.' And that's why I came, Claudia. To help. I am JAK."

She laughed. "No—no—you're not JAK. You can't be JAK."

"J-A-K are my initials. Jared Adam Kelley."

"You are a liar. JAK is a grown man. He works in a lab. He's on the outside. He can't be you."

Jared placed his forehead against the back of her head. "I'm sorry, but no. I am JAK. People don't contact me out of the blue, Claudia. I go to the camps with some—bullshit about the plants. Then I teach the workers the code and how to contact me. It's all very clear."

"No." She shook her head again. "You can't be JAK. You just can't be."

"I know. I'm a sorry excuse for a knight in shining armor."

"A knight in armor?" she exploded. "I was hoping for some cops in Kevlar!"

"I am sorry. How did you even know how to contact me?"

"It was just a rumor," she said. "A myth from a transfer that you could contact someone through the sheets."

He nodded. "I have no interest in killing you, Claudia. Can I put my knife away, or is Steve here going to brain me?"

"Steve will stand down. Right, Steve?"

"It doesn't matter." Jared stowed his knife. "Regardless, I'm not going to kill you, but please, leave Katie out of this. She's done nothing wrong."

Claudia held her throat as she moved away, but Steve did not approach. "Let the girl go. We should talk more about this in the light."

"Agreed. We have much to talk about." Jared relied heavily on the wall to right himself now that the adrenaline had ceased. Holding his stomach, Jared limped back to their corner, and Katie join him on the way.

As Katie lay on her bunk, he sat at the foot of her bed. "Are you guarding me?" she asked.

"Yes." He leaned against her bedpost and brushed his fingers over his ribs, wincing as the pain roared.

"Should I stay awake too?"

"No," he said through gritted teeth. Clenching his shaking fist, he dug his nails into his palm and forced his breath to steady. "I don't feel much for sleeping now. Go ahead and rest." Within moments, Jared heard Katie's even breathing and wondered how the heck she did that.

UNDER A BUSHEL

Katie sat up rubbing her eyes as the bare bulb attempted to blind her awake. Once her vision cleared, she noted the figure still sleeping against her bed post. "Jared!" she cried.

"What?" He jolted awake. "What's wrong?"

"No, it's just . . ." Katie scratched her head. "You're covered in blood."

His face was bruised and swollen from where he had been beaten the night before. In the darkness, he had smeared blood across his face and onto his clothes. Jared flaked some of it off onto his fingers. Groaning, he swiveled his legs to the floor and braced his ribs to stand.

"Are they broken?" Katie asked.

"Bruised, I think." Wincing, he hobbled past the bunks to the sink on the far wall. As he passed, Claudia bit her lip, but Steve leaned against his bunk and glared. Upon reaching the sink, Jared doused his face with water.

Claudia approached them, grimacing. "Here." She handed him a bit of cloth. Jared ran it over his face, but it only removed the first layer of grime. "Let me." She reached for the cloth.

"I'll do it." Katie practically pushed the other girl out of the way. She brought the cloth to Jared's face and sponged away the blood.

Claudia stood aside wringing her hands. "About last night . . ."

Jared's face remained neutral, neither angry nor accepting. Claudia shook her head and fell into silence. Katie tried to decipher his thoughts as well, unsure as Claudia in what he planned to do. But she followed his lead, held her head up, and said nothing. In her opinion, after getting the crap beaten out of you, one had a right to hold a grudge.

When Katie finished, Jared took the bloody cloth and washed it in the sink before handing it back.

"Thanks." He stepped past Claudia toward their bunk.

"JAK, wait!" Claudia said, and he turned to her. "What are you going to tell the Watchers about your face?"

Jared bit his lip and walked away.

*   *   *

Four Watchers patrolled the room at breakfast with their semi-automatic rifles at the ready, and Katie kept her eyes firmly on the table for fear of catching their ire. They had said nothing to Jared about his bruises, but when Addison entered the room, even the sound of eating ceased. Jared did not raise his head until Addison was at their table.

"Whoa," she said. One of Jared's eyes was so swollen he peered at her through a slit. "What happened to you?"

Jared played with a splinter in the table. "I fell off a bunk bed."

Addison narrowed her eyes. "A bunk bed? Really?"

"I had a bad dream," he said.

Katie winced and averted her gaze.

"And how many times did you fall off this bunk bed?"

"I don't know," Jared said. "I was asleep."

"You know what?" Addison said. "It's way too early to deal with your bullshit. Come on, Linus is waiting."

Katie helped Jared rise as he clutched his ribs, and they followed Addison to the door. As they moved past Claudia, she nodded to them. Although his face remained flat, Jared offered a quick wink.

Addison stopped outside the door. "Give me your hands." Before zip-tying his wrists, she studied his hands. "Didn't even get in a punch. Goldie, what happened?"

"I fell off a bunk bed."

"The bunks are stacked three high," Katie said. "It was a heck of a—"

"Now you've got her lying too?" said Addison. "Why are you protecting them? They aren't your people."

"They are all my people," Jared said.

Addison frowned and pulled a bag over his head.

*   *   *

"What happened to him?" Linus asked the moment the bags came off.

Addison sat down in the upholstered chair as Katie and Jared continued to stand in the office entryway. "He fell off a bunk bed," she said.

Linus narrowed his eyes. "Yes, I've heard those bunk beds can be quite vicious."

A small smile tugged at the corner of Katie's mouth as Jared kept his eyes on the floor.

Linus leaned back in his seat. "Tell me, Golden Boy, what do you think about my little operation?"

"Your irrigation system needs flushing," Jared said.

Addison stifled a laugh as the man's face fell.

"I'll make a note of it," Linus sneered. "Did you find the cause of the pH conundrum?"

"I'm still working on it," Jared said. "I'll give you a preliminary assessment tomorrow, but the final evaluation won't be available until the labs come back."

"And when will that be?"

"About a month," Addison said.

"I also have concerns about your workers," Jared said. "Their diet is lacking in some essential proteins. We upgraded our food a few years ago with some notable positive effects. Addison has that information if you would care to see it."

"Hmm," Linus said. "You're here for the plants. Not the workers."

"I'm here to increase your productivity," Jared said. "Your workers are an integral part of that."

Linus narrowed his eyes again. "Indeed. Any other—suggestions?"

"Not at this time."

"And how about you?" he asked Addison. "Any update from your boss about my offer?"

Addison shrugged. "He's not interested in selling. He's got a good thing going, and he plans on keeping it for as long as possible."

"Fine," Linus said between clenched teeth. "Back to work, I suppose."

Addison led them away. Once they reached the elevator, however, Jared asked, "Is it me, or is that guy creepy as hell?"

Addison laughed. "It's not just you. Were you afraid we'd actually sell you to him?"

"I'd be lying to say it hadn't crossed my mind."

"It would be hard for Ian to make a deal he knows nothing about," Addison said. "I told you, Goldie. No way in hell."

*   *   *

"To send you 'A,'" Claudia said as she leaned over the datasheet. "I would prick a 5 and a 3?"

Claudia, Katie, and Jared sat on her bunk as Jared showed her the details of encrypting their communications.

"Right," Jared said. "And if you want to indicate the number you've chosen, prick it twice."

"But what if my next 3 is at the bottom of the page?"

"That is the beauty of decimals. Say your temp is 74.4. That 0.4 is negligible. Change it to 74.3. Fudge some of the numbers—within reason of course." Jared looked to Katie. "Do you have it finished?"

She handed him the notebook filled with squares starting with the seventh letter of the alphabet. The letters then went by sevens the whole way through, omitting Z. With this method, he would be able to recreate the code once they were home.

"Put this code somewhere safe. Memorize it if you can, then destroy it." He tore the paper from the notebook and handed it to her. "There is another matter we need to discuss, and I don't think you're going to like it. There is actually a pH imbalance going on in the grow beds."

Claudia rolled her eyes as she tucked the paper into her pocket.

"Exactly half of your grow beds are too acidic," he continued. "And the other half are too alkaline."

"That has nothing to do with us."

"So . . . you didn't put all the lime in half the beds and none in the others?" he asked, and her lip curled. "Next you'll be telling me you haven't been pissing on the plants either."

"Why do you care, anyways? So, they don't make as much money this year. Big deal. Those bastards don't deserve any better."

"Claudia," Katie said. "Exactly half of the grow beds. That's not chance. The Watchers are going to see through that easily."

"Then fudge the numbers."

"I will," Jared said. "To cover my own tracks. But you still need to fix the problem."

"Why?" she said. "If you keep fudging the numbers . . ."

"They'll catch on," Katie said. "When the production numbers don't increase, they'll know something's up."

"Those morons won't notice anything. They haven't yet, anyways."

"How long have you been here, Claudia?" Jared asked. "Two, maybe three years? And you think that's impressive, don't you?"

She crossed her arms.

"I've been doing this for ten years. I know these people better than my own damn parents. If I don't give them real, lasting results, they will catch on. And at the end of the season when nothing has improved, they'll get someone else to look at your product, and I won't be there to help you."

"Claudia," Katie said, "he knows what he's doing. You need to trust him."

Claudia was silent for a long time. "What do you want me to do?"

"In about a month," he said, "you're going to receive some instructions from me. Follow them."

"That's it?"

"That's it. I'll take care of the rest." He stood. "Now, if you'll excuse me, ladies, there's a matter I'd like to discuss with Steve."

"Oh, please, don't get into a fight with him," Claudia said. "Last night was my fault, not his."

Jared smiled. "Steve's liable to kill me if I fight him. I'm just going to show him how to tie a proper knot is all."

Jared crossed the room to where Steve sat chatting with some of the other workers. Bewilderment filled his face as Jared explained what he was going to teach him. He borrowed Steve's blanket and wound it tightly. Claudia shook her head, and Katie laughed.

"I don't know if I've ever met anyone quite like your friend there," Claudia said. "Friend, boss—lover?"

"He's not my lover," Katie said.

"Hmm," Claudia said. "But you have feelings for him, am I right?"

She sighed. "That's a complicated question. I just found out he likes me."

"He's a complicated guy. At first meeting, you just want to smack him."

Katie stretched and leaned her head against the wall. "My friend once told me that Jared is a good kid, he just forgets it sometimes. It took me a while to figure out what he meant. He's super loyal and very protective—especially of his sister."

"Protective, huh?" Claudia said. "That's a damn valuable thing to have around here."

"It's just—he's not the kind of guy I would typically go for, you know?"

Claudia laughed. "What do you like? Tall, dark and handsome?"

"Maybe? Kind of?" Katie said. "There was this kid at school I liked. He had the whole coiffed hair and all. He played in this band and talked about music all the time. He was really passionate about it, you know? But all that seems silly now."

"He sounds adorable," Claudia said.

"Yeah," Katie laughed. "That's one way to put it."

"So, Jared's a five-foot lightweight." Claudia shrugged. "You know it's not his fault."

"Of course, it's not his fault. Nobody picks that stuff."

"No," she said. "You don't understand me. He's been here, what? Ten years, he said? With the stuff they're feeding us?"

"You think his growth was stunted or something?"

"I'd say in the real world, your friend there would be as handsome as your at-home sweetheart."

Katie watched as Jared secured the blanket around Steve's hands and gestured for him to try to get free. Of course, Steve was unable to do so. An impish smile played at the corners of Jared's mouth as he continued to give pointers to the crowd. Meanwhile, a humiliated Steve tugged at the blanket. In frustrated surrender, Steve held his hands to Jared. "You gonna untie me?"

"Oh, sorry," Jared said. Steve glared at him, but he waited patiently as the knot was undone. Claudia giggled.

Katie smiled too, but the smile did not reach her eyes. Anger boiled at the atrocities done to him—to her—and to all the people who had become so important to her in such a small time.

Jared suggested they say goodbye that night. There was, after all, not much else for them to do. All the samples had been taken and sent. Claudia had been trained on the correct way to collect data with some added secret instructions. It was only logical to assume they would be leaving soon.

Right after breakfast, Addison fetched them, and they were taken once more to meet Linus. "You told me you were going to give me a preliminary report?" he asked.

"Yes," Jared said. "It all goes back to your irrigation system."

"You think a clogged pipe is causing this?"

"No, but I noticed a bluish-green discoloration around your pipes. That's typically indicative of acid contamination. Are we near a city, by chance?"

"We're in the middle of a city, boy," he said boredly. "What's your point?"

"Acid rain. Wherever you're getting your water from, it's contaminated with carbon dioxide. They make products that can neutralize—"

"I was told there was a high pH problem too?"

"That is where the clogged pipe comes in. When I advised you to put lime on the plants, it was based on the assumption that some of it would rinse off. It did not, so the soil became too alkaline."

"Fine. Your recommendation on that?"

"Flush out the system and reapply the lime to the needed areas. Exact amounts will follow in the comprehensive report."

"Alright. I'm done with you now." He shooed Jared back and looked to Addison. "You, however, did not level with me about the deal I was trying to make."

"I'm sorry?" she said.

"You didn't tell me he was defunct." Linus shook his hand in the air mimicking Jared's tremor. "As a serious buyer, I expected to have been given that courtesy."

"He wasn't for sale," Addison said. "I was not required to tell you anything."

"Don't think I won't keep this in mind the next time I do business with you," he said, but Addison rolled her eyes and led them out.

Clayton rejoined them at the car, still a little intoxicated from his bender. He said nothing, but climbed into the passenger seat and kicked his feet up on the dash. Jared sighed before climbing into the trunk. He scooted over to allow as much space as possible for Katie, and soon they were plunged into darkness once more.

"I'm not sure which is worse," Jared said. "Coming and not knowing how long it will take to get there, or getting back into this thing after being out of it for a while."

The trip was long and boring, but Katie was able to nap easier. She startled awake, however, when Clayton's voice croaked over the intercom. "Goldilocks," he said.

Jared's head hit the ceiling. "Yes, sir?"

"You're making dinner tonight. Chicken parmesan."

"Chicken parmesan?" Rubbing his head, he repeated the absurd request under his breath. "That's a bit intensive, isn't it?" he said aloud.

Suddenly, the tires locked, and Jared collided into the wall of the trunk with Katie landing on top of him. The sound of a horn honking penetrated through their cell.

"Okay, okay!" Jared said. "Fine, chicken parmesan it is."

"Wonderful," Clayton said. "What ingredients do you need?"

Jared rattled off a list.

"Sounds good." He clicked off.

"He's a real piece of work." Katie extracted herself to the other side of the trunk. "Son of a—"

Jared placed his hand over her mouth. "Shh—"

Clayton was listening.

*   *   *

"Never been here before," Jared said gazing around the garage.

"Neither have I." Addison gestured for him to go forward before pulling Katie out of the trunk. "Can't say you're going to like your quarters."

Katie's lip turned up as she surveyed the cell for the night. It was a small room beneath the stairs lined with bricks. The floor was a bare slab, and a single bulb lit the room, casting odd shadows on the ubiquitous markings—names and addresses carved in the brick. There was no mattress or blankets. Neither of them could stand upright unless they went to the end of the room.

"It's better than the trunk," Katie sighed.

"I half expected the door to be covered in fingernail marks," Jared said, and Katie shuddered.

Addison returned a few minutes later with an air mattress that filled the entire space and a set of sheets. Jared found a nail that slid easily in and out of a hole in the stairs, and they set to work carving their names.

A quarter-hour later, the door swung open, and Katie hid the nail behind her back. Clayton peered into the poorly lit room. "Come on, Goldie. Ingredients are on the counter."

After tying Jared's hands, Clayton pulled him into the hall. "Don't be getting any ideas. The curtains are drawn in all the rooms.

You're going to do your job and nothing more. I'll be watching." The door closed, and Katie was left alone in the room.

Katie lay on the mattress and stared at the bulb. After a few moments, she looked away and followed the blue blotches that appeared. Afterwards, she stared at the walls, counting the number of kids who had come before her.

Finally, the door opened again, and Jared appeared holding a paper plate with one of the most delicious-looking meals Katie had ever seen. Either that or she was so hungry that a normal meal looked amazing. As Addison cut his bond, he handed the plate to her and she shoved noodles into her mouth.

"That's for both of us," he said as he joined her on the mattress.

"Sorry," she said with a full mouth.

Having nothing else to use, Jared separated the chicken and the noodles into two portions with his hands.

"This is good," said Katie.

"Thanks," he muttered.

"You've got—you've got a little something on your ear." She brushed away some tomato sauce.

"Clayton threw his sauce at my face."

"He's relentless, isn't he? He reminds me of this kid at school. I can only imagine what this kid would be like if he had unlimited power like Clayton does."

Jared slid a noodle around the plate. "Yeah, well, Clayton's a grown-ass adult. I wish he'd pick on someone his own age—or size."

"So . . . Addison?"

He laughed. "If he wanted to end up dead, he could try that. Actually, I wish he would. An attack against Midas's niece would be an insult to him, and Midas would cut out his entrails. I wonder if there's some way we can arrange that . . ."

They spent the rest of the evening imagining schemes to dethrone Clayton or cause a conspiracy. Katie fell asleep next to her friend feeling safer than she had in months. Jared, however, dreamt all night about being buried alive.

*　　*　　*

"Breakfast time!" Clayton grabbed a sleeping Jared by the shirt and pulled him out of the closet. The door closed behind him.

Jared blinked in the sudden light as night-time crusties tried to keep his eyes glued shut. Clayton cinched the zip ties tight around his wrist, biting into his skin, but Jared forced his face to stay neutral, determined not to give him the satisfaction.

Clayton scowled as if his fun has been lost, shoved Jared into the kitchen, and snarled, "Go at it."

Laminate floors, cabinets, and countertops filled the room. Jared could have set up his own laminate shop had it not been for the smell of skunk weed and burnt something. Burnt shoe? He had tried last night to locate the true source, but without success.

Between the stove and food-encrusted sink was a workspace the length of one cabinet. This countertop had been sticky and gray yesterday too, but Jared had bleached it white. Couldn't Midas hire a maid for these places? But then again, he'd have to find one who wouldn't look in the creepy closet.

Last night, Clayton had left groceries on the counters, but there were no ingredients out this time. Jared didn't want to talk to Clayton as their conversations generally ended up with him slammed up against a wall, but not clarifying the meal orders would result in the same treatment. "What do you want for breakfast?" he asked.

"There's eggs and bacon in the refrigerator. Figure it out, genius." Clayton smacked him on the back of the head and moved to the table while Jared glared at his back. One day—just one day without getting smacked around by him would be nice. At least he didn't live at the camp anymore. Jared would be out of teeth by now.

Jared found the supplies in the refrigerator and set to work. The task proved much harder with his hands bound, but he dared not complain. Clayton sat at the table across from the kitchen with his ridiculous hat next to him, spinning his gun in a circle.

Addison flipped her crazy, pink hair as she came into the kitchen some time later. "Good morning." She nodded to Jared.

"Morning." He added a slosh of milk to the eggs but then paused to sniff the carton. The smell wasn't coming from there.

He leaned over the sink and caught a nose-full of burnt shoe. What the hell was rotting down there?

"Did you get a hold of your girlfriend?" Addison asked Clayton as she poured a cup of coffee and joined him at the table.

Jared paused with his fork in the scrambled eggs. *How the hell do sociopaths get girlfriends?*

"She called this morning." Clayton holstered his weapon. "She said she had a busy day and went to bed early."

"That sounds reasonable."

"Yeah," he muttered. He didn't sound sure, and Jared rolled his eyes.

"You turned the jammer back on after you spoke with her though, right?" Addison asked.

"What do you take me for?" Clayton said. "Of course, I turned it on."

Jared divided the food onto two plates. Damn, why did the bacon have to cook so quick? But, knowing Clayton was watching his every move, he did not dawdle longer. Jared closed his eyes and took a deep breath before turning to them. He tried to still the tremor, but his hands shook as he set the plates rattling onto the table.

Moment of truth.

Even Addison watched with breath held as Clayton raised his fork to his mouth. His face screwed up, and Jared winced.

"Augh!" he cried, spewing the eggs onto the plate. "These are horrible. What the hell did you do, Goldie? I wouldn't feed my dog this shit."

Jared braced for impact. Clayton grabbed his hair and smashed his face into the plate of eggs. Blood oozed into the eggs from his nose and his eyes watered.

"Clayton!" Addison said. "Don't do that."

Clayton smeared the eggs into his hair and face. "Are you trying to poison us?"

"I'll make another batch," Jared said through gritted teeth. "Tell me what you want in them, and I'll make them." *Like you should have the first time, asshole.*

"You'll fail at that too. I don't know why Midas still keeps you around, you worthless piece of shit." Clayton poured his coffee over Jared's head.

Jared gasped as the hot liquid doused him.

"Clayton!" Addison tried again. "Come on. Leave him alone."

Like that's going to work. Jared eyed the gun at Clayton's belt. He inched his hands closer to it. Then a knock sounded at the door, and everyone froze.

"Open up!" a voice shouted as another knock rang through the house. "It's the police!"

The police? Shit. Jared wished he were back in the closet.

Clayton slid his gun out of the holster and let go of Jared's hair. "Get rid of them," he said to Addison. "If you don't answer it, they'll break down the door. And if he does that, I'm putting two in Goldie's chest."

"What?" Addison exclaimed.

Clayton yanked back on the slide, and Jared jumped. "Midas's orders. He knows too much. Now answer the damn door."

Addison met Jared's eye with a look of terror before moving to the next room. Clayton pointed to a corner beside the refrigerator, and Jared slid against the wall to the floor in the indicated spot. He brought his knees to his chest in hopes of giving Clayton a smaller target. A bit of egg slid off his head.

The door in the next room opened. "Hello? Can I help you?"

Clayton put a finger to his lips and sat at the table; Jared continued to stare down the barrel of the gun. *Come on, Addison. Work your magic. Get rid of him.*

"Officer Vermire," the man said. "There was a disturbance reported here by one of your neighbors." Jared tilted his head. A disturbance? The house had been silent all morning.

"I don't know anything about that," Addison said.

"I'd like to come in, please," he said, and Clayton pulled back the hammer of the pistol. Jared gulped.

"Why?" Addison said. "There's only my husband and me inside, and we're just eating breakfast."

Vermire paused. "You know, you're pretty good. Thing is though, I know who you are and why you're here."

Jared's heart beat like a jackhammer.

"I'm—sorry?" she said.

"Let's cut the crap, shall we?" There was scuffling in the other room.

"You can't do that!" Addison said. "This is private property."

The officer rounded the corner, his hand on his holster. He stopped short upon seeing Jared on the floor with Clayton holding him at gunpoint. Jared held the officer's gaze, shaking his head, begging him not to pull.

"What's going on here?" asked the officer.

"What does it look like?" Clayton asked.

"I'd say it looks like a hostage situation." The officer folded his arms across his chest. "Who's the kid? One of the marks?"

Jared dropped his head to his chest. Of course.

"He's a Comm." Clayton un-cocked his gun. "Marks are the parents. How are you doing, Harry?"

He frowned. "It's Harold. What the hell is a Comm?"

"A Commodity." Clayton stowed his gun, and Harry nodded.

"You two know each other?" Addison said.

Duh, Addison. It's why I'm still breathing. Jared stared at the baseboard on the opposite wall. Damn dirty cops. It was better than eating a bullet, but still, bad guys pretending to be good guys set his teeth on edge. Why couldn't he ever meet one the other way around? An undercover or something?

"We do," Harry said. "Clayton's my confidential informant."

Addison's eyes widened, but Jared rolled his eyes.

"Vermire is on the payroll." Clayton popped a bit of bacon in his mouth.

Officer Vermire smiled at Addison. "And who might you be?"

"Get bent," she said.

"Vermire," Clayton said, "why the hell are you here?"

"I got word you might be coming by. I want to talk."

"You have a way of contacting us," Clayton said, "and this isn't it."

"I'm tired of going through your damn call center. Press one for English. Press two for Spanish. Then sit on hold for twenty minutes while you dickheads round up the nearest manager who actually knows something. Then they say they'll run it through HR and get back to me, which they never do."

"Okay!" Clayton held up a hand. "I get it. What do you want?"

"I want a bigger cut."

Clayton frowned. "A raise? You barge in here like this because you want a raise?"

"You see this button?" Vermire tapped on the radio fixed to his shoulder. "All I have to do is press this button, and back up will be here in less than a minute. And I wonder what they're going to do when they see you here with a missing kid."

Moron.

"So, I suggest you get on the phone with your boss and get me that raise." Vermire grinned.

Clayton cleared his throat. "And how much do you want?"

"Ten thousand," he said. "A week."

"Ten thousand?" Clayton said.

"You heard me."

"Okay," Clayton sighed. "I'll make the call." He went into the other room, and Jared resisted the urge to roll his eyes again. This guy was out of his mind.

"Whose kid is this?" Vermire's heavy shoes thudded across the linoleum as he moved to lean over Jared. The hair on Jared's neck rose, and he kept his eyes on the floor.

"I believe that would be filed underneath 'none of your business,'" Addison said.

"House-broke, I take it. Otherwise, I assume, he'd be locked up and not out here." Vermire squatted down in front of him. He lifted Jared's chin with his finger, but Jared didn't meet his eyes. The shaking started again, and he cursed himself internally.

"Damn, you do have him trained," said Vermire. "Do you got some girls hiding in the back too?"

Addison frowned. "No, only him."

Jared made a note to thank Addison for that later.

Vermire grinned at Jared showing a tooth broken in half. "This one does whatever you tell him to, huh?"

"He made breakfast this morning," Addison said.

"Did he now? And supposing I were to take him into that back room—what do you think he would do for me in there?" he asked and tightness gripped Jared's throat.

"Yeah, that's not going to happen," Addison said.

"Hold on there, honey. I don't think that's your call to make. Let's wait until the boss man comes back round off that phone."

Addison laughed. "Listen, you little weasel, you have no idea what's going on or who you're dealing with. Do you think your little stunt here is going to work?"

"Come off it, girl. I know how this works. I've been a valuable employee, and I deserve to be compensated. Now, about the boy?"

"We're not in that line of work. He's a farmhand."

"Farmhand that knows how to cook. He might be capable of other skills." Vermire pulled his baton off his belt and ran it against Jared's cheek. "Am I right about that, blondie?"

Jared turned his head away. Damn this man. If he thought he would have him easy, he was mistaken. The knife hidden in his secret pocket at the small of his back pressed into him.

"Look at me," Vermire said, and Jared's lip curled into a sneer.

"That's enough," Addison said.

"Uhm . . ." Clayton returned. "What's going on?"

Vermire stood and put the baton back into its holster. "What did they say?"

"They'll be here in twenty minutes."

"Twenty minutes." Vermire smiled again. "Then we have time to kill. What if I offer you a deal? For one hundred dollars of the ten thousand coming to me, how about I take the boy into the back room for twenty minutes?"

Clayton sneered. "Hundred dollars, huh?"

"We can negotiate."

Clayton's eyes lingered on Jared. "I don't give a shit about what you do to him," he said, and Vermire's smile widened.

Jared paled.

"But my boss has a deal worked out with the kid," he continued. "I don't think he'd be much in favor of me selling him like that. Sorry."

"Two hundred. And your boss doesn't have to know."

Addison laughed. "Oh, he'll hear about it."

"A word of advice," Clayton said. "Learn to take no for an answer."

Jared's brows knit. That was not the answer he expected. Midas wanted him alive, sure, but otherwise?

Vermire frowned. "What the hell is he good for then?"

"He makes good scrambled eggs," Clayton said. "Goldie—cook the man some eggs. And fry up what's left of that bacon."

So, Clayton liked his eggs after all. Jared needed no further prompting to leave his spot and set to work quickly. He had to slow himself down and control his heartbeat, as his tremor was so violent it would cause him to drop the utensils.

"Come on over here, Vermire, and have a seat." Clayton patted the chair closest to the kitchen.

Jared set up his supplies on the counter and pondered the probability of finding Drano nearby. He pulled the eggs back out of the refrigerator.

Reluctantly, Harry took the chair. "These eggs better be as good as you say."

An explosion rocked the room, and the carton of eggs crashed to the floor.

"What the hell?" Addison shouted.

With his shoulders raised to his ears, Jared turned to see Clayton standing behind Officer Vermire, his gun still smoking. The cop slumped from the chair to the floor, and blood pooled around him, mixing with the eggs Jared had dropped.

"What did you do?" Addison said. "I thought you said—"

"I told him they would be here in twenty minutes," Clayton said. "They're coming to collect the body. Vermire has become more trouble than he's worth."

"But he's a cop," she said. "You just killed a cop."

Jared touched his hair and saw blood on his fingers. Addison and Clayton continued arguing, but he didn't hear it. Instead, he stared at the crumpled body. The man's eyes looked up at him.

"Jared!" a muffled voice called from the other room. Pounding came from within the house.

"What the hell?" Clayton pushed past Jared into the next room. The door beneath the stairs creaked open. "Quiet!"

"Where's Jared?" Katie cried. "What did you do to him?"

"I said be quiet!"

Jared continued to stare at the doorway until Clayton returned.

"What are you gawking at?" Clayton said. "Go get some towels and clean this up."

CLEAN DEATH

"What the hell is this?" A woman in her sixties and two men entered from the garage into the kitchen. "Please, tell me that's not a Comm."

Jared sat back on his haunches. He had wrapped Vermire's body in a shower curtain and was busy mopping blood up with a towel. Blood spatter littered the room, marring the cabinets, the walls, even parts of the ceiling.

"He's fine," Clayton said as he sat at the table playing with his gun. "Kid's a relic. He won't cause trouble."

"Amateurs," the woman muttered. "Kyle, get him a spare set of clothes from the car. That's good enough, boy. Get up and go take a shower."

Jared closed the lid of the bleach and tossed the towel onto the body. Blood streaked up Jared's arms to his elbows, and he had been contemplating on how to get it off without a sink. A shower sounded fantastic.

Kyle returned with a set of clothes, and Jared followed him to the bathroom. When Jared saw himself in the mirror, he startled. His blonde hair and shirt were bloody in patches, and his back was covered in spray. Not to mention, his face was still bruised from his encounter with Steve, and a trail of his own blood ran down from his nose after his other close encounter with a plate of eggs. After undressing, he flipped on the water and stepped into the curtainless shower. He scrubbed and scrubbed at his hair and neck. The water around his feet turned pink.

After Jared had showered, Addison took him back to the room beneath the stairs. Katie looked over her shoulder from where she lay face down on the mattress. Clayton had bound and gagged her, but she looked relieved to see him.

"Listen to me," Addison whispered. "I'm going to tie you up."

"A bit redundant isn't it," Jared said. "Tying me up inside a locked room."

"Shut up, will you? We're in some deep shit, don't you get that? I swear you'll be the death of me." Addison cut the bonds in front and secured his hands behind his back. She lowered him onto his belly and tied his feet. "I don't care how uncomfortable you—or Katie—get. I don't care how badly your nose itches. You stay tied up and gagged. Take a nap even."

"Take a nap?" Jared scoffed. "How the hell am I supposed to take a nap? Some guy got his head blown off in front of me."

"Figure it out." She slipped the gag into his mouth. After blindfolding both of them, she closed the door behind her.

"Jared?" Katie said through her gag.

He rolled to face her. "I'm here. Are you okay?

"Huh?"

"Are you okay?" he tried to speak clearer through the gag.

"I'm scared. Are you okay?"

"My ears are ringing."

"What?"

He sighed. "Never mind. I'm okay." But he shook so badly, the whole mattress quaked.

"Are we going to die?" Katie whispered.

"No, we're going to be okay," he said, but she started to cry. Jared scooted close to her on his stomach. With some effort, he took her hand and held it. "We're going to be fine." Meanwhile, the vision of Vermire's exploded head remained frozen in his mind.

∗   ∗   ∗

They waited in the room for hours. Jared kept flip-flopping around, and soon the air started seeping out of the mattress causing them to roll toward each other. Finally, the door opened.

"What the hell is this?" the cleaner woman said above them.

"What?" Addison asked, exasperated.

"The markings on the walls. What is this? Ted Bundy's kill room?"

"I don't know," Addison sighed. "They all do that."

"And you let them?" The woman muttered something beneath her breath. "Get them out of here. And get lost. We'll paint this room over before we go."

After cutting their legs free, the Watchers led them to the car still bound and gagged. They stayed that way until an hour later when they stopped for lunch. There was no time, however, to stretch their legs, and they ate on the road.

"Jared," Katie asked, "what just happened?"

Jared split his burger in two with his fingers. "A cop showed up, and Clayton shot him."

"A cop? Clayton killed a cop?"

"Don't get too torn up about him," Jared said. "He was dirty."

"Are you sure? Because a lot of people would say my dad is a dirty cop. He could have been undercover."

"He wasn't your dad, Katie. And he was very dirty, alright? Just—trust me." Jared rolled his face away from her to hide his tears. Even if she couldn't see them in the dark.

Katie rubbed her raw wrists as she stood on the hill of their camp in the near twilight. How strange. It actually felt good to be home. Addison nodded to both of them before heading inside, and Katie smiled vaguely after her. Was she starting to like one of the Watchers?

"Stockholm Syndrome," she muttered beneath her breath. "Stay away from Stockholm Syndrome."

"Let me see them," Jared said. At first, Katie didn't know what he was talking about, but then realized she was still rubbing her injuries. She showed him the red sores that used to be her wrists.

"Come to my hut, and we'll get them looked after," he said.

After lighting his oil lantern, Jared had Katie sit on his cot while he gathered supplies. "This is going to sting a little," he said as he poured liquid onto some cloth. "Okay, that was a lie. It's going to sting a lot." He wrapped the cloth around her wrist.

"Ah!" Katie pulled away. "What is that stuff?"

"Vodka. Stolen from a stash in Ian's room. Let me see the other one."

Katie frowned at him but begrudgingly held out her other arm. She held her breath in anticipation. "Yeow!" She leapt up from the bed as the cloth touched the wound. "Ow! That burns!"

Humor flitted in Jared's eyes.

Katie snatched the cloth away from him. "Let me see your wrists so you can know how it feels."

He laughed. "I know how it feels."

She grabbed his wrist. There was nothing there but a pink spot. "How the—? Why aren't you all cut up?"

He shrugged as Katie inspected the area closer. His whole wrist was one big callous. "Perks of being a veteran. There aren't many, but . . ."

"That is bizarre." Katie studied the area closer.

"Okay, quit. That's getting weird." He rubbed his wrist. "Here." Katie allowed him to tie the bandage around her wrists.

"We had quite the ride this week, didn't we?" Katie said. "You're alright, aren't you? After Clayton and all, that is."

Jared rubbed the back of his head. "I'll survive," he muttered. "Just another memory to shove into the back."

"How often should I stop by to have you change my bandages?"

He shrugged. "Once in the morning, once at night."

"I'll be seeing a lot of you then?"

"You already see a lot of me."

Katie chuckled. It was time to go to her hut, but she didn't really want to go. After all the time they had spent together, she felt safer here with him. Her hand continued to linger in his calloused grip. He made no move to let go, and neither did she. *What do you want? Tall, dark, and handsome?* Claudia's words floated back to her.

"I don't think that's a bad thing," Katie said in answer to his statement.

He considered her quizzically.

Katie played with her hair. "I guess I should head back to my hut." But she made no move to stand.

Jared laughed. "There's about a 75% chance that I might be getting this wrong again, but . . ."

Jared leaned forward, and Katie closed her eyes. His soft lips met hers, and warmth spread through Katie. He kissed her again, then slid his arm around her waist and pulled her close. Excitement flooded her—but also fear. Katie ran her fingers through his shaggy hair—the smell of soap still lingered on him. Jared kissed her neck and tingles skittered down her arm. He slid his fingers under her shirt and onto the soft skin there. As he kissed her, his hands slid up her body.

Her eyes flew open. What was wrong with her? She didn't want him to stop, but she wasn't ready either. But how could she do this to him again? How could she—but she couldn't keep going either.

"Stop," she whispered.

He didn't hear her, and Katie had to work up the nerve again.

"Stop," she said, and Jared hesitated.

"I'm sorry," she said, her eyes filled with tears. "I'm so sorry."

"What is it?" He slid his hands back to her waist. "What's wrong? Did I hurt you? Did I—?"

"No, I'm sorry—I can't." Tears slid down her face. "I just—I can't."

Jared ran his hands over his face. "What the hell, Katie? These are some mixed-up signals I'm getting."

Biting her lip, Katie glanced at the door. What could she say? He wasn't wrong.

Jared grabbed a rag from the bed and tossed it to her. "If you're going to go, fine. Just wipe your face first. That last girl who left here crying like you caused a world of trouble for me."

"Jared," Katie said, but he sat in his chair with his back to her. She knew she should say something, explain herself, but she didn't know how. So, she wiped her face and left.

"You're back!" Leida slammed the book closed and leapt off her bed when Katie arrived at their hut. "How did it go?" She stepped over the boys playing in the middle of the room. One of them glared at her as she overturned a rock.

"It went . . ." Katie's mind blanked. "It went. Can we talk about it in the morning?"

Leida frowned. "Sure—I guess. How's Jared?"

"He's fine," Katie sighed. She pushed her way past the boys to her bunk, pulled the covers over her head, and pretended to fall asleep. Instead, she let the tears continue beneath the blanket. How could she explain to him what she was not sure of herself? She had feelings for him, but it had all been too fast. Could she even speak to him again?

*　　　*　　　*

"So . . ." Ian leaned on the doorframe of Addison's office and surveyed the chaotic room. Her coffee cup collection had caused a shortage in the kitchen, but there was no point in telling her to return them. They'd all be back in a week. "How did it go?"

Addison glanced over her shoulder before continuing to unpack her travel bag. "Clayton shot a cop."

"I heard about that. Midas said it was long overdue." Ian closed the door behind him.

Addison rolled her eyes.

"I got a call from Linus while you were gone."

She started and turned to him. "How did he get your number?"

Ian frowned. "He asked Midas. Did you really think I wouldn't find out about his wanting to buy Goldie?"

Addison played with a strand of hair.

"That was not your call to make. The boy is close to cracking. It's time we off-load him, the sooner the better."

"He's not some used car you can just off-load like that, Dad," she said.

"He's not your pet either, Addison," Ian said. "He's a Commodity. Nothing more. And if he's not bringing in value . . ."

"He's a child. A boy. And he's this way because of what you've done to him."

"I've barely touched him, Addison. This is Richard's camp. I run the finances, but—"

Addison stood. "You think because you sit all day in your office with your back to them you are not responsible for this? You are the head of the camp!"

"I never wanted any part of this!" shouted Ian. "I'm a tax attorney, not a human trafficker!"

"Says the man sleeping with a teenager!" she shouted back. "That boy is more of a man than you'll ever be. Even after he's been beaten, flogged, threatened—even after you schtuped his girl!"

Ian smacked her with the back of his hand. Addison stumbled back against the blow, tripped on the printer hidden among the clutter, and struck her head on the desk as she fell.

Ian stared blinking at his daughter's body draped awkwardly over the scattered boxes. It was just one blow—it was nothing. Why had she? He knelt next to her and felt under her nose for breath. There was none. Eyes wide, Ian scrambled backward from her body.

Leaping to his feet, Ian sprinted for the door. The halls blurred as he raced past them until he entered his room. Hidden behind his bedroom doors, Ian paced up and down the carpet. He hadn't just—surely that hadn't just happened. He hadn't just killed his daughter.

But if he had then that meant . . .

Ian yanked his suitcase out of his closet and tossed clothes into it. All these years Midas had been threatening to kill Addison if he didn't work with him. But if Addison was dead . . .

Ian was free.

The customary siren roused everyone from their sleep. Then it stopped abruptly and started again. And again.

Katie's hut-mates sat up, rubbing sleep from their eyes when the siren came on again with the same pattern. Everyone was to meet on the hill.

"That's different." Leida scratched her head. "Do you know anything, Katie?"

Katie shook her head. As far as she knew, nothing from their eventful trip would impact any of the other workers here.

Upon leaving their huts, the Watchers ushered the workers up the hill. Jared went with them, stumbling along while putting on his new shoes. Katie offered him a small smile, and while he saw it, his face remained unreadable as he moved past her to speak to Bartram.

Katie continued up the hill with her hut, disappointed but not defeated. She would have plenty of time to talk to him later.

As Jared made his way past the others to the front of the group, Dakota took hold of his sleeve and asked, "What's going on?"

"They won't tell me," Jared said.

"They won't tell you? That's worrisome."

Jared sidestepped Dakota and slipped a shiny silver lump into Leida's hand. The hamburger from yesterday? It vanished under Leida's shirt, and Jared continued on his way.

Katie didn't even know he still had the little morsel and could only imagine the level of self-control it had taken not to eat it. And a realization hit Katie in the gut. Claudia had mentioned how Jared's lack of food might have caused his height to be stunted, but Leida did not appear to be this way. How many meals had Leida received at her brother's expense?

How did a seven-year-old take care of a four-year-old? Any way he could.

Katie's stomach gnawed at the thought. Something told her that while Jared had suffered severe, scarring injuries to his back, Leida had not a mark on hers. Twenty-seven times? Doubtless, nearly half belonged to her. She regretted leaving him last night. He deserved an explanation. If only she had one.

Jared strolled to the top of the hill overlooking all the workers. Their curious faces peered up at their leader, the seventeen-year-old know-it-all who kept them alive by his wits and sacrifice. Jared folded his legs and sat in the grass.

The workers stood looking at each other, wondering what this could mean. Was there no explanation to be given? No orders to be followed? Then Bryan sat down too, and, as his hut followed his lead, the others did too. And they waited.

And waited.

Katie kept feeling Jared's eyes on her, but every time she looked at him, he looked away. She hadn't expected to wait this long to see him and now her mind refused to let her think about anything else. The best explanation she could provide was this: she wasn't ready.

As far as she could tell, there was nothing wrong with him, it was all her. This would be her first time to be with a boy after all, and things had felt a little rushed before. Not that she blamed him for that either—he had just watched some guy get his head blown off and probably wasn't at his best last night either.

The sun rose high overhead, and stomachs growled with hunger, but still, they waited. Katie popped heads off clover flowers while the boys played their silly rock game. Finally, long after noon, Bartram tapped Jared on the shoulder, led him to the side, and spoke in hushed tones. Jared dabbed his eyes and stared at the ground. Was he crying?

"This is not good," Leida whispered to Katie.

Not good indeed. The only time Katie had seen Jared shed a tear was when he told her about Landon. What was going on now?

After giving Jared's shoulder a squeeze, Bartram mounted his stump and addressed the crowd, "A co-worker of mine died last night. Addison is dead."

A couple of kids gasped.

"Addison?" Leida whispered to Katie. "Weren't you with her last night?"

"I was. And she was fine!"

Bartram continued, "We have determined the cause of death, and the events surrounding it, and do not believe any of you were involved. Everyone is to go to their jobs. The next siren you hear will be for lunch. Since you missed breakfast, you will receive double portions for this meal, and then back to usual." He stepped down and nodded at Jared.

"Hut leaders' meeting after lunch," Jared said. "Katie." He motioned to her. "Everyone else—go."

Katie waited for the others to clear out before approaching Jared. "Addison is dead?"

He pinched the bridge of his nose. "This is bad, Katie."

"What happened?"

"She and Ian got into an argument last night. He struck her, and she hit her head on her desk. Tripped over a damn printer—you've seen her office. Anyways, they found her this morning. Ian's halfway to Aruba by now. He called from an airport to confess what he did."

"If Ian's gone, then who's going to run the camp?"

"Bartram for now. Midas's on the way. He'll pick someone when he gets here."

"Jared, I'm sorry."

Jared cleared his throat and started back down the hill. "I need you to help me write a letter to Camp 7. If we have any hope of sending our location, it has to be now."

*   *   *

It didn't take long to put the letter of recommendation together and puncture the necessary holes. Afterward, Jared sent Katie back to her field where kids shuffled around little piles of dirt. They were too weak from hunger to do much else. Finally, the siren sounded, and they trudged into the mess hall.

Katie lingered behind with the other hut leaders after the meal. Jared had taken a bowl back to his hut, so they mingled as they waited for him. No one knew what to make of the news. Addison was dead. Ian was gone. The absence of further information only increased their anxiety.

"Katie," Michelle said. "Can I talk to you for a second?" Katie followed her to the side of the room. "How are—things?"

Katie reddened. "Oh my gosh, he told you. I can't believe he told you!"

"Calm down."

"I don't believe this. Why on earth would he tell you? Is there something going on between you?"

"There is nothing going on between us," Michelle said. "We're just old friends."

"Old friends? Please. Your boyfriend's halfway to Aruba by now."

Michelle bit her lip at the word 'boyfriend,' and a lump lodged in Katie's throat. Of course that wasn't the arrangement.

"Katie," Michelle said, "if there was ever anything going on between us, it's all in the past now. That ship has sailed. Some bridges can't be rebuilt."

"Enough with the clichés, Michelle. What do you want?"

"All I want is to make sure you're alright." Michelle touched her arm and smiled.

"I'm fine," Katie said. "But I don't really want to talk about it."

"Okay." Michelle nodded. "Sorry to pry into your business."

She walked away to talk to Bryan, and suddenly, Katie felt like everyone was looking at her. Did they know? Who else did he tell? She was about to leave when Jared arrived and took his usual seat. Hesitantly, she took her place beside him.

Jared spread his arms wide. "Any questions?"

Katie barely listened to the details of the meeting. There wasn't any additional information anyways. She guessed his asking Michelle to check on her was understandable, especially after Courtney. But there is nothing like talking to your ex about a current interest.

Katie looked between Michelle and Jared. Ian was what stood between them. They had experienced a lot of life together and Katie could not hope to compete with that. Maybe it wasn't meant to be. But that only made her want it more.

Jared heard scuffling behind him and looked over his shoulder. Bryan's head popped over the edge of his hut as he mounted the wood pile onto the roof. He sat down beside Jared and dangled his legs off the edge before offering him a joint.

"No thanks."

"Suit yourself." He lit it.

"You're on a roof. Don't get caught."

"If anyone comes, I'll just hand it to you." Bryan blew out a large puff of smoke. "Who do you think is next in line?"

"You've been here longer than I have. Who do you think?"

"I've been here a month longer than you," he said. "Although, I appreciate the nod. Gives me a badass edge."

Jared smiled.

"Bartram, maybe?" Bryan suggested.

"I doubt it. Bartram sold his gang out to a rival back in the day. I don't think Midas trusts him."

"Probably not Matt. He's too twitchy."

"Honestly," Jared said, "I don't know who he'll pick. I hope it's not some guy like Camp 7's boss. Man, was he creepy." He lit his own cigarette and let out a puff. "Going to these other camps reminds me of how bad it could be. With Addison gone . . ."

"Remember that time she smuggled us an entire lasagna?" Bryan smiled. "Carried it down in her backpack. She never did get the tomato stains out of it."

"Remember the Home Ec. food?"

Bryan laughed. "That was some weird shit. Those kids had no idea what they were doing."

"I'm not going to lie, man, I'm scared," Jared said.

Bryan tapped out the joint.

"Things were looking better for a bit there. We've only buried what? Three people this year? If this new camp head cracks down again—if we're back down to five per day in the kitchens . . ."

"Hey," Bryan said. "We'll figure it out. We'll keep our numbers up and keep them out of our shit."

Jared drew his knees to his chest. "I don't know how much more I can take of this." He buried his face in his hands.

Bryan grabbed his arm. "Stop that. You stay with me, do you understand? We have survived so much, you and I. We will survive this too. But you've got to believe that. You have to trust me."

Jared ran his hands through his hair but nodded.

"Come on." Bryan slapped him on the back. "Show me what you got from this last trip."

He and Jared slid off the roof and entered the hut. Together, they moved the bookcase away from the wall. Jared dusted away a layer of dirt from the ground covering a sheet. Grabbing the edge, he pulled it back revealing stacks of loose papers and notebooks inside and selected the one with the blue cover.

"Okay." Jared slid on his glasses. "The warehouse was approximately 10,000 square feet. It was at least three stories high with an elevator. Concrete floors. . ."

Bryan wrote this information on the backs of the data sheets and hid it with the rest.

*　　　*　　　*

The next morning, Jared took a deep breath as he stood before Ian's office door. He opened and closed his hands several times, attempting to still them. The motion was ineffective. He knocked on the door anyways.

"Enter," Midas's voice came from inside. The door opened, and a knot formed in Jared's stomach to see Clayton standing there.

"Hey there, Goldilocks." Clayton grinned.

"You sent for me?" Jared asked, ignoring him.

"Indeed, I did," Midas said. "I have been in touch with Ian. He's found a nice little beach in Aruba and has no intentions of returning. It seems he finally found the stones to break free." He paused as if expecting Jared to say something, but Jared kept his eyes lowered, so he continued. "Since I am otherwise engaged, I found a new camp head to take his place. You know Clayton, so introductions aren't necessary."

The knot in Jared's stomach tightened.

"Aren't you going to congratulate me, Goldie?" Clayton smirked.

He would rather stab him.

"It's a big promotion, don't you know? The head of a camp—and my mama said I'd never amount to anything."

Jared bit his lip. Still don't.

"You know, Goldie," said Clayton leaning in. "I've been saying for years that you have lived your life with far too many privileges. I've seen how lax this place has gotten since I left. Don't think you're going to be getting away with much anymore. Not while I'm here."

Moisture collected in Jared's eyes, but he forced it back.

"There's a secret to keeping Goldie in line," Midas said, rounding the desk. "You see—Ian was lax with Goldie. He had been for years, but that's because he knew the truth." He pulled a pistol from the small of his back. "Goldie has had a bullet with his name on it for years now, and he'll do anything to avoid meeting it. All you have to do is remind him of that."

He placed the gun against Jared's head and cocked the weapon. Beads of sweat collected on his brow, and the shaking in his hands grew to include his whole body. He closed his eyes.

"Isn't that right, Goldie?" Midas pressed the pistol harder into his temple.

Jared envisioned the bullet passing through Landon's head. His body falling into the empty grave. The feeling of the hot metal against his own skull.

"Because he has to know that at any second—the moment he slips up—you're going to pull that trigger."

The gun clicked, and Jared jumped.

"Oh dear," Midas said. "I forgot to load it again. Silly me."

Jared drew breath between trembling lips. His legs wobbled.

"Gentlemen." Midas bowed. "I have funeral arrangements to make, so I'll be seeing you." He paused at the door. "Ah, the grieving candidate—looks good on any ballot."

Jared continued to tremble as Clayton examined every inch of him. Sizing him up. Looking how best to devour him.

"Where's your little assistant?" Clayton asked.

"She's with her hut," he breathed.

"Have her here by 1 pm. Daddy's requesting another photo."

"Yes, sir."

"I can see now we're not going to have any problems, are we? You are about as harmless as harmless can get. You're a spineless, gutless, toothless dog. And you're going to go out there, and you're going to do whatever the hell it is you do. And when I ask you to do something, what are you going to say?"

"Yes," Jared said.

"Yes, what?"

"Yes, sir."

"Good. Now, get out of here."

Jared sped down the hall as flashbacks of the meeting and of Landon's death played continually in his mind. He ducked into the bathroom and vomited.

"Jared?" Katie asked as she opened the door to his hut. He had told her to come back after lunch, but after several hours of playing the same imaginary conversation in her head with him, she could not wait any longer. But as she entered, a pungent smell burned her nostrils. It was as if the entire camp had been stuffed into his hut and burned.

"What's that smell?" Katie asked.

"It's—nothing," said Jared, who sat at his desk. He knocked over a box, spilling the contents as he turned back to her. "What are you doing here?"

"You told me to join you after lunch, but . . ."

"Right, the photo," said Jared as he moved to the door. "Let's go."

"It's not even noon yet."

"What? Then why are you here?"

"I don't know." She shrugged. Already the conversation was going in a way she did not anticipate. "I thought we should—you know—talk. About the other night. Why are your eyes so red?"

"Hmm?" he said. "Allergies."

"Allergies? Since when have you had allergies?" Then Katie saw the bag of green herbs sitting on the edge of the table. "Have you been smoking pot?"

He frowned. "No."

"But you said you don't smoke it anymore."

Jared tried to move to the door, but she stood in his way.

"What's wrong?" she asked.

He smiled at her. "You know, you're still pretty. You worry too much about your face."

"Jared, I'm serious. What happened?"

"Nothing," he said with exasperation. "Okay?"

"I spent an entire week glued to your side. I know when you're lying."

Jared tapped a finger on her table. Finally, he said, "The flashbacks wouldn't stop. Or the flash-forwards or whatever the hell they are. My brain—" He moved his hands away from his head as if it were exploding.

She took his hands and led him to the cot. "What triggered it?"

"Nothing. Don't worry about it. The stuff will wear off in a bit, and I'll never do it again. I swear."

"I don't care about the weed, Jared. I care about you. Is it Addison?"

He shook his head.

"Then what is it?"

Jared pressed his forehead against hers. As she didn't expect this, Katie didn't brace, and his head sagged down.

"Clayton's the new head of the camp," he said.

Katie's eyes grew wide. "Shit! What are we going to do?"

"Whatever I'm told," Jared said, then he laughed. "Because I'm a spineless dog."

"What? That's not true."

"Of course, it's true. It's always been true. That's why my hands shake. It's why we're all still here. Because I'm gutless."

She cupped his cheek. "Jared, what happened? What aren't you telling me?"

"He did it again." Jared imitated a gun being placed to his head. "Click. And I just stood there. Didn't fight. Didn't say anything. Just—waited on the bullet. It was empty—again—but I fell for it—again."

Katie wrapped her arms around him. "It's okay. It's going to be okay."

"No, it's not." He shook his head. "I'm going to die here. Die like the damn dog I am. We're all going to die. It's coming, and I can't do anything to stop it." He cried into her shoulder.

Katie's eyes darted around the room for help. This boy had been her rock, her savior. And he wept into her shoulder. Katie never felt so scared.

"Whoa." Bartram stopped Katie and Jared at the door of the communications room. "Are you okay, Goldie?"

"I'm fine," he said as he rocked in place. Bartram looked at Katie, who shook her head.

"Thank God, it's a photo op," Bartram said. "You know what to do."

Katie picked up the most recent copy of the New York Times from the table in the back and stood still against the wall as Bartram took the picture. Then they were dismissed.

"You're going to go lay down for the rest of the afternoon," Katie said as they descended the hill.

"I'm fine. Do you have any food?" Jared asked.

"You have three Hershey's kisses stored on your desk."

"My gosh! You're right. How do you know that?"

"Go eat your candy," Katie said. "And take a nap. I'll be by with your dinner later."

He saluted her hazily and entered his hut. Katie rolled her eyes and moved on to the field. She was about to rejoin her hut when she got an idea.

*   *   *

Katie rounded back to the mess hall with Michelle. She had called a hut leader meeting and most had already gathered by the time she got back.

"Is it true?" Sam stood as she stepped inside the mess hall. "Is Goldie walking around the camp totally baked?"

"Where is he now?" Bryan asked.

"Taking a nap," Katie answered.

"Great," Sam muttered. "He's turned into a pussy."

Katie took her seat in her usual spot. "I'm sure you have noticed our latest addition to the camp as well."

"You mean the new Watcher?" Sam asked. "I noticed him. Did anyone else?"

"He's replacing Ian, isn't he?" Michelle asked, sitting next to Bryan, her face creased in worry. Of everyone there who had a right to be nervous, it was Michelle.

"Yes," said Katie, "it was announced this morning."

"Well, who the hell is he?" Olivia said. "Because I've never seen him before." Olivia, the newest hut leader, had caramel skin and kinky black hair. Katie guessed her age at fifteen.

"That's because you're lucky." Bryan put his hands together in a peak. "Clayton is about as bad as bad can get. No wonder Jared fell off the wagon. I haven't had a joint in ten minutes, and I'm about ready to throw in the towel."

"Does Jared know you've called this meeting?" Michelle asked.

"No," she admitted. "But I didn't feel like this could wait until he sobered up. Clayton's pretty much a textbook psychopath, would everyone agree?"

"Not far from it," Bryan muttered.

"Sociopath," said Michelle. "That's what Jared calls him at least. Midas is the psychopath."

"The question isn't what they are," said Olivia. "It's 'what are we going to do about them?'"

The door opened, and Jared entered the room to plop down in his usual spot. His eyes were red and his head bobbed as if he were struggling to keep it still.

"Glad to see you're still standing," Sam muttered.

Jared glared at him. "Shut the hell up." To Katie, he said, "I told you, it wears off."

"You're saying you're not high anymore?" she asked skeptically.

"No, but I'm functional."

The rest of the hut leaders looked less certain, and Jared pulled a granola bar out of his pocket.

"And you're on the larceny wagon too," Bryan said. "Great timing there."

"I stole it from your stash," Jared said. "Payback for all the weed you take from me. Now, I assume Katie's told you who the new camp head is?"

"So, he's a bad dude." Olivia shrugged. "If I'm not mistaken, we've been dealing with bad guys since we've been here."

"Not like this one," Jared said. "Clayton is a sadist. He's insecure, erratic, short-tempered, and he destroys everything he touches. And he enjoys taking things he views as good and defiling them anyway he can. How am I doing there, Michelle?" She looked away, and he continued, "He's already raped and murdered one girl, and I watched him blow a cop's brains out two days ago."

"Then what do we do?" Olivia said.

Everyone looked down the table at Jared, but he leaned back in his seat. "I am open to suggestions."

"What if you got Addison to—oh—hmm . . ." Dakota said.

"We have to kill him," Michelle said. "Before he kills us."

Everyone fell silent as they averted their gazes from each other. Murder might have always been on the table, but to have it spoken about so openly, churned stomachs.

"Does anyone disagree with this?" Jared said, but no one else spoke. "Then it's time we closed this meeting."

Bryan opened his mouth to protest, but Jared held up his hand.

"We will discuss it later in a more private location," said Jared. "Meet at my hut after lights out. And keep this in mind: even planning something like this is enough to get every one of us killed, so anyone who decides not to come will not be thought of as less."

*   *   *

"What do you mean you're not coming?" Leida blurted at Dakota that evening. Katie had told her about the planned meeting—or rather, Leida had extracted that information after repeated sessions of questioning.

"Exactly that," Dakota said as he rolled a thin joint and leaned against the bunk bed next to his own.

"But they're going to need help!"

"Look Leida, I'm all for grand plans and the like, but I'm not about to sacrifice myself trying to take out some guy. If we're not talking about escape, I'm not interested. I've heard the stories. Clayton's a mean snake, but we've never talked about killing any of the Watchers before. This is a revenge mission, and I'm not going to risk my ass over it."

"Coward!"

Dakota barked a laugh. "Don't call me that unless you're planning on calling your brother the same thing."

"Jared's not a coward," Leida said.

"Not only is he a coward, he's also halfway out of his mind. He's spiraling, and I'm not about to go down with him. If he pulls this off, you know the next bullet that flies will be coming straight for him."

Leida glared at him, but Dakota crossed his arms. She turned on foot and retreated to her bunk. "Don't worry, Katie. I'm coming with you."

"I don't know if Jared—" Katie said.

"I swear, if you bring up what my brother would or wouldn't allow, I'm going to punch you in the face."

*   *   *

"Nope," Jared said as soon as Leida and Katie stepped through the door to his hut. "I don't think so. Go back. Now."

But Leida marched past him, Bryan, and Michelle to take a seat in Katie's chair. "I'm staying right here."

"I have not watched your back for this long so you can—"

"Goldie," Bryan said. "Chill. Leida's good."

"I don't care," he said. "She's not getting wrapped up in this."

"Beth was my friend, too." Leida leapt back to her feet. "She was the closest thing I ever had to a mother and that—bastard!" Her voice caught. "He killed her. And I want him dead as much as any of you. I'm not going back."

Jared opened his mouth to retort, but Michelle interrupted him. "Jared, Leida is at risk more than anyone else because of you. She has a right to be here."

And he clamped his mouth shut. Dammit, she was probably right. Of all the things that worried him about Clayton's presence, this was number one. Through gritted teeth, he said, "Fine. You can stay, but you're not going to be the one who does it, is that clear?"

"Yeah, yeah," Leida said.

"Don't yeah-yeah me," he snarled.

"Dammit!" Bryan hissed. "Can you two please move on? I forget how obnoxious your bickering can get."

Jared scowled and flipped her the bird. Leida returned the gesture, and Bryan rolled his eyes.

"How are we supposed to kill him?" Katie asked as she sat on Jared's bed, her legs dangling off the floor. "Is someone going to just walk up to him and stab him?"

"Someone could do that," Jared said, "but only if they wished to die a few seconds later."

"So, we have to kill him, but not get caught," she said.

"That's typically how murder works," Bryan said, and it was Katie's turn to flash an obscene gesture.

Jared could not help but smile. If she had ever flipped anyone else off before, he had not seen it. Katie had changed a lot since the beginning of the summer. It wouldn't be long before she was indistinguishable from the other veterans. Whether or not that was a good thing was up for debate.

"We could break into his room and stab him in his sleep," said Leida as she played with the stack of papers on Katie's desk. The violent suggestion did not surprise Jared, but Katie's brows popped upwards. If Jared wore the 'standoffish asshole' mask, then Leida wore the 'rainbows and butterflies' mask. She, however, was just as tough as the others, and just as devious if the time called for it.

"What if he wakes up?" Katie asked.

"Whoever did it would have to overpower him." Bryan leaned against the wall. "Damn, I wish Trevor were here."

That would have been a bonus, if Trevor would have been willing to work with them. He wasn't always a team player and often leaned more to the side of Dakota and Sam.

"What about poison?" Michelle asked.

Jared perched on his desk with his feet in his chair. "We'd have to get it in his food or drink, but most of the food he eats is community-made. We've never been able to get enough poison to dose everyone, so we'd have to isolate him a plate of food."

"What about his drugs?" Bryan said. "Could we lace them with something?"

"Opioids perhaps," Jared said. "Something he could O.D. on. Actually . . ." He dropped off his desk, removed the false bottom, and dumped the contents on the table.

"Saving up for an occasion?" Michelle muttered.

Jared ignored her comment. He knew she didn't approve of his keeping the stash after kicking his habit, but when one had nothing...

"The problem is getting him to take a lethal dose," Jared said. "We're going to have to account for several variables. Height, weight . . ."

"Tolerance," Bryan offered.

"And we can only put enough in each thing so as not to make him suspicious," Leida said. "He'll notice if his drink tastes too bitter."

"Or if a puff of white powder comes out the end of his joint," Bryan said.

"We might get him to take enough to knock him out," Jared said, "but I don't know if it will kill him."

"Someone will need to be there to follow up," Michelle said.

"Jared," Bryan said, "do you remember when we installed the air ducts on that wing? There's one large central duct with branches going off into the different rooms. How wide do you think those air ducts are?"

"A foot by three feet, maybe?"

"A small person could squeeze through the duct. Then we wouldn't have to worry about opening the door and being seen. Whoever it was could slip in, finish the job, and get out."

Jared nodded as he imagined the dimensions. No doubt it would be tight. "A young one would fit, but we're not involving any of them."

"I—uh—wasn't thinking about a young one," said Bryan.

Jared frowned at this, not quite getting Bryan's meaning. Then it hit. "Oh," he said. "Naturally."

*   *   *

When the door to Jared's hut opened unexpectantly, he spun in a circle, checking to make sure he had not failed to hide any contraband, but it was Katie who entered.

"How did it go?" she asked.

Jared shrugged. "I fit." He and Michelle had tried out the ducts that morning to see if the plan was even feasible. The idea of going back into the air ducts made his stomach churn, but it was, at least, possible.

Katie plucked little tufts of dust off of his previously clean shirt. A good idea. Walking around with garden soil on his clothes would be one thing. Dust bunnies, another.

"Are you nervous?" Katie asked.

How could she read him like that? "I could use a smoke," he said, "but why are you here? I didn't send for you."

Katie bit her lip. "We still haven't talk about . . ."

Jared grimaced. After everything that had happened, the other night was barely a blip on his radar. He had acted like a dick and she deserved at least a little explanation, but now?

"Yeah, I don't mean to be rude," said Jared, "but I've kind of got this whole murder thing on my mind right now."

"Oh. Sure," said Katie.

Jared winced. Sure, he didn't want to get distracted by relationship nonsense, but he also wasn't quite ready to end things. Sending her away might do just that, so as she turned for the door, Jared said, "Hang on a second, though. I have an idea I'd like to run by you."

She lingered, which was good, and Jared continued, "I've been thinking. I could kill Clayton no problem if he's gorked out of his head, but there might be a way to make it look like an accident." He lifted the leg of his table, unscrewed the base and slipped out three hypodermic needles.

"Is that entire desk hollow?" Katie asked.

"It might be a bit lighter than expected," said Jared with a grin. "What if I take the rest of these drugs, grind them up, and inject them into Clayton until he stops breathing?"

Katie's lips parted, and then she scratched her head. "That would work. In theory."

"And if that's not enough, I could smother him with a pillow."

"Does it bother you? Talking so casually about murdering someone?"

At this he paused. "Not really," he admitted, but didn't tell her he had been dreaming about this moment for years.

"You haven't actually, you know, killed anyone before. Have you?"

Jared tapped his thumb against the tabletop. "Not intentionally."

"What?"

That was not a question he was going to answer, so instead he asked, "Want to help me grind up some pills?"

*　　　*　　　*

Not long after, the time came to put the real plan into action. Jared and Katie made their way to the second-floor bathroom with little hassle from any of the Watchers. The one benefit of being Goldie: unfettered access to pretty much anywhere without a second look.

The bathroom was small with only enough space for a sink and toilet. After a final glance into the hallway, Jared locked the door and scooted past Katie to the toilet, above which stood an air vent.

After unscrewing the grate with a penny, Jared passed it back down to Katie. "Put this in behind me, wait fifteen minutes, then go signal Bryan. Be sure not to burn yourself."

Katie rolled her eyes. "No, duh."

Stepping onto the back of the toilet, Jared shimmied his way into the small, dusty space, ignoring the warning bells of claustrophobia. The job came first, his feelings second.

Katie supported his legs as he army-crawled through the duct until his legs were fully inside the metal shaft. As silently as possible, he slid through the ducts of the East Wing. Occasionally, the walls would creak and shift, and in a couple of places the floor sagged under his weight. Again, he silenced his anxiety with a quick prayer to a God he wasn't sure existed.

Jared counted the branches as he passed. One, two, three, four. He turned right at four. He grimaced as he contorted his body around the awkward turn. For the first time in his life, he was thankful for his small frame.

As he continued on, his belt loop got caught on a loose screw. Jared heard a small tear and froze. No sounds came from the other side of the thin metal wall separating him from assured destruction.

He slid back a bit. The snag held firm. Jared whispered an expletive under his breath. His arms were in front of him, and there was no reaching back to free the belt loop. Beads of sweat formed on his brow. He had to get free. No matter what. He couldn't be found here. He couldn't stay here locked in the trunk. It was getting too hot. He was going to suffocate and die if someone didn't crank the car soon.

A blast of cold air swirled around his ankles, and Jared rested his head on the metal floor. "I'm in the air duct," he whispered to himself. "I'm not in the trunk. It's a snag. Breathe, dammit."

Damn anxiety. No matter how much he tried to ignore it, it still seemed to get the best of him. Jared closed his eyes and forced himself to take long, deep breaths, refusing to let his terror take over him. After shoving his emotions into the overflowing pit of his mind, he slid forward and then back. He shifted sideways and up. The loop came free, and he breathed a sigh of relief.

He pushed on and came to the open grate sooner than expected. Clayton sat on his bed watching TV. Jared's first instinct was to retreat, but he forced himself to be still. Slowly, he eased away from the grate.

*   *   *

Katie peeked out of the bathroom once the fifteen minutes had passed. Still no Watchers to be seen. She tiptoed to the stairs and caught sight of Bartram heading up them. Katie was about to hide, but realized how foolish that would be. Instead, she descended the stairs as normally as possible.

Bartram grabbed her arm as she tried to pass. "Where's your boss?"

"He—he's in the kitchen," she said.

The Watcher's eyes narrowed. "I just came from there."

"Oh," Katie said. "He was there when I was there, but they needed toilet paper so I came up for some."

"Toilet paper?" Bartram said. "For the kitchen?"

"For the downstairs bathroom," Katie said. "But I couldn't find any extra, so . . ."

Bartram's brows came to a pinch, and he motioned for her to follow him. Katie's breath caught as he stepped into the second-floor bathroom. She looked toward the grate and prayed he wouldn't notice the missing screws. Bartram opened the cabinet under the sink to show two dozen rolls of toilet paper tucked inside.

"That cabinet. I see what he meant now." Katie tucked as many rolls as she could under her arms.

Bartram looked around the tiny bathroom. "What other cabinet is there?"

"Thank you." Katie ducked out of the room and headed down the stairs in haste. She stopped by the first-floor bathroom and shoved the superfluous rolls into the already packed space.

When Katie stepped into the kitchen, Bryan's head craned over his shoulder. "Where were you?" he mouthed to her, but Katie waved him off. The boy rolled his eyes before turning back to the stove. He shook his skillet vigorously and grease spilled over the sides. A spark caught in the oil.

"Fire!" Bryan cried.

"I've got it!" Katie grabbed a glass from the dishwater.

Bryan scooped up a curious young one and pulled him away from the stove as Katie splashed water onto the fire. Flames roared to the ceiling, some blowing back on Katie as she ran back. What a horrible idea! Did Jared know that would happen when he told her to do it?

"Holy shit!" Ruby, the kitchen Watcher, tossed her phone in the air. "Put a lid on it. Where's the fire extinguisher?"

Katie stood back, mouth ajar as fire licked the range hood and surrounding cabinets. But Bryan discharged the fire extinguisher, and the flames shrank. Ruby glared at Katie, but she raised her arms in wonder.

"Go get Goldie," Ruby ordered, and biting her lip, Katie obeyed.

*　　　*　　　*

Jared rested his head on his arms as he reviewed the list of crop varieties for the coming spring. This was the safest place for his brain to linger, but the lump in his throat only abated slightly. No matter how hard he tried to concentrate, Addison's face kept coming into mind.

Stop it. Stay on task.

The intrusive thought prevailed, and his throat went dry. Jared pressed his forehead into the metal floor.

"Clayton." Clayton's radio cracked to life, jarring him back to reality.

"What?" Clayton said into the radio.

"There's a fire in the kitchen," the voice replied.

"Then put it out." The fire alarm sounded. "And turn that thing off."

"It's a pretty big fire. We're going to need you on this one."

Clayton sighed and slid off his bed. Absent of haste, he put on his boots, shirt, and hat and trudged out of the room. Jared slid the grate out, and the door opened again.

Jared froze, grate suspended in mid-air, his hands visible behind it. Clayton trotted inside, grabbed his taser, and left again.

Hands shaking, Jared turned the grate sideways and pulled it in with him. He then eased back down the passageway and turned the corner backwards. Leaving the grate at the junction, Jared slithered down the shaft to Clayton's room feet first.

Jared lowered himself out of the duct until he was suspended by his fingertips, then dropped to the floor, crouching to ease the impact. A bottle of liquor sat on Clayton's dresser, and Jared removed a plastic bag filled with powder from his pocket. After dumping the powder inside, he stirred it until the little white flakes disappeared. A jar of queso and left-over chicken wings from the mini-fridge were doused as well. Clayton's weed he swapped out with his own rolled joints—the paper being some of his rare plain white stash. He even sprinkled some on Clayton's toothbrush.

Jared pocketed his leftovers, jumped to grab the edge of the shaft, and pulled up. With help from the wall, he pulled himself up inside the duct and slid down to the junction. After returning with the grate, he peered over the edge to check for any odd footprints he might have left on the wall. Finding none, he covered the hole and slithered his way back down the air shaft.

"Jared," Katie's voice echoed down the vent as Jared continued to shimmy through the air ducts.

"Coming," Jared whispered back.

"They sent me to find you."

"Good job then, I suppose." He pushed himself through and into her arms. Katie helped him onto the floor and swatted dust off of him. "Is the fire out?" he asked.

"Yes," she said. "When you suggested throwing water on the grease fire, did you know?"

"That it would erupt in a fire ball?" Jared asked. "Yup."

"A head's up would have been nice!" said Katie. "I nearly lost my eyebrows! Oh, and we're in trouble."

When they arrived in the kitchen, a black tower of soot clung to the wall behind the stove. White foam dripped off the countertops and the ceiling.

"Look who finally showed up." Jared turned his head in time to face Clayton's incoming fist. Katie gasped as he went down on one knee.

"And where the hell were you?" Clayton said.

Jared held his nose, but blood continued to soak his chin. "I was taking a shit."

Clayton eyed him. "Shit in your pants next time. When I call, you come immediately. Get up."

Jared rose to stand as blood continued to pour from his hand and onto the floor. Bryan, who sported a similar dried blood pattern around his lips and chin, tossed him a dish towel.

"I want an estimate for repairs," Clayton said. "You have an hour."

"I'm going to need to look up current prices," Jared said.

"One hour. And we start repairs in the morning, so get the demo out of here. Nobody eats, nobody takes a break, until this is done. There will be half-rations tomorrow and for every day after until the kitchen has been fixed."

While the workers began cleaning, Clayton fetched a hard lemonade out of the refrigerator before kicking his boots onto the island and watching them wipe away foam and debris.

"We won't be able to salvage this sheetrock." Jared continued to hold his nose as he inspected the damage. "Katie, go get a couple hammers and a crow bar. Bryan, help me with this range hood."

Clayton sighed loudly as he swiveled his legs off the island. The bottle swung in his hand as he lumbered to the door and stepped outside.

"Asshole," Bryan muttered.

"Honestly," Jared said, "he let us off easier than I thought he would."

*   *   *

Leida pushed a wheelbarrow full of scrap weed plants, plants not good enough to sell, up the hill toward the composting pile while Ivy carried a bucket full of the same. All day she kept looking toward the house as if she could see what was going on inside. She hated being away from the action, so when Dakota offered up the job to roll the plants up the hill, she took it.

Of course, her view from outside the brick walls was not improved by being closer to them. The trip was taxing and disappointing.

Little Ivy dumped her pile onto the kitchen scraps, then helped Leida scrape the contents of her wheelbarrow out. As Clayton exited the kitchen, Leida frowned. He swung a glass bottle in his hand, taking an occasional sip, but when he saw the two girls watching not too far away, he stopped.

"Let's go, Ivy." Leida gave the wheelbarrow a quick shake before turning the contraption around. About halfway down the hill, Leida turned around expecting her ever-present shadow to be still on her heels, but Ivy was not there. Neither was Clayton. She scratched her head.

Then Leida caught sight of a door to the hut closing. "No-no-no-no!" Leida abandoned the wheelbarrow and raced for the door. She flung it open to see Clayton and Ivy inside. Ivy sat on the bed holding Clayton's glass drink. Tears slid down her cheeks.

"Leida!" Ivy jumped off the bed and crossed the room to her.

"Run Ivy," Leida whispered and turned to follow her, but Clayton grabbed her arm and pulled her back inside.

"I know you." Clayton pushed her against the door frame. "You two—you share such an uncanny resemblance. But I must say, you are quite prettier than your brother."

"Leave me alone!"

"Sh-sh-shh—now, none of that." He kissed her cheek. Leida pushed him, but he grabbed her and dragged her to the bed.

"Stop it!" she cried as he pinned her down. She tried to smack him, but he grabbed that hand and held it above her head. He slid his hand under her shirt.

*　　*　　*

The wind on the hill sent a chill through Katie as she stepped out of the kitchen. Was summer ending, or was it a cold snap? She made a mental note to ask Jared later. As she headed to the toolshed, she spotted Clayton on the other side of the huts. He continued to swing his bottle as he walked, taking the occasional sip.

How she hated him. It was an unfamiliar experience for her, hating someone this much, and she pondered on this distaste as she stepped inside the toolshed. Katie was about to return to the path, tools in hand, when she spotted a young one running from Trevor's old hut.

"Ivy?" Katie cried. "What's going on?"

"Katie!" The little girl sprinted to her. "Clayton took Leida. He's going to hurt her." Ivy handed Katie the glass bottle.

Katie's eyes grew wide. "Trevor's old hut?"

Ivy nodded.

Dropping the tools, Katie ran for the hut. As her hand reached for the knob, however, she hesitated. She had no plan, no excuse. If Clayton was raping Leida, what could she do?

"Somebody, help me!" Leida's voice came from inside.

Katie ripped open the door. Clayton's head swerved to her from where he lay on top of Leida, pinning her to the bed. "Get out of here!" he yelled, but Katie stood frozen in the doorway. "I said go!"

Taking advantage of Clayton's distraction, Leida wiggled one hand free and tucked it behind her back. With a swift motion, she jabbed a thin blade into Clayton's belly.

Clayton cried out as he came up off her. "You little bitch!"

Leida rolled to the floor and made for the exit. Tears streamed down her face. Katie closed the door, knowing the action was pointless. He would be fast on their heels.

"Jared!" Leida cried, and Katie turned to see him coming out the back door with a load of sheet rock. The girl raced to him, and he tossed his load aside. She buried her face into his chest. With wide eyes, Jared swore as Clayton stumbled out of the hut with the hilt of the blade still sticking out of his belly.

Katie backed into the alley between the huts and ran her fingers through her hair. "Help," she whispered. "I need to go get help." But from where?

Two Watchers stepped outside as the commotion continued. "Shoot her!" Clayton shouted to Bartram as he made his way up the hill. "Now! She stabbed me."

Bartram's gaze darted between the two. Jared moved Leida to stand behind him, and his hand went to the small of his back. Katie knew he was reaching for his knife. Another Watcher approached from the greenhouses.

"Shoot her! Kill her!" Clayton continued to stumble up the hill.

Jared stood firm, but Katie could see him shaking. She urged herself to do something, anything, but her legs were frozen in place.

Bartram drew his taser and fired it at Jared, and he convulsed and fell to the ground. Another Watcher grabbed Leida and dragged her inside.

ANOTHER'S TREASURE

Katie's legs decided to move, and she raced to Jared's side. "Jared!" She grabbed his arm. "Jared!"

Jared stumbled for the door, but Bartram pressed the trigger again, casting him back to the ground. "Stay down, Goldie," he said, "if you know what's good for you."

Jared let out a moan.

"And you stay back too," Bartram told Katie.

"He was trying to rape her!" Katie said.

Bartram watched as Clayton hobbled into the house and sighed. "Goldie, when I let you up, you're going to walk back down the hill and to your hut. You will not come up the hill until you are sent for. Do you understand?"

"I understand," Jared grumbled.

"You know disobeying me will get you nothing but a bullet to your head. That's not going to help your sister any, so let it go."

Jared winced as Bartram ripped the barbs out.

"I'll be at the door, watching."

Katie helped Jared up, and he limped down the path. Mournfully, he gazed over his shoulder. Katie berated herself for having done so little.

*   *   *

Jared pressed his hands onto the surface of his work table. Cursing loudly, he flipped it, startling Katie where she stood next to the door. He pounded his fist into the plywood wall before sinking to the floor, burying his head in his hands.

Katie took a seat on the floor beside him, not knowing what to do. Jared gripped his hair and tugged, pulling out a clump. He reached into the matted mess for some more, but Katie grabbed his hands.

"Stop that," she whispered.

He let out a torturous cry. She wrapped her arms around him, pressing him against herself, shielding him. Tears flooded her cheeks as his body trembled against hers. She searched for something to say.

It'll be okay?

No, it wouldn't.

They had Leida, the best of all of them. And they were powerless to help her.

Bryan entered the small hut, but stepped back outside, probably to preserve his best friend's dignity as he continued to weep against Katie's shoulder. He returned a few minutes later and set a cigarette on Katie's table. She nodded understanding, and he left.

The weeping did not last much longer, and what followed was a brooding silence. Jared took the cigarette left for him, lit it, and puffed it down as he stared silently, miserably at the opposite wall.

Katie tried to drape her arm back over his shoulder, but he shrugged her off and continued to puff. So, she wrapped her arms around herself. She tried to think of a solution, but nothing came to mind. Why had she done so little?

From the belongings scattered on the floor, he picked up the silver rosary with the blue stone and ran his thumb over it.

"I didn't know you were religious," said Katie.

"It was Beth's," he said, and Katie felt as if she were stabbed in the gut. Clayton had murdered her too.

An hour later, Michelle entered and sat on the edge of his bed as Bryan stood in the doorway. "She's alive," Michelle said. "For now. She's to be shot after breakfast."

Katie dropped her head, and Jared let out a cloud of smoke from his fifth cigarette.

"We're still set to go for this evening, if you still want to kill him," she said.

"I want to kill him, alright," Jared said. "Lot of good it will do though. They'll still kill her."

"And they'll know who did it," Bryan said.

"I don't give a rat's ass about that. They can kill me too for all I care."

"Don't say that," Katie voice caught. "Please don't say that." She looked pleadingly to Michelle and Bryan, but they said nothing.

"Where is she?" Jared said.

"They're keeping her in a closet on the first floor of the West Wing," Michelle said. "Bartram is guarding her."

"Am I allowed back into the house?"

"Nobody is guarding the door. People are still working on the kitchen demo. Clayton mentioned something about still wanting an estimate."

Jared laughed. "He can go to hell."

"What are you going to do?" Katie asked.

Jared smashed his cigarette into the dirt. Turning to his overturned desk, he undid the false bottom. "I'm going to see if Bartram will accept a bribe."

"He won't let her go," Bryan said.

"No, but he might let me talk to her. Then at least I can say goodbye." Jared gathered up the rest of the drugs and pocketed the caramel candies. As he left the hut, Katie gripped the collar of her shirt and dug her fingernails into the skin beneath it.

"This is going to kill him," Michelle said.

"You think I don't know that?" Bryan said, ramming his hands into his hair. "Geez."

"We have to do something," Katie said.

"Do you have a satellite phone hidden where the sun don't shine?" Bryan said. "Because that's what we need."

"Don't be a jerk," Michelle said.

"Katie, if you think there was a damn thing any of us could do, don't you think we'd be out there doing it?" Bryan grumbled something unkind before slamming the door behind him.

Michelle winced as he left. "I don't know if you pray, Katie, but now would be the time to start."

*   *   *

"Goldie, you shouldn't be here," Bartram said as Jared approached him in the hall of the Big House, just outside Leida's closet.

"I just want to talk to her," Jared said.

"Out of the question. Go on back down the hill."

Jared pulled out the giant bag of pills from under his shirt.

"What the hell?" muttered Bartram.

"For your trouble."

Bartram inspected the bag. "Are these from your stash? The ones you've been getting from us?"

He shrugged.

"How long have you been off of them?"

"Do you want them or not?"

Bartram frowned. "I'm sorry kid, but these are worthless. These aren't oxycodone like you thought they were. Most of it is a cocktail of other stuff. Acid, coke, meth." Bartram laughed. "Enough to make for one terrific high."

Jared blinked several times. "But—why?"

"Because you were getting used to the Oxy. They were never for your enjoyment. They were meant to keep you under control."

"I figured that. But LSD?"

Bartram shook his head. "Look, it was Midas' idea. You were always too smart for your own good. That deal of his—it wasn't meant to last forever."

"He was trying to make me go insane?"

"Not a first, but as you developed a tolerance for the stuff, they started adding more to it. We thought that's why your hands started shaking, but when did you stop taking them?"

"It's been a while now."

Bartram chuckled. "I'd recommend you not taking them now, or you're in for the ride of your life."

Jared stared down at his worthless pills.

"One thing about it though. If it's not the drugs causing your hands to shake, then what is?"

"How the hell should I know, Bartram?" Jared looked longingly at the door.

Bartram sighed. "Tell you what, kid. I may know a guy who can sell these on the street. What they don't know won't hurt us, right? You can see your sister, but for only five minutes, understand?"

"Yes, I understand."

"Don't make me regret this, you hear?" He unlocked the door, and Leida stared up at them, blinking in the sudden light. Jared stepped inside and sat opposite her. The door closed, plunging them back into darkness.

"What did you do?" Leida said. "Please, tell me you're not here to be executed tomorrow too."

"I bribed him for five minutes. Ten if he's feeling generous."

Leida wrapped her arms around him, and Jared closed his eyes as tears threatened to re-emerge. "Thank you for coming," she said.

"I'm so sorry," his voice caught. "I'm sorry I couldn't protect you."

"It's not your fault. You did everything you could." The tears came, and Leida held on to him tighter and cried as well.

"Will it hurt?" she asked.

He shook his head, and his voice cracked. "No, it won't hurt. I promise. It will be quick."

"Did it hurt Landon?"

"No," he sobbed. "It was fast. Like the blink of an eye."

"I'm so scared," Leida said.

Jared closed his eyes and placed his chin on her head. "I know, but I can be there with you if you'd like."

"What?" She pulled away from him. "What do you mean?"

"I can kill Clayton," he said. "That part's easy. It won't stop tomorrow, but then you wouldn't be alone."

"Jared, no!" Leida said. "You don't deserve to die!"

"I swore to Dad I would keep you safe. I failed. I don't deserve anything."

"You kept me alive for ten years. That's more than anyone could have asked of you. Kill Clayton, sure, but do it smart. Wait at least a week so his guard will be—"

He shook his head. "I can't do this anymore. Not without you."

Leida tugged on his collar, bringing him to her face. "You can't die. If you die, then who will make them pay?"

Jared blinked, and his mouth parted.

"Make them pay, Jared. Promise me you'll make Midas pay!" she sobbed.

The door opened. "Sorry, Goldie," Bartram said. "Time's up. In fact, time was up a few minutes ago."

"Jared!" Leida took his hand. "Promise me. Do it now."

"Come on, Goldie," Bartram insisted.

"Promise me."

"I love you, Leida. And I always will." He kissed her on the forehead and slipped the caramels into her hand.

"Jared!" she cried, but he stood and slipped into the hallway. "Jared!"

By the time Bartram shut the door, Jared was already down the hall.

*   *   *

"Jared?" Katie slid her hand into his. He barely flinched as he continued to stare at the electric fence ten yards away. He did not, however, pull away. "It's chilly out here. Don't you want to come inside?"

He didn't respond.

"Have you decided what to do?" she asked. "Are you still going to kill Clayton?"

"The pills don't work," Jared said. "The Watchers—they laced them with other things."

"What other things?" Katie asked.

"I don't know. LSD? Meth?"

"How do you know this?"

"Doesn't matter." Jared shook his head. "It won't work."

"But how do you know? Maybe it will still work? Maybe if he's given enough?"

Jared laughed. "Can't overdose on LSD. Might howl at the moon, but it won't kill him. Hell, he might not even sleep tonight. Too many variables. Don't know what he got. Don't know what I'll be giving him."

"Then we'll think of something tomorrow," she said.

"Tomorrow," he laughed bitterly. "I'm going to kill him, Katie. I will kill him. I just need to figure out how."

Katie tugged on his arm. He came with her willingly, and she led him to his hut. Jared sat in the dirt against the wall while Katie took a seat on his bed, hugged his pillow, and wished for home.

Bryan and Michelle stopped by. "Stay with him tonight, will you?" Bryan asked, and she promised she would.

Katie prayed and prayed and prayed all through the evening and into the night as Jared sat brooding on the floor. Unsure how, she fell asleep.

A hand clamped over Katie's mouth, instantly waking her. She expected next to be dragged out of bed and tied up by some angry workers, but it was Jared. "I have an idea," he whispered and let go of her mouth.

"And you about gave me a heart attack because . . . ?"

"Sorry. Come with me."

"Jared," Katie said, "I'm not going on a suicide mission with you."

"What about an escape attempt?"

Now that, she could get behind.

Jared moved to the door and peered down the corridor.

"What time is it?" she asked.

He studied the sky. "Two o'clock. Dumar went by a couple minutes ago, so we have a small window."

Taking her by the hand, Jared led her out of the hut and through the shadows of the shacks. Stopping shy of the last building, he peered around the corner. One of the Watchers lit a cigarette at the top of the hill. A small cherry red flame glowed at the base of the roll. Jared held up a hand for Katie and counted down from five. At one, the Watcher walked away.

"Show off," Katie whispered.

They ducked behind the bushes at the edge of the house and inched their way to the door. Before they reached it, Jared stopped, and Matt emerged from the shadows of a building. Jared waited until he was three buildings away before he slid from cover and pulled bits of metal from his pocket. The deadbolt was picked in under twenty seconds. He opened the door slowly, preventing the customary pop, and motioned for Katie to enter.

The stench of smoke still lingered in the kitchen, and the appliances cast strange shadows across the floor. Katie tugged at her collar as she considered the repercussions of being caught here at this time of night, but then she looked to Jared and the pounding in her chest slowed. He knew what he was doing.

Jared had her wait by the door while he went to the cabinets. They were no match for his lock pick, and soon he had what he wanted. He then held a finger to his lips and peered into the dining hall. After a moment, he motioned for her to join him.

Katie inspected the item he had procured. It was cocoa powder. "What are we doing?"

"Shh."

Jared and Katie slunk along the dark hallway until he stopped at Addison's door. After picking the lock and typing in the code, the door clicked open.

"Careful," he said. "It's messy."

As Katie stepped over the bits of junk, a chill ran up her spine as she realized this was the room in which Addison died. Jared crossed the room and pulled the heavy shades. As he turned on a lamp and powered up the computer, Katie's eyes grew wide once more. "What are you doing?"

"I'm getting us out of here," said Jared as he rummaged through Addison's things. He selected a coffee mug from the bookshelf and carried it to the lamp, holding it by the rim. A smile appeared on his face. Without explanation, he tossed the leftover liquid into the trash and laid the mug on its side.

Katie rounded the desk as Jared sprinkled a light dusting of the cocoa onto the mug. Gently, he blew across the mug removing the excess powder. Left behind on the mug was a blurry fingerprint.

"Holy crap!" cried Katie.

"I need a brush or something," Jared said. "See if her purse is lying around somewhere."

Katie searched the cluttered office and found Addison's travel bag. Inside was a makeup brush. She handed it to Jared.

"Perfect." He brushed away more of the cocoa powder, but he smudged the print with his shaking fingers. "Dammit!"

"Calm down," Katie said. "Here's another mug. Let me try." With her steady fingers, Katie captured a good print.

"Add some tape," said Jared.

Katie placed the tape over the powder and lifted the print.

"And now, the code." Jared picked a notebook off the top shelf and flipped through the first few pages before closing it. The third on the shelf had the password. He typed it in and hit enter. The computer unlocked, and Katie punched the air.

"Don't get too excited," he said. "We don't have internet access yet."

"How do we get that?"

"We don't," he said. "Two people from two separate computers have to authorize internet usage before it will connect. I only know how to get into one."

"Then—what do we do now?"

"Addison could log on to the video call account, but only contact people already on her list. If any of them are online right now, we can call them. It's a shot in the dark."

"But it's a shot," she said. "Who do you have in mind?"

"Why do you think I brought you?"

"My dad!"

"Mmhm." Jared pulled up the program and typed in the code. Before having Katie upload the fingerprint, he hesitated.

"What?"

"Nothing," Jared said. "Do it."

She pressed the print to the scanner, and the program opened. "Yes!" She punched the air once more.

"Do you know how to run this program?"

"Of course!"

"Good. Because that's the extent of my computer knowledge. It's all yours."

Katie slid into the seat and pulled up her father's profile. "Ready?"

"Ready."

She dialed the number.

Jared winced again and rubbed his temple. "Try it again."

Katie sighed and clicked the button once more. The now-familiar ringtone played over the speakers, but nobody connected. They had tried ten times.

"Dammit," Jared whispered. The clock on the computer read 3:00 a.m.

"We can try it every fifteen minutes," she said. "He has to get up eventually."

"No," Jared said. "The longer we're in here, the riskier this is. We need to shut it down."

"Thirty more minutes?"

Jared buried his head in his hands. "Fine. Then we're leaving."

The minutes on the clock ticked by faster now that a time limit had been set. Jared and Katie discussed the idea of calling someone else on the contact list, but then saw Midas and Clayton listed. If they called a Watcher, all would be truly lost.

Katie was scrolling down the list of names, then suddenly, she stopped. "Alec? That's my brother!"

'Backup for Peter Thompson' was listed underneath his name.

"Jared—should I?"

"Try it."

Katie called, and once again, they listened to the now obnoxious ringtone as they waited—and prayed—for Alec to pick up. The call connected.

"Katie?" Alec's voice boomed through the speakers. "Is that you?"

"Shhhh!" Katie hissed at the screen as Jared scrambled to cut the sound.

Alec covered his mouth with his hand. "Sorry!" he mouthed.

"Try again now." Jared increased the volume to no more than a whisper.

"Katie, where are you?" Alec said. "Is that one of the kidnappers?"

"No, this is Jared. He's a friend," she said. "Alec, we need your help. You need to wake up Dad and—"

"Dad's at the office. He's been staying over almost every night now trying to dig up anything he can to find you."

"We don't have time," Jared whispered.

"Alec," Katie said. "You need to run the program—the one that hacked them last time."

"I don't have it anymore. I didn't bother rebuilding it when—"

"Fine," Jared said. "We'll have to do this another way. We're in the Cherokee National Forest about forty-five minutes from a tiny town called Reliance, Tennessee."

"You're still in Tennessee? I thought you'd be halfway around the world right now," Alec typed quickly. "Reliance, Tennessee. I've pulled it up in Google Earth. Where now?"

"There's a river that flows through it. The Hiwassee River. H-I-W—"

"I got it," Alec said. "It looks like this river runs all the way to North Carolina. Can you narrow down for me?"

"There's a store on the river called Hiwassee Rafters," Jared said. "It sells boats and rafts and stuff like that."

"Okay, I found it," Alec said. "Are you there?"

"No, that's the closest landmark I know. Follow the train tracks and the river until it turns east. We're five miles south of there."

"Uhm—whoa."

"What?" Katie said. "What is it? Do you see us?"

"I think I do, but there's a greenish gray blob directly over the area you've described. At first, I thought the image hadn't finished rendering, but I think it's you. It's been airbrushed out."

"That's us," Jared said. "Definitely."

"But—this is government-level restricted access stuff."

"It's us, Alec," Katie said. "These people are super well connected."

"Are they government? Like CIA?"

"They don't wear name badges," Jared said. "But they have government connections."

"We have to tell Dad," Alec said. "We have to call the FBI."

"The FBI is involved," Jared said. "At least some of their agents are."

"Agent Watts i—" Katie said.

"I know about that guy," Alec said. "Dude tied me up and left me in a bathtub for like hours. But what do we do?"

"I don't—I don't know," Jared said.

"Jared," Katie said. "What about your cousin?"

"Sedonya?"

"Sedonya?" Alec said. "Sedonya Ryder?" Both of them stared at the screen in surprise.

"You know Sedonya?" Jared said.

"Yeah, she runs this alternative media site focusing on the Midas cases. I contacted her last month. Are you—are you Jared Kelley?"

"Yeah," said Katie, "he's the kid from Dad's first Midas case."

"Holy crap!" said Alec. "No offense, but I thought you were dead."

"We'll talk about all that later," said Jared. "About Sedonya . . ."

"What if we got Sedonya to come with you guys?" asked Katie. "She could do a live stream."

"GoPros," Alec said. "I could get Dad to wear a GoPro and have the feed going to Sedonya. We need Dad though."

"Fine," Jared said. "You go tell your father. We need to go before someone sees the light on."

"I love you, Alec," Katie said. "Please hurry. Jared's sister is to be executed in the morning. You have to make it before that."

"Wait, what?" Alec said.

Jared's face crumpled. "She has until after breakfast. Please hurry."

"I will do my best. I love you, Katie." The clock read 4:00 a.m. when the call ended.

"We need to go," said Jared picking up his mess.

"Okay, okay," Katie said. "Don't knock over anything."

Katie followed Jared through the halls to the kitchen door, but just as they were about to go outside, Jared said, "Oh shit. I left the stupid lamp on."

"Are you sure? I thought you—"

"I'll have to go back and turn it off. Follow the shrub line until you're even with the huts. Wait for Matt to come by so you can know where he is. Ruby will come up row two and down row three all night every night. Dumar's probably off in a corner smoking. If anyone sees you, head to the bathroom as if normal. Okay?" He opened the door and pushed her behind the shrubs. Jared closed the kitchen door, and Katie frowned when the deadbolt locked.

Jared went back to Addison's office, clicked on the lamp, and sat back down at the computer. He made the call again.

"Hey, Katie!" Alec started. "Oh—hello."

"Hey. There's a bit more."

Katie considered heading back to her hut, but diverted to Jared's. Bryan had, after all, told her to stay with him. She waited on his bed for him to return and woke there at the siren. Jared still wasn't back, and Katie didn't know what to do upon finding him missing. Should she go look for him?

Still deciding on what to do, Katie wandered out of the hut into the morning light and headed for the water spigot. Jared was not there either, nor was he at breakfast.

"How is he?" Michelle said as she and Bryan joined her at her table.

Katie stared at them blankly. "I—I don't know. I stayed overnight, but when I woke up, he wasn't there."

Michelle's eyes widened. "Do you think he went to the Big House last night? That he tried to carry out the plan?"

Katie scratched her head. "Maybe he's in Addison's office."

"What?" Michelle said. "Why would he?"

"Tell me he didn't!" Bryan said, and three consecutive sirens sounded. "Freakin' hell!"

*   *   *

At 8:30, the door to Addison's office flung open and punched a hole into the drywall behind it. Clicking feverously, Jared attempted to close the open tabs as a pale Clayton leapt across the desk. The Watcher flung Jared and the swivel chair over backwards and spun the monitor in his direction. "What the hell?"

A nude picture of Addison stared at him.

"Uh . . ." Jared disentangled himself from the chair and tried to grab the mouse. Clayton elbowed him in the shoulder.

"Ha!" Clayton clicked on a few more of the tabs finding more of the same. "You broke in here for these?" He grabbed Jared by the hair and dragged him from around the desk. Forced into an awkward crablike crawl, Jared went with him with only verbal resistance.

Clayton tossed him into the hall where Bartram stood with a taser drawn. Jared received a kick to the stomach, and he collapsed into a heap, clutching his middle.

"Watch him." Clayton ordered before returning to the computer. "Where else did you go tonight, Goldie?" asked Clayton, clicking through screens. "I know you've been doing more than looking at smut."

"I wasn't looking at anything," Jared managed. "I happened by and saw a light on. I was as surprised as you to see—augh!" Bartram boxed his ear.

"Shut up," Bartram snarled.

"The man asked me a question."

"Stop the bullshit, Goldie." Clayton raked his arm across the desk, scattering bits of green leaves into his lap. His sleeve came away covered in the stuff. "What the hell?" He sniffed the herbs. "Reefer? Have you been smoking reefer?"

Jared sniffed as his itchy eyes darted around uncertainly. "No."

Clayton knocked the leaves off his lap and into the floor. Upon rounding the desk, he grabbed Jared by the throat and pinned him against the wall. "You think you're funny or something?"

Wincing, Jared clutched his fingers around the choking wrist. Clayton pushed harder.

"I know you did something," said Clayton, "and I'm going to figure out what. Then I'm going to skin the flesh from your bones for this."

He released his throat, and Jared collapsed onto the floor coughing. To Bartram, Clayton ordered, "Tie him up. I need to make a phone call."

Bartram forced Jared up by the arm.

"I didn't do anything, Bartram." He coughed. "I swear."

"Shut up!" He shoved him into the dining hall. "You stupid, stupid son of a bitch."

Jared took off running. Cursing, Bartram raised his taser and shot him, and Jared collapsed into convulsions. Bartram kicked him in the head, knocking him out.

*   *   *

Once the camp was gathered on the hill, Michelle, Bryan, and Katie inched their way through the crowd to meet together. "Are they executing Leida now?" Bryan asked.

"No," Michelle said. Before rejoining them, she had met with her girls to gain intel on the situation. "Apparently, Jared wasn't the only one missing this morning. Clayton was too."

"He did it, didn't he?" Bryan asked.

"Bartram had to break Clayton's door down this morning," continued Michelle. "He's alive, but the drugs worked. They had trouble getting him to wake up. As soon as he did, he ran down the stairs and found Jared in Addison's office looking at porn."

"I'm sorry—what?" Katie said.

"That's what they said," Michelle said. "They said he hacked the firewall and was high as a kite looking at porn."

"It's a cover," Bryan said. "He was doing something else, but is trying to hide his tracks. He's off his rocker, but he's not stupid."

"But why was he in there at all?" Katie said. "He should have been back by now."

Bryan grabbed her under the arm and pulled her to the edge of the crowd. "What happened last night?"

*   *   *

Bryan's face pinched in rage while Katie told him the tale. She was confused at this reaction. This was supposed to be good news. Help was coming, right?

Michelle placed a worried hand to her mouth when she told them about hacking onto the video call account. "Why would he do that?"

"I don't understand," Katie said. "Jared said it would be fine. Addison had to log on so often they didn't make her receive authorization every time."

"No," Bryan said. "But every time she did log on, a notification was sent to at least three other people. Ian, Midas, and some other guy. And since she's dead, her logging on would raise more than a couple of eyebrows."

"But—I . . ." Katie shook her head. "He didn't tell me that. But why did he stay behind? We were done. He could have left."

"And when the Watchers see someone contacted your dad," Bryan said, "who do you think would be on the top of their suspect list?"

Katie started and stammered before burying her face in her hands. "Jared, you idiot! But—but he still got through. Right? We spoke to my brother. My dad is on the way."

"It won't matter," Bryan said. "Where's your dad coming from? Nashville? He has to get a crew together, figure out how to get here, drive all that way—"

"He can't use the FBI," Michelle said. "They're blown. They'll never make it in time."

"In time for Leida's execution?" Katie asked.

"For starters," Bryan said. "But they'll be too late for the trucks also."

"When Jared and Landon got through the fence," Michelle explained, "the Watchers thought it was over. They called for some transport trucks to come to the camp. They were starting to load us into them when they found the boys."

"One hour and thirty-seven minutes," Bryan said. "That's how long it took for the trucks to get here last time."

"That's if they called them," Michelle said. "He was sitting at the computer looking at smut and smoking weed? He's trying to look like he failed and—"

"And if the threat is minimal," Bryan finished, "they won't call the trucks."

"So," Katie hesitated, "there's hope?"

"If they believe him," Bryan said. "Which is unlikely."

"What probability would Jared give it?"

Bryan rubbed his eyes. "For his survival? I don't—I'd rather not think about that. Our rescue though—I'd say sixty percent."

"That's rather precise," said Michelle.

"Jared pitched an idea to me the other day. He thinks he has enough information to find six, maybe seven of the other camps. If he can get Katie's dad the information, then there's a sixty to seventy percent chance they can find us at the other camps."

"You're kidding me," Michelle said. "You think that's his plan?"

"But I thought he was trying to save Leida!" Katie said.

"Katie," Bryan said. "Chances are, Leida isn't going to make it. He couldn't kill Clayton last night, but this—this is his revenge."

"But he'll die. They'll kill him," she said, and Michelle and Bryan exchanged a glance. "This is what you meant when you said this was going to kill him."

The kitchen door opened, and they turned to see Bartram and Clayton exit. An unconscious Jared hung over Bartram's shoulder as he trudged past them and entered a greenhouse.

"I don't like this," Michelle muttered.

Clayton stood on the stump to address the others. "Hut leaders, get your crews to package as much of the product as possible. Have it on the hill in one hour. Go!"

"One hour," Bryan said. "That's not a good sign."

Jared woke in the greenhouse to voices speaking as if far away. "You know," the voice said. "I had some of the weirdest dreams last night. Ever had a bad trip?"

"Couple times, yeah."

"It was like that."

"We were worried you weren't going to wake up." Bartram's voice.

"Midas called me ten times. And I heard it. I just couldn't wake up enough to answer."

Jared shook his head, and the cobwebs slowly lifted. He sat in a chair with his hands secured behind him. His head ached. He wasn't sure if it was from the kick to the head or the copious amount of weed he had consumed.

"Morning, sunshine." Dread filled Jared as he heard Clayton's voice a couple meters away. He trembled as a thousand thoughts flooded him at the same time. All of them bad.

"I've got my tech guy looking into what you did," Clayton said. "He hasn't figured it out yet, but he will. Unfortunately for you, that gives us plenty of playtime. Now, I'm going to give you the option of ending all of this, but only if you tell me what you did."

"I already told you." Jared's voice cracked. "I didn't do anything."

Clayton's fist crashed into Jared's face. As he pulled it back for another swing, music erupted startling them all. Pulling his cellphone from his pocket, Clayton stared at it as if not perceiving what it was.

"This is Clayton," he answered finally, and Jared released a pent-up breath.

As Clayton stepped away, Bartram whispered to Jared, "Goldie, what the hell? You're smarter than this. You think there's a chance you're going to survive this?"

Jared stared at the floor.

"Why are you resisting? End this. The trunks are already on their way. It's over."

He cleared his throat. "I didn't realize you cared so much, Bartram."

Bartram cringed. "I'm not saying that I do . . ."

Jared said nothing.

"Fine then. But whatever happens from this point is on you."

"Whatever helps you sleep at night."

Contempt grew over Bartram's face as Clayton returned.

"That was my tech guy," Clayton said. "You covered your tracks well, Goldie, but he's already making progress. We know your call connected. Let's cut the crap, you lying sack of shit. Who did you contact?"

Jared sneered. "Go to hell."

*   *   *

Katie winced as she heard Jared cry out from the adjacent greenhouse. He had been in there for a while now. At first, she had forced herself to ignore the sounds. She trusted him. He knew what he was doing, but with each cry, her heart tore a little more. "We have to do something," she whispered to Michelle.

Michelle swatted away moisture collecting in her eyes and continued packing her crate. "He's buying time. If they are torturing him, then they're not killing Leida."

"Then can we buy him time too?"

"Look at the guards, Katie. They're watching us closely, and they're wearing guns now instead of tasers."

"But they're going to kill him," Katie said, and Jared's cry reached them again.

"We have a job to do, Katie," Michelle said. "We have to look after the young ones and be strong for them. Focus on that."

Jared screamed, and Katie stared longingly at the doorway. The young ones were the last thing on her mind.

Michelle took her arm. "This is his choice. I know—I know it's hard, but . . ."

"I can't do this."

"You have to let him do his thing. You have to."

"No, I don't." Katie headed for the door.

"Katie, no!" Michelle cried, but it was too late. Katie was gone.

*   *   *

Jared's eyes found a corner to stare into. His focus was waning, and he didn't know how much more of this he could take. Blood dripped onto the floor from where Clayton had carved the word "LIAR" into his side. Multiple ribs were broken, and every breath hurt.

All of those times Clayton had beaten him were in preparation for this moment. He had one last move to make, but the timing wasn't just right. He had to focus.

Clayton glanced at the bloody knife in his hand. Sweat covered his brow, and he kept clutching his side where Leida had stabbed him. At first, the pain from his belly seemed to make him want to lash out at Jared more. Now it just made him look tired.

Bartram stood nearby puffing on a cigarette bent in half from where he had bitten it.

"You little shit," said Clayton. "You just never know when to quit, do you?"

Jared reached for a quippy comeback, but he had none left to spare. Instead, he refocused on the corner, determined not to give in to the fear.

"It's time we took an ear off." Clayton grabbed Jared's ear and started his cut at the top. Jared closed his eyes, and his face pinched.

"Stop."

Jared swerved his head to see Katie standing in the doorway. She stared at him, face frightened. What the hell was she doing?

"Little Miss Scarface," Clayton said. "How nice of you to join us."

Ardently, Jared shook his head.

"He didn't do anything," Katie said. "He's lying."

"Shut up," Jared mouthed.

"Jared didn't hack the computer. I did."

"Uh, no she didn't," Jared said. "I hacked the computer. She's lying."

"I used cocoa powder to lift Addison's prints." Katie took a step forward. "I found her passcode hidden in the notebooks above her desk."

"Katie, shut your mouth," Jared said, and Clayton smacked him.

"I couldn't get onto the internet," Katie continued. "I came back and told Jared what I did, and he made a diversion."

"You can't be buying this, Clayton," Jared said. "She's a moron. She couldn't come up with something like that on her own. This was my job, not hers."

Clayton looked between the two of them. "Wow, Goldie, who knew you were such a stud? Getting a pretty girl like that to lay down her life for your worthless one."

"Katie is lying," Jared said.

"Seems to be going around," said Midas leaning against the door frame. Even Clayton jumped at his sudden arrival. "Obviously, they're both lying. However, I might be able to simplify this." Midas drew his gun and pointed it at Katie. "You have until the count of five to tell me what you two did."

"Dammit, Katie," Jared breathed.

"We've told you what we did," Katie said. "We tried to get on the internet and failed."

Jared hung his head. She did not know the Watchers were aware of the connected call. Her lie spiraled from there.

"Five," Midas said. "Four. Three. If you don't tell me, Goldie, I'll go fetch your sister. How much of her will I have to carve off before you talk? Two—"

"Sedonya Ryder," Jared said, and Katie's eyes widened. "I called Sedonya Ryder. Sedonya is my cousin. Addison was feeding her information, which is why her name was on the contact list."

Midas smiled wryly and lowered the gun to his side. "And suddenly it all becomes clear. The reporter? Really? You should have at least contacted someone reliable. Then you might have had a chance. Bartram, contact Watts. Tell him to track down the reporter. If she's contacted the police, tell him to stall. If she hasn't, kill her."

"Right boss." Bartram left.

"What do we do now, boss?" Clayton asked.

"Until we hear from Watts," Midas said. "We proceed as planned. Load up the workers in the trucks. If this all blows over, we'll bring them back. Oh, and shoot Goldie."

"No!" Katie said, but Jared closed his eyes.

"What about the sister?" Clayton said. "And this girl?"

"I don't give a damn about the sister," Midas said, but he eyed Katie. "You know, I'm going to take out an insurance policy." He seized Katie's arm.

"Let go of me!" She tried to pull away.

"Handcuffs?" Midas held out his hand, and Clayton produced a pair from his back pocket.

Katie cried out as her arm was wrenched around, and her body forced against the raised bed. Midas secured her hands behind her back.

"Midas, no!" Jared said. "You can't take her."

"Shut up, Goldie," Midas said. "Clayton, I'm going to borrow your car."

Jared slid the small blade from its hidden pocket and sliced through his bonds. He raised the knife to stab into Midas' back. Clayton landed a punch against his temple, and he stumbled back. Midas turned around with brows raised.

Jared grimaced as he clutched his ribs. He was in no shape to fight, but he readjusted his grip on the blade and tried a go at Clayton. The man grabbed his arm and dragged him forward. He kneed Jared in his damaged ribs and wrestled the knife free. Jared went down gasping, and Clayton flipped the knife neatly in his hand.

"Pathetic." Clayton tucked the blade in his pocket. "Here are my keys, boss. I'll take care of this filth."

Katie screamed as Midas dragged her out. All the way up the hill, she thrashed and clawed at him, but to no avail. Clayton's car was waiting for them at the fence. Midas popped the trunk and shoved her inside. The lid slammed down, and Katie was trapped.

Jared's ribs screamed as he knelt in the grass, the mansion to his back. As the other workers trudged up the hill, they blurred and pulsed as his eyes refused to focus. As if his vision wasn't bad enough already.

His hands were tied behind his back, and his chest heaved as he took each painful breath. Blood continued to drip down his chest. He was unsure what had happened to his shirt in the scuffle, but it was no longer with him.

Bartram exited the house with Leida and shoved her to the ground next to him. She looked at him with tear-filled eyes. He knew he was quite the sight, all beaten and bloodied, but there was nothing to be done about that.

"Hey, there." He smiled at her and tried to force the pain from his face, but he wobbled and almost fell. His focus returned to staying upright.

"You're really stupid, you know that?" Leida whispered as a tear dripped off her face and into the grass.

"Yeah, I know, but I couldn't let you have all the fun." He looked back over the crowd to see Bryan chewing on his thumbnail. Tears streamed down Michelle's face, and Jared looked away.

"You said you were at least going to kill Clayton." Leida nodded to where he chatted with Tweedle Dee. "I see he's still standing."

"That's hardly my fault," Jared said. "What kind of knife work were you doing yesterday? I taught you better than that."

"I'm sorry," she said. "I was busy trying not to get raped."

Jared laughed, but it turned into a cough. Grimacing, he spat a wad of blood from his mouth.

"Stop talking!" Clayton marched up the hill to them. "This is not a social gathering."

Jared looked down at the ground until Clayton moved away, then his eyes went once more to Leida. "I love you," he whispered.

"I love you, too." A tear slid down her cheek, and his heart broke. He tried to mask his pain, his fear, but he shook so hard he thought he could hear his bones rattling.

"I'll see you on the other side." He raised the corner of his mouth, and Leida nodded fervently.

"Listen up." Clayton gained the crowd's attention. "This is an execution. Midas wanted everyone to be present so you all will know what happens to those who cross us."

"Clayton," Bartram said, radio in hand, "the trucks are at the base of the drive. Should we?"

"Sure, let them in." Clayton turned back to the crowd. "The girl stabbed a Watcher, namely me. Goldie, here, placed a call to the outside. Now, don't do that!" He pointed to the children's faces. "I see that. Don't look so excited. He contacted a no name conspiracy theorist. It's being handled. No one is coming for you."

A murmur spread through the crowd.

"This should be a lesson to all of you," Clayton said. "This is your life. No one is ever coming for you. Accept it." He placed a gun at the back of Jared's head, and Jared closed his eyes.

As the barrel of the weapon pressed into Jared's hair, he found himself transported to the woods where Landon knelt beside him. He could see the flash of the barrel, the surrounding blood.

Music played in the deathly silence. Clayton frowned as he pulled his phone from his pocket. He flipped open the phone, and Jared swayed.

"What?" Clayton listened to the speaker as the trucks approached the fence. The electric motor rolled open the gate, and Bartram waved them in.

"You're a little late on that," Clayton continued. "We know who he called—some reporter named Ryder. Sedonya Ryder."

Jared stared up at the blue sky through his puffy eyes. A couple of birds launched from the trees beyond the fence and danced through the air across the camp. What a beautiful day.

"What do you mean?" Clayton asked. "Who the hell is Alec Thompson?"

A smile tugged on Jared's lips, and he returned his gaze to the grass. Clayton clicked the phone closed.

"What the hell is this, Goldie?" he said. "Sedonya Ryder isn't even on the contact list. The only outgoing call went to an Alec Thompson. Who the hell is Alec Thompson?"

Jared looked him dead in the eye. "Your mom."

Clayton narrowed his eyes, raised his weapon, and fired. Jared hit the ground.

Leida screamed as the gun fired and her brother fell face forward into the grass. A sob caught in her throat as she stared at his body.

Clayton stumbled forward. A red blotch in the center of his chest expanded, and he fell to his knees.

"Boss?" Bartram said. "Boss!"

Clayton collapsed next to Jared, and Bartram spun around with his gun raised. Another blast sounded, and he fell to the ground as three men in Kevlar jumped from the transport truck parked inside the gate. Matt was the next to fall to the assault team.

"Drop your weapons!" one of the men shouted. "Get down on the ground, now!"

Seeing their leader dead in the grass, the other Watchers did not resist. Hands went up as weapons were cast to the ground.

Leida knelt in stunned silence at the chaos all around her. She looked back to Jared who lay unmoving in the grass. Her vision blurred as sobs racked her body.

Michelle ran up the hill to them. "Is he? Oh, Leida." Michelle cut through her bonds and wrapped her arms around Leida.

Leida pushed her away and leaned over Jared. "He can't—he can't be!" She touched his blood-streaked hair. "Jared—Jared? Please, no."

One of the men in Kevlar approached and cast his helmet to the side. He sank to his knees next to Jared. "Oh no," he breathed.

"Are you Katie's dad?" Michelle asked.

He shook his head as he rolled Jared onto his side. A sob caught in his throat as he brushed Jared's hair from his face.

Jared let out a soft moan.

"Was that?" Leida asked, and the man's eyes widened. He swung his pack from his shoulder, removed a water bottle, and poured it over Jared's face. Jared started coughing.

*   *   *

Ringing roared in Jared's ears. He tried to open his eyes, but they refused to work. The pain in his head throbbed, and as someone rolled him onto his side, his ribs screamed.

Jared tried to sit, but nothing moved. Was this death? Being trapped in one's body for all eternity? Oh God, he hoped not. Visions of dirt covering his face during his burial floated through his mind.

Someone touched his face. Pain erupted from the area, and he tried to shout. It came out as a moan. Cool liquid cascaded onto his temple and fell into his mouth. Jared coughed and sputtered.

"He's alive?" Leida's voice. "He's alive?"

Finally, his eyes fluttered open. The blinding light seared into his vision, and he closed them once more. The light hurt. Why did the light hurt?

"It's going to be okay," a male voice said. "You're going to be okay. Thompson! We need an ambulance!"

Stop yelling. Jared's head continued to pound. He opened his eyes once more, but everything was red. No, it was just that one eye that was red. Was he blind in that eye? Jared closed it and tried to manage with the other. Blades of grass inches away were all he could make out.

"Jared?" Leida said. "Jared, can you hear me?"

Yes, you're screaming, Jared thought, but his words wouldn't come out. He managed a nod instead.

"You're going to be okay," she said. "They've sent for an ambulance."

An ambulance? Who the hell is they? Jared tried to raise himself up, but the pain in his ribs stopped him. "I can't see," he managed.

"Hold on," the man said. Water poured down his face once more and a cloth was wiped across his eyes. The red disappeared, and his vision cleared. The man held pressure to his temple. "It's only a graze, thank God."

Jared looked over to see Clayton staring at him, and his brow knit. Why was Clayton on the grass? Why didn't he move? Then he saw the red blotch on his chest. Had he been shot?

The man holding pressure shifted his position and pulled Jared's head into his lap. Jared winced with the movement but did find himself more comfortable. He was able to look at the man now but still didn't recognize him.

Or did he?

There was something familiar about him, but he couldn't place it. He wore a vest that read "FBI" in yellow letters. Was this Katie's dad?

No, he knew what Katie's dad looked like. His hair was brown, and this man's hair was blonde and curly.

"His chest is bleeding too," Leida said.

"There are more bandages in the bag," the man said.

Jared squirmed as his sister pressed gauze to the cuts Clayton had made all over his chest.

"I know," Leida said. "I have to."

He nodded.

"Is he going to be alright?" Michelle appeared in his field of vision.

Leida passed her a worried look. How bad was his head? Jared reached up to touch it, but the man wouldn't let him. "Relax," the man said. "Help is on the way."

"Am I dying?" Jared said.

"No!" A sob caught in the man's throat. "No, you're not dying."

Jared frowned as he looked up at the man. He knew him from somewhere. Where did he know him from? Was this a dirty FBI agent?

He didn't think so. But dammit! Who was he? This was going to bug him all day if he didn't figure it out.

"Wayne!" Another man came into view. This was Katie's dad. Agent Thompson. "Alec called 9-1-1. An ambulance is on the way."

Wayne swiped at his eyes as he continued to hold pressure on Jared's head.

"Excuse me," Agent Thompson spoke to Leida, "I'm looking for my daughter, Katie. She's fifteen—"

"I know your daughter, sir." Michelle interrupted. "Midas took her fifteen minutes before you got here."

"What?" Thompson said. "But—why? I thought—"

"Insurance," Jared said.

Thompson's mouth parted. He ran his fingers through his hair and wandered away. Jared shook his pounding head as tears threatened to breech his eyes, but he met the eyes of Wayne as he looked back up.

Wayne. Wayne. He didn't remember any Wayne. Not that he had met recently anyway. His dad's name was Wayne, but . . .

Jared's eyes grew wide. He looked over to his sister—same blonde hair. Same nose. Same cheeks. Wayne? Wayne Kelley?

"Dad?" Jared said.

A sob erupted from Wayne's chest. He nodded emphatically. "Yes, son. It's me."

"Dad?" he repeated in disbelief. "What—what are you doing here?"

Wayne smiled as he petted his hair. "It was the damnedest thing," he said. "I got a call from Agent Thompson this morning. He said some kid claiming to be my son needed help."

A tear slid down Jared's cheek. "Leida," Jared reached for her hand, "this is Dad."

Leida stared wide-eyed at the man. If she had any memories of him, they were few. But as she looked at her father, her eyes filled with tears.

"Leida?" Wayne breathed. "Leida? My Leida?" He pulled her in close and kissed her on the head. "My children," he cried. "My children are alive!"

Jared leaned up on his elbow to see Matt lying still in the grass. His head had cleared a little bit but still swam. "Did you kill all the Watchers?" he asked Dad.

"Uhm, no," Wayne said. "The kid over there is guarding them."

He rose further to see Bryan standing on the stump. He had a pistol pointed at ten handcuffed Watchers kneeling on the ground.

"You guys are really winging this thing, aren't you?" Jared asked.

Wayne laughed. "A little bit, yeah. You didn't give us a lot of time."

"What are you going to do when the Feds get here?" Jared said. "If they're in Midas's pocket . . ."

"We've been live-streaming this whole time." Wayne tapped on the GoPro fixed to his shoulder. "There's no way they will be able to put this genie back into the bottle."

Music started nearby, interrupting the reunion. Wayne fished a cellphone out of Clayton's pocket. "Richard Dunn?"

Jared shuddered. "That's Midas."

"Thompson!" Wayne hollered, and the man came over. "Jared says it's Midas."

"Richard Dunn?" Thompson said. "The guy running for congress? We cleared him after—"

"Slender guy, black beard, talks through his nose?" Jared said. "Richard Dunn is Midas. And who the hell else would be calling?"

Wayne and Thompson exchanged a glance.

"If Midas finds out you raided this place, he's going to try and turn things around. How many guys do you have with you?"

"Me, Thompson, and your Uncle Nate," Wayne said.

The phone rang again, and Agent Thompson snatched it up. "Hello?" he said. There was a pause. "This is Special Agent Peter Thompson. What do you want, Midas?"

Jared craned his neck to try and hear the conversation but was unable to make anything out.

Thompson raised a hand to his forehead. "I can't do that," he breathed. "God help me, I can't do that." He pulled the phone away from his ear and stared at it. "What did I do?"

"What did he say, Thompson?" Wayne said.

"I lost her," he said. "He wanted me to turn around and leave, but, obviously, I can't do that."

"Thompson," Jared swallowed. "Turn off your camera."

"What?"

"You might not have lost her," Jared said, "but you need to turn off your camera. There's something you need to know."

*   *   *

Katie heard the sound of the key entering the lock of the trunk, and her heart pounded. Soon, Midas hovered above her. "Out you go," he said, grabbing her arm.

"I can do it myself." She maneuvered out of the trunk with her hands tied behind her back, and Midas raised his brows, impressed. "Where are we?" she asked.

"Safe." He took her arm. "At least I am."

Midas pushed her to the door. Once inside, he led her to the living room where all the curtains were drawn. A support beam stood next to the couch, and he secured her hands to it.

"What are you doing?" she said.

"I figured you might like to watch the news," he said. "After all, it concerns you too." Midas produced a bandana from his pocket and gagged her.

Katie cursed him with muffled oaths. Midas ignored her and surfed through the channels as he sat back on the couch.

Katie's eyes grew wide as the screen filled with images of the camp. Her camp. It was drone footage of the gigantic compound. The news anchor told of a massive FBI raid that had taken place where forty-seven children had been rescued.

"In a strange turn of events," the anchor said, "a live-stream video that later went viral was uploaded to multiple media sites showing the actual raid taking place. While one member of the raiding team has been identified as Special Agent Peter Thompson, conflicting reports are still coming in regarding the other two members of the team. The FBI is not giving details regarding the incident at this time. It is speculated that all of this was part of a larger drug operation run by the criminal mastermind, Midas, who has been at the top of the FBI's most wanted list for years."

"Hmpf," Midas muttered as he left the couch for the kitchen. He returned with a beer.

The anchor continued, "Reports are saying all of this took place in the middle of the Cherokee National Forest in Tennessee. The camp was hidden and only accessible by a fire road. We have clips of the video. I must warn you: it is disturbing."

Katie watched from her father's camera as they drove up and through the open fence. She couldn't help but smile to think of her father commandeering one of the trucks to get in.

"What the hell?" Thompson slammed the brakes, and the camera caught the blur of a rifle being raised. Two children sat on a hill kneeling. The video blurred their heads, but Katie knew it was Jared and Leida. A man stood behind the children with a gun.

The camera mic shrieked as Thompson fired the rifle shot, but it was Jared who went down. Katie screamed in her gag while Midas took another sip of beer. Clayton went down a few seconds later.

Then the camera began to bounce in a chaotic motion as Thompson leapt from the vehicle.

When the video stopped, the anchor spoke once more. "We are told the boy was taken to a local hospital and is currently in critical condition. We do not have a confirmed identity of the victim, but our hearts and prayers are with him and his family."

Katie didn't hear much else as she sagged to the floor. Midas, however, smiled as he sipped on his beer, and her stomach burned.

"Intensive Care, huh?" Midas muttered. "We'll see about that."

Turn out the freaking lights, Jared thought as he winced at the fluorescents above his head. What were they trying to do, blind him? His head pounded, and he tried to sit, but his ribs complained. Jared inhaled deeply to calm himself, but it felt like his breaths were coming from a water hose. Damn ribs.

Jared tried to brace his ribs to sit, but his hand was stuck. He tugged harder. It was the damn handcuffs. Stupid things. Folding his fingers upward as far as he could, he felt along the edge of the manacles. Instead of metal, he found soft foam. Well, that was different.

A thick strap came off the side of the cuff. He followed it as far as he could but was unable to locate the end. The familiar panic crept into his chest. In an attempt to calm himself, he took another deep breath but coughed instead. Jared licked his lips and frowned. There was something in his mouth, and he bit it. Was there an actual water hose in his mouth?

Jared opened his eyes wide. A giant tube protruded from his mouth.

He sat up, ignoring the pain in his ribs, and coughed and sputtered. Why the hell did he have a tube down his throat? He strained against the restraints, but his hands held firm.

A loud beeping started over his right shoulder, and Jared craned his neck to see a screen filled with lights. He shook his head wildly trying to dislodge the tube. What the hell was going on?

"Hey now, hey now!" A woman in blue entered through the door at the foot of the bed. "Settle down. You're alright."

You're shitting me, right?

"Dr. Black!" the woman called. "He's awake."

Jared thrashed, and the woman grabbed his shoulders and held him down. Jared glared at her. If only he could get his hands free.

"Okay, okay!" A woman in a white coat came to the head of Jared's bed and wiggled the tube around. Jared choked and gagged.

Dr. Black pulled on the tube and it slid out. Jared's eyes grew wide at the length of the device. Once it was out, his chest heaved with coughs, his ribs screamed.

"Welcome back, Jared." She smiled at him, but Jared glared back. "Anna, I'm going to go let them know."

"Jared, you might not remember me," Anna said. "But I took care of you when you first came in."

Jared tugged against the restraints, and Anna pulled the cord, releasing the line. Jared, seeing what she had done, found the other line and released the slipknot. He scooted to the edge of his bed.

"Wait! You can't get out of bed!"

Jared flipped his legs over the side of the mattress, and Anna grabbed his arm. He grabbed her wrist and twisted. Anna cried out as her arm torqued behind her back, and Jared shoved her face-first into the mattress and wrapped the restraint strap around her neck. A pole next to the bed toppled from the movement, and Jared yanked out the tubes he found in his arm.

"Jared!" Anna cried. "I'm not going to hurt you. Please—let me go!"

"What's going on?" Dr. Black returned. "Anna!"

Yanking Anna up by her hair, Jared turned so she stood in front of him. "Back up," Jared told the doctor hoarsely. "Back up, now."

"Jared, just relax," Dr. Black said. "You're in the hospital."

"I said back up!"

She took a couple of steps backward.

"How do I get out of here?" Jared whispered in Anna's ear.

"It's not safe for you to leave," Anna said between sobs. "You're not well."

"I won't ask you again." He tightened the hold on the strap.

"Th-there's a stairwell. Down the hall to the left," she said, and Jared pushed her forward.

"You don't need to do this, Jared," Dr. Black said. "You're in the hospital. You were bleeding in your brain and had to have surgery. You've been on a ventilator. The restraints were to keep you from pulling out your tube, nothing more."

"Bullshit!"

"Jared?" A small, melodic voice reached his ears. Jared hesitated, his eyes searching for the source. A young woman with a long golden braid resting on her shoulder stood in the doorway. Although her clothes had been changed and her cheeks were pinker, she was unmistakable.

"Leida?"

"She's telling the truth," Leida said. "That's Anna, your nurse."

Jared's eyes darted between the two women, and he ran his hand over his closely shorn scalp. His fingers brushed against thick metal bands holding the skin together.

"Let her go, Jared," Leida said. "It's over. We're safe."

Hesitantly, Jared released the tension on the cord and flipped it over Anna's head. The nurse sprinted into Dr. Black's arms, weeping as Jared slumped against the wall. His ribs screamed once more, and he slid toward the floor. Leida grabbed his shoulders, catching him before he fell.

Leida slipped beneath his arm and helped him to the bed, and Jared collapsed onto it, grunting.

"You're bleeding." Leida wrapped his arm in a blanket.

A crowd had gathered at the door, a blur of faces peering in. But Jared's gaze rested on a small, mouse-like woman standing in the corner of the doorway. She clutched and unclutched the handle of a worn-out leather bag. Gray strands of hair collected among the brown, and premature lines of worry marked her face. Yet to Jared, she was the most beautiful woman in the world.

"Mom?"

The woman placed a hand to her mouth and nodded. She rushed to his bed, and tears fell down their cheeks.

Ten years. Ten long, horrible years had passed since Jared last buried his face into her shoulder. The softness of her embrace flooded him with a myriad of emotions he could not identify. Was this truly happening? Or was another cruel dream about to end? Was he about to wake once more in his lice-infested bed? Yet the smell, the touch, the sound of his mother's heart was too real to be a dream. He was home. Finally home.

Book Two: Escaping Midas Now Available.

Scan the QR Code below to claim your copy!

The QR Code can also be used to leave a review for Surviving Midas. Please consider doing so. Surviving Midas is not just an entertaining tale, but a story that demonstrates the real-world psychological effects that child abuse has on those who have suffered from it. As the daughter of a social worker, kids from hard places hold a special place in my heart. My hope that kids or even adults who have suffered trauma will find comfort and strength from seeing their experiences reflected in others. But the impact of this story will only be felt if that know that these books are out there for them. Leaving reviews does not just let others know you liked this work, it incentivizes platforms such as Amazon to advertise it to others. It does not take much time to leave a review, but the help that it brings to the author is difficult to understate.

Thanks so much for reading! I hope to see you in the next installment of this series!